Emsky
Chronicles

James Hendershot

Order this book online at www.trafford.com
or email orders@trafford.com

Most Trafford titles are also available at major online book retailers.

Printed in the United States of America.

ISBN: 978-1-4907-4093-5 (sc)
ISBN: 978-1-4907-4092-8 (e)

Trafford rev. 06/27/2014

 www.trafford.com

North America & international
toll-free: 1 888 232 4444 (USA & Canada)
fax: 812 355 4082

Dedicated to

Dedicated to my wife Younghee with special thanks, and to my sons, Josh & Lilly and John combined with daughters Nellie and Mia, and then publishing services associate Evan Villadores and check in coordinator Heidi Morgan (not pictured) .

CONTENTS

CHAPTER 01

Spiritual chaos and sanctuary

Accordingly, countless stories fill the ages, as most reveal the same tales. Each and everyone around me knew me as Sénye throughout the days of my existence on a planet called Emsky of the Chuprin Galaxy. Our galaxy was one of many, which had no deity. Therefore, when we died, the righteous spent their eternity running from the evil spirits. These changed thousands of years later when the Empire of the Good and the holders of the Sword of Justice and Freedom (EGaSOJAF) accepted annexation. When the EGaSOJAF accepted Chuprin's bid for annexation, a process that took two millennia to complete, as they have so many galaxies begging for appendage to their two and half-million galaxies. Once they accept the request for annexation, the Empire begins collecting the virtuous spirits and capturing the wicked spirits. This event happened for Chuprin far pass this story. My story recounts the chronicles of Emsky. A world filled with hardships, loves, wars, death, plagues, and life, all which changed when the Empire annexed Chuprin. Our world had its range of strange mythologies and religions, as they tried to explain the mysterious. The unknown is the creator of realms that a rational person would believe insane. This unfamiliar ruled those who roamed Emsky, nonetheless; the anonymous has ruled many worlds, taking away any unique trait for Emsky. Special or not, the original Emsky was my world and my honor to tell her story.

After my death, I roamed through the other worlds in Chuprin. I actually roamed with extreme caution, eluding the wicked spirits, which I quickly discovered ruled the lofty obscure empty space. I saw the other worlds had people with different color skin. Emsky had totally pale orange people, throughout all its history. Even without the color of their skin to discover ways to hate and kill, Emsky still found other reasons. On drifting through Emsky, I discovered the wicked spirits caused most of this aggression. There were many who were in the middle, and they were our safeguards. Initially, I was tremendously terrified believing my eternity filling itself solely with torture and misery. An eternity existing entirely while chased with no sanctuary in existence offered no hope. When the middle spirits captured me, I believed my eternity would end soon. A few spirits told me that many virtuous spirits were missing. I believed my captor had put me on my final road. So quickly my end came. However, my predictions were wrong. They convinced me that I was protected, teaching me that a few borderline wicked acts would make sure me a secure future. I wondered what these works would entail. They would include mustering up a few storms, droughts, starting fights, and fires, essentially actions the people had an avenue for escape. My first, middle spiritual companion was a spirit of the far part of our universe. She did not appear as we did. She revealed her name to me as Orosházi. She was my indoctrinator, teaching me most things I needed to understand. The middle spirits told me the worthy souls simply escaped to a galaxy, which had a deity to request admission into their heavens. Few deities rejected their appeal. I wanted nothing to do with these requests. I belonged around Emsky and Orosházi was going to show me how to do this. She was fashioned as a dark-brown woman, with bright pink and white spotted wings. She had a crown of colorful flowers supplemented with long green leaves. Her eyes are large and powerful, as I almost expect lasers to shoot all, she sees. She kept the form of her species, as this is before the Empire, which converts all to one species. She has a pink strap wrapped around her breasts and another around her pelvic area that droops in the back so when she stands forms a skirt covering her legs to the knees. When she sits, the long, slender legs support her spiritual body unexposed. Green birds fly around the orange, blue, and purple, white spotted butterflies swarm around her whenever she stops. My many attempts to discover how they attach themselves to her while in flight were always fruitless. Her hair was a black wool perfectly styled and held in place by her flower crown. Her flawlessly shaped, pink lips had a magic to them that would pull her comrades under her spell.

I had to understand how she devised an image of the body she once lived. I was barely a white smoke. I had been fortunate during my life to have a wife and children, misfortune to lose them to raiders, who took my family life with it. My eyes could not believe how gorgeous Orosházi was, nevertheless I needed her to exist, therefore I could absolutely admire. She had the food for my soul, which had nowhere to hide and no chance of survival. Once Orosházi claimed me, all others ignored me. I asked her how she could appear as she did, considering I was still a puff of smoke. To my great delight, she promised to take me to the Jarunka, the guardian of the red door. This door was not like the ones I always knew. This door had a five-inch brick frame while arched at the top. The door had three thick stone steps in its front. The oddity was the absence of a building to surround the door. I saw winter trees with a sky plastered with dark black clouds. Before the door stood a woman wearing a fluffy milky bottomed gown, which exposed her shoulders and appeared to be low enough not to reach her breasts, which I would not recognize her as she kept her back to us and front to the red door. Her long white hair reached down to the center of her back.

We appeared behind her as Orosházi told me to hover in her hands, while we waited. I wondered if Jarunka even knew we were here. Orosházi assured me that she knew we were here, for if she did not distinguish us, we would be suffering from her massive retaliation. We wait and wait. Finally, she asks, "Orosházi, who did you bring to me?" Orosházi tells her, "Jarunka, I have brought my new mate, Sénye." Orosházi asks her, "Why is Sénye still as smoke? Does not that make your relationship difficult?" Orosházi confesses to her that this is almost making their relationship nothing more than words. Jarunka asks her, "Do you wish for me to bless him? Furthermore, if I bless him, will you stay together or separate?" Orosházi explains, "Jarunka, he appears to be sincere, and heartfelt with his words, I would hope we share many adventures together; however, as you know, the choices are his." Jarunka discloses that she understands. She then calls my name, and I reply, "Yes," hoping she will turn around, not knowing who spiritual women appear when their chests are exposed. Jarunka asks me, "If I give you the gift of my special spiritual body, would you desire to stay with Orosházi?" I ask her, "Is there any in the high skies who fairs better?" She asks, "What about me?" I tell her, "I have not seen your face." Jarunka informs me, "Nor will you, for Orosházi's sake." I believe that she may be overstating herself, because Orosházi has me sold on her, especially as she is not afraid to face new situations and spirits. I do not experience easy with someone who keeps her back facing me. Nevertheless, I need her for this special spiritual treat.

Jarunka tells me I must walk up behind her, then bypass her, open the red door and enter behind it, keeping my hand on the door handle. After this, I must keep my eyes closed, and return through the door, walk around her and once three steps behind her open my eyes again. She stresses that I must keep my eyes closed and hold on to the door handle with my complete strength, for if I let go, I would be lost for eternity. I ask her how one can hold on without hands. She reveals that I will discover the answer for this question. I hate uncertainty and explore Orosházi, whose angelic face winks at me signifying that I can do this. That was all I needed. My spirit swerved around her and locked onto the door, struggling hard to push it open. Finally, as if by this strange force, I could turn the door handle. I kept all my force concentrated on the handle needing no force to open the door as it accomplished this feat itself. I hung on tight, feeling my legs and arms expand from a growing torso. At last, my head popped out of the torso causing my eyes to open. I closed them immediately swinging, my other arm to the inside part of the door handle. Next, I swung my legs and clamped them to the door. Thereafter, I could sense the door swaying inwards, accordingly I leaned my spirit body into the sway, bringing it closer to the brick frame. Subsequently, I took my gamble and reached my leg out for the doorframe. I could get far enough for my heel to anchor against the bottom part of the frame. I used my anchored leg, bending it, to pull my body all the way around the door latching my remaining leg with the first leg. Now with patience, struggling to maintain my secure grip, worked my legs inward until my knees were on the door's foundation. Afterwards, I straightened up my body in the door's frame closing the door and turning the latch to secure it. Staying in reverse, while keeping my eyes closed, I said, "Be careful Jarunka, as I do not recognize where you are." She informs me there is no need to worry, as she is without substance now, asking me to walk backwards four steps. After that, I may turn about, and open my eyes. I did as she said and after the four steps, turned around, and opened my eyes. I had the appearance of the body I had on Emsky, and when touching it, could experience this substance. Jarunka later told me this was imaginary for our self-satisfaction. She properly tied her top securing her breasts and turned around facing me. She was correct, as her beauty was unmatched.

I knew the unique chance that I had now was to rush back to Orosházi as she was watching me carefully. I asked her if she was disappointed in my appearance. She examined me as one would in the purchase of livestock. As she completed her inspection, a smile flowed across her face. Orosházi reports to me, "Except for, no wings, I guess I will ask Jarunka now to cast you through her door she has just opened." I looked and verified she had indeed opened the door. Jarunka pleas, "Orosházi, you appreciate that I love the way men scream as the beasts crunch their new bodies." I looked at Jarunka, as she appeared serious. I studied Orosházi who smiled and said, "I want to keep this one, for a while, at least until he turns bad." I told her the exclusive thing that I hoped to do that was bad was to love her. She focuses her big eyes on me and explains to me that she will teach me how to do this. I think that life after death may not be all the bad after all. She drops to a fallen tree, sits on it anchoring one leg in an upside-down V shape, and allows the other leg to hang. This is her favorite position, as it has also been mine. Her legs are perfect beauties and hypnotize me to no end. She asks me if I like her legs. I confess that I like everything about her, and that she is a dream come true. Orosházi teases me by accusing me of saying that with all the women. I tell her that each woman had one special thing; however, none had as many exceptional features and qualities as her. I decided at this time to tell her my true situation. I said, "Orosházi, I am totally dependent on you. When you cast me away, I will perish. If you refuse my love, I exist without love. Without you, I am lost. What should I do?" She tells me, "Stay this way, and we will do fine. I knew you were lost when I found you." I had to know, therefore, I asked, "Why did you have mercy on me and select me?" Orosházi chuckles and asks, "Why do you ask so many questions? I felt sorry for you, and you are a little cute." I told her, "You are beautiful." She giggles and says, "I had better instruct you how to love while you are still hot." I could not pinpoint what she thought; therefore, I just pretended to understand and said, "Great idea." She, once again, smiled, this time grabbing my hand and whisking me into the sky.

Orosházi explains to me that she will teach me now the primary reason she wants and needs me. We sailed in the clouds while she held my hand. I was still adjusting to this complete form, which is not as easy to maneuver as a puff of smoke. I am not afraid of being detected neither as one glance at Orosházi's character and confidence convinces me she knows this environment. She shifts our direction to straight up, for we are heading directly for the large clouds in the upper sky. Thereafter, she takes us into a thick cloud and slows down considerably. We soon enter a large opening, which has red hearts floating everywhere. Orosházi explains to me that this is her loving world, and that solely she has this place. I ask her how she can hide this from all the other spirits. She answers, "By scarcely allowing me to see it, and now you." I ask her, "Glamour woman, what do you do in your loving world?" She winks at me and whispers, "Take a guess. Why would I allow a man to follow me? Why would you take a female to a loving world?" I am now embarrassed and confused. Could my dream be coming true? I am not used to a woman being the planner and the aggressor, although I remember seeing my sisters operate on a few helpless boys. I laughed at them, as I am sure, they would laugh at me now if they saw me. I examine my body and discover I do not have the equipment to perform what she wants me to do. Surely, she would have known this, unless Jarunka was playing games. I humbly and now within full depression, as a child in a candy store being handcuffed, point to the missing part and tell her, "Orosházi, I think Jarunka forgot something." Orosházi asks me, "Are you serious, did not you learn anything during your orientations?" I tell her, "They began the orientation as a band of wicked spirits launched their invasion, thus they simply told, us to hide somewhere. That was the end of my orientation." She reminds me how lucky I am to have her and begins to teach me some important things. Orosházi discloses, "Sénye, sex between people is physical; however, as we do not have flesh, our sex is my touching our lights and drifting in each other's radiance." She had a fallen tree appear that she laid on sideways, not to cramp her wings. Next, she asked me, "Sénye, when you touch me, we will share our spiritual wine. Are you sure you wish to seduce me?" I have never been surer of anything else in my life.

I looked into her eyes and said, "I am so sure, for this is a dream come true for me. Tell me what to do." She raised her hand, and told me not to let go, and to grip her hand vigorously. I did as she requested and that was the beginning of our wonderful wine drinking days. Our lights merged as I could sense myself floating inside her spirit. What was better, I could also experience her flowing through me? This was special as we were totally inside each other. She could hear my thoughts and bear my emotions. Orosházi tells me not to be ashamed, for she knew nothing about Emsky when she first arrived here. It was harder for her, as she is clearly from another species, although fortunately close enough where it counted. While I roam through her, I am so comfortable, and secure. I ask her if it is common for a man to be this afraid. She explains, to my delight, it is normal if you want to be playing in her light. I notice she has a few locked doors and I ask her about them. She explains those are bad memories, and she never wants to release them. I had not locked any of my doors yet, mainly for fear that, I could end hiding in those rooms, if possible. Orosházi compliments me on how beautiful my wife was. She tells that proves I truly select the best, and this puts her in the prodigious company. She reviews my two sons and daughter, complimenting how handsome my sons are and beautiful my daughter, as all looked like me. Her face becomes stunned as tears begin flowing down her eyes. She says nothing. I recognize what she is looking at now. She is watching the wicked raiders kill and butcher my family. I notice that she turns different colors rapidly. I ask her what she is doing. Orosházi tells me she is collecting their soul identifiers. If those spirits ever roam around us, she will destroy them. I felt so complete now, in that my woman, of life source, was also going to revenge those who were my family. I told her that was such a wonderful thing to do. Orosházi tells me that when she selects a male as her mate, that male will never doubt her loyalty and love.

I find myself, completely exhausted, and lying on Orosházi's fallen tree with my face resting on her foot. She asks me if I enjoyed having her. I told her it was the greatest experience so far in my existence. She asks me if I want to return here with her someday. I asked her, "What about every day?" She winks at me and tells me, "That is the spirit, my partner." I ask her, "Orosházi, did you ever have any children, as I did not see any in your books." She reveals to me, "Sénye, family life, and procreation were exceedingly different in my world, which is called Jaroslaw of the Laurentius galaxy. It is extremely far away, as it took me ten years zapping through space to make it here. I never wanted to see another from Jaroslaw again. In our world, a couple is one male, one seducer female, and one reproducer female. The reproducer female, oddly, never has contact with the man, as all the genetic material to fertilize her eggs our kingdom provides. Seducer females do not have the internal organs to reproduce. Once our kingdom decides we have enough children, they take our reproducer and give her to another couple. They replace her with a servant woman who cares for the children and runs our household." I agree that this is truly different and ask her why she hates Jaroslaw so much. She confirms this not the way that her kingdom set up their family unit. This way was extremely efficient in producing a younger generation of soldiers. She hated all the wars. I ask her why she stopped at Emsky, as our history is flooded with wars. She reminds me that she does not have to fight in these wars. She settled here because she could make important contacts and discover how to survive. She also reveals to me that when the Empire takes, control of Chuprin, she will travel around the parameter of the Empire and exit the other side zapping in space for a

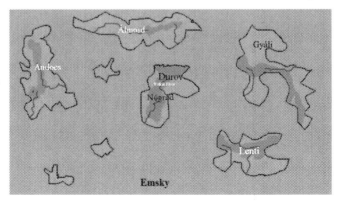

9

few years, staying ahead of its expansion. She is the first I have ever known not to want the Empire. I asked her, "Why?" She explains, "They would convert my species to yours, and I wish to keep my species for eternity. When I leave, will you join me?" I told her she would have to be awful sneaky to get away from me. She flapped her wings hovering over me, giving me a warm hug. I felt something good inside her, as if she had been searching for someone to share her destiny. Even though our union is young, I want her to keep her species as well. With her being of a different species, sharing our lights does not seem to conflict with my previous relationship responsibilities, if they even exist.

Orosházi enlightens me that she did not see much information about the geography of Emsky when she was inside me. She takes us to the upper worlds showing me each continent or big island as she calls them. She begins with the large island in the Northwest called Gyáli. I knew of these places and names from the books in our school. I never believed these places were real, and even if they were, it did not matter. While they stayed in their lands, I would stay in mine. Gyáli has the longest mountain range on Emsky. I was always amazed how all the large islands had two rivers. Emsky had a large island in the north we called Álmosd. The southern shores were habitable; however, the northern half, suffered bitter cold most of the year. Our long history accommodated abundant trouble in these areas. The next large island in the southeastern seas we called Lenti. Unique memories packed Lenti, who avoided many of the other four huge islands and their senseless squabbles. Orosházi swings me around our globe as we hover over the large island that represents our western lands. We called these lands the Andocs. These lands were the ones who dealt with our galaxy and struggled to bring Emsky up to the Empire's pre-standards. She coasted me eastward across the sea to the large island in the middle of Emsky to my homeland, Nógrád. I spent my life struggling in and out of Durov, a kingdom that occupied the lands above the Yolkin River. Emsky was not as huge as Jaroslaw, as told by Orosházi. I told her bigger worlds emphatically meant larger problems, and I never would wish anyone to live in a world with as my problems as Emsky was famous. I sense that Orosházi is enjoying Jaroslaw by enjoying Emsky through me. The other large islands were completely stories from a schoolbook, or wild tales our elders used to spice our lives. We glided over Emsky, and even though the sites were new, my mind was fixated on Orosházi. She knows how to play her game, as a newbie to Emsky, she knew more than I did.

I asked her which large island was her favorite. Orosházi confessed that Nógrád was her favorite, because it produced me. I shook my head and asked her to be honest with me, as there is no reason for someone, consequently, beautiful to be so fascinated with me. She orders me to wake up to reality. First, she is from another species, and she is not going to switch to the species of Chuprin. Orosházi never discovered one who she could control the way she needed for her existence and spiritual harmony. Second, she knows me completely, as I was the easiest male to bond. She saw my book and I had the character, loyalty, and stories she respected and felt had the words to fill the missing pages in her book. She told me to think of it as a formula, and I had the elements that she did not have. She questions me if she was over controlling. I assured Orosházi that if I had my way, I would demand that she takes more control of me. Orosházi further explains that the Jaroslaw click with another, and she never understood how it worked, but it does work. She believed that she would never click again, and that is why she is so far from Jaroslaw. Clicking or bonding is an overwhelming and a life tormenting experience. This click unexpectedly shattered her when she saw my puff of smoke zip by her. Orosházi additionally tells me there is no requirement or need for her to be the dominate one in our bonding, she will be the servant if I so desire. I tell her it does not matter to me, while we have our relationship. I am not going to play games with her and wiggle around for an overpowering position; she deserves better and is my savior. I fear to think where I would be now. I may be foolish for clicking with her, nevertheless, the lone alternative is clicking without her, and I do not want that thought in my mind, especially with her roaming in my mind. She unloads those innocent eyes on me. Orosházi asks me one more time if her being of another species bothers me. I reassure her; it is no problem. Now, we need to go playing somewhere or do something.

Orosházi tells me it is time, to visit the recharger or znovunačíst. I looked at her and repeated znovunačíst is in what is this? She takes me to the other side of Chuprin to a site whose first appearance overwhelmed me. I see a giant hole, with many different colored squares and the sides are a cluster of packet hermetic color rays shooting out everywhere. It is like firecrackers exploding on top of, and within, packed so impervious that it erases the black of space. We circle around it first, as its size is larger than a planet. Its rays are constantly exploding into space. I ask Orosházi where these rays end. She tells me they eventually blend into all the elements. She tells me that our special spiritual bodies need recharged at least once every five years. I ask her what would happen when we leave Emsky and travel to far-off parts of the galaxy. She grins and tells me that most galaxies have one in the center of their stars. Chuprin is odd in that it spins on one of the star spirals. Orosházi explains that she hope we share our lights frequently in her loving world. I promise her I share the same hope and intense desire. She guides me into the hole. We drop deep and then deeper as the color rays now pound us as needles. Our special spirit suits are, for the most part, immune from pain. Orosházi recommend we close our eyes and, save our strength, as we must pass through this hole and shot out through one of the rays. As the lights crash into our spiritual body, I can experience the new energy absorbing into me. She wraps her long legs and arms around me, as we now appear as a ball. I see the lights bounce of her through my occasional glances. We spin in circles as the beams' swat us as it would a ball. Nevertheless, we land on a flat surface and out of the reach of the bashing beams. Orosházi unwraps herself from me and while holding onto me, tells me that we must walk down into the tunnel ahead of us. I hold on tight, as the sound, here is extremely loud and forceful. We drop into one of the side tunnels, and the wall's collapse packed on us and began forcing us out. She tells me the znovunačíst is attempting to remove any foreign objects, which we are. The process is slow; nevertheless, confidently steady. Thereafter, I could see a few blinking lights ahead of us, and the forcing out pulses intensified speeding our exit. It shot us out. We spin in the rays as they shot deep into space. Orosházi tells me these ensure we pick up some extra and that our souls completely recharged. I notice that there is less difficulty maneuvering now. Orosházi tells me I am just imagining the surplus.

We float side-by-side, both feeling as if we had just showered when we were alive. Orosházi explains that the Jaroslaw did not shower with water, but showered with the sunrays. The sunrays would add a chemical to her skin's chemicals, which destroyed any foreign matter or life forms on their skin. I ask her if Jarunka gave her the darker tan, which she has. She discloses that Jarunka gave her the tan she had during her life. Her tan almost has a golden glow to it. It reflects light, adding to its shine. I notice that we are going back quickly; therefore, I ask her. She reveals that we are not in the middle virtuous space and the wicked spirits enjoy patrolling this area. Next, I ask her why we were not worried on our trip here. Orosházi reveals that now with our extra znovunačíst we are easier to detect. This convinces me, and we zip quickly, no more than discovering this might not be our lucky day. Orosházi opens her mouth and sucks me into her insides, compressing me to the size of a hand. She then begins to spin, flip up and down as if going through a maze. I can see through her eyes, as, she synchronized our lights. I simply see the conglutinated space around us and am trying to see what she is avoiding. She answers me by informing me there are dark black balls floating in this area. These gloomy balls are dangerous, in that they will explode and wrap themselves around their victims. Once they have their victims wrapped, they take them back to the malicious dens, where the wicked spirits imprison them. She continues carefully to weave around these balls. I would estimate there are over one million of them surrounding us. Orosházi maintains her control, precision, and course changes. I wonder why we go up, and after that, we go right, next left, and then up, continuously changing our headings. Orosházi elucidates that the black balls are steadfastly trying to guess our heading and then form a blockade. By changing our headings, they cannot block all the potential exits. A few times, they guessed correctly, in which Orosházi simply stopped and exited through the most advantageous opening. It took her over an hour; however, we made it through this. She told me that I needed to stay inside her, because, both of our znovunačíst lights were too obvious, moreover, this made it difficult for her to spot any rogue black balls. I agreed, feeling as a child in her womb, a sentiment I did not mind. She got us back and coughed me out of her. I tell her how impressed that I am with her determination and the care she is exercising to protect me. I have a secure feeling around her, which I could never say enough.

Orosházi reminds me that if I wish to survive here, I must learn how to detect the wicked and study their habits. She promises to take care of me until I get a lot more experience, when we can take care of each other. She emphasizes that we must be careful now, because her attention is not as focused as needed to live safely. I ask her what has her attention distracted. She gives me her wink and probes me to take a wild guess. Orosházi exhibits excitement by our arrangement. I am wise enough to realize that without her, I would still be a puff of smoke. Orosházi tells me there are many dangers around Emsky, yet since the Empire is barely about ten galaxies away from here, they have been sending in the wicked demon zappers, so the rate today in about one-half of what it was just ten years ago. I knew the Empire always had long-range capability in capturing malicious spirits, because, when they discover evil, they go after it, destroying all vicious spirits long before the annexation. Orosházi shows me how to form as a wicked spirit and how to form as a righteous spirit, plus the important middle spirit. There are massive alerts when Empire forces are in the area. Orosházi alerts me the Clotilde has cells around, and in Emsky. These cells are dangerous, because they pose as righteous spirits, capture you and then put you in their terrible spirit prisons. The Empire has discovered and freed a few of the prisons; however, the Clotilde is moving them deeper into space. She has heard a few of the prisoners' stories. The Clotilde created a universal method that produces the ability to experience pain. When they capture a spirit, they read their book to determine their status. If they are moral, they are in serious trouble. Their available hunting grounds are limited, as they cannot find righteous spirits in galaxies that have a deity, which protects their righteous dead.

I thought, oh the Clotilde. A dangerous and serious group that can destroy my eternity is all I need. I ask my Orosházi how we detect them. She has discovered their spirits have a low pitch vibration, in which she can sense. I inquired if there was a way I could sense them. She did not see a way. She could sense that I was terrified. I asked her, "Orosházi, if they attack us, how do we defend ourselves?" She revealed some crystals she had. I asked her how she could store crystals. Orosházi told me it was easy, she simply changed their chemical composition into elements that attached to her soul. Once again, I found myself asking her, "Can I do that?" Once more, she tells me, "No." I asked her, "How could I survive without you?" She tells me, "You cannot survive with me, nor can I survive without you." I am flattered that she claims the dependence on me. Nevertheless, I can find no foundation for her claim, so I tell her, "Oh Orosházi, I commend you on your words that give me a credit I do not deserve." Orosházi reveals to me, "I will always be honest with you, to a degree that sometimes the whole truth is not appropriate, yet with timing and tact revealed. The Jaroslaw clicking has another unique feature, in that if my click leaves me, I will suffer with crippling abnormalities. I am still puzzled that we clicked, as you are Emsky and I am Jaroslaw. Whatever force decides the clicking must finally have caught up with me. I am so thankful that it was you, as I believe we click well, even without this internal burning bond." I tell her, "Precious Orosházi, I realize that we were not clicked when I first saw you, as you surveyed all the fresh confused puffs of smoke, I was burning. Because I was new, I concealed this burn." Orosházi chuckles and confesses, "I appreciate my Sénye, which was one of the first times I investigated a candidate when our lights allowed me inside your mind. I hold that activity as, so flattering. When I saw that, I knew our relationship was going to last. Now, if we do not get to a sanctuary, the Clotilde may want to test how our bond works under fire." I do not like the thought of these Clotilde and the possibility of them thrashing us. I sense her grip slowly getting tighter as her eyes are probing the vast space in front of us.

She slowly moves us to a new heading and once in that heading flashes us to under the surface of Emsky. This is a special sensation, as I can see the wide variety of rock layers and a few random layers of dirt, after the surface of course. There were also large pockets, many filled with water, the others with oil. Orosházi tells me that a few planets use this oil as an energy source. I ask her why they would be so foolish, as even my nation, which lived as close to the way our ancestors did, rely on solar energy and some devices use 'hydro' foundations. I never gave this much attention during my school days, as I knew where to put the cup of water and how often, which of course was rare. I identify that my schoolbooks talked about selected primitive cultures using wood, but at no time did they talk about this black thick waste called oil. I am glad I never lived in a world that used this oil, as I can tell it would make the air dreadfully dirty, and affect the way cells react in their bodies. I can tell this just by drifting through it. Orosházi verifies my thoughts in telling me that they forbid the burning of fossil fuels in her Laurentius galaxy. They discovered that those worlds, which depleted this material, began to have orbital fluctuations because of the planet's weight change. In addition, these rocks and oils helped control the internal planet's heat exchange. The wider range of heat responses, made the core hotter, which added to the pressure on the surface causing large cracks or deep earthquakes. Naturally, many cracks made it to the core, which released that intense heat into the planets breathing gasses, while also releasing noxious gasses trapped inside the planet. The other dire side effect was the toxic emission, which reprogrammed the cells in the organs causing them to reproduce without control. When she finished revealing all this to me, I gave thanks to something that we never had to use fossil fuels. The primary source is solar for the planets and hydro for space travel. Either way, we are still drifting inside Emsky. I ask Orosházi why we are drifting inside the planet, as the resistance is slightly higher. She explains the Clotilde does not like to go inside worlds, because they have trouble releasing themselves from the internal gravity, which pulls them deeper into the core. She also tells me that there are usually certain fun spirits to play with in sanctuaries splattered under the surface, and that she would like to relax for a while. The Clotilde was attempting to zone in on us, so she wants to spin around down here for a short time to make sure they are not still tracking us. I reminded her that she just said they did not like to go under the surface. Orosházi tells me this is true; however, they will track our under the surface movements so they can capture us when we return to the surface and space above it.

I ask her, "Orosházi, how do you comprehend all these things?" She explains that when you go to live in a new place, you study everything, taking nothing for granted. She has witnessed the hunting techniques of the Clotilde, who specifically need that one irresponsible second to claim their prize. She additionally reveals that they like her legs more than I do, and they have placed her under their high-priority capture list. I ask her, "Why do you remain in this area, as it would be better if you found a new home?" She explains the exclusive places that do not have these bands of organized evil are galaxies ruled by a righteous deity, and the lone way one can live in those galaxies is to submit, for eternity, to that deity. Here, she knows how the evil operates. She usually does not go into dangerous space, except for an occasional scouting of the new spirits, which is safe and the trip to her loving world. The wicked hate, the love vibes released by her sanctuary transmitting love, and thus they evade her place. She adds the trip for the znovunačíst few spirits are aware of, and with the traffic so low, the wicked groups avoid scouting the outer parts of the route, and instead concentrate on the reentry points as they did today. She is merely floating on the borders with me, so I will understand these dangers. I report to her that this information is valuable while we are safe, and that she can explain many things to me without jeopardizing our security. She winks at me and tells me, "Do not worry; I will not put my favorite light in danger. Now, help me locate any packets of light down here. Those lights will be a few safe sanctuaries where we can relax for a while." I ask her how long, a while is, and she responds that maybe a year or so. We shall, of course visit my cloud when the sanctuary we find becomes too crowded. I confirm that a little rest time would be wonderful. Oddly, I had expected much rest time after death for all the children I saw sacrificed throughout my life. I ask Orosházi if she has any idea why my world sacrificed so many people. She reports that the wicked spirits read the minds of those who fear and the thing they fear is unleashed on them. After they sacrifice the person, they remove the thing they feared. The easiest one is a drought, although occasionally, a middle spirit will sneak a little rain as the relief. Afterwards, the wicked spirits merely intensify the drought. She tells me we will mess of a few of their plans for fun someday.

I spot a small cluster of white lights ahead. We drift over to the lights, when suddenly one light turns bright on us and asks, "Who are you and why do you come here?" I tell them I am Sénye, a new arrival from Emsky and I search for a place to rest awhile. Next, they ask, "What is that thing with you?" I tell them, "She is Orosházi, my eternal mate. I am with her as she is with me." Every one of the lights now burned on us as a loud voice declares, "You may not enter here, as anything not from Emsky is from evil. Go away with your trash." I lashed back at them, shinning my new recharged light on them pushing their lights back and said, "The single thing evil on Emsky is you. I will send your signals back to the surface and vibrate them so the Clotilde will realize you are here. I wish you a pleasant future in their prisons." At this time, I pinched each one, grabbing their soul codes. They tried to grab ours; however, Orosházi has placed a blocking shield around us. I then vibrated their codes shooting them at our large moon, so they would stay in this area. I could hear them screaming at me, "What have you done to us?" I told them, "Fools, I have condemned you for your evil, which you may live with the evil where you belong." Orosházi tells me we need to leave as the Clotilde scanners are heading this way. She slaps me in her womb, and we drift my home large island Nógrád. Understandably, I have no idea where we are going, therefore, I ask my mate. She tells me we are going to her favorite land mass, Nógrád. Orosházi reveals to me that I surprised her by my actions, especially how fast I was able to put together the little elements, which created an effective weapon. She desires to understand why I became so angry. I answer her by explaining that they called her trash after I had told them she was my mate. I now let her grasp how sad I am on the way; they treated her, and that it was wrong what they did. For the first time, she softly put herself in my arms, with no tension in her substance. This felt good, as I believed she was telling me that she is at peace with me. I just cannot imagine spirits being so hateful to her simply because she has such beautiful wings. All the other parts of her enjoy the perfection of an angelic female creation. I would believe the other spirits would enjoy the security of her wings and their ability to maneuver traps set by the wicked. I realize that I sure do.

Cruelty, even from those who profess themselves as virtuous pesters me without ending, as my desire for rage increases. If they had looked at her eyes, the windows to transparent soul, they would have known. Instead, when they found the one easy thing that was different they blockaded their hearts and blinded their eyes. I explain to her that I do not want anyone mistreating her. I added the partial second of thinking about being without her sent a wave of fear and emptiness through me that I could not control. Orosházi thanks me for claiming her as my mate. It had been so long since someone confessed her as his mate, and it felt wonderful. It did something special inside her when she saw me fighting for her honor. She winks at me as her head rests on my shoulder and responds, "And you thought I did not need you. Now, if we do not find something soon, we will have to go to my loving world." I smile and tell her, "I hope we do not find anything."

However, as destiny would have it, a cluster of white lights appeared before us. A great light questioned me, "Who are you and where do you come from now?" I asked Orosházi if we were under the northern part of Nógrád. She tells me, "Absolutely." I tell the lights, "I am Sénye from Durov above the Yolkin River. The wicked invaded my indoctrination to my afterlife. I have been so fortunate the one beside me saved me so many times that we are now mates, as my life without her would be one of being a prisoner of the Clotilde. I seek entry here show that I may show my mate how wonderful the Durov is." The lights became dimmer as a soft female voice welcomes us, "Son, bring your bride to us, so that we may thank her for saving and loving you." Orosházi hold onto my hand as I could experience a slight tremble. I asked her why she trembled. She tells me because I identified her as my mate. She wants others to honor me and not to bring shame to me. They open their gate or really lower their protective shield, and in, we go. As we go in, the large group surrounds us. One-woman claims, "I recognize that woman; she saved me once from the Clotilde." Everyone applauded her, as she turned to face my side, wrapped both of her arms around my left arm, and rested her head on my shoulder. A male spirit commented, "Sénye, many have tried unsuccessfully to talk with this fleeting angel, nevertheless; we can easily see she is smitten by you. Congratulations on capturing her with that Durov charm." Orosházi smile and replies with a soft, charming voice, "He has me under his trance, so much that I can think of nothing else. I never knew that Durov charm was so powerful." A female spirit tells her, "I hope you do not get angry with us for not knowing; however, we always believed you to be a special angel for Emsky. Is this true?" Orosházi tells them, "I am sorry, for I am merely a spirit of a world so far away. I was searching the universe for my true love, and I found it. I belong completely to my master the great Sénye." The group applauded as I heard one female adult say to a few child spirits, "You can go touch her wings, and she is a kind spirit and now our friend." A swarm of young spirits came rushing around her. We noticed that they all had transcendent forms such as us. I asked one man in front how they could obtain their spiritual suits, saying suits not knowing of a better word to describe them. He reports that this group, which called themselves, the Leontina discovered the spirit body creator at this location, and that is why they stay here. The only reasons they leave is to scout for children's spirits and bring them here before the wicked, groups' capture them. Many times, they will hover over a sacrifice and collect the child spirit as it leaves their body.

Orosházi appears accordingly happy now, as all the children are touching her wings and touching her body. They continue to repeat, "She feels like an actual person." There is usually the older child who will say something like, "Dummy, she can talk so she has to be real." The children have no fear around her. One of the adults asks her, "Angel, are the children bothering you?" Orosházi tells the adults that she loves this attention and that is so much better than the way they usually hide from her, as if she were a monster. I told the adults how rudely the previous place under Andocs was to her, calling her trash. An elderly spirit, tells Orosházi, "Honey, those Andocs have always been trashed. You have a home here or should I say you are now a prisoner here as the children will never let you leave." Orosházi looks at them and smiles, "Well, while I get to serve my Sénye, you can throw away the keys." My mind became puzzled now, as I asked them, "Why do you have children and elderly spirits. Cannot your machine create everyone in their prime?" An elderly woman told me, "Son, this takes all the fun out of our relationships, as your poor sweet Orosházi has discovered the enchantment of a child spirit." Orosházi answers, "Oh, you speak the truth; however, I have a great need now, which I need help." The adults asked her, "Great friend, what do you need?" Orosházi explains to them that she needs my light in her, or she will explode. I was shocked when she said this, embarrassed as the men all looked at me, and grinned. A few of the older women came up, put their arms around her, and said, "We understand. You are truly in love with your Sénye." She confesses to them, "He floods my heart with his love and makes me believe like a true living spirit." The old woman pats me on my back and says, "We are so proud of you young Durovian." They examine their mates and tell them, "Take her to the number-one special tunnel."

They wrap us up into their unique force and off we go. They actually have a special setup here, as it is quite large. Into a tunnel, which appears to be off in a secluded area, they take us. The men tell me when we are finished, go down to the lake, and relax. The group likes to glide through the lake before retiring into their assigned family units. They will assign us to a family unit tomorrow. I ask Orosházi how she can ask for a place that we can make love to a group we just met. She tells me, "Just like all men, you do misunderstand these things. Now, give me your hand and get your light inside me currently, or I will swallow you." I grab her hand and allow her to pull my light inside her. Once inside, I begin to understand what was happening inside her. She actually was alone for way too long. This loneliness had caused so much of the pain she kept locked in those special rooms. A few of the doors were open now, and the ugly ooze was pouring out. I grabbed a nearby suction hose and began collecting this ooze as it was pouring out of her spiritual body. I am not going to explain these hoses being so conveniently located nor am I going to explain this ooze. The hoses remove the ooze. They created this way for our spiritual bodies. My mate is slowly beginning to heal inside her soul. I have to respect her in that when I could see no trouble in her life, she continuously confessed to me; she had trouble. I believed that she was simply trying to make me suffer less for being so weak and foolish. She brought me great honor today by portraying her devotion and loyalty to our relationship. Accordingly, I have no problems is confessing that I am her mate. She can be totally destroyed inside and still paint a picture of total contentment. I ask her why she is like this. She tells me that without a mate, the mission is simply to survive. To be weak around Emsky is to invite a living death, which is worse than all the ooze inside her. I must agree with her on this one, as I find myself agreeing on everything, the other part of me says.

I did allow my ego to elevate itself today when Orosházi claimed to all to belong to me. I saw all the male spirits stare at me with envy and that felt good. I naturally stood taller and behaved as if I were stronger. I ask Orosházi if that was a good thing, I did or a bad thing that I did. She tells me it was a good thing. That is why she submitted herself to me, and when I behaved, as I was durable, that made her appear greater in having a strong protector. She begins to spray me with her special spiritual wine. The spray elevates me into a new peaceful bliss. At this point, in my existence, I am my whole. I am inside the greatest creation that I ever met, and we are in a sanctuary with spirits from my existence, while outside is a raging sea of wicked danger. Of greater importance, someone special needs me. Throughout my entire life, I had difficulty understanding relationships and always searched for a meaning. I am now in my relationship and ask myself, why I would need to have or understand a meaning. It exists, and it is real. The greatest credit for this peace of mind is that I am in Orosházi, as she is in mine. I do not worry about her being in my mind, as the greatest thing on my mind constantly is when my light is inside her once more.

Through her aggressive and openness in her desire to have my light in her, we agree. She did not care about any great honor for herself; instead, she struggled for a way to give her mate, what her mate wanted, claiming it to be her wish. This was to the delight of all the male spirits and surprisingly to the respect of the female spirits who felt she was professing her complete devotion to her mate and relationship. If a man had asked those questions, they would have looped him to the nearest fire pole and burned him. Nevertheless, when a woman asks it, she is a hero and dedicated mate. They realize how and when to make these requests, while preserving their label as heroes or vessels of purity. I have no complaints about her loyalty and the creativeness she uses to cement our bond. After all, I am the one who is relaxing under the spray of her heavenly wine of love.

Orosházi has a tight lid on her previous relationship, as I see that her kingdom arranged it. I witness the limited happiness in the early parts of the relationship and then intensive hate and disappointment. After a few highlights, I move on to something else, not wanting to stir any bad memories for her suffering through once more. It is sad that someone who needed so little hand to wait this long to receive something. I regret that she must depend on me, mainly because I am accordingly dependant on her. Because others abused her, it gave me no license to abuse her. I witness cases such as this in the days of my book, or commonly known as the book of life, which is the record of my days. I saw how that when someone unjustly became labeled, or even justly, everyone went for the kill. Knock them down, and keep them down for good. I will not let this happen to the extremely gifted Orosházi, who at taking advantage of opportunities. We were on the line when I introduced us, I played the, 'I am part of your line, and she is part of me.' Orosházi in turned played the 'I cannot survive without him and I am just for him line', which worked wonderfully. Floating inside her heart and soul as I am now, I can see that she is for real. She gave herself to me, and held onto a hope of real love. Sadly, some lived no more than to find love when they are dead, yet, then again, it is better late than never. Instead, I tell her, with a loud, forceful voice, "I am going to abuse you Orosházi as you have never been abused before by a mate. You will suffer from my light staying in you too much. You will suffer from me refusing to be separate from you. You will suffer from someone who will never stop loving you. You will suffer from someone who will follow you through this universe. You will suffer from someone who is hypnotized from your eyes." She rushes into the room I am yelling at her and hovers over me, motioning for me to be quiet. She then tells me to make her suffer as she has never suffered before with a mate. We share a great hug as she drips with some more of her heavenly wine. I surprise her with a soaking of my heavenly wine. She falls to the floor in her room and just lies there frozen with an appearance of total shock. I ask her, "Orosházi, have you ever been soaked with heavenly wine before this?"

She looked and appeared as one who had just drunk a gallon of Lecia, or 250 proof firewater, the extra fifty proof coming from a secret discovered on Emsky in the early days. When we drink, we dance or trip in the stars, which was the lone thing that we ever did in the stars. She is plastered and completely in ecstasy. She has earned this. I asked her if she had ever had any great experiences during sex, which after I asked her, I realized I had put her in a compromising position. She calmly enlightened me the Jaroslaw has heavenly wine in their physical flesh. Her mate used his wine on his mistress or his secret love, never accepting her as his kingdom established mate. She could have reported him, and the kingdom would have executed him, yet instead; she held onto her official title and lived without love. She accepted that love was for some people and not for others. She tells me that we live in the lots allocated to them. Some have wonderful, happy lives, while others have barely lived. Some start at the top and continue to be elevated; others start at the bottom and constantly enjoy merely the joy of losing. The choice is when you are down, do you stay down, or do you stand up and fight, fight for every inch. Some get the pronounced break or opportunity while others got the great break or shattering. She confesses to hold onto a dream of a better day ahead and after so many years she had one choice, keep hoping or give up forever; however, she knew I would show up someday and that one day came. It did come easy, yet it was worth the darks' days, as she wears sunglasses basting in the reward of brighter days, and nights filled with armies that chase away the losers of the old days and usher in wins today. The aspect she appreciates the most about this is that she finally did die; the hate and emptiness died, and love equally important enjoyed its long-overdue day of birth.

Relationships change everything; nevertheless, they do not give everything, as they demand everything. You pay to either receive or pay when you lose. The price of losing is too high; therefore, the commitment to the new gift must be complete. I am willing to pay this price because Orosházi paid it in full just to be in the game. She went into the store and bought it, nevertheless, agreed to pay it repeatedly, until I knew what was alive in us. I appreciated the dignity; she demanded that I receive from her. Her eyes owned me, yet she fell before me willing to beg for what was hers. Perplexing and hypnotizing, as it forced me to merge my light to hers. I ask her why I must live outside as a light beside her. She explains that I am her mate to help her face our challenges. If I hide in her, I will lose myself, and we will lose our relationship. Orosházi explains that she is not always strong and needs a shoulder to cry on at times. I can understand and appreciate this. She was tough to survive, and this toughness had a price, a price thankfully she paid. Now, I must work with her to rebuild her savings. We float around above this lake enjoying the view. These Nógrád spirits have done a wonderful job carving out a home in this underworld. We zip down into the lake and explore the world under the surface. The water is clear, yet the life in this lake consists mainly of a few scarce minnows and snakes. Orosházi believes the Nógrád spirits permitted the snakes to remain to keep those from the surface from swimming in these waters. I asked her how the people from the surface could make it to this lake. She tells me that usually a network of caves will lead to an opening somewhere under the lake. I remember my cave explorations and find myself agreeing with her. An excitement runs throughout her body that I can touch as it grows. I ask her about her fresh excitement. She reveals to me that she is excited in our new membership with this group. She senses that they are genuine and will allow us to be contributing members. I wonder why contributing means so much to her. Apparently, she can read my mind and tells me that by being, contributing members, we will have a purpose filled with objectives and contributions. I tell her these objectives and contributions are headaches for me. Orosházi explains to me that when your lone objective is to survive, you will welcome a change. Instead of running for so long, you can chase for a while.

On finishing our relaxing exploration, we walk along the lake's shoreline. Subsequently, a group drops to greet us. The elders have a new spirit with them. They introduce him as our leader, Kleofas. Kleofas ask us if we would like to become citizens of the Nógrád underworld. Orosházi agrees instantaneously; however, I ask Kleofas what responsibilities being a member would include. Kleofas tells me the primary duties, he enforces are, working as a team, sharing the community duties, joining in the defense, not working for any wicked groups. He transmits the complete community agreement to Orosházi and me. I scan it and agree. The big thing that they emphasized was helping to defend each, which I would believe to be a given, that by being a combined group, we expect our security and must agree to provide it and that we accept a post or function in this community. Kleofas explains that usually for mated spirits, as, so few mates, one member in that mate would perform a role. He continues, nevertheless, for your group we would hope that Orosházi would accept the post for our family by becoming a teacher for their young spirits. Kleofas qualifies this by saying that they understand that to survive in the future they must learn to cohabitate with other species. He smiles and confesses that they realize not all foreign species will be as beautiful as Orosházi, nonetheless, the children need this exposure, as our adults will also gain from this exposure, as parenting rotated, and the parents remain the same, just the children rotate to new families. He looks at Orosházi and further explains, "You are in no danger of abusive treatment here, and any who do will lose their membership. I just believe that if we can make this into a natural concept and not a behavior-modified concept, which we will benefit. You will also gain through experiencing our childish emotions and experiences, which will allow you to share theirs and formulate your foundation." My love was bubbling as never before this miracle. She looked at me, and I nodded my head yes. She rushed to Kleofas, hugged him, and accepted telling him she would do her best. Kleofas glances at me and comments, "It was a lucky day for the Nógrád spirits when you arrived." I smile and then, feeling overambitious, a trait I am not famous for, volunteer for a post. He asks me if I believe that my relationship could handle it. I tell him, "I hope the times would be the same; therefore, we both can have the same free time. It is not like we are in the days of our lives and must return home, cook, clean, and perform or get tired." Kleofas reveals to me that he has a special function for me, which he will discuss with me privately. He looks at Orosházi and asks her, "Do you think your mate would enjoy preparing a chronicle of Emsky, with his book included?" She tells Kleofas, "You would have to ask him, although I can assure you I will recommend that he accept it. I am inquisitive about the history of his world and would enjoy exploring the history of this wonderful world." Kleofas asks her, "Are you curious about his book?" She tells him, "No, because he already shared his book with me. I appreciate everything about his life, mind, and heart. That is why I made myself his slave." I gaze at her and tell her, "Orosházi, we understand who the master is in this relationship, and it is not me." Orosházi lowers her head and responds, "I wish it were you."

Kleofas ask her, "Precious and beautiful Orosházi, so many, including myself, wonder if you have any sisters or girlfriends in the area who would enjoy sharing our community?" She smiled and told him, "I love your flattery and even myself wish I had sisters or girlfriends from this area. Unfortunately, I traveled a long time and distance to arrive here. I realize that others with my adventurous spirit will pass through someday." Kleofas tells us, "Well, we are lucky to have you. Now, follow us and we will show you your private home." They took us through some rocks and soon to the space; they reserved for us. They gave us a space that we enclosed by rock. Spirits do not need space such as, we did while alive. The primary thing is an agreement that others will not take it and use if for any other function. Orosházi tells me we are lucky to be in the rocks. Rock areas are prized commodities for spirits. I ask her if she truly wants to be a teacher. She confirms her desire, sharing with me how much she always wanted to have children; nevertheless, her mate would not accept a reproducer for their marriage. Because her body did not have the reproducing organs, she had to submit. This submission guaranteed her life would be empty and lonely. Orosházi asks me if I noticed how the children adored her. I tell her, "Children love unknown things; nonetheless, new things get old fast. Notwithstanding you will be a teacher and be able to keep your material fresh for them; therefore, you should not have any problems." She corroborates that keeping the new material is extremely important. She always favored the teachers who made the material exciting. The key factor for her is that she gets this opportunity and understands that a few of the other teachers may become jealous and cause problems; however, this is normal social behavior and although some, based on the species differences, those who favor her species will balance against those who do not. She knows that any difference between the other teachers will warrant a form of negativity. Her strategy is to concentrate of her class and avoid the faculty as much as she can. Her need for companionship and love was purely satisfied with me. She falls into my arms and tells me, "If you give me love; I will have love. If you do not give me love, I will be without love. I am your female and have no options of choice except to obey me." I tell her, "Orosházi, that may have been your way while living, nonetheless, that is not the way of the Nógrád spirits so reprogram your mind to, I will kick his hind end if he does not treat me with respect and honor. I am equal and he promised me his love, and he will keep that promise, or we will have troubles."

Orosházi confesses that it will take a little time, and that she does not understand why her way of thinking disagrees with me. She believes that I should enjoy this power, especially because she is so happy to give it to me and needs the security of belonging to someone. I think for a few seconds and then understand where she is coming from, therefore I tell her, "Orosházi, will you also allow me to belong to you so I can have security in this relationship. I still believe you are of great value, and a wonderful dream come true mate. We can think your way and work on adding my thinking so that the road we travel will be ours. Can you compromise?" She agrees to compromise, especially since she will spend much time with the children. She simply wants everyone to recognize her devotion. I quickly tell her that I will also share my devotion and honor of her to all that I will meet. Utterly, a fool would have a mountain of gold and tell everyone it is unquestionably worthless rock. She acknowledges the joy she receives when I compliment her. Around me, she claims to be in the ambiance, which is fantastically special. The miracle of me opening a few sad doors inside her and pulling out those bad memories give her hope that someday, I will be able to travel through all her rooms and go places inside her that even she may not go. This spiritual intimacy far exceeds what he had when living. I wonder if the reason she insists on being so subservient is from something in my spirit that I am not aware. I agree with her concept of the security on a tight bond. We share, and we care. Orosházi asks me what responsibility I believe Kleofas has in mind for me. I tell her that I suspect it will be something perfunctory totally to keep me occupied so they can keep her happy. Orosházi disagrees with me believing that Kleofas has something special in mind for me. I tell her we will soon know. Orosházi asks me if I am ready to come out of her now. I tell her yes and spin myself out of the light tunnel reforming in front of her. Oroshází asserts that she already misses having me inside her. I tell her not to worry for I will soon reenter. Oroshází tells me the next time is her turn and she will be in me during the spiritual quit time tonight. I tell her I am looking forward to this time. I truly enjoy having her inside me. She calmly finds my empty spots and fills them.

Our predictions of the leaders soon visit proved true. When he sounded the alarm requesting entry, Oroshází pushed me to the side and rushed to lower the spiritual walls, so Kleofas could enter. While he was entering she confesses to me that what she did was wrong, it is just that she so much wants to appreciate my position. I told her not to worry about this. Somehow, I understand why she is concerned. She wants to ensure that others treat me fairly. I cannot condemn her for this. She boldly asks Kleofas if he is ready to reveal her mate's now position and responsibilities. Kleofas glances at me as I shake my head in agreement. I explain to him that my special Jaroslaw has great concerns over the quality of my existence and will search for ways in which she can support me. Kleofas acknowledges how lucky I am. I tell him that every day and night is exciting now. Consequently, we do not sleep; however, we do have quiet family or friends' time. Most share stories about their lives. The mates who foster the children use this time to teach the youngsters the values and customs of their clan. Kleofas ask us to seat ourselves, which really did not make sense to me, as sitting or standing, we are in solid rock; therefore, it should make no difference. I begin to suspect that he may not have the great news that we hoped to receive. Oroshází sits beside me, although at first she tried to sit in my lap, nevertheless her wings would not support this, fittingly she sat as close to me as possible and wrapped her arms around my chest. Kleofas senses, our apprehensions, and asks us to relax. He has good news for us; it is that to sell it to us, he will have to explain the concept initially. Oroshází, who always speaks her mind, now displays her bargaining and pleading skills. She tells Kleofas that her mate's position is more important to her than the teaching they gave her. Kleofas tells her that he will take care of her mate. He also advises her not to act so subservient when with her mate when in public. This behavior puts the other female mates on the edge and would soon breed trouble.

I confirm this telling her I believe it would be better if she did her total release when we are in private. Stand beside me as an equal, even if you do not believe this, become an actor, and play the part. Kleofas recommends that she stand tall, proud, and strong because she does represent the Jaroslaw. Kleofas reminds her that here she will be treated as the ambassador for Jaroslaw. He confesses to her how they are so hungry to learn about the other worlds, considering that they cannot explore them until the Empire takes over this galaxy. Kleofas reveals to her that it is scarcely a matter of time before the Empire annexes her Laurentius galaxy, and when they do, she will have a huge advantage. Orosházi reveals to him that she does not understand, if she is ready for the Empire, and may need much more time to consider joining, as it does take away much of her freedom. Kleofas informs her that he will provide her with the updated spiritual annexation program. She will find many misconceptions the wicked ones have spread. He has been in conference with one of the advance disciples just before coming to meet us. He told this disciple about us. The disciple explained that all spirits were free to travel wherever they wish. The main inconvenience is that if they wish to travel in an area, the Empire believes is dangerous, they will have the spirit soldiers escort them. They believe that any who belongs to the Empire, if they wish to travel and explore elsewhere may do so, and if they wish to return will have an avenue making this possible. If they wish to leave, the Empire removes their claim and releases them. They may rejoin later if they wish. Kleofas revealed to him the disciple shared a map of Laurentius with him, and they actually reviewed some landscapes on Jaroslaw. They are concerned with the lowering sea levels as their scans report large cracks under the sea is draining water into the planet core, which turned to steam causing other dangers. They also need to settle more on the twenty-two moons around Jaroslaw, as they are dangerously settling in land gained from the decreasing sea levels. Orosházi looks at him stunned claiming it is impossible that they could view her galaxy, as it is clearly too far away. She asks Kleofas how he knew about the twenty-two moons. He tells her that he counted them, and he did see her Jaroslaw and was impressed with the organization and discipline. Orosházi asks him how this is possible.

Kleofas tells her to relax; the Empire has gates, which open in other distant parts of the universe. They have armies dedicated to fight wicked spirits anywhere they can find them. If their sword of justice or sword of freedom reveals many vicious spirits in an area, they will use their nearest gate to deploy large armies in that area. Once they win, the armies return. I ask him why they are fighting so many long-range battles when we still have wicked spirits in this galaxy, which they approved for annexation. Kleofas tells us that he asked the same question, and the disciple explained that a total cleaning such as ours is much more intensive and executed following the universe's divine laws. These laws forbid the injury to blameless spirits, and the wicked spirits in our galaxy are hiding among these innocent spirits causing the delays. Their ends are near, as they exist trapped inside this galaxy, and the slow, intensive sweep from all four sides of Chuprin will end when they connect in the center. I confess to him that it is an amazing process. Orosházi now worries about others coming after her. She confesses to Kleofas that her mate abused her, and she escaped holding onto a dream of someday finding love. Kleofas tells her to relax, as the disciple reviewed all reports about her life, and he reported you as a qualified saint. Orosházi comments, "I finally found a mate who believes in me, and now an Empire who wants me. My existence has changed for the better for sure." Kleofas asks her why she did not list the Nógrád solely of not believing in her, but also wanting to have her as a part of their family. Orosházi admits to the error in her statement and explains to Kleofas her strong desire to prove she wants to be a part of the Nógrád family.

Notwithstanding, Kleofas switches our topic back to me. He begins his presentation by explaining to us the Empire collects, chronicles of important events in the history of the worlds they assimilate. The Empire is serious about education. They have discovered the more, their people understand about each, another, the more unified and willing they are to exist as one large family. The histories of the various worlds are strangely similar; however, each world has important events in their history, which is a source of pride. The Empire works hard to preserve the special histories of the worlds before entry. Freedom for all to know, share, and respect are a concept they enforce. Orosházi asks Kleofas why the Empire does not have their lights prepare this chronicle. Kleofas explains the lights concentrate on rational objectivity omitting any allegiance or emotions. Remember, they are allowing us to chronicle our emotions and subjectivity. Additionally, they have as many as twenty different supporting chronicles for each world. If the first chronicle claims one kingdom to be evil and wicked, they will have a spirit of that kingdom prepare a chronicle filled with their emotions, allegiance, and subjectivity. These helps define the whole picture. I acknowledge to Kleofas that such endeavors sound worthy and clearly assist the other worlds in knowing who their previous neighbors who now live in the same house are. He tells me this news makes his mission here much easier. He continues, "Sénye, we believe that you would be able to prepare this chronicle, with Orosházi's help as no army is great enough or foolish enough, to pull her from your side. We appreciate that your existence is limited to Durov and the remaining reports of the other parts of Emsky will be new to you, or confined by what they taught you in your school. We believe that you have a hunger for truth and the energy to find it and define it. Moreover, we are comfortable with your Jaroslaw, who has survived in the wicked upper worlds for way too long." I explain to Kleofas that my partner and equal, knows much more about Emsky than I could ever know. Kleofas explains this is one primary reason they think I am the one to execute this project. We will have our eyes, plus the eyes of our honored adapted Jaroslaw Saint. He looks at Orosházi big glaring eyes and tells us that he has no reservations about those in the Empire seeing us under the influence of Orosházi's perceptions.

Next, I ask him how she will be able to teach and help me at the same time. He tells me that since all their schools are demanding to have her; they have decided to assign her to different schools on a rotating base. She will teach random classes, no more than three each day and strictly three days or less each week. They have also agreed to allow me to join her, if we so desire. Orosházi yells out, as she is jumping for joy, "We desire." They pore over me and with her wonderful glowing eyes innocently begging me to agree, I say with enthusiasm, "We desire." Thereafter, it became obvious to me that I had just agreed, and I knew I had to qualify this by adding, "If we accept this assignment, as you can respect we need some more details." Kleofas comments, "Just as a true Durovian, always suspicious. I do respect and understand this, a skill I have learned to master from all the Durovians who share this community." He then decided to talk about the process. The Empire has provided Emsky with advanced history scanners. We will be competent to explore events almost as if we were there. We may read selected memories, so long as it does not invade their personal privacy or reports information that would dishonor them. We merely have to review these events, explore them as much as we desire, and then chronicle them. There is no right or wrong, therefore, want some emotion in these chronicles. We understand that it is impossible to record all events, so a large part of the value in our chronicle is the events or people we reveal. Kleofas adds that he think we will truly enjoy this historic adventure. Orosházi looks at me and discloses, "Sénye, I believe we could do this with the justice it deserves. I have faith in us and our great abilities." She then turns to Kleofas and asks him if we can include my life in these chronicles. Kleofas agrees that this would be great, in the readers would be able to understand more about the author. I glance at him and tell him we will do it. Kleofas invites us to the chamber room the Empire has set up for us to prepare these chronicles. I tell him that this is amazing, that the great Empire wants to see our feelings and adventures. Orosházi asks Kleofas if it is true that all spirits are the same species. Kleofas acknowledges this and asks me if all the suffering I have endured worth being different. Even the Emsky spirits are changed, we go through this, the same way, and come out a unified member in a great family. Orosházi confesses that this does have some great merit. She looks at me and asks, "Mate, are we ready?" I stare at Kleofas and say, "We are ready!" Kleofas adds one more request. The Empire approves of you expressing your feelings, emotions, and views in these chronicles. He believes that if we do this, it will strengthen our rock solid relationship. Orosházi squeezes my hand, which signals agreement, so I tell Kleofas we have no trouble with this.

CHAPTER 02

The six stones

Orosházi and I followed Kleofas as he led us to the center of their sanctuary. We saw a giant red door, with strange appearing angels guarding it. I asked Kleofas where he had found these male angels, as I put my hands over Orosházi's eyes. She pushed my hands off and rested her head on my shoulder telling me not to worry, as we are bonded. Kleofas explains to me; they are from the Empire and are here to protect the writers of the chronicles. There are others inside our limitations who make sure the wavelengths you received had nothing altered. Orosházi eagerly rushes into this special capsule, which has over fifty windows, all which are black. As we scanned them, the inside filled with a bluish-green fog. Next, a tree with many branches appeared, and on the top branch, sat a black bird. Afterwards, the windows began to vanish, all draining into a small hole that appeared on the wall before us. My mind begins to wonder what is happening, yet I realize we must hold onto our faith that this is not from evil, but instead of the righteous Empire that eventually will accept Emsky. Someday this will be after our chronicle is finished, and when the Empire has removed all the wickedness from our realm. For now, I can simply dream of this. I am so happy that Orosházi is considering this amalgamation. Back to our current situation, all windows have poured into this hole as the hole vanishes. We are in a room with a dead tree and the tranquil black bird staring at us. Subsequently, a new hole appears before us with a fresh window then expands. We watch it expand so large that it covers one complete wall. The black bird flies to it and then through it, vanishing in the thick yellow fog that fills its opening. I ask Orosházi if she can guess at what is happening. She tells me that she can guess all day; however, she believes the yellow window is the history we will be watching and the lifeless tree in our cavern continued tied to it someway. She believes the bird flying into the window established the link. I agree with her. We stand together, patiently staring at the yellow thick fog. Finally, an image appeared in the window. It was a stream flowing and then in the front appeared eight stones, of varying sizes stacked on top of each. The stone on top was the largest. I have never seen stones stacked like this in my life; therefore, I can no more than propose that they are connected or held together by something, because they should have fallen and be scattered in the rushing stream beside them. Orosházi does not want to make any guesses about this image because she believes it has a definite message and unquestionably is a symbol for something. Orosházi additionally recommends that we wait at the large window, because we do not understand what is happening and could find ourselves on the wrong path.

I inform Orosházi that while we are waiting would be a good time for her to shine her light inside me. I promised this gift to her. She looks at me and declines the invitation, "Not here Sénye, because, if we get caught, I would be so humiliated. We must appear as ethical spirits if we want the Empire to help us in this mission." I tell her, "You are just like the women on Emsky, always worried about what others may think that you cheat yourselves out of available opportunities." She winks at me and explains, "I am not cheating myself; I am simply temporary changing the start time." As we were talking, the window changed and is now displaying a blue sky with white clouds. In the center, a small golden sparkle began to move toward us. Thereafter, an image began to appear as the golden sparkle approached us. This image was an angel with large golden wings. Unlike other angel wings, she has had solid gold bones that appeared like ram horns as the upper frame for her wings. She wore a white hood with gold trim on her head, short dress under a long white opened robe. She had a thick golden band with a diamond packed emblem on the front around her neck. She also had a huge gold necklace with large golden fruit platters, which hung on and between her sizable breasts. In her right hand, she held a golden wand with a powerful torch on top. My apprehension decreased because her left hand, which she held out from her upper left leg, while pushing her robe against her wing revealing her fingers spread open. She came to the window and asked us if she could enter. Orosházi invites her in, as long as I do not focus on her breasts. I tell her not to be accordingly silly and worry so much about every other female in our world. She enters our cavity and introduces herself, "I am the angel called Vinik and was sent here to be your guide while you prepare your chronicles. Orosházi, have no jealousy over me. I am neither male nor female, but a creation of the throne. We simply chose an appearance in which the other spirits will have little fear." Orosházi thanks her for understanding as she once more confesses, "I have searched so long and hard for a click, and this click I need to serve so I may survive." Vinik calms Orosházi by explaining, "I understand my child, the throne requested that I review the personalities and customs of the area on Jaroslaw where you lived. I have also searched Sénye heart, as have you, and discovered your click will solely click with you. If any relationship problem could have occurred, the throne would have selected another."

I ask Vinik, "Now that the one who just a few minutes ago refused to shine her light in me is at ease, what is your purpose concerning us?" Vinik looks at Orosházi and questions her, "What were you embarrassed by being caught. I do not understand much about the light sharing, except I have witnessed so many sharing this activity. I am with you from this day forward. I will not be pretending as if I am gone. Your needs are more important than me. Never be embarrassed around me, for I am a special species created by the Power Spirits of the throne. Your privacy is with me, nor from me." Orosházi looks at her and replies, "Somehow, I understand your words." Vinik's mission is to guide us through Emsky's vast and varied history. Vinik explains that Emsky's history is unique, in that like the other worlds, so many space Empires set up colonies, yet the oddity is that all these Empires were of the same race. Moreover, many deities established thrones her, yet were either defeated or lost interest, making Emsky a world with a deity. I tell her for a world without a deity, the priests sacrificed so many children. She reveals that Nógrád was not the lone place, which sacrificed children. Vinik looks at Orosházi and explains to her that she is also a special feature in the Chronicles of Emsky, by being one of the extremely few spirits from other species to exist here, and the single one to survive. Now the Nógrád spirits have added her to their clan, she is the first foreign species accepted here. She is amazed at how we clicked, considering the extreme complexity of her clicking process and the first ever Emsky click. She suspects something else could have played a role and assures us if the Empire discovers that force has an evil purpose, they will destroy it, and because we have given our wills to each other, replenish that will with an extra strong potion.

Orosházi has a special glow flowing over her now, as she confesses to Vinik that, even though I am so ugly, I have grown on her and she would extremely be pleased to care for such a pitiful creature. I thank Orosházi for that wonderful endorsement. She kisses me and assures me she was playing. I realize her real mind, and that she was indeed playing. I tell her, "My love, there is actually a strong element of truth to your words." She looks at me with fire in her eyes and declares, "Sénye, there is no truth in those words, because every word was false." I wink at her and say, "Ha-ha; I got you." She winks back and says, "Paybacks for you will be especially rewarding." I released some tension when she told me this. I had to tell her, "Orosházi, you are so special and wonderful." She tells me we need to focus on Vinik and stop wasting her time. Vinik explains this is not a waste of her time and recommends we include it in the chronicles, as it adds some validity of our ability to accept change and others. I tell Vinik that not all shared my views. She rebuts with, "Nor is there any world we have annexed that all shared the same views. The marvelous thing is that, after we annex them, they share or encompass the Empire's views, which do give way for individual variations." Orosházi shares with Vinik that she always hears wonderful things about the Empire, yet never hears anything pessimistic, which makes her extremely suspicious. Vinik explains this is because the Empire works hard to prevent negative situations from occurring. She cites the Empire has experienced disruptions and internal conflicts, yet has handled them through those involved. Any world or person who wishes not to be in the Empire they expelled. If they do not want the great peace, love, and security the Empire offers in our demon-free Empire, we place them outside our expanding borders. The Empire has too many loyal worlds to care and share. Vinik further adds the Empire's flesh dwellers usually live for at least one millennium before resting in the Empire's vast heavens. The Empire also has large Armies composed of Saints who voluntarily share in the spiritual security missions. Orosházi watched the large window as it displayed visions verifying what Vinik is reporting.

I ask Vinik where a good place to start our exploration would be. Orosházi adds her question, "Vinik, what does this tree behind us and the vision of the stacked rocks mean?" Vinik tells her the tree is the outline of the history of Emsky, as; so many tangles small branches touch the other main five branches. The branches in the tree will become obvious as we travel through Emsky's history. The stacked rocks symbolize the different dispositions that Emsky has evolved. This too will become more obvious. Orosházi asked Vinik which stone represents Emsky's current disposition. Vinik reports to us that Emsky is in the rock immediately below the large uppermost rock. The huge top rock represents the Empire, which is why this stone is polished and shining. The color variation between the two uppermost stones is minimal showing the compatibility for assimilation. The flowing stream that surges on both sides represents the Empire. Orosházi wonders if there is a relationship between the tree and the second rock. Vinik confirms this association. Curiosity is killing me, as I need to comprehend what this means. Vinik tells us the different ages and worlds existed; each one before the current one destroyed itself, or extinguished by aliens. The first one Emsky1 existed during a time when the orbits were much different. At the beginning of their disposition, thirty-five planets composed this galaxy, which floated in a group, as ice balls, through space. Then an enormous, powerful spirit, who had escaped from a mighty spirit, now considered deities, discovered these small floating balls. In those days, deities formed as giant clusters. Then they slowly began to explode, creating throughout the universe collecting galaxies. Emsky floats on one of the outer spirals of Chuprin in an empty branch that barely stays in the galaxy. This probing power child, whose name was Emsky, roamed through certain mystery space dust without flowing with the vibrations and on departing, suffered particular mystery reactions. He collected dense masses of gasses and radiation. His disrupted guidance sense made him crash into four of the Chuprin planets, which hurled him into the Emsky solar system. The combined weight of these worlds caused him to vomit, and out of his spirit shot a large mass collection of the dense gasses, he had absorbed.

The friction from these dense gasses created an explosion that formed a star. The star's gravity took hold twenty of the loose worlds, spinning them around as they slowly established orbits. Emsky lost control of the other worlds, as many crashed into each, another, creating the many moons that flow around the remaining worlds. The heat released from this star melted the ice on these worlds, and slowly life evolved. Emsky pulled this solar system out of Chuprin far enough that just sufficient gravity would keep it from roaming as a free solar system. Emsky once more had a reaction to the space dust he had consumed. This time, he expelled space dust, which had collected traces of his spirit and during its journey to the surface of the worlds mixed with the surface minerals creating life forms. Eight of the planets had Emsky's child flesh beings on their worlds. His divine coding created the genetic codes needed to produce a male and a female. Klimek was the first man and Benina was the first female to produce the first couple or parents of Emsky's first disposition. Their survival was harsh compared to the other stones or dispositions; nevertheless, they prospered. They adapted to the harsh environments by developing their worlds under the surface. Even to this day, deep under the surface remain the remnants of their civilization. They worshiped Emsky as their god and in return, he did great works for them, giving them advanced technologies. Some of the other planets in the Emsky solar system that had life also prospered, yet above the surface as their orbits gave them special life sustaining environments. One world became angry and jealous and searched the other worlds for life forms, destroying all they discovered. They had difficulty tracing life on Emsky; however, their scans verified a healthy civilization under the surface. They elected to flood the secret air vents with biological hazardous agents, spreading disease throughout this underworld. When Emsky discovered what they had done, he became dreadfully angry. He had given this world his name as it was the one he visited most. In his wrath, he destroyed the life of the invading world. When he finally realized all life on Emsky died from the devastating plague, he sealed the air vents and crushed two moons, spreading them over Emsky sealing the plague until it would eventually destroy itself. Emsky departed from his little solar system, going deep into the universe to find another home.

Our eyes filled with tears as the visions revealed to us how much Emsky cared for this solar system. Over one billion years passed until another creator, named Klothild, came scouting through this area. Klothild lost his galaxy in a state of war with her neighboring deities. She fled far across the galaxy searching for a small solar system, which had no deities. Klothild had accepted an appearance as a human, because she had detected that this life form was appearing everywhere, and she felt comfortable with this human shape. Naturally, she formed herself with great beauty. She had fluffy red hair and soft silky skin. She wanted to be special; therefore, she had one green eye and one brown eye. She wore a unique two-inch thick green necklace with a large egg shaped gem hanging down from it. She carved special symbols from the language of her former divine creator. The necklace held her power, and by actually being a part of her shape, she could turn the power on or off as she desired. This proved beneficial for her as she drifted through space, as many evil divine forces also floated through space, looking for weaker divine gods to destroy and take their power. These evil forces gave no mind to straggling flesh dwellers. Accordingly, Klothild would transform into flesh when confronting these god killers. They ignored her allowing her to pass through in her custom-designed space ship. She elected to stay in this divine created an advanced spaceship, which transported her into the deep universe, when she discovered the Emsky worlds. Emsky created an invisible sign with his name on it over the upper atmosphere around Emsky. He did not label any of the other worlds in this solar system. When Klothild saw this sign, she searched for any evidence that a divine spirit was in this solar system. Once she verified the solar system was without a god and worlds with merely animals flooding their surfaces, she elected to make Emsky her new home. She erased the name sign in fear that evil forces would detect it and capture her. This was the main reason she decided only to create life for one world. Her loneliness compelled her to become actively involved with this world. She had to create people, yet could not create the proper elements to form a couple. This was when something unusual ensued.

Klothild needed to create people in her world. She decided to take an animal species and reprogram its DNA (Deoxyribonucleic acid) to form a male father in her world. She wanted one that was tall and strong; therefore, she chose a large guerilla, which at that time on Emsky, stood ten feet high. Klothild reprogramed the DNA to produce a male around six feet, six inches. She did not like too much hair on the male so she altered these genes as well. When she first saw this new transformation, she immediately knew they would spend much time together. She named him, Benoit, and each day walked with him. Klothild carefully programmed his reproductive organs to produce his genetic material with the new DNA so his children would be a version of human and not an animal. Klothild discovered that Benoit did not have appropriate defense abilities against the animals. Accordingly, she built a high rock wall around his large garden, which was about one hundred acres. She gave him beautiful flower gardens, fruit trees, and many acres of vegetables. Emsky was in the second orbit of its new sun, which kept it hot. It had many mountains, more than today with a, much lower sea line. The mountains formed many rivers that flowed through the continental islands, supporting life. Klothild has designed Benoit's new garden land with a large stream flowing through it, with fences under the water tight enough to prevent animals from gaining access, yet open enough to allow the fish to pass through it. She also added a large net in the middle of the stream as it passed through this garden. This allowed Benoit to catch fish if he wanted to eat fish. Klothild decided to live in this garden; she called the Home of Benoit. Her deep affection for Benoit changed this animal ruled world.

Klothild fell deep in love with Benoit, who did not realize she was divine. All that he knew came from what she told him. She reported to Benoit that he had hit his head on a large rock from trying to climb a neighboring cliff. Klothild even showed him the cliff, which she had sealed in blood on a nearby rock as proof. Benoit had no choice but to accept this, considering Klothild was the only other living, being. Klothild did her divine work when Benoit was sleeping. She did not like the way Emsky was accordingly hot and dry. She determined that Emsky was too close to their sun; therefore, she moved it back to the third orbit, which it would share with another world. She placed Emsky 180 degrees opposite of the other planet in this orbit. This new orbit cooled Emsky and created a winter season, which helped kill many of the excess animals, who had never experienced the bitter cold and the absence of vegetation. Klothild, in her deep love, gave Benoit dominion over all the animals that lived on Emsky. She gave him a hunger for animal flesh, and the skills needed to trap and hunt animals. She would clean the animals that he killed and prepare them for consumption. She created an invisible dome over the Home of Benoit, and opened a hot spring, which released heat when they left the entry point open. Klothild informed Benoit that they had always slept together. One day, when they went to do their daily walk around the garden, a strange new event occurred. This event was the first rain on Emsky. This process occurred without Klothild's intervention, and at first; she was terrified. This fear disseminated when the rain stopped, and she noticed it not only cooled down the land, but it also gave the plants a healthy drink of water. This expanded the vegetation throughout Emsky. As the large grasslands filled dry, sandy lands, the animals began to migrate. This shift by one orbit was enough to allow Emsky to prosper. Benoit invited Klothild to join him in a hunt one day. This hunt changed their relationship by adding intimacy.

Benoit spotted a large beast grazing. He had not eaten so far that day, as he preferred to hunt while hungry. The hunger would convince him to kill. He drew back his bow and shot the arrow straight into the beast's neck, where he had aimed. Benoit consistently tried to hit those fleshy parts, because, if he hit a bone, the arrow would bounce. He always did the initial field cleaning immediately after the kill. On this day, he handed his knife to Klothild for the cleaning. She cut along the animal's body to remove the organs. She attempted to cut off its head, yet could not do so. Benoit could cut and twist sufficient to remove the head. His great might was not adequate to carry this trimmed carcass. He asked Klothild to help him. Klothild, who had her divine powers turned off, struggled hard to help carry this animal with Benoit. When they entered the Home of Benoit and took the animal in their cleaning room, she noticed something strange between her legs. She had blood between her legs. She removed her white bloodstained gown and ran for the stream where she cleaned herself and her gown. She wondered what caused the blood, and she used her fingers to explore inside and discovered the part that broke was sealing a new passage between her legs. She did not understand anything about sex. Klothild had no idea how the female and male bodies could create a new life or child. That night, after Benoit was in a deep sleep, she used her divine powers to explore the area that had caused her to bleed this day. She determined that this passage lead to her ovaries, which she knew were her eggs. She studied Benoit's genitals, as she suspected this had to be his contributing part of their reproduction. Her divine powers discovered where Benoit's procreation liquids were stored. She had witnessed animals doing a strange act where the male would pump himself into his female partner. This had to be how they would perform this function. She was determined to do this soon, as she so much wanted to have a child. She did not recognize for sure how to initiate this, yet she just went natural in her stimulating Benoit who through his instincts finished the mission. They both enjoyed this experience and decided to practice it often, such as every night. Each night, when Benoit was asleep, she would explore her womb to determine if anything changed. One night she discovered as change, and a big change that it was.

Klothild noticed the two of her eggs were activated and expanding. This had to be her blessing, yet it was also her misfortune. Her divine powers departed from her, as she had broken the great law. This law declared it illegal for a god to reproduce with a human. The vast majorities of these violations were from male gods, enjoying the daughters of humanity. This was a delicate issue in that she may have violated an even higher taboo. Benoit was actually a guerilla whom, she had transformed into a human. The divine powers had their laws programed inside them and their mandatory responses. Klothild had forever lost her divine powers, and she was completely human now. She at present slowly became paranoid, knowing that even a beast could kill her. Without her powers, if she were to die, she would no longer exist, because her divine powers were her spirit. Each day was a painful learning experience, as these children grew larger. Benoit discovered from watching animals that their newborns came out of the female's womb existing from between her legs. He believed that Klothild's body would do the same thing. Benoit explained this to the future mother of his children. Her delivery day came; however, her children were reluctant to depart from her body. She pushed as hard as she could and many hours later, one came out. The second one was easier for her to deliver. She kept pushing hard and finally; he dropped from her body. Benoit congratulated her for creating two sons whom, they called Koloman and Amilleus. Klothild had painful damage inside her and had to rest for two months before she could walk and function in a normal manner. Their two sons grew tall and strong. Klothild found herself alone usually as Benoit enjoyed hunting with his sons. One day, Klothild saw a space ship land in the next valley from their home. The ship had serious mechanical problems. She rushed to the crash, entered the ship, and discovered three women unconscious, and three deceased men. Klothild pulled the three women out, one at a time, and lugged them into the nearby forest. This mother of the new Emsky found a few weapons and tools that they might be able to use in the future. Soon thereafter, the ship exploded. She struggled, and one by one moved them around the hill that had the smoking ship. The smoke flooded the sky. Benoit saw it and rushed with his sons to the site, finding Klothild along the way. After they determine nothing more could be salvaged the help pull the three women back to their garden. One woman was older and became Klothild's great friend and second wife to Benoit. Beatrix gave him seven children, while Klothild had given him eleven, being able to produce no longer. The woman's two daughters who were among the three rescued from the ship married Koloman and Achilleus as they left the garden and built their own fort city.

Klothild grew old, outliving Benoit by over twenty years, until her body no longer functioned and both vanished from history. Benoit had no soul, as he transformed from an ape. Their children did receive souls. Twenty-two thousand years later, ships from the other worlds in Emsky's solar system began their three-hundred year invasion, taking the captives back to the other worlds to work in their deep mines, which they quickly perished. The immunities were different, which led to mass plagues throughout Emsky's solar system. Emsky was at a great disadvantage with her sister planets because Klothild had written that those who travel through space would meet their demise and that to survive, they had to stay away from the other worlds. Their sister planets accused Emsky of purposely starting the plagues and eventually destroyed all who were from Emsky. They developed deadly biological agents and within one hundred, years killed all who were living on Emsky. They forbid Emsky captives from reproducing, to the extent that their reproductive organs, both male and female, no longer remained. Disagreement over how the Emsky had suffered their genocide led to great wars in the Emsky solar system coupled with an unexpected wave of meteors lead to the destruction of life in the Emsky solar system. Emsky lay as wasteland, taking another billion years to rebuild a world capable of supporting life.

This disposition characterized itself much different from the previous ones. A god named Kelemen established a strong and powerful throne in Chuprin and within one thousand years controlled all the worlds in this galaxy. His Armies passed through the lone and the secluded solar system that was lifeless, other than disembodied spirits who once lived on Emsky from two dispositions. Kelmen's spiritual Armies collected these spirits, punishing the wicked ones and placing the virtuous ones in his heavens. He enjoyed walking on Emsky and wanted no surprises. This divine power decided to create a post for a governor of Emsky and brought ten couples spreading them out among the five large island continents. The humans slowly, yet with diligence repopulated Emsky. Kelemen, as had the other gods, favored Emsky and would occasionally visit repairing any damage and supplying them with advance technologies. The other planets felt betrayed by Kelemen's favoritism, nevertheless could do nothing than issue warnings of false crimes against Kelemen, for fear of his wrath. Many clans began living against the seashores, and with the powerful digging equipment Kelemen had given them created large tunnels that we far beneath the sea. Kelemen, knowing of the prior dispositions did not want his people accidentally to dig far down and open a tunnel from the Emsky world, for fear of releasing any plagues. He forbade digging deep tunnels under the land yet permitted digging under the sea. Because of the lack of digging machines, this large time-consuming project provided a ripe opportunity for the first evil and the wicked conqueror to pluck away at the virtuous as if she were taking fruit from a tree. There lived a Queen known as Mira. The King forced to marry his son, the Prince, who later killed his father and became King. Mira hated this as her King was sadistic in all fashions, he would have her clothing removed and parade her in front of his Armies. Many of the people sympathized with her, as they could experience the anguish in her heart. The King ceased parading her when his wicked counsel, taught him about ways to torture her. He would bind her in chains and cut her with his razor knives. Next, he would starve her for weeks at a time. All who worked in their castle could hear her pleas for mercy each day. Subsequently, he would wrap a fleshy part of her body and beat it with a thick club. This gave her the pain and internal damage while minimizing any external signs. Her beatings continued as those who worked on the castle's ability to remain silent decrease. Change had to happen.

Mira's sanity gradually escaped from her. Each day gave only misery and torture to the Queen, while the King paraded regular women into his bed making many of them pregnant. These women registered their children as his sons and daughters, and then escaped into the highlands fearing for their lives. Many disloyal clerks hid these registers planning to expose them when the King eventually would die. To their great surprise, the King's death came earlier than many projected. Each night while she lay in her prison cell, which was in the King's room, because he enjoyed having her watch him seduce the common women. The servants who had to watch this would no longer kill the normal women who slept with the King, setting them free. One night, they tied the King to the bed, and cut out his tongue. Mira had them retie him to a new door that the King had made to decorate his private torture chamber. At this time, she began driving nails into his body, beginning with the feet, legs, and arms. She had each injection sealed to minimize the blood loss. The King died the next day, having suffered her revenge. Something sparked inside Mira as; she found great joy in this revenge. The counsel of the people reconvened at Mira's plea. They did, without any hesitation coronate her, as the divine ruler of their Kingdom. She requested the counsel help her; as a semi-regent performing many of the Kingdom's ordinary day-to-day activities. During these days, many of the Kings former nighttime adventures brought back their sons claiming that they should be Kings. The counsel of the people disagreed, claiming that while the Queen lived she would rule. The Queen quickly had a new law passed by the counsel of the people, who loved her dearly; the only heir to the Kingdom had to be born from the Queen. She based this on Kelemen's laws against adultery, and that no child born from adultery could receive a heavenly appointment, nor would that child receive celestial blessings, but instead would put this Kingdom under the divine wrath of Kelemen. The temples and priests supported this claim; therefore, convincing the Kingdom, that unless they made this the law, Kelemen would unleash his wrath. The Queen had secured her Kingdom and now was the time for her to move onto her next mission.

Mira's next mission changed the lives of all who lived on Emsky. Her mind was a psychological tornado, and she needed so much to unleash the anger from her life of suffering. She loved her subjects and considered them her children, although this did not quench her desire to kill. During these days, a small Army from a neighboring Kingdom invaded her borders, massacring many of her people, including women and children. This was too much for her to handle. She called for a great Army, which she would lead in revenge. To show her Kingdom, she was serious, the Queen declared she would wear no clothing until Emsky paid the price for this invasion. Her counsel had discovered the Kingdoms from the far islands had supported this invasion. When the priests published this news to the people, they dedicated to her every able-bodied young man in her Kingdom. She called for the elderly men to teach her eighteen million men Armies how to fight. They organized these Armies into groups of ten-thousand, providing her with 1,800 Armies. She worried about how to feed them. While they trained, her Kingdom feed them abundantly. She also allowed many of the Kingdom's women to work in the shipyards while they built her many ships. She knew these ships would not be available during her wars to control all Lenti, which would require that she capture as many of her neighboring Kingdom's ships. Many followed her cause when they saw the dark bruises and scares which covered most of her body. Even as she stood naked in front of them, it appeared as if she was wearing a black gown. This intensified the Kingdom's devotion to their Queen, a devotion mistakenly, yet welcomed; she had created. One year later, another neighbor attacked her borders. She asked her advisors if any Armies were ready. They gave her

1,000 Armies, of which she took 500, appointing Generals to command these remaining 500 Armies as they invaded the first neighbor who attacked. She knew that she attacked both; any allies would need to divide their support on both fronts. She invaded the first neighbor Kingdom, as they were no match for her 500 Armies, merely having forty-two. Neither Kingdom expected an attack of this magnitude. During her first battle, she killed many enemy soldiers with her long knife. Her Kingdom had developed a method to make these blades' razor sharp and unique small stones the soldiers could take with them and maintain this special cutting power. They mowed through their enemies with ease. Mira knew that she needed something else to make these victories even easier.

That night, she walked over her battlefield searching for an answer for her dilemma. While walking, still in her deep trance, she tripped over an enemy's body and landed on another severely slashed body beside him. As her body smashed against this flesh, she became soaked in blood. Accordingly, she stood up and discovered she loved the feeling on blood on her and thereafter covered her entire face with blood. When she returned to her camp, the soldiers moved away from her. She called her Generals and demanded that everyone splash blood on their faces and uniforms. The Generals asked why. Mira explained to them that in war, the victors defeated or killed their enemies. When they see the blood on my Armies, they will realize they have killed. The sight of blood will startle some making them easier kills. If this saves just one hundred of my soldiers, which I can return to their families, the endeavor would have reaped great rewards. The Generals agreed, as many believed it was a divine inspiration that Kelemen had given her. They sent dispatches to the other Armies so that all 500 would receive this new and original war strategy. The strategy worked; with such great success, the Generals sent, dispatches to the other front so those 500 Armies could gain this advantage. Mira did not take prisoners of war. She executed every one of them, claiming the burden of feeding them only took food from her Armies. Mira had every male child killed by claiming that these young men would grow up to revenge her Kingdom when she was old. She permitted the women to live, allowing her soldiers to divide lots for them after their battles and receive them as slaves. Mira knew the war would last for a long time, and her Kingdom would need new sons. She needed pregnant women to produce these sons. Mira joked about how her soldiers would understand an advantageous way to exploit the opportunity she gave them.

Her Armies defeated and depleted the two neighboring Kingdoms. Mira sailed all their ships back to her harbors converting them into naval ships. She still had two Kingdoms on Lenti that she needed to rule the entire continent. Both these Kingdoms were landlocked; therefore, she sent diplomats to offer them a chance to surrender. They refused, not knowing her military power. This time she deployed the 800 fresh Armies, leaving her 1000 battle tested Armies to defend her expanded Kingdom. Once more, she took 400 and had other Generals attack the other rogue Kingdom. Painted in blood, and with their razor sharp long knives, they plowed through these Kingdoms, killing all males and receiving the women as booty their victories. She wasted no time, assembling 100,000 large ships attacking every harbor they discovered on Gyáli. She collected all the ships she found, sending them back to Lenti. She deployed 700 of her Armies on the Kingdoms, hitting from the borders and seashores. Her terror caused many of the smaller Kingdoms to surrender, which she demanded to be unconditional. She executed all royalty, claiming that she was now their Queen. She developed a new strategy in Gyáli, and that was taking their prisoners of war and placing them on the front lines. She gave these prisoners her soldier's uniforms and therefore, had no choice but fight or die. She formed another 1400 Armies, using 600 of them to guard nonnative former Kingdoms. She added the other 800 with her 800 and headed to Durov, where she added another 700 Armies attacking Andocs and Álmosd. After flushing out deserters on the three small islands, she became the first ever to rule all Emsky. She transplanted the men from one continent to the others for the four continents she conquered. As she believed, they soon mated with the women in the lands they now lived and began new families.

Her Kingdom reigned for 15,000 years, receiving great technological blessings from Kelemen. This propelled them into advanced space travel and mass destruction weapons. Mira's Kingdom had defeated every other Kingdom in the Emsky solar system by their 5000 year, long after her death. They declared all these lands by the name of Kelemen. This reduced the likelihood of rebellions. This was the golden age of Emsky, the ruler of this solar system. They fought hard against many wicked invading Empires, surviving for an additional 10,000 years. Emsky fell when Kelemen was defeated, as large groups of malicious deities sweep through this region of the universe. They destroyed all life that they discovered, and this did include the highly advanced Emsky world, which they blasted to bits and poisoned the atmospheres. All Chuprin lay in ruins, as the third rock not only ended for Emsky, but for all in this galaxy. Kelemen faced destruction with so many other deities. It took another one billion years before this evil devourer destroyed itself from within itself. This created a huge void of life in such a large section of the universe. Reigning deities saw this as an opportunity to gain new galaxies, as other deities finally accepted their first galaxy or galaxies. A fresh wave of evacuees passed through this quadrant, looking for new worlds to settle. One such small fleet discovered the Emsky solar system, and needed a world with an environment and animal Kingdoms as Emsky possessed. This colony began the fourth stone in the rock ladder, the only dull-gold stone. They had traveled for generations, and the newest generation desperately wanted to settle into a world and Emsky floating along the deep end of Chuprin's border. This offered the privacy they had searched so long to find. Their need for freedom created the reasons to stay.

The founding fathers of the fourth disposition stood called the Jarousek. They spent their journey escaping from the Jocki, their bitter enemies. Oddly, throughout the ages, a few drifted over to the other side and mated. These couples elicited strong reactions and caused many controversies, as the local priests demanded they continue to live; however, the Kingdoms always had them sterilized, so they could never reproduce. The Jarousek was able, around fifty years ago to break aside from their long-range scanners and changed their original heading from east to west to north and south. This assured that they would remain out of their search range, as the Jocki increased their speed, actually pulling farther away. The Jarousek had one unique feature, in that they had to remain in subzero freezing weather. When they built their cities on Emsky, built large domes with decorated walls that looked like snow clouds. The top of the doom they designed as a two-way mirror, in which they could see out and no sunlight could enter. The Jarousek had special machines to produce the extreme internal cold they needed. The Jarousek soon discovered the frigid lands in the northern parts of Álmosd and flourished in these lands. Their domed cities were designed the traditional Jarousek fashion which emphasized neighborhoods formed inside a circular pyramid. The center of the dome had a large freestanding platform the enclosed their administrative buildings, with some towers almost reaching the dooms upper window. The open space included, frozen lakes and wood spiked elevated ice sidewalks. They also built, clusters of upside-down ice picks the rose from the surface to the top of their dome. They only used gray or shades of gray, as their exterior colors. We saw the images appear before us now on our screen. The city actually looks spooky, yet at the same time special. They were a private race, and gave no attention to the other planets in Emsky's solar system, except for a few of the outer frozen worlds. They lived on Emsky for over five thousand years. In their last days on Emsky, too many modern spaceships were scouting the area, thus they decided to migrate to the deep outer five planets. They built their new cites level with the ground, allowing the ice glaciers to almost completely cover them. They carefully disassembled their Emsky cities and rebuilt them on the far deep worlds. After they removed all their structures, they unleashed their old weapons, leveling the surface, attempting to erase all traces of their existence here.

This was a special disposition for Emsky in just as the current disposition their transition was without bloodshed. Jarousek's most famous tale is the tale of Princess Bela and Countess Beatka. Princess Bela was the eldest of King Arrie, who was the Jarousek's fourth King of their new frozen planets. The Jarousek was a strict society, as they all lived so close and compact because of their architecture and cultural customs. Sex was for procreation solely, and any caught over enjoying this act placed in a warm room, which usually meant death within a few hours. Princess Bela was extremely popular among the Jarousek, as her mother had died many years earlier. Princess Bela labored hard for the children and family issues, ensuring her father's ears always knew the common people's problems. The people shared their hearts with her and served them faithfully. Princess Bela cared for the Jarousek, as they cared for her. Nevertheless, something was missing. She was empty inside. The King introduced his greatest Generals and public officials to her; nevertheless, she felt no attraction for any of them. Her father provided her with demanding male teachers during her childhood; therefore, she had the natural repulsiveness for strict authoritative men. There were wonderful men in their castle that she enjoyed, yet the royal rules were harsh; she could hardly talk with them, and never permitted to be alone. Then one day, all the trumpets sounded in the castle when Princess Bela's younger brother selected a damsel to marry. She was the Countess Beatka and by the royal laws, had to stay inside the castle for one year, while the courts thoroughly investigated her past actions. She was initially terrified when she moved into the castle. Her fiancé could not be alone with her, and anytime they met; strangers chaperoned them. She quickly became a secret depressed woman, afraid to do anything except to smile. Princess Bela detected how the Countess was suffering and decided to remedy it.

Princess Bela invited Countess Beatka to her chambers. They relaxed and shared issues each other had. Princess Bela was a master at easing people and making them share their feelings. Countess Beatka broke down on her second visit. She could be alone with Princess Bela, as no one monitored their activities, and actually promoted this union, recognizing how the new Countess needed a special friend before her wedding. Princess Bela began inviting Countess Beatka to her royal visits, as this introduced the Countess to the Kingdom. She soon became a popular figure on among the Royals. The Countess had her occasional visit with her fiancé, which was tearfully seldom. He was accordingly busy as the Kingdom prepared his schedule years in advance. The Countess found herself completely dependent on Princess Bela. Princess Bela also enjoyed the Countess, who almost lived with her twenty-four hours each day. The Countess wanted to serve the Princess in all ways, and chased the chamber servants out, as she would have bathed the Princess. The chamber servants permitted this because the Countess was not royalty, yet, and as a subject was obligated to serve the royal family. The baths would last for hours as Princess Bela confessed that she enjoyed being naked with the Countesses' hands roaming over her body. When they finished with her bath and retired to her chamber, she would bathe the Countess with her cleaning rags. The Princess requested that when they slept together, as they had for many months now, they sleep nude. Then, during the third night, the Princess and Countess shared a romantic kiss. They both enjoyed it, yet knew they had to keep it a secret. They went to the library to research women with women relationships. They fell in love and could no longer deny it. As they searched through the books, they discovered some stories of many of their female deities being lovers. There was no law of their gods forbidding it. Only the high priests made judgments on it. They knew either way; they would have to keep this a secret. The books also described how the goddesses made, love to one another. They decided to try these things, and if they did not enjoy them, they would no longer perform them and would recognize if they were to be lovers or simply great friends. This night, after pretending to be just friends throughout the day, often even ignoring each other with grace and style, they performed all the activities described in their sacred books. This exotic ecstasy fulfilled all their wildest fantasies. They knew this was their destiny. Each night, they further cemented their bond. They knew that they could never live apart. One night, Princess Bela realized that they would have to escape into the open frozen tundra to be alone. The Countess told her she knew how to get false identifications and exit to one of the other worlds, where she had friends.

The cold night came when they slipped pass, the sleeping guards she drugged. They escaped through come secret tunnels that lead to some normal Kingdom vehicles for when the royalty wanted to travel in secret. They changed their clothing while in the tunnel. That night they went to the friends of the Countess, obtained their passports and transportation passes, and were on the late-night freight flight that moved trade goods. They arrived on a world three planets from them. A special old classmate to the Countess took them inside her house, gave them haircuts, removed their Kingdom chips, and replaced them with new ones. Actually, they had their chips removed when they obtain their fresh identities. The removal of the new chips was to erase their association with their former planet. The King was frantic about the disappearance of these two royal children. They searched everywhere. The Princes run a bundle of their clothing through the palace's shredders, simply to put a little confusion and doubt into the search. The King intensified his search, nevertheless; those on her home planet stayed loyal. His son explored the other worlds. This kept Bela and Beatka in constant fear. Once they had established their new identity, and modified their habits and personalities, they were passing by strong. They had a small apartment, always ensured that they made no noises when making love, and maintained two beds, rotating which bed they slept. Things worked well; however, the males in each area would complain because they did not date. This forced them to continuously move and mix up their occupations. Their years were hard, yet the King and the Prince continued searching. One day the Prince spotted his sister working in a small machine shop. This shop was making some special personal modifications to the crown's equipment. He pretended not to notice her and one of his guards see where she lived. This was when Bela and Beatka's love met the challenges they feared.

The Prince waited at Bela's residence in disguise. When he saw how Bela's roommate resembled Beatka, he had his guards apprehend them. They involuntarily returned to the palace where their chamber maidens and the King inspected them. They all confirmed that the resemblance was too close. The King then demanded that they confess, or they would stay in his dungeons. They chose the dungeons for three years, as they were together and late at night shared their love. However, after three years, their resistance wore down, and they decided to take their chances with the judges. Their previous chamber maidens cleaned them, and appeared before the King giving their confessions and story. The King was angry and demanded they imprisoned until they agreed to terminate the relationship forever. They sat in prison, refusing. Many priests wear horrified at this disobedience of the judge's laws and demanded an execution. They could not execute the Princess without a public trial because she was next in line for the crown. The trial began, as the Princess and Countess claimed exception under the tales of the gods. They quoted the tales, as all knew them yet considered, it permissible. They swore their lives for each other were clean and permitted by the gods. The representatives argued, yet the judges ruled in their favor claimed their rulings represented an update to the divine laws. The punishment was harsh; they would have to stay in a heated room, temperature seventy degrees until they died. The King offered his daughter and almost daughter in law one last chance to renounce their relationship. The public switched their support for their beloved Princess and the Countess, believing that because they were royalties, they had the right to live as the gods lived. Unfortunately, the Judges and King believed differently. The day of execution came. Just before their execution, the King and his son begged them to renounce their love. Bela and Beatka once again declared their undying love, and they had not hurt the crown because they had gone into voluntary exile. The judges ignored their claims. The King and Bela's brother already gave up on her. The people began to riot; therefore, the judges decided to expedite the execution. This was when the tale became a part of their history and this chronicle. Bela and Beatka died within two hours, and as they broadcasted the visions, riots erupted. All the lights in the Kingdom turned into dark. The Kingdom had only the light of the snow to block all the darkness. Then, before their highest mountain, a giant image of sculptured rock appeared. The inside of this image was as great as the mountain, which was behind him. His image was the image of Mirek, as the stories of the gods told he would someday return to demand a rebirth of his justice. The priests ran to the temples and closed them, fearing the people would destroy all the temples and to hide from their punishment. Mirek sacrificed all judges and priests, and made all the King's sons sterile, so his line would die. The new priests and judges destroyed all the old laws. The people erected statues of Bela and Beatka and placed them in the palace courtyard. The King made a law that no other statues would exist in the palace courtyard, which gave Bela and Beatka greater honor. One month later Mirek's statue vanished, although he did not turn the lights back on for three months.

The fourth stone remembers Bela and Beatka each year with a one-week festival, the highlight of the year. Included in this festival is the festival of Mirek's return, and the celebration of the new order. The Jarousek still survives today on the out frozen worlds in many solar systems in Chuprin. After the burning of Bela and Beatka, they relocated most of the settlements to other solar systems, only keeping the city that Mirek's stone appeared in, declaring this sacred land. The Jocki finally discovered their search was in vain and was returning to the native worlds of their distant ancestors.

The Chuprin will belong to the Empire when they pass around, and thus the Jarousek will be safe. They continue to survive on the frozen worlds as does the memories of Bela and Beatka.

The fifth stone or fifth dimensions are the round white stone, in that this represents the sole disposition in which Emsky two non-human species ruling it. They arrived about ten million years after the Jarousek had placed most of their people in other solar systems. Any pilgrimages or trade run to their Mirek monument were in the far-distant parts of the solar system and were almost on the verge of being out of Chuprin. The Jarousek was masters at sneaking undetected, as they had perfected their cloaking abilities. The primary species or more specifically, the ones who ruled the surface were the Itchok. Their species was much different from the others. They were once complete demons and destroyed everything they could. The reason they returned to Chuprin was the joy, as they had previously been ravishing this area. They became too self-confident and ravaged a galaxy, which had three power spirit deities, which were among the most powerful. These three mighty forces captured all the Itchok and judged them. They allowed one out of time to survive; however, to ensure they never again harmed another, they trapped their spirits inside dried clay with special inside containers, which they at no time could be free. They also gave them no brain, with a limited free will. They would think as a group, as just one had a central mind per twenty. The three gods did this, so they could not roam separately. Never again would they have a self-identity. Their heads were open above their necks. They had a special peace, which held on their identical white bland facemasks. They could see through the eyeless holes where eyes would normally be. Their mouthpiece moved no more than one inch. They could not turn these masks in any direction and have to move their bodies instead. Their white masks only had about one inch of cemented mud behind them, so they had to be careful with flying objects. Their mud had to have new mineral with water daily. Most times, they would eat crushed rock or sand. They drank water every day to keep their mud from turning into cement. They had to avoid the extremes in weather, because too hot would explode them and too cold would shatter them. The females had no reproduction abilities as they closed all the female parts with no possible entry. Even something gained access; no internal womb existed to begin the recreation process. The other special feature was their hands, which replaced themselves every year. The old hands were disposed. They could not run, and survived by staying in groups. They built their homes out of stone. Their society had no weapons and used underground tunnels usually beside streams to hide. They needed the water to maintain their mud even while clandestine, and this is where streams and notwithstanding underground rivers that, when they found one, they exploited running large tunnels to follow the river for sometimes over 100 miles.

Life was slow, hard, and lonely for the Itchok. They languished along their pathways into groups; and when danger was near, they would sink into the forests and venture for their tunnels. Their constant grinding of rocks helped make the soil of Emsky softer and easier for vegetation. The Itchok developed a taste for blood. To get blood, they had to learn how to trap. They developed many types of traps catching all types of animals, who was overcrowding Emsky and needed thinning. This was not the motive of the Itchok, as they enjoyed drinking, the blood, believing it helped lubricate and soften their mud casings. They buried the animal's flesh, after grinding and eating its bones. One day, the event which changed this age occurred by an accident. The Itchok male Ártánd was strolling along inspecting his animal traps when he came on a wide meadow. He saw many trees on the other side and decided this would be a great place to add some more traps. As he was walking across the field, a strange creature crashed into him. This creature was from the Pécsi species, which barely existed in this universe, yet do still appear in a few other dimensions or universes. They at most appeared three times in our universe, and this was one of those times. They are unlike any other species in that they are just female, one-third fish, one-third bird and the remainder a species related to humans. They can breathe in the air and underwater, making the switch instantaneously. They seldom venture out during the days, as sunlight dims their eye vision, yet, to the contrary, they can see perfectly in the dark, which helps them in the high sky at night and the dark deep seas. They can eat anything, and their ovaries will produce offspring from any male hereditary material from any animal or species. They have the unique ability to reproduce both, themselves and one host from the genetic material from the provider. This daydreaming Pécsi, whose name was Bábolna had been swimming in the trees about half way up their branches, when she hit the open meadow; she wanted to make a swooping dive and the fly and swim straight up from the surface. The Pécsi can make this special move by using their fins and wings in conjunction. The sudden flashes of sunlight, which had just appeared as clouds had moved passed them, blinded her. She hit the ground first, rolled and bounced up knocking Ártánd down. When he regained his consciousness, he saw her lying in front of him severely injured. He carefully dragged her out of the opening, placing her in the forests. He then sounded his emergency horn, yet no one came. Meanwhile, he saw that Pécsi's wing and damaged fins, as were also many of her bones. He tied some branches to her injuries hoping they would hold them until he could cast them with some mud. Ártánd next snuggled her in some branches to an evergreen hoping to keep her off the ground and not visible. She did not appear good. He knew this was an emergency.

As Ártánd rushed to his group, he wondered how he would describe this creature or person. When he described it, many began to laugh. The clan leader refused to send a rescue party and instead recommended that Ártánd not work in the sun or walk in open areas. Ártánd was desperate and finally some of his friends agreed to take a wagon to this site and rescue this beast. They wanted to wait until the next morning, yet Ártánd told them this could be too late. Therefore, they immediately departed on their rescue. When they arrived, Pécsi was barely living. They gave her water and placed her on their wagon. They had eight people in their group; therefore, Pécsi recommended that two return and get some wise ones, or the ones with the brains to return and help keep this creature alive. Two brainers, or the ones with whole heads, as also Pécsi was fortunate to be a young brainer, were now dedicated to try a find a way to fix this special creature. They grabbed more branches and packed rocks beside her, trying to prevent any movement. One of the brainers examined her quickly and then returned to their dwellings to prepare for some special procedures. He assembled the brains that helped with the healing issues, although this was not mud, they would have to follow somewhat along those lines. They had no idea what was coming to their large table. The messenger recommended that they have a lot of the cement mud. This mud was easy to apply and became hard quickly. They knew that if she had broken bones, they would need a cast to hold them together so they could heal. No one could have ever guessed how many bones.

Ártánd and his friends carefully pushed this wagon back to their camp and delivered her to the brain healers. No one knew exactly what to do, nevertheless, they had chopped enough animals for their blood and bones, and they had an idea of what had to happen. They slowly spread, her out, reassembled the broken bones, moving them back in place and casting them to hold them. When they had finished, accordingly, they plastered her wings and fins were all in plaster, her backbones, legs, neck, and arms as well. The brain healers took down inside a tunnel to a river shore before connecting all the plastered areas. Once they connected them, her wingspan was over twenty feet as was also the distance from her head to the tip of her fin was twenty feet as well. Everyone just stared at her, not knowing what she was. They guessed from her long hair and large breasts; she must be female, even though bird and fish females did not have breasts. The Itchok women have extra mud on their chests that could resemble breasts. Likewise, the human women have breasts much like this creature. They searched her carefully for any weapons or information that could tell them something about her. The Pécsi searched throughout the night for her. Finally, one night they found traces of her blood in the open meadow and on the evergreen Ártánd had secured her. When they placed her on the wagon, all traces of her blood vanished. The Pécsi believed predators ate her, especially a bear, as they favor fish. They returned to their underwater city, held a memorial for her, and believed she was forever gone, ceasing their fruitless searches. A total of eight months went by, when finally Ártánd received his first surprise.

The morning started as normal, Ártánd slowly poured some liquid food into the mouth of his mysterious friend. The medical brains were afraid to give her solid food, not knowing how long it would take her insides to heal. They monitored her wastes to study her internal organs. These brains were concerned how these organs were performing relative to the decreasing quantity of blood. This morning, as Ártánd stuck the first spoonful in her month, she coughed and flinched away. Her eyes blared at him as she tried to move her body. Ártánd smiled at her and motioned for her to calm down. Unable to break free she stopped attempting to do so. He took a rag and wiped her face, patting the rag in some cool water as he hummed and massaged her cheeks, careful not to cover her eyes causing her fear. He tried to explain to her what had happened by using hand signals. She calmed down. When he finished feeding her and prepared to leave, she screamed, "Stay." He looked at her, as the medical team came rushing in and told her he would stay. She kept him there and each day she made some more progress. The brains originally feared that she would not speak the human talk. The Itchok had learned the language of the stars when they were raiders and kept it, in case they were ever to contact some other visitors. Emsky sits so far out in the openness that most do not consider it worth their time to investigate. This has spared Emsky of any visitors, which is not what the Itchok wanted. Ártánd never left Bábolna's side, which he could not have if he tried. She guarded him, and even though she knew no one was going to hurt her; she thought that everyone listened to him, and that he would not harm her. Actually, Ártánd continuously bathed her and her casts, applied the oils the brains had prepared, massaged any non-cast places to enhance blood flow, and removed the containers that had her body wastes, and cleaned those areas as she let no one else touch her. The brains believed her human parts had healed enough so they began to remove the casts from her ribs, back, arms, and leg bones that ran along the skin of her fish sections. They could determine from the broken leg bones that both legs had a fish skin wrapping that sealed them into one part, and had additional muscles for swimming and controlling her fins attached. They kept the wings' cast on, as they were composed of a lighter element and needed more time to heal, as well as requiring her back to heal primary for the solid foundation. The casts were off, now her initial test was at hand.

Bábolna watch as they removed her casting from these target areas and as Ártánd applied the special oils to begin the skins final healing. He also massaged and exercised these areas to begin the blood circulation to the healing muscles. They asked her if she needed sunlight to heal, and she told them she did not. They set up a physical therapy program to fashion her torso strong enough to perform all the special functions for swimming or flying. Pécsi worked extremely hard and progressed ahead of their earlier projections. Her wings also healed solidly. She filled each day with intensive physical therapy. Then their big day came, a day she confessed never to believe possible. Even with their advanced medicines, she not at any time knew of anyone who had recovered from such an extensive array of injuries. The special group that had endured with her during her recovery stages held her upright, so she could practice with her wings, and placed her in a nearby stream, so she could practice swimming. Her mental processes appeared to be stable as she was much more comfortable around the Itchok, knowing that if they had wished to harm her, they could have long ago. Her swims progressed, as did her flying. She would fly for an hour, and then the next day swam gradually rebuilding her body.

Muscle strains and setbacks occurred, yet they worked together and overcame them. Bábolna was so homesick and wanted to return to her people, but also wanted to take Ártánd with her. He explained that this would be impossible as his link to his group could never be broken, and even though he was a brain, the brains were locked into groups, and unable to survive if a part too long. This was their curse of the ages. Bábolna confessed to Ártánd that she had a great love for him, and thanked him for all the Itchok had done for her. They both agreed that they belonged to separate worlds and the day for her to return had arrived. Actually, she left in the night, wishing not to allow the sun to blind her, as what day vision she once had been slowly returning from being underground in the tunnel beside the river. Under the lights of the moon, her team stepped away from her for what could be their last time, if she was completely healed, which all believed she was. She flapped her wings as they lifted her body straight until only her fin was touching the ground. Bábolna said goodbye to the Itchok and Ártánd, swearing always to love them and to visit some nights. She would first leave a letter telling the night she would visit, so if any wanted to see her, they could meet her in the dark. Her clan would not allow her out in the day for a long time. She did a fancy swirl and maneuvering her fins as if swimming just for a show and balance drifted into the unknown dark, wondering how this voyage would end.

Life over the next six months was drastically different for the Pécsi than the Itchok. Bábolna returned to her homeland under the sea. She was so happy swimming in the waters, as she previously could escape from any deep-sea predator. The sea offered more escape options, as compared to the sky, which, if the injury occurred while the victims were in the sky, the crash to the surface could destroy you. An injury on land could leave the victim stranded. Not everyone would be as fortunate as she was; to have an unknown species save them. The Pécsi was so shocked when she returned, believing they saw a ghost or a vision. Her mother and priestess examined her and confirmed her identity. Only her mother was available with the priestess as the Pécsi just had females. Their bodies cannot produce males. They do have peaceful relationships with many of the other species under the sea, trading their offspring, newly produced by the Pécsi women in exchange for more genetic material. Bábolna appeared before one of her Kingdoms judge panels who questioned how she had survived. During her absence, the Pécsi suffered from much unease among their neighboring species. They were worried if the Itchok might be allies with one of these warring neighbors. Bábolna swore to them, the Itchok were not the Pécsi's enemies. Moreover, during her absence, the Pécsi judges put them under martial law, and anyone who contacted a species who were not in the treaty list faced prison, and scheduled for execution. Because she was not with the Pécsi when they declared the military law, they would spare her life. Nevertheless, she had an obligation to return at her first possible date and not when her injuries, no longer existed, and therefore, they judged her imprisoned for the remainder of her life. She argued the date of return should have made no difference, and that the risk of injury warranted her additional stay. The judges refused to listen. Bábolna's return to her people would now be a life of incarceration. The guards prevented her from escaping and forced her forever into the prison. She wondered if life were better for her love, Ártánd. Bábolna knew that if she confessed this love for Ártánd, immediate execution would take place.

After a long rest, life for Ártánd slowly slipped back to the boring, empty life that the Itchok curse provided for them. He always reluctantly remembered the glory days when they raided and destroyed. Ártánd never enjoyed this unleashing of wickedness, yet as with so many of the others, who gloom through each day now, the great wicked leaders forced them to stay in the clan. They would pretend to be destroying when, in reality, they were attempting to save their appointed victims. They were lucky their books recorded these actions in the judges spared them with a life of quiet, often bored, empty days. There was that one year of excitement and worry, filled with hope and success in which the wonderful Bábolna recovered from a horrific accident. All who helped in her recovery discovered this was a great source of excitement. This was the greatest event is so many thousands of years and a chance to show how moral and giving they could be. Most intelligent species take one glance at them and run in great fear, giving them no opportunities to display virtuous actions. Even though Bábolna was frozen in a caste, she could have refused to eat or drink, and other such self-destructive actions. Instead, she placed her life in the hands through a trust. Ártánd missed this so much. His heart filled with true emptiness, would guide him into all eternity. Yes, once again, became the zombie he was destined and cursed to spend eternity. He pictured Bábolna living her happy life with her family and friends, swimming the deep seas or gliding in the high skies. I wished there was a way to discover what she was doing.

This wish clearly burned in his heart as the world around him merely told him how this was a fantasy that caused even the stars to mock him. Accordingly, they had enjoyed so many places together, with all the physical therapy and training to build her wings and fins. These places haunted him. They repeated those events as if they wanted to watch him suffer in agony. The pain came when he reached out to touch her sadly to find empty air. This became a way of life, as if it was his punishment for contact with another species. He had no prison walls as Bábolna had, primarily because he was his prison walls. He knew his breaking point was approaching quickly, yet had no solutions. If clearly he had known, his love was in the same situation. Bábolna's breaking points had already slammed her. Her prison walls trapped her misery inside as if tons of torment would freeze her every move. She felt worse than when she had worn her casts. Subsequently, one day her mother elicited the help of a priest who forced a judge to give her visitation rights. Her mother reported to the priest how grim her situation was. The priests complained to the deaf ears of the judges. The tide changed unexpectedly one day when a species of whales called the Benji decided to change the ecological balance in the area by removing all the Pécsi. The grievance lies with the claim the Pécsi were eating or destroying all the small fish and sea life needed to support the other species. The Benji were not the only who believed this, as also many other species currently had serious grievances with the Pécsi, believing they should live on the land and not crowd them in the sea. The Benji could unite all these enemies and begin striking hard at the Pécsi. On the first day of battle, the Benji captured and dissected two Pécsi, releasing their parts into the Pécsi underwater caverns. The Pécsi immediately prepared for war by first sealing themselves so no one could penetrate their lines. They could fight must easier than their enemies with the use of their hands were, although with the rock solid blockade, the fighting was limited defending their borders. The sea now filled with blood, which invited in other predator species, much to the delight of the Pécsi. Even with this small break, the Pécsi knew that starvation would soon destroy them and accepted their time as near at hand. They released all prisoners. When Bábolna discovered this news and idea came to her mind.

She might have discovered a solution for her future, which is if a future for the Pécsi was still possible. She asked the former guards to take her to the high judges. Standard protocol no longer existed; therefore, they rushed her for a meeting. She pleaded to the judges for a chance to petition the Itchok as an ally. The judges agreed to allow her to make this petition, believing the Itchok could in no way help them, nevertheless, permitted her to bring five friends with her for security and to find a place to continue their species. They released them through a few undersea rivers that flowed into their caverns. The judges expected never to see them again, and placed all their hope in the survival of their species on Emsky through Bábolna. Bábolna; however, believed differently. She knew that Ártánd would find a way to save them, even though they were deep under the sea. She believed in him and the love they shared. Bábolna swore to her friends that this meeting with Ártánd would continue until she died, for she would never leave him again. Her excitement and hope radiated into the eight friends with her, as three more joined, and the judges offered no resistance. They swam slowly in the river, going against it flow, knowing that its source would come from the surface. Bábolna simply wanted to make it to the surface, as she was comfortable in the air and believed she could easily find her former home. Shortly thereafter, they spotted the daylight on the surface above them. Bábolna would soon get her chance to test her confidence.

They swam to the surface, looked around detecting the water flowing through a main passageway. They swam up it and into a surface large stream. Here, they shot into the sky, because Bábolna wanted to get a solid aero view. She finally recognized a land feature and led her small group to it, carefully working her way back to the Itchok fort that had cared so well for her. When the guards saw her arriving, they celebrated and alerted their comrades. Bábolna's friends commended her on the truth about the Itchok, which was so contrary to all the reports the other species had about them, as being former wicked killing demons. When the news arrived to Ártánd that his former love who departed two years earlier was among them once more he rushed into the fort to welcome her. Ártánd and Bábolna's hearts knew they would never part again, as it was up to their minds to determine the path. Bábolna explained their situation to Ártánd, after which they explained it to the brains who asked Bábolna and her friends for all the information they had about the Benji. The key information that they learned was that the Benji was a species of whale and needed air to breath, thus surfaced regularly. They would need for a couple of Bábolna's friends to fly them over the waters so they could visually see them. Once a few sees them, the brains would share this vision among themselves. They knew that these whales depended on great quantities of smaller fish to eat. They prepared the razor sharp long spears as harpoons needing to kill at least one and bring it to their medical brains, so they could analyze their organic material. They brought the one back to the medical tables, and the research began. The brains discovered an easy to formulate the chemical compounds that were deadly to the Benji, actually flooding their lungs with water. They gave the compound to the Pécsi with little crossbows to inject it from the air while they were breathing. When they came up for air, a Pécsi would dive in close, shoot the small dart, and then vanish. The Benji became over confident believing the Pécsi were fleeing from them. Bábolna sent four of her friends back with a large quantity of the poison and small dart shooters. Their warriors could take these with them while roaming under the sea and kill the lagging Benji. The Itchok brains told them that they would need to chase down the escapes and kill them to have future security and to break up the coalition that challenged them. The Itchok agreed to help them erase these species as well and to sign a peace treaty. The question remained, would the Pécsi accept this treaty or reduce it. Her four friends departed, hoping to find the answer.

When her friends returned with this news, the judges were in disbelief, thinking that Bábolna was teasing them in revenge. The group revealed the poison. There were a couple of Benji bashing at one of their defense supports, creating great damage. The friends volunteered to go out into the water and inject the poison. They bravely went out, shot their darts, which immediately paused the Benji's nervous system and began work on their lungs. Within a few short moments, the three large, fierce Benji warriors floated dead to the surface. The judges were amazed and at once began distribution of the poison. The friends recommended these warriors also shoot them at their breathing points from the air. Bábolna's friends showed the judges the peace treaty and offer to assist in dispersing the remaining enemy. The judges agreed and returned with Bábolna's friends formally to establish the treaty. The Itchok brains apologized for not taking an active part in the fight, as serious constraints still bound them under the established laws for their freedom. Excitement flared throughout the Itchok lands as they had finally made friends. This would help make the ending days of their unique species somewhat bearable. The Pécsi invited a diplomatic group to return and live with them. In exchange, they left Bábolna and her friends with the Itchok to represent their diplomatic unit. This was the beginning of a strong alliance, which would outlive them, as, both species were so eager for something new. They would search for that something fresh together as one united two species merger. The Pécsi at no time cared for surface areas, as the Itchok never gave mind to the sea or sky, because of their mud constraints; therefore, the two species were not conflicting with the other's common interests. Excitement flooded both large Kingdoms, as the news spread through all Emsky. The Pécsi believed they now had a land Army, while the Itchok currently believed they had a Navy and Air Force. Their combination would add to the common defense of Emsky. Little they knew that the greatest news was yet to come.

Bábolna and Ártánd struggled to be alone, notwithstanding Bábolna could not abandon her eight friends who were still working hard to become comfortable with their new fellow citizens. Ártánd discovered he had a group of eight friends hanging close to him as well. These friends were special in that they were the ones who initially helped him rescue Bábolna. He would not deny them any opportunities better to acquaint themselves with the Pécsi. Bábolna, who was friends with everyone in this combined group decided to have the introduction games, in which all would be embarrassed and challenged. She believed that they would soon pair off throughout these games, as alliances formed. Bábolna knew they all had common interests, because they were their friends. Her friends were fascinated and loyal to her when it came to issue concerning the Itchok. She knew Ártánd's friends were what her friends wanted through all the hours they worked hard for her recovery and shared their hearts with her. Bábolna's game worked great, and as they began to pair off into groups of two, she would tell the two all the great things about each other. This gave them an open platform to enjoy. It is almost like someone taking your clothes from you in front of this new acquaintance, although clothes do not do much for fish skin and mud bodies. A unique new custom began this day as the male Itchok flew on the backs of the female Pécsi as they searched for a safe place to learn about each other. There were so many differences and even though these differences broaden the advantages of their new relationships, these couples were having difficulty in finding that special spark that would bind them as Ártánd and Bábolna remained bound. They had faithfully based this bond on something invisible that they could not pinpoint. The danger of such a small fire burning in a secret place was when that fire went out. How would they restart it? Even Ártánd and Bábolna were aware of this danger, nevertheless knew that living away from each other was not an option. They had to find the key to this mystery. Little they realized the answer was already at the tip of their tongues.

Ártánd and Bábolna elected to return to the place he first discovered her on this night. She wanted to begin their lives again in the same place that it began. Ártánd agreed, although questioned Bábolna as to the value of any romance in their relationship. She told him that it was the idea that would bring them the joy. He agreed, like any male simply to appease the female. Bábolna was convinced she would find a way to repay the great love the Itchok had given both her and her nation. They talked about anything they could think about now; as they finally discussed many games, she played as a child. Then, as if she should have known way before this, she asked Ártánd where they kept their children, as the Pécsi kept their new children in special child lands they had in their under lands in a few converted caverns. She always assumed the Itchok did the same. Ártánd told her they had no children, nor have they had any children since their judgment. Bábolna asked him why. He explained that their females had no reproductive organs, therefore, made their genetic material worthless. They had tried to mate with other species, yet their material had too much mud and acids, which harmed any possible host. Thereafter, they erased any hope. Bábolna asked him how they extracted their genetic material. He explained how to extract this, and she explained to him how they received the foreign material. She asked him if he gave her some. He told her that it could be too dangerous, as he was afraid to chance it. She got him to test a small sample. Bábolna had no reaction, therefore he gave her a complete portion, and it worked, as she knew within hours that the process was positive for both babies. He asked what she meant by both babies. She had explained this to him previously; nonetheless, he never gave it any mind, not believing such a thing to be impossible. Once more, she explained that inside her was a female Pécsi and male Itchok. Ártánd asked her she knew this. Bábolna explained that her organs could solely reproduce male Pécsi, as her species had no males and that they could merely produce male babies for the donating provider of the genetic material. Ártánd said that was perfect as there was no code for Itchok women with reproductive organs. They sat there in shock, wondering why they had not put this small puzzle together earlier. The Itchok would not be able to reproduce sons, and the Pécsi would have a source of genetic material providers available. This news was too great, thus they decided to share it with their families.

They presented this new miracle to their friends, and when the Pécsi discovered this readily available source of genetic material, they rushed for their share. The nations forever locked themselves as one, and built a clean virtuous Emsky. Because of their situations, they voted not to venture into space beyond defending Emsky. They launched an effective defense network that did prevent many invasions. The Itchok could not enter space because of their judgment. The Pécsi could not function well in confined areas, working best in the sea and air. The construction of a ship to accommodate these needs was not practical, or defendable. They instead developed Emsky into a world that fit their needs. The skies had the beautiful Pécsi flying to visit their Itchok relatives, as their other cousins came up from the sea bringing fresh mud for their brothers. The Pécsi's reproductive systems had evolved only to accept the Itchok reproductive materials, and both species evolved effective organs successfully to transfer this prized species saving substance. The stigmatisms between their appearances vanished, as the woman accepted the mud men and their mates and fathers. The Itchok original women served as maidens and other forms of childcare duties. They enjoyed the rich source of new children who kept the homes occupied. Emsky did suffer from a few severe plagues, which kept their population thinned to where the planet could support them. The Itchok always believed their curse at judgment caused these mystery plagues. Stray microscopic killers who followed their spiritual vibrations enforced this curse. Knowledge of this great civilization on Emsky spread throughout all Chuprin, and to other galaxies throughout the Empires who traded. Unfortunately, not all accepted this as good news.

The legends of the Itchok were permanent in the tales and histories of so many galaxies. This caused the unification of the greatest space force ever, before the Empire to invade just one world. Billions of ships unleashed a wave of destruction that it even removed the remains of the first rock or disposition buried miles deep under Emsky's surface. History recorded this as one of the greatest massacres of the innocent in this universe. The souls of Itchok and Pécsi cried out to the heavens for justice. The day came when the original three power spirit deities discovered this injustice. They gathered their Armies and invaded all the galaxies that participated in the massacre, destroying any area-ruling gods and their thrones. The fire burned from all the worlds in the six local galaxies, except for Emsky, where the power spirit gods flooded with the blood of those who killed the innocent Itchok. The blood soaked deep into Emsky cooling its inner core. This caused Emsky to stop rotating for over one billion years, the time it took for the blood of this injustice to reenter the surface and drift off into space. Each world the blood entered, all life perished. When the last drop of blood spun from Emsky, the core began rotating once more and after another billion years, animal life once again flourished throughout Chuprin, never again would a god of scarcely a few galaxies rule Chuprin. The Empire reached an agreement with the three power spirit gods in exchange for agreeing to approve their annexation when the Empire reaches their quadrant and to dedicate three Emsky moons in memory of the Itchok and Pécsi rebuilding giant museums so history will never forget them. All moons and Emsky will have three-hundred foot high statutes of Ártánd and Bábolna. Chuprin will also create a one-planet sanctuary for a few thousand Pécsi who the Empire will provide and protect. The three power spirit gods destroyed the genetic coding for the Pécsi when they judged the original Pécsi. They are lost to history. Emsky stands proud as the world where they found love and honor dying in their innocence. They are the symbols of pure love. Love not based on reason, but entirely in the heart. Their love is the symbol of blind, enduring love bound by their oaths, which became a power greater than those who made it. Their differences had united them. They reminded us those things so opposite, such as light and dark, when united could form a day.

The sixth stone or gold stone were a special age of horrifying evil, which remnants still torture the virtuous spirits in this disposition. The wicked spiritual Kingdoms had lost much of their former strongholds throughout the universe, much through their wars against their many groups who all were searching to rule. They were continually searching for new galaxies to hide in for their long-range attacks. The universe could now purely be thankful in the fact the wicked spirits were firmly against each, another, as no virtuous deities, other than the rotating Power Spirits, could defeat them. Many aging Empires from the far corners of the universe were planting fresh colonies to advance the human populations in new sections of the universe. Fortunately, they were not the lone planters of the humans, as this genetic coding was a favorite among many of the gods, especially for the ability to attach souls with them and use the first flesh cycle as a testing stage. This is something like how the caterpillar turns into a butterfly, which is the most popular planet decorating species. Emsky was to receive a special treat by random chance. The normal colonization explorers believed Emsky to be too far from the center of Chuprin and thereby ignored it. These people known as the Patrizius had a small fleet of three ships with forty-three people remaining from their long exodus. Their world's sun went nova and destroyed their solar system. They had moved their people to another solar system in the same galaxy; however, wars with the natives made their resettlement almost impossible. A group of one-million Patrizius elected to search for a home deep in the universe. Space battles with pirates coupled with mechanical disasters and meteor storms reduced their fleet to the current three ships. They agreed to settle in the next galaxy on a world far from the center. They believed the stars in the center of all galaxies were heading into black holes and when they saw Emsky, decided it could provide them a lengthy future. They based this on their theories. Theory or not, they landed on Emsky and began the sixth stone, the gold one. The gold labels had a significant symbol for this age.

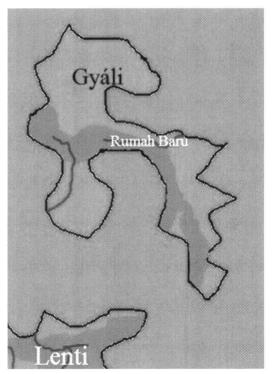

The Patrizius earned their gold label from sacrifice and suffering, and not from great riches. They salvaged some construction equipment from their ships to construct their first few cities and a road to connect them. They settled along the great south bay of Gyáli along the mountainous seashore between the northern shores of this southern bay and the long river that flowed to the west. They called their first city Rumah Baru, a city that survived the entire cycle of the sixth stone. Emsky had once again become overflowing with wild beasts, unlike previous stones, this time they were huge with many of them carnivorous. Therefore, the Patrizius built large walls around their cities and high stone fences along great portions of their thick stone roads. The survivors learned the benefits of a protein-rich diet, especially with such a rich source of meat available and considering the wild beasts were so destructive to the vegetation. They enjoyed Emsky without any new visitors from the stars for almost ten millennia, during which time they built large cities on all five great islands. Emsky offered them all that they needed, with the legends and their tales taste in their mouths for any future space exploration. They knew space with big, empty, and dangerous and that was enough for them. They created institutionalized cultures, which ignored the family unit. Males lived in male institutions, whereas women and children lived in the women's institutions. Children moved to the educational institutions when they turned six. Education was the highest priority for the Patrizius, who had managed to save much of their original knowledge from their destroyed home planets. To maintain peace and order among all the city-states, the Patrizius would continually be randomly reassigning individual citizens to new city states throughout all Emsky. The Patrizius did not accept any form of deity and believed everything they based on technology. Even if they had accepted deities, no deities existed on the galaxies in this area since the revenge of the Pécsi and Itchok. Even with the absence of gods, they were strong moral and virtuous people. Everyone, except for the planet and city-state administers were treated the same. An occupation produced, work-credits, which they traded for personal items. They were a competent culture, suffering only from the danger of being too efficient.

The lubricant needed to keep their machine spinning that was scarce was love. Better defined or qualified, the missing part was enthusiastic love. The Patrizius existed rigidly disciplined loving the production from their technology more than each another did.

Other Patrizius lost during the production process was a simple cost of producing. There came a generation, which challenged this concept. This generation wanted to reinvent the family unit, a concept that appeared in the literature only as proof of the many disadvantages, and the dangers it created. Their raging leader was Oshun, a tall longhaired dressed savage style. She was a strong orator, and an extremely beautiful woman, who used her words to create her followers. She established a large base in her initial days until the administrators forbid any public release of her streams. This merely slowed, her down, as it did not stop her. Instead, she traveled the city-states delivering her message. Oshun was non-violent and spoke harshly against any who was violent. She dedicated her life to this mission, which even to her death remained unfulfilled. She; however, forced many of the city-states to pass laws that permitted a couple to live together and keep their children, as long as these children passed the annual state education tests. The parents had the option of sending them to a state education facility or teaching them in their home. Unfortunately, for Oshun the Patrizius never widely accepted the value of a family unit, and viewed it more than an inconvenience and a disadvantage for the children, who seldom continued the custom. As the number of family units continued to decrease, the number of states increased that created the laws permitting it. This created the appearance of an administrator who was concerned about the people's freedom.

Although the Patrizius did not choose to follow Oshun's family unit concepts, they did love her and her words. Her arguments became a part of the Patrizius literature. Her timing was wrong, in that during the latter part of her life; wicked alien expansionists were forcing more Patrizius to depend on underground shelter for the regularly attacked Emsky. This made the concepts of family, and freedom took on more risks than it offered value. The states called more men to fight in the planet's defenses, and as more died, the females had to depend on fewer men to impregnate them, thereby also making the family unit unpractical. Her concept of a love between male and female did become popular; however, just for temporary relationships, as few wanted the constraints of an imperishable bond. The permanent bond did not simply restrict a female from other males; it also pulled her away from the female institutions that had a great hold on them. When Oshun died, her revolution went dormant with her as well. The space attacks continued for over two millennia, when finally, the planets of the Emsky solar system united with a space fleet and chased them back to their home worlds and severely attacked those home worlds, reducing their fleets to rubble. Unfortunately, they omitted the production facilities. Emsky enjoyed a few centuries of peace, nevertheless; the attacks resumed, and this time they were for revenge and not capture, targeting civilian structures and locations. The created much destruction to their internal networks and left many without arms, or legs, and destroyed faces. The solar system elected to trace the warring vessels back to their worlds and this time not just destroyed the fleets, but the production facilities, and as a bonus, larger populated areas. After enjoying this virtually free destructive campaign, they returned to Emsky to finish off the invading ships. During their absence, these ships had limited successes against their civilian targets on all but three worlds, which lost their security shields. These three worlds received the bulk of the invasion attacks. Their worlds lie in ruin. Emsky's shields experienced a few provisional shutdowns, which exposed the populations to some serious blasts. Emsky technology kept most barely alive in temporary medical advanced clinics. They converted approximately thirty percent of the structures to medical facilities. The Patrizius desire for survival was now up for their largest test.

The worlds agreed to establish a strong solar system defense force, as this could not happen again. The weapon with the greatest destructive impact was the acid missile. This weapon contained a powerful mixture of airborne acids or chemicals, which burned skin, ate through muscle and bones, leaving it scarred and crippled. It was a living acidic creature that when released, would search for people. When making contact it would attempt to work its way through the host's body. The lone thing that gave the host a chance for survival was the acid could not live long in a ninety-eight degree body, needing a lower temperature to keep it from over expanding. Sadly, these left injuries that were sporadic that cut through nerves, separated veins, and occasionally made it to the lungs causing permanent internal damage. Technological advances created temporary new machines like faces to cover the scared skin and repair damaged nerves and tissue. For many, this included external device to perform particular brain functions for the brains damaged area. Their medical technology discovered that rather than replacing small sections of an organ, it was easier to replace the organ. This made future maintenance almost nonexistent. The other social impact was these victims with similar injuries tended to form new groups. They reversed the previous concept of working hard for the greater tomorrow with the concept of trying to survive today with the help of others. The medical strategy changed also, if some came in complaining that their hands hurt, they would replace that hand with an artificial one, and routine organ replacement based on age became the medical norm. It was not until a few centuries later, when the attacked generation had all died, the new effects from these organ replacements surfaced as if nature's way of trying to stop this. Normal Patrizius tissues contained their ancestral antigens that could fight certain diseases and plagues. The replacement organs did not have this ability. The replacement tissue had enough flesh elements (mostly from animals) to attract and host these previously dormant viruses. Once in the victim, they would destroy all replaced organs. If they replaced the replaced organs again, they would also destroy them. This left death as the one possible result and if the Patrizius were to survive this death sentence the only remaining question.

This was a question, which the answer was almost no. All the people who had replacement organs, which included everyone about ten died. The administrator's mass developed incinerators to cremate all the dead, as the young children would not be able to handle the ancestral burying of the dead. They destroyed the organ replacement technology and concentrated on helping the children prepare methods to survive. Within four years, all the adults died, and the children's senior age group had grown to fourteen, which was old enough to guide the Patrizius into their second stage. As to be expected, the children wanted little to do with the children's institutions. The younger and older children, bonded into small units. The senior children also cared for the infants who needed constant intensive care. The girls discovered that if they had a male mate, this process became much easier. This elicited the rebirth of Oshun's philosophy. The females also discovered the procreation function could also help in keeping their male mates. Within one century, Oshun's ideal family unit was the foundation of the new Patrizius society. Rather than advancing their technologies, they devoted a large part of their mental energy to music and streams with love, happiness, and family as the core themes. Poets and actors emerged as emotions became the rulers of behavior. Unfortunately, as with so many times in the current stone or dispositions, emotions many times get out of control as the results are painful at best.

Emotions, a world dedicated to the pursuit of happiness found one obstacle they had expected, and that was whose happiness was the determining factor. No one liked large governments; therefore, families pretty much merely joined with other families in activities that they had a common interest or need. This decentralization eventually left much of the planet-wide functions in ruin. Services such as energy, waste removal, food distribution, for the family homes slowly disappeared; their transportation and communication resources also began to fail. Many functions or jobs did not attract the later generations, as they all competed for the special functions, ignoring the maintenance and mechanical fields. These functions did not make them merry. They unfortunately later discovered the absence of them as well did not make them happy. Struggles and violence broke out when certain families would attempt to assign these lower functions to the children of other families. Many considered this degrading as an insult worthy of execution. This swiftly led to no one attempting to organize the public services. More families departed from the cities and settled in small self-sustaining rural locations. Nonetheless, these locations rapidly became scarce and to obtain a farm one would have to kill for it, and then kill to keep it. Next, food became an item worthy of killing to obtain. As the food became almost nonexistent, simply knowing that another existed provided an opportunity to kill, because, if they were alive, they were eating, so in killing them, one had a chance to find his or her food source. No one married, nor did any reproduce, as children were too dangerous to raise. They made too much noise and required special foods, which were not available. Within one century, the Patrizius on Emsky perished, as the generations of the three ships were extinct. Twice, they had tried for the ultimate civilization, and two times, they failed. The first they based on reason, while an invisible enemy killed what the Patrizius had created defeating logic. Long existing functional human bodies that they altered from the way their creator produced them fell outside the protections the same creator had provided. If they had used this advanced biological technology within reason, such as replacement absolutely when the life was in danger, they would have overcome their invisible assassin. The precise reasoning that they were trying to advance was the reasoning that sat the ambush that surrendered their world to their children. Their children were intelligent enough to understand that a work wholly and never love philosophy was not the road to travel. They did not appreciate that a little sleep could lead to an unfavorable ending.

A little sleep and a little slumber, and in a flash poverty can destroy the sleeper. This was the demise of the second Patrizius civilization whose desire to be different put them on a dead-end road. Unfortunately, for the new generation, they had few choices as just one had dedicated her life to the concept of a reformed social foundation, which she had copied from the tales of ancestors of the three ships who spoke of this from the home worlds that burned in their exploding sun. Oshun never had the time to advance her theory into a functional society, spending her entire life simply defending the foundation. The younger generation became overwhelmed with love and loving. They had the huge emptiness to fill. They did not grasp which way to take this new lifestyle, as the only thing, they knew was they could not do as the previous civilization had done. The argumentative personalities and total disagreement in their interactions with the other planets concerning their contribution to the solar system's defense forced the other planets to refuse any contact. The Emsky planets avoided them and treated them as if they were a primitive world and path that they soon traveled. Total love and denial of any existence of hate secluded them. Unfortunately, they discovered the hate would grow in their fellow-Emsky when food became scarce, as hungry people had no laws. The assumption that what you have today will be your tomorrow will not hold true when those around you do not have and decide to take what is yours, not because of lust but instead because of the need to survive. The denial of the depletion of life sustaining resources and refusal to engage in activities to replace them was almost the same as driving a knife into your heart, because the results were the same. Love without caring and sharing could not function. The caring, involved providing, as the sharing involved giving. These pillars needed to keep love alive. Emsky now watched her sixth cycle, the golden cycle of love, surrender her back into a dead lonely decaying empty world. It would be another million years, as all from the Patrizius was buried deep under her surface before the next disposition would attempt to bring life back to Emsky.

CHAPTER 03

The seventh stone, the stone of wonder

Oroshází and I sat staring at each other, as the visions we had just seen, filled us with wonder and astonishment. I confessed to her that I had no idea about the rich history of the world that I existed while in my flesh. My world had no more than existed either on foot or on horse throughout the Durov Kingdom. We always believed Andocs to be the cradle of the great advanced civilization and wonders. I now have witnessed much greater come forth from Emsky and the events, which made them, tumble. Staring at Oroshází I tell her, "Oroshází, these visions can impartially prove the advantages of Emsky joining the Empire, because every stone we have seen fell, and I do not want to see Emsky fall again. It would be so much better to be a tiny fish in a large sea, especially with the largest fish providing protection, then a huge fish in a small pond with fish hunters covering the shores. Which was your favorite?" She smiles and tells me that Ártánd and Bábolna, because they were such extremes, put aside what was different, and let their love show them how to create their new love. Reflecting on what she had just shared with me, I began to wonder about the next visions the window would show us. As I investigated around our special room, I noticed our guide was gone. I asked Orosházi if she had seen our host. She scanned our room with her eyes as well and told me that it appear, we are alone. She asked me if I believed our visions had finished. I told her that they could not be finished because so much of our history is unrecorded, and I would not be able to complete the chronicles they wanted. At this time, darkness filled the room, the tree that previously stood behind us, now vanished, and new tree appeared. This tree had totally a trunk that stopped at its first two branches. A warm stream of white light dropped from above us, circled the trunk beginning at its roots, and continued to spin until it reached the two branches. Now it appeared horizontal in front of us with the blurry top section of a woman appearing. The woman of light shot lightning with her left hand and broke free of the lightning, commanding it to stop. The lightning stopped and now before us, we could see to upper half of a giant female spirit. The spirit glared at us and said, "Welcome Sénye and Orosházi. Orosházi I brought from Jaroslaw and Sénye I saved from the Clotilde. We are Borsod-Abaúj-Zemplén or the three Power Spirits you have witnessed during your visions of the stones. We are the spirits, which recommended to the Empire that you record the Emsky Chronicles. You represent what Emsky represents, and that is accepting that which is different." I waved my hands wanting to ask a question.

Borsod-Abaúj-Zemplén asks me to speak. I ask them, "The love that Orosházi gives to me is from a rare spark in her being, a spark she cannot control." Orosházi hits me in my back, which means she wants to stop talking. Next, she confessed to me, "Sénye, I might have stretched the truth about the spark to build your confidence in our relationship. The spark I speak of now, I made and will keep it burning, forever my love." Borsod-Abaúj-Zemplén continued, "Your sparks will add the dimension to the Emsky Chronicles that we seek. You will now begin your vision of the seventh stone, and the tree that represents it. The seventh stone we created different from the other stones, in that first formed a solid foundation before each branch reached for its destiny. We will send you your new guide." The lightning reappeared, and she jumped into it as it retreated through the rocks that formed our ceiling. Orosházi smiles at me and asks, "Do you forgive me?" I told her that, of course I forgave her and thanked her for knowing I needed extra confidence boost to accept my great fortune. She winks at me and adds, "Today is a day for much fortune as we have been visited by Power Spirits." I asked her who the Power Spirits were. She explains that they are the strongest of the deities and that these easy ways to think about it is they are each about one-thousand times more powerful than a regular deity is. Suddenly, we hear a voice confirm what Orosházi has just told me. We both sit patiently waiting for an image to appear, showing our confidence that one appears. Our faith proved fruitful as our room turned a peaceful shade of orange and yellow combined. Next, yellow large fluffy flowers began to fill our room after which a human female arrived wearing a gown made of small yellow flowers. She appeared normal, although she had so much hair that it flowed to pass the length of her laying body. Her hair was a rich brown with many yellow streaks going down throughout it. A yellow grass table begins to rise in front of her. Accordingly, she sits up and leans both elbows on the table, as her hair instantly forms into a giant stylish ball on her head. Her smile and blinks her decorated eyes and introduced herself as Pankrati. We welcome her. Pankrati welcomes us to sit beside her as we watch the visions of the seventh stone, the stone of wonder. We sit one on each side of her. Oddly, Orosházi has no reactions and displays no jealousy. Therefore, I invite her to sit between Pankrati and me, explaining that she will have a better view and that by doing this; I will be able to hear the questions she asks with more ease. Orosházi smiles at me and tells me she prefers that we sit as we are so both of us can share in Pankrati's guidance.

Pankrati smiles and reports, "Great, this way when I bite one, the other will not know." We laugh at this joke as Orosházi comments that she believes the vision we shall witness joyfully in a spirit of fun and laughter. Pankrati begins her story that we summarized for the chronicles. Borsod-Abaúj-Zemplén found themselves once more saddened by the misfortune of Emsky, agreeing that they should have intervened and enlightened the children of love about the laziness that destroyed them. They scanned Emsky searching for any survivors, yet could find no one. These Power Spirits considered going back to the time line and pulling a few for replanting. Their lights revealed to them that this was against the laws of virtue, in that all must be treated equal, and if they were to give rebirth to chosen beings, they would have to allow all the spirits they kept in their heavens the same opportunity. These spirits decided that they would control the future of Emsky by selecting its next inhabitants. The five largest islands gave them a unique opportunity to study these inhabitants before they went global. The waves of the last refuges from the distant parts of the universe were scarce currently, as the bands of wicked forces made passage through this quadrant. Most would now circle above this quadrant. Borsod-Abaúj-Zemplén began a one billion year war against these wicked powers, attempting to destroy them. They formed a giant inescapable blockage and slowly pushed and fought inward attempting to destroy them. They found themselves fighting both the inside the blockade and attacked from the outside, as the wicked forces throughout this universe were converging to free their comrades. This was always the strong point of the evil forces, because they will unite and fight for each, another. The deities stay within their boundaries, watching the others fall that surrounds them. The Borsod-Abaúj-Zemplén found themselves forces to create an opening in their barricade, providing the wicked, an avenue to escape. Many did, while the others stayed and held their original domains.

This began the great demon wars with the Borsod-Abaúj-Zemplén, who found the wicked demons attempting now to blockade them. The wicked ones could not hold the barricade as the Power Spirits broke through at will. The constraint was that, after they broke through they returned, wishing to hold on to their domains and servants. The Power Spirits unleashed a great wrath on these vicious forces, and after one-hundred thousand years, the central base of the wicked giant retreated. This still left remaining strong pockets within their domain. The Borsod-Abaúj-Zemplén began fighting to remove these pockets, who would, after a solid fight, reform in another section, and the fighting continue. The Borsod-Abaúj-Zemplén was effective in blocking new wicked spirits in their galaxies. Many ages later, virtuous refuges began to drift through our galaxies. They were few, and avoided Emsky as it sat on an end spiral of Chuprin. Chuprin did receive its share of new alien settlers, as Emsky sat barren, covered with scars from the ravaging attacks of evil spirits who injured hurling meteors into planets. They usually selected worlds that had inhabitants. The meteors that missed their targets would continue in space until finding another world. Emsky sat far on the outside Chuprin, and unfortunately; the Emsky solar system's gravity would pull these meteors into their orbits. The Emsky worlds had enough density in their atmospheres to reflex many of the meteors back out into the vast space beyond Chuprin. Those which broke the atmospheres splattered spreading their destruction throughout smaller, more numerous, crashes. These rare splashes were enough to cause concern for Borsod-Abaúj-Zemplén, whose favoritism for Emsky forced them to steer away from Emsky. Moreover, the ages pass by as the battles between the Spirit Gods and wicked one continued. Then came an age when the wicked ones began to depart for other quadrants, leaving those behind to spread out into small groups, which the Spirit God's scanners could not detect. This required intense solar system investigations, which clearly provided the wicked ones the desire to destroy where they were and go ahead to another solar system, as the process repeated itself continuously. Borsod-Abaúj-Zemplén slowly began to shift their emphasis from Emsky to other sections of Chuprin, close enough to keep any large force or meteors from harming Emsky. Their shift also shifted the wicked ones who began concentrating on new opportunities. Emsky had been barren for so many ages and time; a time for rebirth was quickly at hand.

The space refugees now consisted more of explorers searching for new places to spread their kingdom's holdings. The Power Spirits steered these away from Emsky, not wanting Emsky to fall under the control of distant kingdoms. Animal life once again flourished on Emsky, with the help from a few alien planters who would use barren worlds to support their preferred beasts whom they consumed. Many of their other garden planets over produced, which soon caused Emsky not to appear on their collection harvests. Emsky's orange grass and clouds began to raise concerns about the safety of eating these beasts; therefore, they agreed not to chance it. The orange pigment was the result of a rare bacterium that had arrived inside various meteors. A unique fleet, now suffering from crippling damages from stray space rocks, limped into Emsky. When the Power Spirits spotted this crippled fleet, they at once opened the orange planet to them. This fleet was so different from the others, in that it carried two species, which depended on each other to survive. The other great thing about their non-aggressive past was their secluded lifestyles. Wherever they existed, they lived in the dark skies or in the deep seas. Enough similarities existed with the Pécsi that the Power Spirits used their divine powers to save them as they were dying in the space outside Chuprin and safely landed them in the orange seas of Emsky. The greatest benefit was that both species ate the orange bacteria that, within a few ages, would choke all life from Emsky. The Power Spirits believed this was a union of destiny and dedicated themselves to protect it. These species called themselves the Benigna-A and Benigna-B. Their similarities ended there.

The Benigna-A were created bottom half fish and top half woman; however, unlike the Pécsi they had no wings and could not live above the water. They also grew while thirty feet and could swim faster than any other sea life in Chuprin. Their species was completely solely female. The planters always planted their eggs with male sperm that they also produced as dissolving eggs. Their sperm could not penetrate eggs produced by the same female; therefore, they planted the sperm with the eggs from another female. In addition, their eggs could not develop in the sea. The planters buried these eggs on the surface under the air, with the sperm from another female. Once the eggs hatch, they crawled to the nearest stream. They always planted, the eggs near a stream, and would then swim to the sea, usually waiting until dark to swim under the escort of the one who planted them. The Benigna-A would meet with their unknown daughters, as the planters would inform them of their arrival. These female warriors of the sea would escort their daughters back to their new homes deep under the sea. The Benigna-A could stretch their arms out to thirty feet in a flash, which allowed them to be excellent hunters. They did not eat much seafood, except for ones that had a high-level of the orange bacterium soaked the seas, to such a degree the ocean's surface had up to ten feet of the orange bacterium in the low places where the currents had settled it. Both the Benigna-A and Benigna-B survived on the orange bacterium, which still floods many parts of Emsky's ocean surfaces. The orange bacterium most times explodes into millions of microscopic bodies. The Benigna-A can syphon the orange bacterium from the water through their gills and the Benigna-B syphon it through their lungs. Their joint efforts offered a cleaning of Emsky within the environment, natural cycles, which pleased the Power Spirits. The Benigna-A were extremely smart and crafty with their hands. They built large underwater cities deep under the sea as their sonar abilities kept them forever out of the sight of the land people. The Benigna-A could not live without their sisters, the Benigna-B.

The Benigna-B was the angels of the night. They could not live underwater nor on the surface during the days. Sunlight would dissolve and kill them within one hour. They circled Emsky at night breathing the microscopic orange bacteria as their primary source of food. They breathed the bacteria above the ground, causing the upper bacteria to vanish. The bacteria on the surface would explode in an attempt to refill the thinning higher layers. The Benigna-B was the planters for the Benigna-A as they also depended on Benigna-A in their reproduction process. The vast mystery is the Benigna-B women generate their eggs, yet generate no sperm. The sperm from the Benigna-A females can also fertilize the Benigna-B female eggs. The greatest difference is the way they deliver their seeds. The Benigna-A or fish women, have unique organs, specifically designed for their angel sisters or the Benigna-B. The angel sisters have genitals similar to humans, although the wombs are vastly different. The fish women have a special pouch below their waste in the fish part of their body. The pouch has an organ that resembles a human male's genitals except it expands to thirty inches. This is because when she inserts it into her angel sister, it will go inside her womb to the egg, dissolve a small hole through the shell, deliver the sperm inside the egg, and seal it. It would then attach the egg to its tubing, pull the egg out, and plant it inside another special organ in the fish woman's pouch. Here, the egg will develop into an embryo. When the egg is full term, it will hatch and a small angel baby girl will travel to the top of the pouch and pull on an unusual organic cord attached to her belly. This connection immerged within hours after planting this egg in a special pouch designed exclusively for it. The fish mother will sense the tug on this cord and deliver the child at once. The water dissolves the cord. The angel daughter will live under the sea for her first four years, the time it takes her to grow large enough to fly and make the special daytime conversion. Then their Benigna-A sperm mother or fish sister will release the daughter with her mother when she releases them for their nighttime feeding. The Benigna-A sperm mother guards her sister Benigna-B egg with all her warrior powers and raises her as if her child, teaching her the ways of the fish sisters and other activities she will need to perform to survive. She would also introduce the angel child to her fish partner. They will meet many times, until they bond around age twenty-five. The fish sister will not produce any eggs or sperm until this sister; child departs on her fifth birthday. The angel sister would not reproduce another time until her daughter mates at age twenty-five. The fish sister will reproduce once more after she releases her angel daughter to her mother. She will never reproduce if the delivery were within eight years of her angel niece's twenty-fifth birthday. The fish sister and angel sister carefully coordinate their reproduction cycles, so no conflict exists. Their mysteries do not end here.

The fish sister and angel sister, oddly spend much time together. The angel sister cannot be around any sunlight, therefore, has a special transformation process; she undergoes in the dawn following a night of feeding. She will transform into a rock and settle inside the unusual pouch her fish sister reserves for her daughter. She does this, as the fish sister will lay on the surface, belly facing up at a time and place they have established. They can use the conditions of Emsky accurately to estimate the time. The angel sister will fly above her sister's belly, open the pouch, and slowly descend into it, shrinking as she enters. Once inside, she will crawl to her special organic pouch and crawl inside where she will transform into a rock. Even more amazing is that she can communicate with her fish sister as a rock in her pouch. They will discuss many things and share each other's daily and nightly experiences. The fish sisters will carry these rocks inside them throughout the entire day under the sea. She would also sleep during the day, because in the deep sea that it does not matter when you rest, it is always blinding dark black, except for the glowing orange ocean bed. If her angel sister has not been feeding well in the high sky, the fish sister will take a spin to the ocean floor and open her pouch, allow the orange settlement to fill this opening, and then reseal it, and continue throughout the day. Her pouch will move the orange bacteria to other openings where she compressed it inside her special tubes, whereas, when the angel sister awakes that night, and departs the womb, she can pull out the compressed tubes and enjoy a filling meal. She will bury any extra and eat it on other non-filling hunting nights. Their average lifespan was one-thousand years. They would never switch mates. On death, both the angel sisters and fish sisters would turn into rocks for ten thousand years, when they would be once again live. This cycle would continue five times. The Benigna had another special surprise for Borsod-Abaúj-Zemplén.

The Benigna had special defenses against demons. Both the fish and angel sisters had sonar systems that could detect demons from within one-hundred miles. Both segments of this species could also unleash a biological laser that would splatter a demon, causing it to vanish immediately. What was even more beneficial was the demons could not detect the angel sisters. The fish sisters never developed this ability, because demons at no time ventured into the oceans nor did they have any interest in sea life, which could easily detect them when under the water. The angel sisters carefully chose when to destroy a demon. They always zapped the ones who ventured off on their own. These were hard to find on Emsky, as it still did not have any human life. Every night, a few demons would venture out alone and not return. This baffled the demons who searched for intruders, yet could find none. When the demons were searching intensely, the angel sisters would extend their rock hibernation. They could hibernate for up to four months. Even though they could have continued their night feedings without detection, they chose not to take any chances. The wicked forces soon attributed these losses to the desertions, and the searches would end. The sister angels would come back out and feast on greater kills, as the demons were careless after four months of no vanishings. The wicked forces seldom would conduct more than two massive searches on a planet, attributing these disappearances to desertions. They would begin imprisoning demons that they suspected would desert. These cages were perfect for the angel sisters, who would wipe out an entire prison in one night, leaving all the cells open. This continued for a few thousand years until the heinous spirits decided to move to another planet four orbits away. Emsky was once again turning green, especially after the demons departed and the angel sisters began feeding on the ground. The seas were turning green. The Power Spirits believed that it was time for life to begin on the large islands on Emsky.

A small fleet entered the Emsky solar system, dividing it among four of the planets to set up colonies. These people were the Ethelbert. Exploration and adventures filled their histories. They had suffered great losses in a battle a few years earlier and were on the run from that enemy. The enemy had stopped chasing them about one year ago, so they changed their heading to straight down, and after one year, discovered Chuprin. They did not want trapped inside a galaxy, and therefore, selected Emsky as it was on the outer spiral. The advantage of an outside spiral is that long-range scanners and other radar systems function much better. This offered the Ethelbert additional needed security. Solar systems inside a galaxy experience many interruptions in their radar scans, and therefore, carry a higher risk. The Ethelbert was extraordinarily excited about starting a new life, and the added benefit of these planets, not occupied spared them any long wars, which they could not effectively fight because of their losses in the Avramiy galaxy. The Avramiy refused to allow them to settle in a vacant solar system. They believed this solar system to be sacred. The Ethelbert was crowded in their ships, and their supplies were dwindling. They asked the Avramiy for any other planet that they could settle and live in peace. The Avramiy chose to attack them instead and destroyed many of their large city ships. The Ethelbert fought back hard, completely destroying major cities in twelve of the Avramiy planets. When the Ethelbert discovered the Avramiy were launching a massive counterattack, they split into two groups.

One group would escape into deep space, while the other group would circle and once the large fleet began chasing the first group they would attack the undefended planets, destroying anything that they detected, could launch into space, and crippled their communication systems. The Avramiy kingdom was one of the smaller ones in the Avramiy galaxy having precisely thirty-seven planets, of the millions within that galaxy. They were actually not Avramiy kingdom, as the Ethelbert gave this name to them. This second group, on completing its mission, went in search of the principal Avramiy force. To their delight, this large force would send back small fleets regularly that would refill with supplies and shuffle them back to the main fleet. The plan was to have two fleets in each section, taking turns collecting supplies from their previous hurdle and deliver them to the hurdle before them. They believed this method would keep a continuous supply line between them and their home worlds. The Ethelbert had other plans.

The Ethelbert destroyed these small fleets, effectively jamming their communication devices, as one planet gave them all the codes and sequences in its unsuccessful plea for their lives. They next destroyed the escort fighting ships, who were no matches to a force one-hundred times their size. They finally pulled the supply ships into their large receiving areas, where they removed all the supplies and refitted these ships for civilian transportation. A small crew would travel three days straight down and then follow the same course. This would keep them far enough away the Avramiy would not worry about them and close enough that they were available as escape vessels if needed. They actually needed, these ships, as damaged Ethelbert ships from the first group lay helpless in space. The attacking Avramiy let these ships float helplessly, giving more attention to the Ethelbert ships still fleeing. The Ethelbert could save their stragglers, and would use the booty ships from the fresh supply hurdles they attacked to move them out of the battle. These new rescues would join the other concerted supply ships that were traveling three days below them. This free picking off the Avramiy ended after one year. The Ethelbert had collected the communication equipment from the Avramiy supply ships and was monitoring all their transmissions. They discovered that because the attacking force had not received any resupplies, which it had to retreat. The Ethelbert changed their headings to straight down, alarming the ships already three days down to drop another three days and keep communications for emergency only. Once they traveled six days down, they moved forward passed under the retreating Avramiy and eventually reforming with their damaged first group. They salvaged all they could and united once more continued traveling on a straight downward course.

When the Avramiy returned to their destroyed homelands, they chose to rebuild their worlds and not hunt for the Ethelbert, who would be as searching for a grain of sand in a giant ocean. The Ethelbert was not known for violence, and used the reasoning that unless the Avramiy was disabled, they would have no place to settle in safety. The Power Spirits agreed with this reasoning, as the Avramiy had attacked first, as the Ethelbert's established history of accepting a potential planet's rejection of their settlement. The Ethelbert landed their ships on the four selected planets and continued to use these ships as their homes, and not build any structures on the hosting planets until they were sure their presence accepted. They would travel, on horses they captured and broke or hike, to many different sites around their ships. The Ethelbert enjoyed the outside fantastically much. They had no gods, and instead worshiped their ancestors, believing they still hovered around their bodies and watched everything they did. This was extremely effective in maintaining their social order, especially preventing any murders or thefts. They were careful to make sure all had the equivalent possessions. Everyone had the same wealth. They made this a permanent law to prevent any greed or dishonest traders. The ship's official channels issued all supplies. They had food generators, clothing generators, and energy generators. Each person had an official duty. They no longer needed most of the duties as the ships sat on planets. The fleets used this time for extra training, qualifying their crew in as many positions as possible, and many learning as many as five. This was more for an unforeseen emergency, even though none of their ships needed repairs. The unanticipated emergency, nevertheless, arrived and changed their destiny.

Emsky4, Emsky5, Emsky6, and Emsky7 were now hosting the Ethelbert, who initially took great care of these worlds, scarcely needing the air, sunlight, and land for recreational purposes. Each world governed itself and seldom had contact with each, another. There came one from the ships on Emsky6, who wanted power, Most likely, a demon or demons had possessed him because his hate and desire to destroy at all cost to get his power caught the peace-loving Ethelbert by surprise. Achilleus began by taking control of his ship with the help of a small group that he promised great rewards and positions for their assistance. Many had no idea how insane Achilleus had become as power was in sight. He alone killed forty-two of his comrades during the battle for his home ship. He even killed and was his mother and father, because they demanded that he not capture their home ship by force. He was wise enough to cripple the ship's communications so no one could request help. After they had control of the ship, he had all the captives line up outside, having the children face their parents or grandparents. He offered that any who killed their parents could join his force. A few accepted his offer. The next made the offer to the parents, as sadly a few also accepted that this offer. Afterward, he had them separate into groups of ten parents and ten children facing each other. He called two groups up to the front, at once killing all in the first group. He then told them that all who were not with him would die this day. He once more gave the children a chance to save themselves by killing their parents. Few parents remained. He offered these parents a chance, which most took. The few that remained, he executed. He ended with a crew of one-hundred fifty that could solely stay with him. They were all murderers now, and faced execution on any other ship in the Ethelbert fleet. Achilleus filled every position needed to fly this ship and operate its military weapons as he had the advantage of their cross training, which provided him with much flexibility. He would select another target, jam their communications, and then land beside them telling them he needed help as their food generators no longer functioned. This allowed him to move a large force into the ship's dining room area, where they began the attacks. Once he had control of the ship's command network, he turned the air generators off in the ship. This forced everyone outside, where they placed their parents against children in these games. This time, he mixed it up placing the children with other parents. This produced faster kills and reduced the risk of a revenge killing. Once he had his fresh crew, he mixed them with his, giving each ship a blended crew. He promoted one of his first friends as the ship's new commander and sent that ship and one-half of his original group off to capture more ships as he did the same thing.

His effectiveness was leaving Emsky6's surface scattered with murdered bodies. Fortunately, for the other worlds, four children with their parents, spread throughout all of Emsky6, survived by bringing pouches of blood with them, and pretending to shoot each other. They were part of a special private club, which had their own communication devices and warned the others. They elected not to warn the masses because they would not believe them and specifically make it easier for Achilleus to slaughter the masses. This extremely small organization could transfer particular communication equipment into selected nearby hills on Emsky6 by claiming to be doing specific long range signal testing. They could not hide in the hillsides as each ship monitored all assigned to it. After the executions, the new crew reassigned the staff, matching each person now assigned to the ship to its monitors, erasing all those they believed dead. This secret club, known as the Hemmelig had their own scrambled private channels, a common practice of special clubs among the Ethelbert. They warned their cells on the

Emsky5 and Emsky7, ignoring Emsky4 because of the distance. They offered the unauthorized movement of stationary spaceships on Emsky6 as evidence. The scanners of Empsky5 and Emsky7 could easily to verify this, mobilize their defenses, and prepare for an attack. They called on Emsky4 for help in blockading Emsky6. Emsky4 joined the blockade, and regrettably, Achilleus picked their positions for his spearhead. He was angry when his ships began their missions for the other Emsky worlds to find such a large force to face him. It was now time to see who had the greatest hunger to survive.

Achilleus was infuriated when he discovered his surprise attack had lost its surprise. They monitored all communications leaving Emsky6 and all coming into his conquered world. He elected to hit the Emsky4 line hard, believing the Emsky5 and Emsky7 forces would not rush too fast to their defense. Achilleus was proving his great military intuition in this move. Emsky4 called for help, yet no relief came. After losing three-fourths of their fleet, Emsky4 opened the line and retreated to Emsky4. This break provided Achilleus time to begin attacking Emsky5 and Emsky7 from both the front line and behind the line. The defenders were using a complete destroy all strategy, which was slow and weapon draining. Achilleus used a disable their shields and weapon systems strategy, which was fast and effective. With their shields down, he was easily able to disable their lives-support systems, leaving enemy ships filled with the dead crew to block the front. These ships provided excellent shields to hide behind in setting up ambushes. His enemy naturally would try to rescue the few still on these ships who were living temporarily in space suits and oxygen tanks. When they contacted their disabled comrades, they would lower their shields, when an Achilleus's cloaked ship would strike the life-support and weapon systems, which also included the shields. They allowed the communication systems to remain, as they would be the bait for more rescue attempts. Achilleus's greatest military strength was his perseverance. He knew that these small numbers would add to large losses for his enemy. His enemy was no longer able to go on a powerful offensive campaign and now was retreating into a circle formation defense. This time, Achilleus used the crippled ships, set on the auto destruct at his signal, giving fake distress signals. The Emsky5 and Emsky7 ships pulled these ships into their safety circle and when they had them inside, Achilleus released, then self-destructs, which crippled the Emsky5 and Emsky7 ships, as they did not have their inside space shielded.

This proved to be the power weapon Achilleus needed. He easily finished off the remainder of the ships slowly by direst disabling their defenses and next, their life-support. After this, he used his laser beams to guide these ships back to the surface of Emsky6, where he would attempt to salvage what he could. He could salvage over seventy percent of them, with a few supply depot ships providing a bonus. To buy a little time, he entered negotiations with Emsky5 and Emsky7. They also wanted to postpone what could be their doom. Achilleus was standing fast to his demand for unconditional surrender. Emsky5 and Emsky7; however, were asking for conditions to their surrender. Achilleus was simply leading them on, as even if conditions existed, he would not honor them after the surrender. His goal was that all would die. He offered them chances to surrender. The person surrendering had to bring another person, caged, that they would execute in front of one of his judges before they started the candidate. They did not realize the initiation would be by joining the force that would give Achilleus Emsky5 and Emsky7. As with his conquered world, once they murdered, they became robots in his service. Even at this, Achilleus still mixed the people into new groups, with several of his spies, so he could monitor their activities. When he discovered a decenter, he or she was tortured and executed publicly with streams to every room within the fleet. He believed that complete fear would give him the control he needed. Just before his invasion of Emsky5, he had fifty Emsky5 members randomly selected and executed on the live stream. This was not a wise move on his part, as he now established himself as a murderer. Therefore, even though in mixed crew teams, the Emsky5 members adjusted whatever controls, they could to hinder the mission's ultimate success. Many even went as far to cause their ships to crash and lay in ruins. Others adjusted their targeting equipment, so they did not hit their targets with a solid hit, allowing a few among the ships to escape. Achilleus did gain control of Emsky5, yet paid a price higher than he should have. He decided someone was going to pay.

When all his fleets rejoined after the attack, he reviewed the attack logs of each ship, comparing their attack accuracy. This was easy for him, as the computers prepared the reports for him. Every ship that returned had missed most of their targets. Next, he collected all the Emsky5 ship members and had his computers retrace the ship's logs of his or her every move; giving details to any contact with any of the ship's adjusting controls. The logs gave no evidence; however, the computer did report several had lapses in their logs, which was near impossible. He collected this large number of his forces and put them into his newly created prisons. Achilleus had something special in mind for them. He leaked a special invasion plan to Emsky7. The plan detailed how he would flash his invasion force to three sites close to their capital ships and remaining military ships. Here, the men would enter one of the ships and install viruses in their command communication devices. They would then release biological chemicals into each of the ships, killing all those who were on board these ships. The surprise in this invasion would be the use of humans on the ground where they could easily penetrate and cause this excessive destruction. Achilleus believed this would cause Emsky7 to mobilize great forces at these three sites in their effort to defeat him, at any cost. Empsky7 did not realize this was a setup. The invasion forces would be his prisoners collected from Emsky5, equipped scarcely with defensive equipment, and dressed in his army uniforms. Achilles goals were to get the Emsky7 to consolidate their forces in these three areas, and once they began their campaigns; he could pick them off easily. The bait in the traps was merely saving him the task of executing them. On arrival around Emsky7, he split his force into five groups with different orbits, yet still within the striking range of the three invasion sites. His communications were on Emsky5 channels, as he had described in his false release. This added confidence to the validity of these plans as Emsky7 waited for their great victory. They were actually celebrating their surprise defensive attack. Unfortunately, a surprise was awaiting.

The prisoner invasion forces appeared as predicted and at once came under attack. For this attack, Empsky7 lowered their shields, so they could release their missiles and lasers. They had no reason to suspect an attack, as they had the attack in front of them and could not give up such an easy and fruitful attack. The Emsky7 believed killing a person was the same as a solid hit on an invading ship, because ships needed crews and crews consisted of people. They begin firing at will against the dispersed invaders. They could merely fire small grenade type weapons, as these invaders were too close to their occupied ships. Additionally, they did not want to destroy their community parks, graveyards, and monuments erected in these areas. Once they began attacking, Achilleus, who had already locked in his targets, unleashed his reign of terror from the sky. Within a few minutes, these three centers of the Emsky7 civilization and power were helpless and forced to surrender. The few prisoner decoys who survived escaped into the nearby hills. Achilleus had a special treat for them and a secret task force to deliver this delicacy. He had tracking chips embedded in their brains during their flash to the surface. His task force could easily locate them and one by one, executed them. Achilleus played the role of honor in this attack, revealing to his Emsky5 members that he had given their natives a chance to regain their honor and that the Emsky7 attacked them, massacring them without mercies. Next, he alluded about the terrible thing that the Emsky7 had done in killing men and women exposed on open ground without a ship. Further, he told them that he had hoped the Emsky7, once identifying these people as Emsky5 would have welcomed them, and thereby giving them a fighting chance for their survival. The Emsky5 members demanded revenge, and therefore lead the attacks on the remainder of Emsky7. They also supervised, the lineups of parents against their children executions, matching them as best they could. The Emsky5 told them that anyone who kills an Emsky7, they would spare. Their heartless and cruel approach left the Emsky7 executing their family members without hesitation.

Achilleus soon had complete control of Emsky7, moving about one-third of their ships to Emsky5 and relocating one-third of Emsky5 ships to Emsky6 and one-third of Emsk6 ships to Emsky7. He was effective in planting his special spies among these populations as the relocations created much confusion. Achilleus no concentrated on his defense, deciding not to invade Emsky4, as he believed that he had destroyed a large part of their attack force, and the history of Emsky4 had been one of the seclusion. He, therefore, entered a peace treaty with Emsky4 not to attack them. He had always heard that Emsky4 had special divine protection and therefore, did not want to risk losing his new kingdom. His kingdom did not unite under his control as he had planned. Rebels constantly disrupted his operations. The further he executed, the more the rebels fought him. Years later, after he had executed forty percent of the Emskies, he faced another invader, although this one was small and had no regard for which side it received its victims. Emsky7 had among its groups a band of renegade scientists who were searching for a biological weapon to deploy on Emsky6 during one if its cargo hauls. The scientists believed that they had found the perfect virus and placed it in a few cargo ships with special explosives that would activate when the container opened. This virus was airborne and multiplied rapidly. Once entering its victim, it would take two weeks to become lethal, and during the interim lived inside its victim's lungs, expelling several of its family when the victim talked. During their lab tests, this virus had a lifespan of two months, after which they would all cease to exist. The scientists believed that they had tested every possible scenario; however, the future held a few surprises for them.

They failed to consider that with so many live people to invade, the extra proteins they consumed enhanced their evolutionary cycle. They had conducted their experiments on lifeless bodies with mechanical lungs, analyzing how these viruses entered the other dead bodies with mechanical lungs. Live tissue was a different process. They also failed to account the simple fact that when these viruses multiplied, their descendants began a new life cycle, thereby permitting this virus to continue destroying. The greatest mistakes that they made were not considering the loading and unloading procedures of the cargo. Emsky6 unloaded the cargo, as the Emsky7 loaders moved their cargo onto the cargo ships returning to Emsky6. The delivering crew always spent the night as guests with the receiving crew. Achilleus wanted them to understand each well, learning as much as possible, which would help in detecting any sabotage swindles. The drawback this time was they all breathed in the virus, securing it until their imminent deaths. The cargo ships returned to Emsky7 as all who had ordered supplies came to collect their resupplies, thereby spreading the virus to all corners of Emsky7. The same was true for both Emsky6 and Emsky5. The virus attached to Achilleus quickly, because he was always among the first to inspect his new treasures from the other worlds. Two weeks later, he was dead. His followers concealed his death as they issued orders in his name. They quickly discovered that the first law was to suspend interplanetary travel until they could pinpoint the source. The two-week lapse, coupled with them having no history of this virus, and the fact that all three planets were dying from it, led them to conclude that it was an invasion from another planet. The sole planet they could think of was Emsky4. Their difficulty now was that they could not launch an attack without a visible Achilleus to order it. He always inspected his launching fleet. They would not ever dare an attempt, because, once the kingdom knew of his death, total chaos would reign. They had to find a way to transfer the power to them or the kingdom would fall.

Achilleus occupied his private ship with the thirteen great judges. These judges handled most of the administrative duties and for usually were the observable leaders. The judges now took turns walking throughout the ship wearing Achilleus's robe and crown, staring out windows, so they would be perceivable. The judges prepared a voice transformer that would change their voice into Achilleus's for all communication orders. Unfortunately, their little secret died with them, as Achilleus had transferred the virus to them as well. When the judges died, their evil kingdom perished and the planets immediately declared their independence, as also did Emsky6. The plague eventually caused the few who were still living off the ships into the forests. Unfortunately, the airborne virus discovered most of them as well. The result revealed that Emsky5 had three living separately survivors, one male, and two females. Emsky6 had four living apart survivors, two females, and two males. Emsky7 also had four separated survivors, one male, and three female. These secluded the hidden survivors had no way to find each other. Emsky4 sent humanitarian ships to these planets, collecting and consolidating the survivors. They relocated these few fresh groups to mountain areas in which they would begin new lives. The Emsky4 ships had basic equipment and supplies to help them build their new homes. The Emsky5 and Emsky7 ships joined waiting for the Emsky6 ship to meet them. The Emsky6 ship notified them that they were still searching, as they had signals, but could not find the refuges. In reality, they had found the survivors easily and relocated them to a safe continent. Achilleus kept this special continent as a retreat for his judges and him. One of the survivors talked about certain pronounced treasures hidden in his capital. The great of this Emsky4 crew lead them in search of this treasure. They searched among the dead and in many ships. Their orders were not to go around any ships. There was an exceptionally good reason for this order.

The early stages in developing this virus existed in dead bodies, therefore, would stay in a body until they invaded all cells. The Emsky4 treasure hunters moved several of these bodies, as they blocked entrances. They believed the bodies were hiding something. Unfortunately, the thing they were hiding was not behind the door, it was in front of the door in their bodies. The virus quickly detected a live being and flooded inside their lungs. Unable to find any treasure and out of time, as the other two ships were returning to help them, they abandoned their treasure hunt and prepared for the trip back to Emsky4. The three ships joined in their one-day trip home. On returning to Emsky4, they unloaded the extra equipment and supplies they took with them. They also inspected each other's ships to make sure illegal items from the other Emskies were not on board their ships. What they could not see found them. They quickly spread, the virus among each, and when they returned to their home ships, spread it there as well. Emsky4 had a practice of randomly selecting humanitarian crews from as many separate areas as they could. This gave the pride and honor of saving others to more of the population; in spite of the pride and honor of these seven who saved included, certain stole ways, which were not interested in reviving. The virus spread quickly among the Emsky4 ships, especially as the Emsky4 civilization was highly mobile. They enjoyed the great beauty of Emsky4's mountains, rivers and the vast oceans. They did explore the ocean as deep as they could; however, they never made it deep enough, to catch the Benigna-A, even when they came to the surface to collect their Benigna-B. The Benigna had excellent biological sonar abilities and were easily able to avoid the Ethelbert. The Benigna-A, or fish sisters, just breathed through their gills, and luckily, the virus could not live in water, as it was strictly airborne. The Benigna-B or angel sisters syphoned merely the orange bacteria and could expel all other foreign particles, to include the killer virus that was quickly turning Emsky4 into a graveyard. When the angel sisters expelled the foreign particle, they expelled it without any life. This was another of the thousands of benefits the Benigna provided for Emsky4. Additionally, when the angel sisters turned into rock at night, any foreign particles attached to them, likewise, converted into rock. This transformation killed all attached foreign particles. The angel sisters mourned over seeing so many of the Emsky dying. They had to find a way to prevent this loss of their mystery world co-inhabitants.

The Benigna examined the dead viruses from the angel sisters' skin when they converted back from their rocks. Regretfully, they did not have any advanced equipment that could prevent the spread of this killing plague. The Emsky believed this virus feed from their ships; therefore, they destroyed all their ships and the items on them. They programmed the ships' course and once launched they activated these ships' autopilot. Within one day, the ships, packed with dead bodies entered space and self-destructed. The Emsky kept nothing, for fear the virus could be in any item. Dejectedly, the virus had spread throughout the population and left Emsky4 with no more than dead bodies scattering her surface. The angel sisters searched hard for any survivors, yet unlike the other Emskies, Emsky4 had solely dead bodies, until one night, an angel sister discovered a young fourteen-year-old girl. She was playing alone, wearing a white silk dress. The young woman had her right hand wrapped in a bandage and was holding a collection of white flowers. Correspondingly, she had long red stringy hair that hung down on her flat chest. She wore a flower wreath over her head. The angel sister became excited when she saw her believing that with the bandage and flowers, she was not alone. The angel sister hid in the thick brush and called out asking the girl what her name was. She answered back with a calm voice, hoping the light from the moons would identify this stranger, "My parents call me Teplov. What is your name?" The angel sister, being extremely careful not to reveal herself, answered her, "I am your friend Tolmachyov." Teplov asks her, "Tolmachyov, why do you hide from me. Have no fear, for I am alone?" Tolmachyov answers, "Teplov, I am not permitted to reveal myself to humans. I have been searching for many days to find survivors. You are the lone person that we have found. I was marveling how happy you were playing." Teplov confesses that she was not playing, but simply collecting flowers for her parents and sisters' graves. Accordingly, she confides in Tolmachyov how lonely she is and that sometimes the large animals chase her. Tolmachyov tells her she saw a few small laser rifles with sun rechargers. She would go and bring them back to her. Teplov points to a nearby forest on the side of a hill and tells her mystery friend, she will be waiting under the trees. Tolmachyov quickly scans within one mile for any large beasts. She sees one and tells Teplov she will be safe for a while. This angel sister proceeds to the large bear, pulls out her long knife, and stabs both of his front legs. She did not want to kill the animal, but just to prevent him from attacking little Teplov. Tolmachyov flew quickly to where she saw the weapon. While flying, she wondered how this little girl could be alone. Something did not feel right here, and she was now determined to find the answer.

When she returned with the small laser rifle and sun recharger, she detected Teplov hiding in a tree. Tolmachyov quietly put the weapon on the branch below her. Teplov was asleep. Tolmachyov wake her, hiding in the tree next to her. She told her to go to the branch below her to collect her weapon. Teplov asked her what she had done to stay alive. Teplov reports that her father heard the ships were returning from the plague planets and took his family in the hills for one month. He knew much about the plague, as he constantly monitored the transmissions from the other Emskies. She added that her mother became sick in the third week, forcing him to take one of her brothers to help him carry our mother back to the ship for medical treatment. This left her with two other sisters. The oldest sister made several spears from various branches as they tried to travel to a mountain that was two days away. Their father told them to stay on a mountain, as the cold thin air would give them a little safety. On the way there, large beasts killed both sisters. This is why she returned this way. Tolmachyov told her she must go back to the mountain. Teplov begged her for help. The angel sister told her she could merely help at night. They would find a safe place for her to sleep during the day. Teplov told her they would collect fruit, berries, and certain wild vegetables while they journeyed at night. When dawn arrived, she told Teplov where to sleep and rushed to the ocean. When she gave the news about the Teplov, the Benigna was excited. This energized the angel sisters to search for a boy or man. Their nightly searches continued to produce no other living human. Tolmachyov and Teplov talked much throughout the nights. Tolmachyov had to think fast a few times as she almost revealed herself to Teplov who was crafty in maneuvers. Teplov continued to beg to see Tolmachyov. Tolmachyov finally told her that she was a spirit and if a human ever saw her, their eyes would completely burn. This held Teplov at bay for the remainder of the trip, as she made sure not to see the desperate angel sister. Tolmachyov scanned the mountains, exploring for a cave that was near various fruit trees and easy to defend. She began to wonder if such a place existed.

Fortunately, one night while they were walking along the base of a long ridge, Tolmachyov spotted the ideal cavern on the next ridge over from her cave. She told Teplov where to go, and that she would be watching from above, because this path had few trees. While watching from above and as Teplov was about to enter the cavern, Tolmachyov told her to wait in a nearby tree. Tolmachyov scanned the cave and found a large bear inside one of the tunnels. She quickly killed the bear and made a fire, placing selected plants that were nearby on the fire. She wanted to make sure the smell of blood was covered. Tolmachyov then went above Teplov and told her there was a dead bear for her to finish cleaning and a fire she could begin cooking. She also had a vein of salt in the next tunnel; she would be able to preserve this meat. Tolmachyov warned her that she must place specific plants that she left there on the fire at least once each hour. Teplov had already hung the animal on one of the cave walls and removed its head. She had the blood running down into the deepest part of the cave. Tolmachyov placed the nonedible organs and head alongside the neighboring ridge. Teplov needed simply to remove and dry the fur and carve the meat, cook what she wanted and salt the remainder, storing it in one of the tunnels. There was plenty of firewood in this area, thus Teplov could live here for at least three months living off the bountiful meat provided by the bear. Tolmachyov felt secure that her friend would be safe during the day, and returned to her fish sister to rest for the day.

To Tolmachyov's surprise, when she returned Teplov was bundled in a corner crying. Because the cave was so dark, Tolmachyov could get closer to her without detection. In the comfort of this cave, although not as appealing as a space ship, yet better than a tree branch and accordingly much meat to eat she asked Teplov why she was crying. Teplov told her that she missed her family and friends and felt so alone. This angel sister reminded her that she would be her friend. Teplov told her, "You are a gift from the heavens; however, as you possess no flesh, you are just an invisible voice. I can hear you, but not see you. I need a friend I can touch." Tolmachyov told her that she truly understood and that is why her friends were searching all Emsky on her behalf. For now, she would help her and at least be a comforting voice. She complemented Teplov and the way she had carved the meat, salted it, and stored it. Tolmachyov volunteered to dispose of the bones. She took the skeleton and loose bones up into the sky two ridges over and broke off the bones spreading them over a five-mile radius. She wanted to keep the predators away from Teplov's cave. On her way back, she gathered several more fragrance plants for Teplov to burn in her fire. They talked for a few hours; however, as dawn approached Tolmachyov fled back to the sea. Once back she asked the Benigna leaders how they could help little Teplov and her loneliness. The leaders called out to Borsod-Abaúj-Zemplén for a solution. Borsod-Abaúj-Zemplén asked for a volunteer. Tolmachyov quickly volunteered. The Power Spirits told her that tonight when she arrived with Teplov, they would give her a temporary human body, and that she could stay until Teplov had another human companion, when she would have to return to the sky and sea.

Tolmachyov was so excited and could not wait until that night to share the great news with Teplov. She knew the flesh bodies would be much harder to care for; therefore, she would have to teach her all she could before another human appeared.

CHAPTER 04

Álmosd's triangle in the seventh stone

The time came when Tolmachyov's fish sister sadly took her to the surface for their temporary separation. She understood the need to care for Teplov, as her heart shared the same desire to care for her. Her fist sister would search the underground rivers and underwater caves to find another entrance. They knew such an entrance did exist, and that it was merely a matter of time. The Power Spirits would not remove Tolmachyov's sonar scenes; therefore, they could continue communicating with each other. Tolmachyov felt sorry for her sister, and in anguish declared, she would forgo this mission. Her sister demanded that she represent the Benigna thereby saving this child so the Ethelbert would somehow continue. They had been the perfect land species, although a future without all their space equipment could prove to be different. Her sister believed this was a risk worth chancing. Her eighteen-year-old daughter, Chemeris who promised to visit her mother every night, also accompanied Tolmachyov. This was a promise that Tolmachyov intended to keep, as her everlasting bond with her daughter. Benigna mothers build their lives around their daughters teaching them everything their mothers taught them, transferring their knowledge of the ages. Chemeris also was close to her fish mother's children or technically her stepsisters. The oceans had many rivers that flowed in from the underground. These passageways always contained air pockets, and most times a small bank on each side. Here the fish daughter would take her angel stepsister, in rock form, to one of these pockets, and they would play together. They had a wide assortment of activities and games that their parents passed down through the ages. These two, once ready to mate would spend the remainder of their lives as mates, therefore, their parents encouraged this. Each new generation of fish sisters had a new-programmed seed, as if it was from a different fish mother.

The fish sister spits Tolmachyov and Chemeris onto the bank of a river close to Teplov's mountain cave. Chemeris was determined to spend the nights with her mother, and then return to the ocean at dawn. Tolmachyov reminded her that Teplov could never see her, or the Benigna would be in grave trouble. She agreed as they established signals that would alert each other of a desire to talk. When they transformed back into their beautiful angel bodies, they flew to the cave. Tolmachyov always flew high the first time, so she could scan where Teplov was. Teplov was crafty in where she would try to set up her ambush. Tolmachyov always kept one-step ahead of her. This night would be her first exception. Tolmachyov transformed into a human woman, having made one small mistake. She was completely nude. She asked her daughter to search among a few female bodies and find her specific clothing. She stressed that after her removed the dead woman's garments, she would need to bury her. Her daughter quickly went to work and within twenty-minutes returned with the clothing. Tolmachyov had no concerns that clothing was wet, other than a casual curiosity. Chemeris explained that rotting flesh was not sanitary, and if she had not washed the clothes, not just would the odor be nauseating for the other humans, but the risk of becoming contaminated was extremely high. Tolmachyov had never studied humans that much. She was thankful her daughter was skilled in this area. She knew the big minute was near and wondered about the reaction Teplov would have.

She had a cause to wonder. Tolmachyov slowly sprang from the bushes behind Teplov giving her greetings. This scared Teplov, who began running away screaming for help. She ran into a pack of wolves who quickly chased her for their next meal. Chemeris flew in front of the wolves hitting them as they tried to pass. Teplov, now aware of the danger from the wolves went to fire her laser rifle, merely to discover she had lost it. Tolmachyov, who followed her, while not alarming the wolves, spotted the weapon and carried it with her. As the wolves came into her view, she carefully killed each one. Teplov heard the sound of her laser weapon and saw the wolves dying. This was a wondrous sight for her. She realized that her life was about to end because she made one careless mistake. This was a night of many moons, and she had heard these wolves howling earlier. Nevertheless, she had another question invading her mind. Who was the spirit that greeted her? It did not sound like her invisible friend. Was her life in danger? Better yet, had another survivor among the Ethelbert, who once roamed this world, currently appeared? She realized one thing now, and that was that this stranger had her weapon and was killing the wolves. If this unknown thing was killing the wolves, then it must be trying to save her. Teplov realized that without her weapon, she was good as dead. She contemplated on what to do in this situation. Accordingly, she came out with her hands up, surrendering to the wolf killer who was saving her. Chemeris currently hid in the brush. Tolmachyov came walking forward and stood in person with Teplov. The question now, was who will talk first.

They continued to stand before each other. Teplov broke down first and fell to her knees begging not to die. Tolmachyov wanted to talk first, yet she had never talked as a human to another human, and her shyness tied her mouth closed. She lay the weapon beside Teplov and began petting her hair gently. Teplov found herself puzzled now. Why would this invader, or fellow Ethelbert because of how she was dressed, surrender her weapon? Teplov was so confused that she froze. The woman was petting her hair. Because she was a woman, she could rule out rape. Her father told her that during times of chaos, several men would rape as many women as they could simply for their pleasure. The other factor that ruled out the woman might have men with her was her invisible friend said there were no men alive on Emsky4. The piece that did not fit now was that she also told her there were no women. So where did this woman originate? Tolmachyov could sense the tension and fear in Teplov and therefore, told her not to fear, that she was a friend sent by the invisible voice to live with her until another arrived. Teplov also could sense the tremble in this woman's voice with her sincerity. Pulling her courage, she stood up and offered her hand to the woman who was kneeling beside her. After pulling her to a standing position, she introduced herself as Teplov. Tolmachyov introduced herself. Teplov declared that was the name of her invisible friend. Tolmachyov confessed the great gods temporarily gave her a body, so she could comfort her while they searched for a man, which she would mate. Teplov declared that she did not want to mate and never wanted children. She cited that her younger brother, and his friends used to torment her continuously. Children are too much work and furthermore, much trouble. She was upset that a man would try to mate with her. She declared that if a man ever touched her like that she would kill him. She knew what those men would try to do, because her older sisters told her everything about it. Tolmachyov now wondered if Emsky would have generations of humans, nonetheless, she began to consider that Teplov was barely fourteen years old and that several humans did not develop as others did. Teplov had younger brothers who bothered her and older sisters who created tales about the horrors of mating. She hoped that Teplov's hormones would change her mind, because the hormones in her new body were driving her crazy. She needed to discover a way to control this.

Tolmachyov asked Chemeris to question the Benigna for a solution. Chemeris confessed to have detailed knowledge concerning the mating habits and conditions of humans. This was a popular activity among couples at night, especially when they were camping in the forests or mountains. As she began, describing the ritual, Tolmachyov began to vomit confessing that such an activity must be horrible. Chemeris argues the women seemed to enjoy this activity. Tolmachyov, holding fast to her position, worries that she will not be able to recommend this to poor little innocent Teplov. Chemeris tells her not to worry, but simply give it a little time. Teplov asks Tolmachyov with whom, she is talking. Tolmachyov explains she is talking with her daughter, who she cannot see. Teplov complains that if Tolmachyov can see her that she should be able to see her. Tolmachyov explains that this is a unique permission from her creator because in her species, the mother and daughter share a special bond as if they were sisters. Teplov remarks that at least she has a real mother as a friend now and one is much better than zero. Tolmachyov begins to touch the weeds she is standing near and how she always wondered how this felt. She can transmit the feeling to Chemeris who transmits it to all the Benigna. Teplov asks her why she is standing in the weeds; now that she is visible, she should stand in the open where it is easier to defend herself. At that instance, the small bug bites her leg. She comes running out of the weeds to show Teplov where something bit her. Teplov explains that the weeds and light attract many insects, and this is another reason to stay in the open. Tolmachyov complains about this pain, and that it felt uncomfortable. Teplov laughs and comments that she has much to teach her mother. Tolmachyov begins to worry that much of her learning may be about pain.

Teplov begins cutting a few large leaves and has Tolmachyov sit down as she wraps and ties them around her feet. She explains that Tolmachyov must cover her feet to reduce any pain from objects cutting her feet from the surface. Their leaves will help tonight, and once they get back to the cave; she will make a pair of shoes from the fur remaining of the bear. Tolmachyov takes a deep breath and comments how well the air feels in her lungs. Teplov tells her to be careful with smoke as this can harm her lungs. She holds her new mother's hand as they slowly walk back to the cave. Tolmachyov hears a noise and motions for the laser weapon focusing on the moving object. She zips her laser causing the movement to stop. She walks into the weeds to discover what this was and finds a large dead rabbit. She picks it up and rushes back to Teplov asking for her knife to begin cleaning the rabbit. The first thing that they do is dug a hole, drain the blood, put the nonedible organs in the hole, and bury it. Teplov then recommends they do the remaining in the cave. Tolmachyov excuses herself and goes into the weeds calling for Chemeris. She asks Chemeris to find her a weapon, solar recharger, knife, and large ax and shovel. Chemeris searches throughout the continent, locates these items on the far shoreline, and places them beside a tree in the path just ahead of her mother. She hovers in the sky above her mother and calls for her when she passes the tree. Tolmachyov thanks her, bidding her good night, as the dawn is approaching. Teplov asks her new mother why she has an ax and shovel. Tolmachyov explains the winter months are soon to arrive, and she knows of a great river to the west comes from the mountains. She believes that will be a great place to make their new home. Teplov does remember hearing reports of the not as terrible conditions along the western areas of Álmosd. This will be her first winter not in a ship. She testifies the winters, here can be terrible, especially in the northern areas. Teplov believes they can make it to the river in three weeks, find an acceptable cave, chop much firewood, and build a stone chimney at their cave's opening. Chemeris will find the path that they can take and scout ahead for places to sleep. She will also find a cave with a small cavern and no animal inhabitants.

They traveled along the side of a lower ridge that spanned this long northern continent. Although the winters were bitterly cold, the summer times were beautiful. The skies were clear, the dew heavy in the mornings and parched by the cool afternoons. Unlike other parts of Emsky, there was seldom any burned withered grass. The grass on this continent had solid roots. The wildlife here was crazier than other parts of Emsky, as the animals had more time away from humans. They adapted to this harsh land and did not enjoy humans, although their prior contact was much different from the future contact had in store for them. They had never experienced hunters hunting them during this age nor had anyone else competed for their lands. Tolmachyov knew what would someday be in store for Emsky, yet even with these drawbacks, new lives and civilizations, with their loves and hates were the way of all destinies. This was the reason for Emsky's creation. She could no more than hope that with the Benigna as invisible chaperones, this time would be different. The thought that the possible mother of this world could actually be holding her hand now was accordingly exonerating. They walked throughout the day. Tolmachyov believed that with the ruggedness of this terrain night walks would be too dangerous. She additionally wanted more time with her daughter during the nights. The pain of not being continuously with her, tortured her constantly. This was the mission that she begged the gods for, yet it was more overwhelming than she originally believed. The issues she never gave attention to before such as pain in just about everything she did, or even on certain things she did not do such as, when she did not eat, the hunger crippled her. Tolmachyov had not witnessed this much with Emsky4 as they lived in, their spaceships usually and had food generators. She constantly wondered why Teplov would continue to cook and eat the bear meat. She unfailingly ate before leaving the cave. They now had the remainder of this salted meat that they smoked before putting on the special backpacks that Chemeris found for them. Pain and hunger sandwiched just with the journey to avoid both. This did not seem to be what she was looking forward to finding. She did not even understand what she was looking for now.

After the three-week trek, they came on the river as evening approached. Tolmachyov sat along the bank of this giant river, listening to the water splash against a few rocks. This sound brought comfort back to her heart, as she so much enjoyed the sound of rushing water. She saw a fish jump from the water. She marveled at how it could thrust itself into the unknown with so much confidence. When it entered the air, the fish maintained its confidence that soon it would return to its home, and simply enjoyed the freedom of this temporary world. Tolmachyov understood that this was she. She had leaped into the unknown, into another world with the dangers and freedoms that came with this new temporary liberation. Tolmachyov dedicated herself to Teplov, which delighted Chemeris so much. Chemeris told her mother, "As I told all the Benigna, no other mothers are greater than my fish mother, who shares her beloved mate with the Emsky and her mother who did not recognize the word fear but slightly appreciate the words of love and peace through exploration." Tolmachyov confided that she was so afraid of this new world and the responsibility for little innocent Teplov, whose young life has already been flooded with rivers of tears that she ignores. Tolmachyov cut a branch, sharpen its end, and spiked a few large fish, astonishing Teplov who had never been near a river or the ocean in her life to date. She had eaten fish before that her father obtained while trading in the markets. She made a small fire for them and cooked the fish, adding a few exceptional plants she had collected during the day. Teplov asked if there was any special place for them to sleep this night. Tolmachyov told her that tonight they would rest on the open ground under the stars and the lights from the moons. This night had many moons shinning; therefore,

Chemeris hovered in the shades, even though the moonlight could not hurt her, she feared detection by Teplov. Tolmachyov and Teplov ate so many fish that they could not move, but just lay on the ground suffering from the sin of gluttony. Tolmachyov asked Teplov why she had not warned her that this could happen when overeating. Tolmachyov thought her body would tell her when to stop eating. They were laughing and having so much fun; their systems ignored the food intake.

Tolmachyov just lay on her back, groaning while still chuckling and staring at the few stars who were sparking from the cloudy night sky. Birds were chirping, while insects were singing. This world is still so close to the manner it once again experienced creation. The animals were the caretakers. Tolmachyov believed the animals knew the new rulers were arriving out of the shadows. How the hills rolled slowly rising into the mountains behind them brought peace and joy to Tolmachyov. Tolmachyov had never experienced it as if she was now, belly packed, feet tired; love filled eyes and soft hand of Teplov as a fellow human. This was also new for Teplov. Teplov was in a critical stage of her life. She was in the middle of her siblings and thus fought to be recognized. Her father understood her and gave her extra attention, yet this attention was on camping trips and other outside adventures. These skills did bring several benefits to her, as she was comfortable outside. Tolmachyov regularly complained that she was too relaxed. Teplov was extremely comfortable around, her father who consistently kept her by his side, especially on their camping trips and hikes. She was in the middle of the siblings and despised by her younger brothers, usually because she told her parents every time they did something wrong. She tried to play with her older sisters, yet all they wanted to do was playing with boys. The thought of boys constantly made her sick, because at school, they were invariably bad. They were always trying to give her tokens to show her privates. They would pay as one of her friends showed her privates to a large group of boys and made a lot of trading tokens. She added that all the children kept this a secret, because the parents would beat all the kids. Teplov was the closet with her mother who gave her three daughters with special attention. She taught all three everything her mother taught her to make sure they knew it as if it were a rock in their foundation. The one thing she had not taught Teplov was a subject her older sisters were experts, and that was about boys. Tolmachyov stopped her here, and changed the subject to something new.

Tolmachyov complained about itching and feeling sticky. Teplov explained that they needed to wash themselves, and the nearby river would be great. She jumped and told her to follow and learn how to bathe. Tolmachyov watched Teplov stand by the shore a remove her garments. Tolmachyov asked her why she was nude. Teplov explained so she could wash her skin and told Tolmachyov to do the same. Tolmachyov complained that we were not supposed to see each other's nude body. Teplov told her not to worry, because we were both women and built the same way. Chemeris whispered from a tree for her mother to listen to Teplov. Tolmachyov did as everyone said and began walking to the water. Chemeris congratulated her mother for receiving a firm female body. Teplov then tells her that she is hotter than her mother is. Tolmachyov asks Teplov how she knows her temperature, as she is just now getting into the cold water. Chemeris falls from her tree laughing as Teplov is also laughing and splashing water at this lost woman. Teplov explains that hot means beautiful and that her body is picturesque. Tolmachyov confesses that she hopes it will last until her new friend arrives, although she does not believe it to be a good idea to eat as much as she did today. Teplov goes over beside her and shows her how to rub the dirt off her skin. She also tells her she must go under the water quickly and shake her hair and when she comes back up, she must wipe her face. Tolmachyov comments that the water is no longer cold, but actually comfortable now. Tolmachyov practices swimming currently and as she ventures a few feet away, her fish sister comes up from underneath her and takes her down the shore a little further so they can talk. Tolmachyov is scared that she may be bringing bad news.

Her fears quickly silenced themselves when her sister told her that all was well. She brought her fish daughter with her. Tolmachyov slid into the water and swam over to her hugging her. The young girl, whose name is Demeris, comments that this is the first time a human, has touched her. Tolmachyov warns her that no other human must ever touch her. They share a bond as deep as the one Tolmachyov has with Chemeris. Demeris swears to bring Chemeris every night. Tolmachyov explains to her fish sister that they will be living close to this river, so they will have many visits. As they talk light flashes into the water, making a robust splash. The next thing that they see is Chemeris coming up out of the water complaining about not being invited. This group of four is tightly bonded. The Benigna women not truly breast-feed their daughter but also their sister's daughter. Chemeris lived in the water during her feeding years; therefore, feeding from her fish mother was easy. This naturally made Demeris hungry. She would swim to Tolmachyov, who would wade or tread in the water, with her shirt removed while Demeris feed. Chemeris and Demeris spend most of their time together. Even when Chemeris is visiting Tolmachyov, she is flying back and forth also to visit with Demeris. Their reunion stops when Teplov now calls for Tolmachyov, who answers all is okay and on her way. Her fish sister quickly swims her close to Teplov who can merely see her friend flying into the water. Teplov asks her how she did this. Her bathing partner explains that one of her friends brought her back, and these are secret friends as well. Teplov asks why they must be secret. Tolmachyov explains that it is the will of the gods and that if her people disobey, the gods will execute them. She begs Teplov not to try so hard to see them, as she could be killing them. Teplov agrees, stating that at least she has a friend for a while. Teplov asks Tolmachyov if she knows much about the female body. She also asks if the new friend knows how they are different from the male body. Tolmachyov shakes her head no; as Teplov stands next to her explaining, they are the same and are females. She points to the areas that are special for females, such as the breasts for feeding babies. Tolmachyov reassures her that her real breasts have fed many babies. She is shocked that these bodies actually develop the babies inside them. After learning, how men are different Teplov warns her that she cannot let the men see her female private parts. Tolmachyov believes this is strange, yet she does not want to break any human laws. She is especially glad that the Benigna had no males. She remembers the visions of Achilleus killing so many people and how his armies were composed of men. She wondered if men were the reason for all the wickedness.

Teplov jokes with her wild mate as she calls her now, that she once believed men were the root of most evil until she met her father and two older sisters. Tolmachyov does not understand this statement and asks Teplov to explain it, which she does. Tolmachyov explains to Teplov that when she falls asleep, she will go visit with her daughters and a friend. Teplov, who is growing tired agrees and tells her they will talk about the daughters tomorrow. Tolmachyov goes back to the water, yet her family is gone doing the work they must do. Consequently, she returns to Teplov, crowds next to her and falls into a deep sleep. They both wake up late the next morning. They lie beside each other as the sun warms their bodies. They agree to relax and talk this day, and when they are hungry, catch just a few small fish and gather a variety of fruits and eat. Tolmachyov explains, as best she is capable of without many details about her other daughter Demeris. They talk about a few places they have visited. Teplov shares certain fun times she had when with her friends. Later in the afternoon, after they ate their fish and fruit, they decided to find their new home. Sure enough, halfway up to sloped hillside, they could see a ledge that looked as if it might have something behind it. It was hard to tell because of the vegetation. Teplov took one bag and went up first. Once Teplov was up there, she yelled back down for Tolmachyov to hurry to where she was. This was a wonderful cave, with a small opening and tunnel, which after they walked about one-hundred feet ran into a large room. They could see light above them. This meant that they could burn a fire inside, as the smoke would go out the above opening, which was most likely located on the top of this large foothill to the mountains. The question now was, "Would this keep them warm for the winter months."

Tolmachyov said they would have to kill another bear for his hide and meat. Fortunately, this cave also had a salt vein in one of its side tunnels. These veins are easy to find, by simply tasting the water that flows from each side tunnel. Emsky does not have large layers of salt, nor does it have salt in its oceans. Through all the billions of years of erasing past civilizations, salt could spread itself in the veins of the mountains. The Ethelbert had no need for Emsky salt; nevertheless, they scanned it and stored this information, in case they would need to trade the salt someday. The plague invasion destroyed these maps, yet at least Teplov knew the salt existed. Searching for something you recognize, exists is so much better than searching for something that you do not realize if it exists. They would then salt the bear's meat and store it for the winter months. One advantage they had is they could ice fish during the medium bitter days. They would also store enough firewood for the complete winter, having extra if the winter in harsher than normal. They had their rechargeable laser weapons cut the firewood. Tolmachyov wanted to cut the wood around their bathing place, so they could better defend themselves. Teplov did most of the work during the day as she always allowed Tolmachyov a long nap, because she spent many hours at night with her family, as Teplov slept in the cave. She no longer tried to see them, because she did not want to be the reason for their deaths. One day, as they were watching several small animals play, Teplov asked Tolmachyov if she knew how the animals arrived on Emsky. Tolmachyov told her they were already here when they come to Emsky and were eating the orange covered grass. Teplov asked about the orange, and her friend explained an orange-colored thick biological dust covered Emsky. That is a favored food of the Benigna and Emsky still has enough particles in the air and at the bottom of the sea to feed for 10,000 more years. Teplov asked if this orange dust was dangerous for humans. Tolmachyov told her it was and within about one-hundred years, it will coat the inside of their lungs causing death. Teplov tells her that is the average lifespan currently, so this should not cause any problems. Tolmachyov now thought about the problems with lifespans.

Tolmachyov questions Teplov on how she plans to extend her lifespan. She confesses that life is day by day now, and if tomorrow comes or not, she does not care. The reward of it not coming is that she would be with her family. Tolmachyov tells her that her family can wait, just as her family is waiting. While exploring close to their cave entrance, they discovered a place they both decided, would be their special place. This was a gorgeous bend in a stream, which fed into the river. It was about a one-acre spotted with trees sandwiched by this forest. Tolmachyov used her laser to remove the trees growing on this plot, and then finished the wood into firewood for their cave. They used their knives to cut the weeds and pulled the weeds that were choking the flowers along the stream's bank. The shoreline was speckled with ultramarine, light blue, yellow, and bright-red flower bushes on both sides. They allow the giant weeping willows along the sides of their lot and next to the stream. Bright purple leaf trees coated the other bank. The water was a deep, pure blue with leaves sparsely covering its surface. Teplov could see certain fish in the shallow waters, therefore Tolmachyov cut two poles from the loose branches of the cut trees and taught Teplov how slowly to wade in the water and spook the fish. Teplov, through trial and error finally spiked three. Once she spiked one, she swings her pole toward their cleared area where Tolmachyov would collect it and place it in their bags. Teplov was so thrilled with her new skill and the pride the food; they ate that day; she provided. Among their security works, they made four to five firewood trips to their cave. Tolmachyov did not like all the snakes who kept appearing. They killed twenty snakes whom the occupied this recreation area. Tolmachyov noted that even their cave had snakes, and that they would have to keep on the guard against these abundances of snakes. Teplov confides that her father told her snakes flourish near water areas. Tolmachyov tells her they flourish everywhere, and that they needed to spend a few days killing them. These snakes were truly trying to bite them. She would need her daughter's help with these snakes as she feared Teplov could be seriously hurt. Surprisingly, the more they killed, the more that would appear. Was this a warning sign, they had done something wrong?

This greatly concerned Tolmachyov. Her fish sister assured her she had done no wrong for if she had the gods would have warned them. Subsequently, Tolmachyov asked her fish sister and Demeris to emit their high sonar waves tonight for her area. These waves torment the snakes forcing them into the open. After that, Tolmachyov asked Chemeris to locate their heat waves and to zap them. Within thirty minutes, they reported that one-hundred thousand snakes in a five-mile radius were now dead. Most of these snakes were crowded in small caves or had created their own holes to hide. They also hid in tree branches. Tolmachyov was surprised at how many there had been. Chemeris tells her mother that more are in the area and that they will zap once per week. More often than that could alert them, in which they would hibernate and wait until a later date to attack. Chemeris tells her that several bears are heading this way, and with the removal of all the snakes, more wildlife will soak into their area. Tolmachyov notes that and after their detailed nightly chats, she returns to Teplov and another day of their routine, clear land, eat, delivery firewood. The firewood was not heavy when they begin; nevertheless, by the time they were halfway of the cliff it grew heavier with each step they climbed toward the cave's opening. Teplov and Tolmachyov grew closer each day, notwithstanding surviving occasional spats. Most spats were due to fatigue. Teplov was able, while blindfolded to speak with fish sister, discovering her name as Siostra with Chemeris and Demeris. Siostra could relate with Teplov quickly as naturally also did Chemeris and Demeris. She felt a part of their family and would spend a few hours with them, each night. On the nights she did not accompany Tolmachyov to the meeting point, which varied, Teplov would climb down to the river, blindfold herself, with her bear blindfold, and call for Chemeris who now had Teplov's voice programed in her scanners. Chemeris would walk behind her verbally guiding, her to the meeting point. This Benigna family thanked her for protecting their mandatory privacy. Teplov always thanked them for accepting her, because having four friends was so wonderful. There were a few times when Teplov would ask various deep philosophical questions, which would put Tolmachyov and Siostra on the defensive.

Teplov was questioning the purpose of life, as Tolmachyov had previously. Demeris and Chemeris explained that life was your friends, helping and living for them. Teplov reminded them that her friends were all dead now. Demeris and Chemeris reminded her that they were her friends. Teplov complained that she wanted more friends like Tolmachyov that she could see and touch, nonetheless, did not enjoy the thought of someday separating. Demeris enlightens her that she will have fresh friends, when a ship comes this way. That could be a little time; meanwhile, she can make a good home for her new friends. Teplov agreed with this and began using her laser to clean the vegetation so their river, resting place would have more area to play. There then came a day that Demeris, Chemeris, and Siostra brought selected special food they discovered, hidden in a small cave. Its owners died from the plague before eating it. Siostra disinfected it and brought it to Tolmachyov and Teplov for a special celebration. Not being able to determine the reason for the celebration, Siostra reminded her that it was her one-year reunion with Teplov. They survived an unusually harsh winter with their bear meat and hides and large campfire. The campfire released, smoke, which escaped through the opening above them that was on the top of their hillside. Little did they discern that one cold April morning, as the girls were still chilled from the winter, thereby keeping their fire high until Emsky once again turned green, that smoke would change the history of Álmosd and the foundation of the seventh stone.

The universe found itself in an evolving state that was beginning to stabilize. New worlds developed, although at different stages, which most slightly varied within 10,000 years from each other. The great evil Empires continued their civil wars, giving the local deities enough space to bring order to their galaxies. New kingdoms still appeared, yet now they were more from diplomacy, and unifications, exploring the benefits of working in a union to provide a better lifestyle. Most travelers stayed inside their galaxies, which naturally provided many opportunities for exploration. There is always that few that wonder about what is beyond their galaxy, and even though it took most ships up to one year to reach these far-distant mysterious worlds, they had to try. Many did not even grasp if they could survive the trip, and unfortunately, many did not. There was a Kingdom on a planet called Yelagin in the galaxy Zhutov, which had an exceptional space exploration program. They had mastered travel to the neighboring galaxies, and now one of their great explorers whose name was Grechko who desired to travel two galaxies beyond Zhutov. He estimated the trip would take two years to go a galaxy named Chuprin, a name they had received from traders in the galaxy who found it in various ancient scrolls. They would use a new space sleep hibernation during the long empty space travel. The Yelagin had no other information on Chuprin and thereby agreed for the exploration, for discovery purposes only. Grechko assembled a crew of two additional men and prepared for the journey. Awkwardly, a daughter of a powerful nobleman complained to the Kingdom's royal administrators that a female should be on this ship as well, so the women could also receive honor in this exploration. The administrators, not wanting their disapproval to reach the Queen's ears, reluctantly approved. This woman was no ordinary woman. Her name was Datsishin. She was extremely well educated in space travel, holding many advanced degrees. Datsishin was also exceptionally dominating and hungry for authority. No one enjoyed working with her. Extremely few men ever dated her. Grechko was radically angry when he discovered she would be on his team, as he had no position, she desired. Nevertheless, he released one of his team members and gave the assignment to Datsishin. She refused the assignment, demanding to be the mission commander. Grechko refused to give up command of his mission and therefore, official offered her his original offer, also citing that if she did not accept this position, she was resigning herself from the mission. He called his friend back, and they continued their training, ignoring Datsishin. Datsishin took her grievance to the Queen, who gave it to the King, as space exploration was his delight. The King upheld Grechko as the commander and further declared that if Grechko did not certify her as qualified by the launch date, she would not be on the mission. Datsishin immediately struggled hard to be qualified in time for the launch. Grechko originally was not going to qualify her; however, the Queen added that they would then delay the launch until she was qualified. Grechko knew that if he did not launch in time he would miss many parts of the route, which would extend the trip to Chuprin up to four years, which he would have no route back for at least one-hundred years. Grechko's hunger to explore Chuprin forced him to qualify Datsishin, which if she did as her team members told her to do, and then they could make it. He loaded extra food, and shortened Datsishin's hibernation, so she could master her new position. She reluctantly agreed, and they launched as scheduled. Her co-pilot ran into several serious meteor showers and needed her help make the adjustments in their course. Grechko helped him as they fired the course corrections to Datsishin, who had to input them. She made an honest error on one input in which her partner became exceedingly angry calling names and cursing her. Grechko ordered the man to apologize and fix the problem. At this point, Datsishin personally vowed revenge on her co-pilot and began working extra hard to obey Grechko, yet any request from her co-pilot given without Grechko she sabotaged. If he said to punch in 112, she would punch in 223, swearing he told her 223, always of course pausing the voice recorders so no evidence would abound. This forced Grechko not to have them working together but each one to one with him. He was already fearful for this mission and wondered that if they continued, would they survive.

They were barely staying on course. If he returned now, they would live; however, he would live in shame. He would be dishonored for qualifying Datsishin when she was not qualified, plus the King would be furious with the great financial loss to the crown's reserves, as many objected to using these funds as many social programs went unfunded. Grechko could not do this and could merely hope that in time, the two would become friends. He believed that by being the first to see a new galaxy, two galaxies beyond Zhutov would create the bond. He sat Datsishin down and with a pleading and explaining demeanor stressed how that if she did not learn this high pivotal position, she was filling, they may not make it back to Yelagin. He added a twist explaining that her position was a combination of many technical positions. With Datsishin's head swelled, he believed they had a chance. Their plan was to awake when they were passing the first galaxy and collect new pictures if possible, as they would be going around it and be able to capture images from the other side. They also needed to maximize the thrust from that galaxy's spiral and get a good fling toward Chuprin. By then, Datsishin would have mastered her position. Once they were spinning of a spiral in Zhutov and on course for the middle galaxy, Datsishin began her studies as Grechko slept in the middle with his first mate to his right. The left side of him, he reserved for Datsishin. Which team member slept beside which did not really matter that much, as they were sleeping in closed tubes. He simply wanted to reduce any chance of friction by keeping them apart. She handled the last few days before the men went to sleep by completely ignoring her mate and serving Grechko as if he were a King. Grechko let this slide, because at least he was maintaining a form of control. Datsishin, having a great mind, mastered not solely her position, but also her mate's position and the commander's position. She was determined to gain control of this mission, even if she were the last one standing, then so be it. She truthfully did not have anything against Grechko, because he appeared to be able to compromise, and she felt he favored her. In fact, he did not favor her; he simply believed it was the single way to survive, as his mate quickly understood what he was doing. Before putting herself in hibernation, she discovered they were off course. She made various adjustments, hoping to keep them in the zone of comfort. She recorded her adjustments, as the computers did anyway and went into hibernation. Datsishin believed they were still on target.

The question now lingered more than before, would they be able to complete this mission, especially with the launch games with the wrong codes had set them off, and as they awoke for their mid-trip adjustments and set up for their fling off a spiral to Chuprin. Grechko rapidly caught that they were off course and almost ready to fling from a weaker spiral. They quickly reversed their ship and burned it to the correct spiral. The danger now was if they had burned too much fuel. It would be six years before this midterm galaxy would fling another spiral toward Zhutov and they did not have enough fuel to position for that spiral, thereby he had no chose, on to Chuprin, they would go and with any luck find a little fuel there. He told Datsishin that if she had not made those adjustments, they would have been lost in space for eternity. He asked his number-one mate, why he had not corrected the confusion in the coding as he had told him that he did. This error was clearly on his shoulders. They had proceeded exactly the way his mate had programmed. They verified their long-range scanners, which would simply produce guesses, as one-year was too long of time to pinpoint any predictions as reliable. Much of their journey was in providence's hands; nevertheless, this was the way of all space travel from Zhutov. The collected much data from the spiral they had hit, by mistake, thus they were already in the uncharted territory. Once again, they went into hibernation. At this time, Grechko stayed awake for an extra month, making sure all was well. He scheduled Datsishin to wake up on the sixth month, verify everything, and make any course corrections. Grechko was extremely impressed with the corrections she made earlier, and knew she had mastered her position. The last wake up would be two months before they enter, and this month would belong to his first mate. Then, one month out Grechko and Datsishin would wake up and take her in, with the first mates help art optional. They flew through space with just a few minor hitches, as the last month before Chuprin was now on Grechko and Datsishin. The first mate elected to hibernate once more, mainly for additional time away from Datsishin. She knew his trigger buttons and kept him angry and agitated. Little they knew that Chuprin had a few surprises that had not shown up on their scanners.

Chuprin was originally two smaller galaxies that blended. This was common throughout the universe, with galaxies having the greatest gravitational pull. The difficulty with Chuprin was that one galaxy rotated horizontally, while the other rotated vertically. Once they settled both centers consolidated, as this center density initially shattered many worlds into large clumps of meteors. The impact of these crashes was the creation of many moons. That is one reason why Emsky has twenty moons. Numerous moon-sized rock bodies fell into the orbits of planets, while others had a weight that propelled them into planets, creating an even greater graveyard of space rocks. Emsky went from thirty-five planets down to twenty because these crashes. The outer two thirds of Emsky still have many moons sized space balls that stay somewhat within their orbit, considering Emsky is at the end of an outer spiral and has no other space systems with gravity to compete. Emsky often finds itself collecting a few strays from outside Chuprin, yet when considering the vast space, this is seldom. Most of the objects drop out of Chuprin and slowly drift through space, and at times may remain stationary such as an iceberg in space. A long-range scanner usually detects, objects by the change in their relationships around them. Therefore, if their objects are not moving and no relationship is changing from around them, then the scanners are blind. Grechko was in store for his first surprise offered by this galaxy so far from his home in Zhutov.

Datsishin braced herself in the vacant mate's seat as Grechko sat in his command seat. Datsishin began complaining that her numbers were not consistent and requested they slow down for a while. The trouble with slowing down was that it took energy and then took energy to resume their course once more, after making so many adjustments for space drop. He explained that he was afraid they would miss Chuprin and instead drift past it, missing the spiral spins. Datsishin afterwards asked him to help her and verify her calculations. One minute a scanner would tell her she had 87,000 light-years, then the exact scanner would change that to 64,000. The numbers were constantly random. Grechko then asked her to find him the shorted safest distance, which turned out to be 57,500 light-years. This gave them twenty-one more days to determine what was happening. As they become closer, their short-range scanners began to report all the floating moons. Grechko now realized he had no choice but to go slower. He elected to change their course to an upward one moving into Chuprin, thereby using the after-drop to align for the spiral shot. He confessed to Datsishin that they could not make it home. Datsishin asked him if we could wake his mate and then keep two on, with one off resting, and visual steer our ship in at this great speed, using no more than their short-range scanners. This would still give them a chance to make it back home. Grechko agreed and woke his mate explaining the situation and told him he would relieve him in about six hours. The first thing that he did was foolishly demanding his pilot seat, not realizing that Datsishin had mistakenly left the commander's chair open for him. Without any form of response, she gave him his chair and took the commander's chair. Grechko was disturbed over this incident, thinking that Datsishin had shown the spirit of teamwork, and his mate was causing dissension. He, therefore, gave the temporary command to his seat and Datsishin who was sitting in it. Next, he went to get a little rest. His mate told Datsishin that if she issued one command to him, he would beat her and make her life a misery. They worked the rotating shifts for the next several days, and with the exhaustion, tempers were beginning to flare. The first two hours of the shift flowed by with a few minor adjustments. It was the next hour that changed their lives for eternity.

Datsishin detected a large object dead ahead with additional objects on her side. She noticed the coast was clear on the mate's side. She told him this turn was on him. The mate feared that he might also have objects on his side and did not want to chance a hit, so he programmed his shift over the object, which was, as Datsishin had predicted in line for disaster. She believed that he was swinging right, as all the data was available for him to verify. Then in the last few minutes the ship swerved up and over with his side hitting a thirty-foot wide meteor. The meteor held its position as their ship spun around it, tearing of the panel and his seat. Into space, he went. Grechko came out and ordered her to get back on course as he activated their backup panels, and they resealed their ship. Their speed was enough to keep them in the ship. Grechko passed Datsishin an oxygen tank as they waited for the oxygen generator to refill this cabin with air. Datsishin complained the generator was taking too long and volunteered to investigate the reason. Grechko began reconnecting any wires that this been split when the panel pulled the mate's seat into space. There were not that many wires as most connections were wireless. He could fix the wiring with ease, as it was one of the skills; they drilled them in during his academy days. Datsishin discovered that one of the under panels in the oxygen generator was pulled up slightly; therefore, she pressed it back on as her sensors revealed it was working once more. Within minutes, the oxygen generator restored the oxygen levels. They were now 5,000 light-years from Chuprin, which allowed Grechko to reduce the speed and use a little power in their drop that he believed that would hit the end of the outer spiral. Datsishin asked Grechko why they did not save his mate. She was actually upset as in all her loathing she did not enjoy death. The answer she received surprised her.

Grechko told her that he barely knew one thing after the impact, and that was if they stopped they were dead. The stop would have allowed the surrounding meteors to pull the ship apart with their reaction to their gravity and the reduced space displacement. He confided in her that he heard her explain why they had to go left, and felt the ship shift up. Grechko told her that he instantaneously knew they were in trouble, as all pilots learned in their first year never to go over a meteor. Grechko adds he killed himself, and that he was determined that he would not kill them. Instead, he took Zhutov away from them, as the emergency panels would never last more than four months in space. Datsishin after that walked over to him and hit him. She told him the game had changed now, that she would allow him to get them to a safe world, and afterwards, they would part. He could have the ship; she did not care, knowing it would not last that long anyway. Grechko was surprised, as he had worked so hard to build a relationship with her, especially now that they could spend the remainder of their days together. He asked her why she hated him. Datsishin tells him that she does not hate him; she hates the world he represents. Grechko reminds her the world she speaks about they will never again see. Datsishin then asked Grechko why his mate hated her so much. Grechko confesses to her that he warned him repeatedly that his type of behavior had no place on this ship. That is why he put her in command. Consequently, he tells Datsishin that was his big mistake knowing a woman could never command a man, and the ship damaged under her command. Datsishin becomes furious and begins throwing her items at him. Next, she attacks him hitting and screaming. Grechko offers no defense and just stands there laughing. After a few minutes, Datsishin realizes that he tricked her. He was merely playing with her. She stops hitting him and asks him if she is going to have to put up with his childish behavior from this day forward. Grechko tells her, that we do this to keep the tension reduced among them. He confesses that if they do not work together, they will die. She lightly slaps him and agrees, telling him that this is what scares her. She did not realize that she had a few real scares ahead of her.

Datsishin depends on her short-range scanners explicitly now. The long-range scanners suffered damage during the crash; therefore, they unhooked them to save energy for the power-hungry short-range scanners. They work together constantly now, merely taking a four-hour rest in their seat in case of an emergency. They are using more energy than they originally projected with all the course corrections. Less than one-half a light-year to go and Grechko does not realize if they make it. They are dropping in at a forty-five angle and there is one spiral, which, if it spins out far enough that they could hit it provided the meteors thin. His side scrapes by a meteor putting certain dents in the open living area behind them. At first, Grechko was going to release it to save energy; however, Datsishin told him they needed the weight from the drop. They are now one day from Chuprin's outer spiral. Datsishin tells Grechko, they must currently release their living quarters and burn their energy in a straight-line shot now. Her scanners are telling her they have a straight shot without meteors. Once they are in the spirals gravitational pull, they can drop in the direction where the spiral is pulling. Grechko knows that gravitational draws will yank harder at objects above them, by collapsing much of the space between them. This vacuum will guide them into the spiral. He goes into their living space and grabs their emergency backpack and closes the door behind him, punching the codes into a special control box along their wall, and away goes their damaged living space module. The release allows their capsule to spring forward. Datsishin had positioned and programmed the ship to jump straight forward. She shows Grechko the course they will take to hit the spiral. The scanners are reporting no meteors along this path. Datsishin recommends that they fire their thrusters toward the spiral before any meteors cross their path. If they drop in, the increase in time would most likely put at least one meteor in their path, and they would have to fire their burners to swing around it. The burning consumes the energy. Once the burners are operational, it takes little fuel to keep the engines running. Grechko agrees, and Datsishin guides them to the spiral's end. When she hits it, she discovers there is not gravitational pull, so they change their course shooting them into the spiral until they get various gravitational readings.

Their fuel is critically low presently and cuts off, as it will maintain enough to land on a planet and there is no way to bypass that safety reserve. They are gliding now, still with no gravitational pull. A day goes by, no gravity. They realize the greater danger faces them now, and that is if they find no gravity, while dropping through the spiral, they could drop out of its bottom and drift forever in space. To give them a longer chance, Datsishin has their capsule titled to drop angled inwards. She calculates two more days. They soon find themselves, less than one day when something strange happens. A half-moon-sized moon comes crashing into the ship from behind them. The crash, cushioned by the moon's gravity, gave them a softly landing on this moon. Datsishin claims that this moon is in a somewhat chaotic orbit. If this is so then they can ride with the moon as it spins inside Chuprin's gravitational pull. Grechko is now rewiring certain electrical components, claiming that he can send an adequate force through the electrical relays in the engine to have sufficient electrical power to launch this ship. Once they can determine it is on an orbit, they can take a breather and pick which planet to launch high enough for that planet to grab them. Grechko looks at Datsishin and tells her, that once again, she will need to be perfect if they will live. He then tells her that he will pull their dinner out of the food processor, so they can enjoy it tonight. Grechko asks her if there is anything special that she wants. She looks at him and comments that she just wants to say one thing.

Grechko braces himself for a first-class insult. She tells him, "I love you." She then relaxes and smiles in her seat, sighing, "I am so glad I got that off my chest." Grechko tells her that naturally he shares the same feelings. Actually, he does not want to be alone, which is not a bad thing. He further quizzes her about the reason she loves him. She tells him that it is because he believes in her and that makes her want to work even harder. Grechko reassures her that values her skills as if they were from a computer. As they are fasting in their newly discovered love, they hear a large crash and can experience their ship bounce up and then back down to its previous position. They each run to a window to see what is happening. Their capsule is so small that any damage would easily be visible. They gaze out and see a large spaceship crashed into this moon. Datsishin looks at other landmarks within a five-mile radius and then tells Grechko that this moon has received many hits quite often, and with its strange orbit, is collecting this space junk, and on its outer orbit, and not enough gravity to hold it on, is releasing them. She recommends that they get off this moon as soon as possible, hopefully within the hour. Datsishin tells her new love that if they are still on this moon when it makes its outer orbit, they will drop off into space hopelessly lost forever. Grechko immediately begins wiring the control box for an electrical launch.

Datsishin is scanning for a planet and finds one. It is the fourth planet in a small one-sun solar system that is in their drop. The atmosphere is solid enough to support their landing. She punches everything in then helps Grechko. They finish in barely three minutes and Datsishin pushes the electric launch button. Up to they go as Emsky's twenty planets and moons, grab them. There is no time to relax now, because, so many dead ships are floating everywhere. Lucky for them, their ships are flamboyant and when they pass by will simply move to the side. This is like having a few toy boats on the water in a tub. If you drop something between them, the force of the object hitting the water will move the two boats. Datsishin did her projections on the target once more than this tiny capsule began to orbit Emsky4. They submerged their ship enough in the atmosphere to miss the lifeless ships, who were falling apart into small pieces that burned on reentry. They sat and looked up at the moon, they just departed from was collecting these dead ships. Datsishin asks Grechko if he can guess what is going on here, then she gives him his first kiss on the cheek. First, he thanks her for the kiss and then tells her that it cannot be war, because the ships have no damage. Grechko then deducts that these ships have not been here that long and yet they have no life aboard them. The main common denominator is everyone on these ships is dead and these advanced ships are far greater than anything on Yelagin is. If all are dead, they were burying their dead in space away from the planet. The lone thing that makes sense is a plague. Datsishin asks Grechko if he thinks they will be okay. He tells her that as the haul burns during

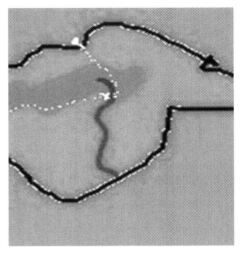

reentry will burn any space dust of material. Datsishin confesses the advanced courses she studied during his hibernation had no instructions on a haul reentry. Everything had the living quarters attached. Grechko tells her he learned a haul reentry as part of his hobby as he hoped someday to drift around Yelagin and take a haul entry to get back home. Datsishin tells him this is his chance, as they should orbit at least three times before they drop into the burn zone. As they circled this globe, they studied the various large continents. After careful thinking, they agreed to settle on the top island. They would have to land in the sea and work their way across a northern forestland, and then go into the mountains, after which they would travel the river and live either in the mountains or at the rivers crossing into the forests. They would need a river that goes into the sea in case of serous hostile forces. They would depend on their emergency backpacks and their pistols, as they had three boxes of bullets, because they would also bring his old mate's emergency bag, pistol, and bullets. Grechko asked Datsishin what forecasts she had for the weather. She tells him they will have to travel quickly to get to the top of the mountain and then the trip down to the river could be in the winter and extremely cold as it is on the top of this world. Grechko comments about how they will be sharing the mate's sleeping bag over theirs. Datsishin lightly slaps her and says, "Excuse me commander, but I do believe we will be sharing one sleeping bag, therefore we can have three of them wrapped around us." Grechko ask whether they will be melting any snow. She tells him that she hopes he is the one doing the melting. Either way, they had to commit now.

They agreed that even though the lower lands were warmer, if there was a plague on this land, and then the danger of catching this disease would be greater. The cold north was the lone viable option until they learned more about the current situation. On the third day, they packed their maps their computer made for them for their journey through the mountains to the river. Grechko had one more concern that he did not want to share with Datsishin. He worried when the large ship crashed into the moon, they were on, and the bounce may have damaged the bottom shield. What worried him was that after the bounce, the ship sat unevenly, which could mean that an object had pierced it. There was no way of checking, so just like everything else, if it burns there will be nothing they can do about it, as the burn will fry them instantly. He had tested the emergency landing system, and everything tested okay; the fuel would release itself. Just as a backup, he had one or two jerry rig tricks that could fire up the system if the program failed. He was too close now for something foolish to trip them. He pushed the button, the emergency system activated and accepted Datsishin's headings, and into the fire, they went. Neither had ever experienced this method of reentry, so their fear was running wild. The reentry was bumpy, hot, noisy, as it seemed like the ship was falling apart. The capsule went into a spin such as a rolling ball. This scared Datsishin as she began to cry. Grechko reached his hand over to hold hers, as sweet rolled off both hands. This lasted for two long minutes, and then the capsule stopped rolling and stabilized as they were simply dropping now. The sea was just one mile from them and approaching fast. Grechko waits, patiently and then pushed the button for the emergency parachute, which springs open fighting hard to slow them. They slow down to a safe speed about ten feet from the sea and slowly splashdown. Datsishin smiles at Grechko and comments the parachute was a great idea. He tells her that it is part of a haul landing.

She thanks Grechko telling him that if not for him; they would both be dead. He quickly corrects Datsishin telling her the calculations and sound judgment that she produced saved them. He then confesses that he is rusty on the code calculates and no faster than a turtle in computing them. Datsishin afterwards asks him that if she had not learned the extra jobs, they never would have made it. Grechko smiles and tells her they would be kissing somewhere between galaxies and trying to decide what to have the food processor make next for them. Datsishin recommends they have the food processor, whip up one week of food for her to carry along with her emergency backpack. Grechko asks her why he cannot carry it. She smiles and reminds him that he will have two backpacks and several other foolish men's things he will create an excuse. He collects his map, compass, and star navigation equipment squeezing it in one of the side pockets to his backpack. Datsishin asks him why they need the star navigation equipment, as they do not even understand the stars. Grechko tells her that he will study the stars and know them, so if they ever get lost or go to sea, he can bring them home. Datsishin winks at him and then returns to the food processor and preparing their meals. Grechko collects a few small tools, such as a hammer, ax, military shovel, and knives. Datsishin asks him to get a shovel and knives for her as well.

Grechko does and then sets the controls for the raft. He flips open hatch, presses the raft buttons, and begins to expand in the sea. He slowly gets out and then has Datsishin hand him the bags. Once everything is loaded, Datsishin asks him if he knows of any way to save the food processor. Grechko explains that the food processor falls under the first contact laws, and therefore, is a solid fixture in the haul. They sit on the raft and go through their lists, making sure they have everything to include the first mate's items. They check and check again as barely a single task remains. Grechko pushes the outside seal button. The door seals itself, and the hull begins to suck in water. Within a few minutes, it is sitting on the bottom of the sea. Grechko comments that in one minute, they went from an advanced civilization to prehistoric men. They slowly row, the raft to the shore. Consequently, Datsishin tells Grechko that their journey is now just beginning.

She tells him that her heart wants solely to allow love to guide them as they make their new family among all the people in this far-off world. She laughs and then comments that when isolation takes them, they do it first-class, such as two galaxies away. As they approach the shore, Grechko alerts her that he has detected movement and light readings on his scanner. Datsishin looks at him and asks where he got that scanner. He tells her it was on the ship. She lightly slaps him and then adds that it is getting dark, so they should stay in the raft and start tomorrow. They have spent every night together for the past two years, so on the water, or under a tree, will make no difference. Datsishin asks Grechko if he dedicates himself to her. He explains to her that it is too early in this world to make a commitment. If they are the lone two remaining, a commitment has no bearing. If there were great civilizations, then they would have to abide by their laws. He tells her that he will be a husband for her, yet will not agree to absolution until they comprehend where they are and what the rules are. She asks him that if she were to bear him a child, would he be a father for their child. Grechko looks at her with a solid, serious appearance and tells her, absolutely. Datsishin then confides in him that she wants to bear his child. Grechko agrees that they will have children, yet once again reminds her they have to settle first. They snuggle together in the raft while Grechko is playing with his star navigation equipment. She asks him if he needs to be doing this tonight. Grechko explains that tonight is the most important night, as he must establish the base for all his projections. Each new strange noise finds her squeezing closer to Grechko. She asks him if she should move to the other side of the boat. He looks at her strangely and tells her that he would appreciate it if she stayed next to him. He asks her if they are a couple. She wraps both arms around him, once more declaring her love for him. She then tells him one of the many things that made her love him was the way he returned kindness when she was giving just insults and criticisms. He explains that when the King denied her petition, he was actually saddened because he wanted her to get the command, so he could step down and get out. The mission seemed so easy in the planning stage, yet as he kept putting the pieces together, it was not pulling into place. He smiles at her and asks her how he could hate her for losing. Datsishin wanted the same miracle that Emsky wanted.

They both were searching for a child to help foster the future generations. This was a time for rebirth, for the old events to pass away and new occurrences replace them. Datsishin's life did not follow the traditional Yelagin's style. While studying in her first university, she began to socialize with members of a lower class. They had great fun privately, nevertheless, always followed the appropriate separatism during the day. She never enjoyed having female girlfriends, nor did she like the boys. Like the boys or not did not matter, because they liked her and swarmed around her. She fought hard to ignore them; nevertheless, situations or events would arrive that she would need a boy. She always had the strongest, most sought-after boys whom, she controlled with ease. They did what she said, or she would leave them on the spot. The other girls hated her because this and vowed for revenge. Many of the boys despised her as well. They discovered that she would vanish toward the markets and not return until late in the evening and on Fridays, until Sunday night. Her classmates agreed something was mysterious and began spying on her. They soon discovered that she was socializing with the lower-class people, and immediately reported this to their school. The school talked to the people she was socializing with, and with this evidence expelled her forever. This instance gave her father no anger, as he was born into the lower class. He worked his way up through their wicked tangles. He simply placed her in a university that catered for all classes. Her, she could mingle with ease, before she emphatically wore her high-class clothes on the mandatory days. She explains to Grechko that the lower-class boys and girls focused more on their studies and not on their rank. She could study all-night with several boys and not once have to slap someone or fight to get their hands out of her pants. When she was with the high-class boys, she always tried to wear fluffy ballroom gowns, so they could not get their hands up her gown. That was all they wanted. She made a few high-class girlfriends who were in touch with reality, as their fathers also advanced through the classes. The four of them took turns visiting each other's homes. They never went there formally, but instead in clothes they could play. This kept all the mothers and fathers happy. Sadly, their garden had a snake in it, and that snake was preparing to strike.

The parents of the four girls became great friends also, and she enjoyed watching her father play sporting games with them. They never cared who was winning or was the best; they solely worried about getting too dirty and their wives, our mothers, yelling at them. They believed that was so funny. The four girls became extremely close, and spent most of their free time with each other. Every Friday and Saturday night, they slept together, rotating between their homes. Datsishin thought this was great, in that when she would go to her bedroom alone, she could sense all the fun times they shared. These were the greatest five years in her life, as they worked their way toward their PhD. Just one-year remaining and then disaster hit. Two of the girls became serious lovers, while the third elected to join with them. Her three closest friends tried to recruit her; however, she just could not go through with it. She had to break away from them, which also meant breaking apart from her family. This was the year she molded her cold defiant personality, never again talking with those former friends. She entered the space program and began serving on small crews to their moons, and a couple of freighters in their solar trading. When she discovered the first trip to a galaxy beyond one of our neighboring galaxies, she knew this was for her. Yelagin had nothing remaining for her. She confessed that she knew she would not be commander, but also knew that the crown would not completely deny her a seat on this mission. They would meet in the middle. She never expected that the first mate would be so bitter and self-destructive. When she saw the first mate die, that was when she decided not to let arguments destroy herself as he had let it destroy him. She wonders now what destruction will take next.

Grechko explains that he was lower class and stayed a lower class until working his way up in the space command. He was married and had one child. His love for the space command choked and destroyed his marriage. Grechko claims that this love engulfed his entire essence. He volunteered for every mission and was merely on Yelagin for less than one month yearly. He was competitive and earned many promotions and the positions that came with them. His superiors had a dream of creating the mission of missions that would give Yelagin fame and honor throughout all Zhutov. They conceived the mission to travel twice as far as all previous missions. He believed that their next attempt on whichever galaxy is possible they will need to jump one galaxy and study the surrounding ones to project a flexible plan. Datsishin asked him about his wife. Grechko then confessed that they had divorced. Nothing messy, she sent him the documents; he signed them and returned them to her. They then began to discuss their beliefs and opinions. The conversation began with both agreeing this was too big of a jump for their technology. They need to perfect intergalactic travel with new space-wave displacement ships. Other galaxies that traded with Zhutov always boasted their new technologies and spoke of what they knew of others. Legends talk about the days when many Empires could flash through the heavens at ease. They knew that they were so lucky to have barely made it to this what appears to be an empty world. When they orbited Emsky three times before landing, they saw nothing. Grechko is suspicious that they saw nothing, no buildings, no ruins, and no roads. With the number of large ships, which appear to have technologies for beyond Zhutov, one should expect to find a great civilization somewhere. He had so many questions, yet scarcely the air to answer them. Grechko was glad when a fish splashed in the water behind them. At least, they were no completely alone. Datsishin complained to him that they should take advantage of the soft raft bottom as it floated on the water, which would be much better for what she had in mind then on the hard ground. She wrapped her arms around him; they began to start kissing, and her hope that she had begun the great goal, she had set. She wanted to have a child and the dream of living a mechanical free or industrial free life. Strangely, just like little Teplov, she loved the outdoors. This is a good thing; in the outdoors is the lone world currently available for them.

Grechko started making modifications to this original itinerary explaining to Datsishin that he wanted to be on the mountaintop within four months; just in case she was pregnant, they could proceed along the ridges making it much easier for her. Grechko had a few surprises for Datsishin as well. The ship had special secret jewelry, which was on board in case they needed to trade with foreign worlds to be in line with their protocols. He had packed this sealed bag in his backpack, and now pulled out a ring and head necklace, packed with gems. He handed it to her and apologized for being late. When she saw them, tears of happiness flooded her eyes. He explains the first time he saw her; he knew she would fall in love with him. She taps him on the side of his face. Grechko comments that she is no longer slapping. Datsishin explains that while he does what she wants, things will be fine. Grechko smiles, and then replies, "Why not." They fall to sleep on the raft and soon find themselves under the peaceful light of so many moons. Emsky has many more moons than Yelagin, which has totally three moons. The one topic they continuously avoid is the dim outlook for Yelagin's future. Over one-half of its people have already resettled on other worlds. Yelagin has a vanishing water supply, which now is completely dependent on human technology to create the rain and keep the vegetation alive. Their projections are that in less than one-thousand years, they will need to abandon the planet. Scientists throughout Zhutov are researching this condition, and Grechko is always optimistic that a solution will come in plenty of time. Datsishin never worried about it, because she did not like anyone on Yelagin and was already in the space program with one foot on another planet, which had positions for her technical field available. She could push her consent button and proceed to the space transporter for her new home. Instead, she received a special island on the empty Emsky. In the morning, they walked on the shore, Yelagin's first steps on a far-off galaxy and were now official the greatest explorers from Yelagin. The slight problem was that no one on Yelagin understood this. Grechko figured things could be worse. He could be stuck her with his mate, which of course would have canceled most of last night's activities. Grechko had a beautiful woman claiming she loved him and behaving accordingly. He hoped the rent would not be too high in this luxury resort. They would soon receive their first bill.

Working well as a team, although Datsishin was understandably still excited over her new gems, they could unload the raft. Grechko pushed the converter button, which changed it into a tent, and then the compressor button that packed it smaller than a book. It had a special place that hooked onto the side of his survival backpack. They began their hike into the forest in front of them. After walking about one hour, they came on an open meadow. Grechko recommended the future mother of their family, take a break while he explored the meadow. Datsishin argued that they had heard nothing, and that she did not want to stand-alone while he was out in the meadow. Grechko understood what she meant and told her to stick behind him. They glided through the meadow, because Grechko did not like being in the open. All was fearfully quiet. They had many clanks and other pestering noises on their ship, yet this world was so quiet. Then they heard a noise in the brush. He went to pull out his pistol, clearly to discover he had not loaded it. Immediately, he dropped his bag, and opened the side pocket that held the bullets. Datsishin was doing the same with her bag. He began loading his pistol when a large lion came leaping out of the brush landing on Datsishin, as the thump forced her to release her pistol. Grechko stood up and began firing, the first shot in the lion's back, second shot in the arm that held Datsishin down, the third shot in the back of his head. This was when the lion became angry and jumped leaping on Grechko, who still had two shots. He shot the first one in the lion's neck and then the second one in his mouth. The lion flinched some; however, took his other hand, and belted Grechko with a solid hit. Down he went. Datsishin did not discern if their happy forever life had ended before their first meal together.

Grechko lay still on the ground. Meanwhile, Datsishin loaded her pistol and began firing at the base of the lion's neck, hoping to damage his spinal cord and cripple him. She fired the first seven of the eight shots with direct hits, yet the lion simply rolled over on the ground beside Grechko with an angry stare in his eyes. Her pistol jammed. She was standing next to the first mates bag, which Grechko had flung when he went to open his bag. She reached into the holster, pouch and pulled out the weapon, releasing the magazine to load it. To her utter shock, it was completely loaded. She reinserted the magazine and fired all twenty bullets into the lion's head, as he dropped dead on the last shot. Grechko began scurrying away from the lion, watching it carefully to make sure it was deceased. By this time, Datsishin had the first aid kit open to begin, treating Grechko's deep cuts in this arm. She disinfected it and then asked him if he was going to make sure the pistols were loaded the next time they began walking. He assured her that he would, as he was actually reloading his as they talked. Datsishin next told him that this was to remind him, in case he ever forgets. She took her needed with the stitch thread and began sewing close the cut. Even though the pain was terrifying, he did not scream, fearing that other predators would be in the area. Datsishin's garment had protected her from a deep cut, and as she finished sewing, she gave him a kiss telling him he was a good boy and that he should be happy the lion did not hit him down there, because then she would have been really mad. She wraps his wound as he lies on the ground laughing. Afterwards, he stands up, takes out his knife, turns on the auto sharpener, and then skins the lion. Datsishin asks him is he is overreacting. He tells her they will need this as a coat, and tonight he will make her a pleasant coat. She tells him to make his coat first because she snuck one in her backpack.

They both laughed at this one, as each had packed their emergency bags with just about everything except the food generator. Now, with their loaded pistols in their holsters attached to their sides and a knife in hand, they began their walk again, still before lunch and having already survived their first attack. They learned that Emsky had predators, and that they would kill. He hoped to avoid the lions if possible; after all consuming, forty bullets to kill one would empty their nine boxes quickly. They also agreed to avoid any large meadows and to stay among the trees. Grechko uses his compass, because under the trees, the stars are too hard to monitor. That night, they ate their evening meal, and Datsishin has them do their nightly ritual. Grechko begs for much mercy, because of his injured arm. She verifies the arm did not hurt for his compass; therefore, he will perform. Grechko explains that working in a palace is not performing. She gives him her new light snap on the side of his face with one of her fingers. Just as she does this a voice from in the trees asks her, "Do not you think a comment as romantic as that deserves a kiss?" They are shocked to hear a voice as Grechko calls out, "Who are you and why cannot we see you?" She answers, "Grechko and your beloved lover Datsishin, I am called Tsigler. I am a spirit and you may not see me, for to do so would destroy your eyes. I am here to be your friend." If a human looks at a Benigna, they will not lose their eyes, they just tell the humans this to keep them from trying to spy as Teplov did so much with Tolmachyov. Datsishin asks her if she was watching while they were making love. Tsigler explains, "I am a female angel spirit, so worry not about those things. We rejoice when we witness this as maybe someday; little ones will once again walk on Emsky. Any ways, someone has to keep an eye out for the lions." Datsishin laughs and comments, "I believe you will do better at spotting the lions than Mr. Commander here lying on the ground complaining that I abused him." Tsigler tells Datsishin that she should remind Mr. Commander there are many men who would love abuse in that manner. Grechko tells Tsigler that he is aware of this, but was just keeping her expectations low, so he could surprise her with improvement. Tsigler informs Datsishin that she is so glad those days are far into her distant past. Grechko asks Tsigler if she can explain the current conditions of this planet. Tsigler surprises them by comparing this Emsky as not the same as Yelagin. She explains that a wicked conqueror witnessed his Kingdom and unfortunately, this world as well falling to a great plague. Their previous tenants were the Ethelbert, from a place over thirty times further away than Zhutov. She explained that the Ethelbert lived in; their advanced ships that had luxuries Emsky could not match except for fresh air and the wild outdoors. They cherished Emsky as most of them elected to take the plague with them in the dead of space. She explains how she helped push them past several of those ships who were trying to pull them into their hauls. Grechko confirms that many times he felt that extra wave. Datsishin asks her about her current mission. Tsigler explains she is to help them go to the place they had originally planned. There they will find the single other living human on Emsky, who is a shy fourteen-year-old little girl. Datsishin complains that if she is pregnant, she does not want a little girl around her husband. Tsigler laughs at her revealing that Teplov is at the stage where she hates all boys, so Datsishin may be doing more protecting than detecting. Datsishin then agrees that it must be terrifying to be alone in an empty world, especially with all those you once knew, gone. Tsigler confides that it would be best if everyone lived in harmony. Grechko agrees with that wholeheartedly. Consequently, he tells Datsishin to be happy, because she will have the babysitter to help her when she needs a break. Datsishin smiles and corrects his statement to claim that she will have two babysitters for when she needs a break. Grechko winks at her and claims he will have to keep a close eye on her. Tsigler, innocent and slightly naïve, tells him not to worry, because she will be keeping her eyes on Datsishin. Grechko smiles and with joy claims, he may finally have a teammate for his side. Datsishin tells him to get his rest because since he has so much energy to run his mouth, she will give him that chance to surprise her tomorrow night. Tsigler rejoices in that there will be a surprise tomorrow night. The question being is this the category of surprise angels they are used to seeing.

As they prepare to sleep, Tsigler explains that she will be gone during the days, and will find them at night to see how they are doing. Datsishin thanks her be helping them and enlightening them about Emsky's current situation. Tsigler tells them goodbye and rushes to Tolmachyov, who is sleeping in her cave. Tolmachyov comes out, making sure that Teplov cannot see as Tsigler explains, there is a man and a woman who should arrive here in five months. Tolmachyov asks her if they are a couple and have any children. Tsigler reports that she hopes they are a couple they make such frantic love, and they have no children, although, if they keep behaving at night as they currently are, she will be pregnant, by the time they get here. Tolmachyov asks Tsigler for a few visions, so she can get comfortable around them. She also tells Tsigler that she hopes Siostra can hang on for another five months. Inside, she knows Siostra can hold on; she is the one who is hurting now, because her time to depart may be much earlier than she originally believed it would be. Tolmachyov would share this news with Teplov, and with five months being in the late fall; they will need to have additional meat and firewood, especially if a newborn is sharing the cave with them. They can make extra blankets and other common items to help these newcomers through their first winter. If the gods allow her to stay, it will be her second winter, and she hopes this one is not as bad as the last one was. She wonders what Teplov's reaction will be. She did not want a man; therefore, this man has a woman, so that the burden will be off her shoulders, and she can remain a child for a little longer. When Teplov awakes in this morning, Tolmachyov already has their breakfast prepared. Teplov asks what the special occasion is. Tolmachyov reveals to her that her friend, Tsigler came by, and told her there is a new man and woman who arrived along the northern sea, a few days ago. Teplov becomes angry and warns that this man had better leave her alone. Tolmachyov further tells her that the man and woman are lovers. Teplov begins screaming in anger at this news. Tolmachyov is shocked and does not realize what to do.

She waits for Teplov to calm down and asks her why she is mad. Teplov explains that both her sisters had lovers who would sneak into their room at night. She still has nightmares about how foolish they acted and moaned. This is my cave and if they want to carry on it will be when I am not here, or they can go up on the mountaintop and howl like the wolves. Tolmachyov tells Teplov that her request is reasonable, before she returns to the Benigna she will make sure they understand that condition. She as well disclosed that her friend told her they were fine people in their early thirties. Teplov complains that they will not want to play games. Tolmachyov tells her that if they do not, she will play games with her, and their children they have. Teplov further complains this is a terrible day, because, if they have children, they will try to make her babysit. She tells Tolmachyov to inform the gods, we want people my age, so we can play without kids for a while. Tolmachyov reports to Teplov that these people no longer have a ship, and landed here to save their lives. Tolmachyov feels Teplov should try to help them. Teplov screams that they will try to be her parents and boss her around all the time. They must find another cave, may be the one that is on the other ridge.

Tolmachyov tells her that they will be here in five months. Teplov strikes again, complaining that they will arrive just before winter and will not have enough time to cut their firewood, so she has to put up with them, this first winter, with a crying baby and horny husband. She will have to watch her every move to keep from exciting him. Tolmachyov tells Teplov that not to offend her or hurt her self-ego; however, she does not have to be that careful, because her exciters are not ready yet. Teplov tells her that this is good, because the last thing, she wants to see is his wife crying in misery because he loves her now. Tolmachyov assures her that they will not have to worry about that this winter.

Teplov is still a bit concerned and reveals to Tolmachyov that she is going to keep her knife beside her at night in case this man gets in the wrong bed. Her sisters taught her all the self-defense moves, because her mother made such magnificent daughters. Tolmachyov agrees that at least Teplov is beautiful, and if they appear like her, then these gorgeous girls need protected. Teplov tells her that if they are going to crowd themselves in her cave this winter, they will need much extra meat because men eat a lot, additional blankets and firewood, because, if there is a baby in here to keep her up to all-night, they will need to keep it warm. Tolmachyov tells her these are great ideas, and that she is so proud of the compassion and mercy that Teplov has. They begin their preparations as Teplov calms down and accepts this new situation. Tolmachyov believes that even loneliness could be giving her a better attitude. That night Chemeris explains that she saw the new people. She adds the woman is extraordinarily beautiful and in love with the man. They appear to be a compatible couple and are almost Emsky's neighbors, just being two galaxies away in the Zhutov galaxy, a voyage that took them two years. Chemeris asks her mother if she knew or knows anyone from Zhutov. Tolmachyov tells her that they were not that advanced so everyone stayed away from them. They must have advanced faster than they projected, by jumping two galaxies. Chemeris tells her mother that Tsigler told her, they were depending on the galaxy's orbits and alignments to make it here, and that she had to save them at the end, as they were lifeless in space dodging all the dead Emsky4 ships. Tolmachyov subsequently adds that at least they had the thirst for adventure and desire to survive. Death must be extremely angry at losing its clutches on them. These primitive space explorers will be among the parents to a new world and a part of a new history. Chemeris also confides that Tsigler tells her the woman is the dominant type. Tolmachyov sums this up as growing into a dreadfully interesting drama, because that woman will go up against Teplov, who will not give her one inch, except as a bump on her head.

Meanwhile, the new couple lugged each day through the forest, greeted by two more lions who they could kill with eight and ten bullets this time. They currently concentrated on the brain and eyes. Grechko was tremendously satisfied with the three lion hides he had now. Tsigler leads them through a few orchards and various thick wild vegetable areas, which they appreciated. They popped a few rabbits each week to add a little meat to their diets. One month later, they were out of the forests and ascending the mountains. Tsigler guided them along the stable mountain ridges trying to keep them on the path that had the least steep climbing. Tsigler asked Datsishin if she was pregnant yet, and why they stopped trying. Datsishin told her they were trying during the day now, as Grechko was not comfortable with a spirit watching them, and that she still was not pregnant. Tsigler told her she would ask several of their medical women about this. The next night, she told Datsishin the medical women told her that sometimes too much stress and equally important excessive activity could postpone her eggs from collecting the sperm it needs to ovulate. They felt confident that once her life stabilized, and she rested she would possibly conceive. For now, her priority had to be to remain living and to help keep Grechko alive. Datsishin felt relieved with this news, as she had read similar reports during her studies. She also suspected her dominating personality could be holding Grechko back, as he could be trying too hard, so she would try to make their times together more relaxed and cater to him much more from this day forward.

She furthermore, reasoned that it would be better if she had her child once their lives were stable, and she had a safe place to raise the child. She was accordingly surprised with herself, as she had never before wanted children, and Grechko was the first time she had ever been with another person. A sense of insecurity was beginning to confuse her. Every man who had ever been around her, flirted with her, and she was always able to deny them. Grechko was different, because he respected her and gave her a chance to prove her abilities. He never made a move on her. The hardest thing, she had ever done in her life was to tell Grechko that she loved him. This made her believe she was so cheap and low. Nevertheless, he played her perfectly not humiliating her and still allowed her to believe as if she was in control. The problem was that she was far from being in control.

She was a train on a roller coaster that was now sailing in midair. All she could think about was Grechko, and ways to please him. When she told him to do something, he did it without question. Whenever he asked her to do something, which he consistently did with respect, she invariably did it before even thinking about not doing it. She had changed the way in which she would talk to him, now always being courteous and giving him a chance to say no, which he never did. He kept her dignity and dominating flaws honorable. When she thinks how she had reported him to their King, she begins to cry. She was afraid of an anger monster that she believed lived in her. Grechko always controlled that monster with ease. The largest question that she had now is why she was not pregnant. She had enough Grechko inside her to flood a river, hence how could she not be with child. She did not want to think about the causes, because to do so tore her insides out. All the bitterness she had given to others, she now felt rushing back to her.

Grechko found himself anxious over Datsishin's push to become pregnant. He was naturally in love with her, and she worked so unyielding to present a worthy sensuous woman. Before, she was hard and brittle, having no room to bend. She was so warm now, and yet she still had that power in her eyes that he found so fascinating. He could experience her suffering when she continued to yield to him. Grechko would search for a way to restore her honor. She had a new habit that was popular on Yelagin. When a woman decided to pledge herself to a man, she would wear a scarf she made from the lion's leg hide. She had one that completely concealed her hair and another partial scarf that hid most of her face, except for her eyes. The wonderful necklace that Grechko gave her, she hung from the center top of this scarf. She wore the ring with pride and walked behind Grechko throughout the day. His complaining about her following him was in vain. She demanded a chance to prove her loyalty.

Grechko told her that he trusted her around all these men. She blows him a kiss and tells him she needs to be strong, in case they do appear. Grechko reminds her that Tsigler told them that beside them merely a small girl lived in this world. Datsishin then concludes that she must set a good example for that little girl. Grechko continues along the open, slightly rocky trail that they are walking. Tsigler told them they had to be careful because large herds of beasts travel this path, as it is theirs. When they see the herd, they must simply get off the path and remain calm. The beasts will not bother them. No sudden moves or a stampede could result. She told them never to fire their pistol around a herd. They do not stampede in scarcely one direction and when they go after a person, that person is going to fight for their lives. Grechko had no qualms with this. Something wonderful was happening in his life. He confessed to Datsishin that after his divorce, he completely gave up on women, and all the time before her hibernation, he was so glad he had. When he woke up and she knew everything, she was his dream come true. Now he had someone who understood the technology they were using to travel the cosmos. When she talked, he knew she was right. Then when she could do the codes for their course, he felt as if he was reborn. Grechko told Datsishin that was when his defenses fell. He was actually relieved when the first mate died and saddened when he disobeyed the course heading. If he voiced his descent or leaned the ship gradually, he would have caught it. He had his compass on his chest, and the ship was going where she had it coursed. When he made the sudden shift, Grechko got up and went to pull his first mate from his seat and relieve him, notwithstanding, the panel and the first mate vanished in front of him. The lone thing that he could think of was keeping the ship moving and activating the spare panels. The motion of the ship kept them in the ship. If they had slowed down, the friction would have sucked them out and pulled the still sealing spare panel that needed the motion of space to seal it and lock it. He then thanked Datsishin for obeying that order, as he saw she wanted to save our shipmate, and he assures her that if he knew ten seconds earlier, he could have saved him. Grechko has a strange question that popped in his head.

Grechko asks Datsishin to review how she killed the lion that cut his arm. She explained how she was putting the bullets in until she believed she had to shoot them to save him. The first seven shots went easy and on target. Her pistol jammed on the eighth shot; she saw the mate's bag and a pistol in the outside holster and grabbed it, ejecting the magazine to load it; however, it was already loaded; therefore, she put the magazine back in and fired until all the bullets were shot, which fortunately coincided with when the lion died. Grechko tells her that he never touched that pistol. He saw it in the holster attacked to the side of their mate's backpack and thought nothing of it, as many astronauts keep their pistol out where they can see it and load it on the run if the need to do so. The number-one rule is never to have a loaded pistol in a ship in motion. He asks Datsishin why that man had his pistol magazine fully loaded. She tells Grechko that it could not be. Grechko tells her the mate was going to shoot one of them, most likely Datsishin if he could get her in a questionable position. He was always asking her to show him, which buttons to push. He most likely planned to have her push the buttons, afterwards push the wrong ones, blaming her and subsequently shoot her claiming she was trying to jeopardize the mission. Grechko consequently, tells Datsishin that if the mate knew how well she was in the raft, and under the tree, he would have killed him. She chuckles at his joke and then shifts her piercing brown eyes to the cliff beside them. Datsishin comments that this is a long way down and compliments Tsigler for finding these trails to glide through these mountains. They have done much zigzagging yet by doing accordingly; they avoided several dangerous situations. That night Tsigler arrived to see how they were doing and to give them a little news.

They told her the day went quite well and asked Tsigler, who was hiding behind a large rock, how much longer to the river camp of the little girl. Tsigler tells them they are not that far, maybe two weeks walk; nevertheless, the terrain was harsh and took a lot of zigzagging as they call it. Therefore, she estimates five weeks, which will put this still way ahead of schedule. They shattered the original five-month estimate, notwithstanding now appears as if they will make it in three and one-half months or about six-week early. Grechko asks her about the news she has. Tsigler tells them that her friend Tolmachyov who is caring for Teplov, the lone survivor of the Emsky, and that they agreed Teplov would do no babysitting and they will not have sex in front of her. The way it looks now, she will allow you to share her cave this winter only, and will help you find a new cave. Datsishin becomes extremely angry and comes rushing around the rock to scream at Tsigler and once she sees her, freezes and drops to her knees begging to be forgiven and not blinded. Tsigler tells her everything is okay. Because of a little upcoming trouble in their journey, the Borsod-Abaúj-Zemplén permits her to be visible before them and to be hanging around during the day. Datsishin asks Tsigler if she was hanging around today. Tsigler confesses and complains, asking what is up with that lazy performance by Grechko today? Grechko comes running around the rock screaming, "I will teach you to spy, oh, forgive me great and pure one," as he falls to his knees. He continues, "I did not realize you were an angel. You have blessed us so much, how will we ever be able to repay you?" Tsigler asks him when he is going to teach her how to spy. She is concerned because she believed she was doing a great job. Grechko's face turns red and then he comments, "When we think about it, angels should be around the creating life rituals." Tsigler tells them that when Datsishin conceives she can see it. She tells them it is such a beautiful sight, and so many of her friends ask her each day if Datsishin has conceived. Tsigler tells Datsishin that one of her friends informed her she watched a couple trying for fifteen years, and then it happened. She tells them the sole way they can guarantee to be without a child is to stop trying. Datsishin stands up proudly, as she removes her nightgown and turns around facing Grechko and says, "Honey, your sweetheart has something for you." He complains about twice in one day. She tells him to do it right this time, with enthusiasm, or he may be complaining about three times in one day.

Tsigler's wings turn bright white for about one minute before she turns off her lights. Grechko and Datsishin do not comment about Tsigler standing in front of them completely nude, acting as if everything was normal. The reason they did not comment is that Tsigler's body is not the same as a human. She looks identical except her breasts have no nipples, and she has no female genitals. Her well-formed body has a coating of shiny grayish tinted skin. She has wonderful fluffy styled black hair that reflects the moons' lights as if that was its purpose. She has an innocent-looking belly button, even though it is hard to define a guilty looking belly button. She has no rings or necklaces; however, does have four large silver bracelets on her right hand. She hovers over the couple while they try to procreate and when they have finished, she sadly tells them they may have better luck next time. Datsishin remembers her original intent to be behind this rock and complains that the little girl will babysit if she wants to be friends and socialize with them. They will procreate wherever they desire. Grechko then complains to her, "Honey, not in front of the kid." Datsishin agrees citing that the little girl might like what she sees and want this. She does not want any competition, until she knows for sure she has Grechko housebroken. Tsigler reassures them, that as the way things stand now, Datsishin has no current competition. She further elaborates that because her two older sisters were promiscuous, many times around her, she is tremendously bitter toward those carnal activities. Datsishin then asks about the staying for just one winter. What made her think they would stay longer? Tsigler tells them not to worry; time will work out the best choice for Emsky and the new world, which will have Grechko as their father. Grechko now asks their private nude angel to show him Zhutov in the clear sky above them. She begins by showing her a few of the planets, as their lights are stronger and will be a reliable reference point. Thereafter, she explains that too many moons are out tonight, but during the first week of the month, Zhutov will be on the centerline, two-thirds of the way from that planet, and one-third back from the other planet. There are always three stars around it. Tsigler then informs Grechko that Emsky is one of the few solar systems in Chuprin that can see Zhutov. Grechko told her just knowing where to find it meant a lot.

Tsigler told him to keep looking forward to tomorrow, as things would be changing soon. Next, she pulled a long knife out of her leg. Datsishin asked her to tell them what she was doing. She tells them that there are about two-hundred snakes in the brush behind them, and that she is going to start killing them. Grechko asks her, "Honey, why do you keep that long sword in your leg?" She asks him if he knows a better place to keep it and afterwards tells them to stay on those rocks across the path and relax, she will be there in about twenty minutes. They sat on the rock as she told them and watched her turn the lights on in her wings so bright that it blinded the snakes, and then she simply swung at will. They were watching parts of snakes, flying everywhere. It was not a fair matchup, when they went to bite her; they fell through her spirit body. She later explained it was her spirit power that held the sword and swung it and the sole reason she stayed visible was, so they could see her. When she finished, she came walking back to the couple she protected. Datsishin revealed to her that she was extremely special and that they loved her so much. Grechko confesses that he is not even shy, loving his mate while she is watching. It helps make the event seem clean and not dirty with an angel watching over them. Tsigler tells them that these events are extremely important for the future of Emsky and recorded in Emsky Chronicles. Grechko therefore adds the children should appreciate how beautiful their mother is. Tsigler looks at Datsishin and agrees that she is beautiful among all women. Grechko played with his papers and compass for a few minutes and then rolled them up and slipped them into a side pocket of his backpack. Datsishin asked him what he was doing. He tells her that he is preparing a map on how to return, just in case they would need to reactivate their dead capsule or if for anything else for their children to understand where they came from along the northern shore. Datsishin did not say anything, because her hopes lie on the having a child first before she planned anything else. She was rather upset, because a few girls in her school claimed they merely was with a boy once and they got pregnant. Why was it taking so long for her?

She decides to concentrate on the hills by day, although, now she has Tsigler to chat with during the hot days and chilly nights.

Grechko is acting uprightly and moral with Tsigler around them. Datsishin thinks he believes she is from a god, which in a way she is, although not directly. They appreciate that she is their lifesaver; therefore, both give her much more respect. She is more relaxed around them as well, most times doing her work as she sees fit appearing and disappeared at will. Datsishin was complaining about the sun being too bright and her fear of accidentally falling off a cliff. Tsigler whipped up a few coal chunks that were laying on the ground, rubbed them thick below her eyes, and coated her eyebrows with it. She asked Grechko what he thought, and he firmly told her that it added to her solid forceful personality and fit her better than a glove. Datsishin looked at one of her small mirrors and agreed. This appeared to have recharged her, as she felt she needed something else now that she felt peaceful inside her spirit. This is the trademark for Datsishin, her black eyelids and eye socket area. Their travel days ensued filled with the warm mountain air and little rain until they reached to mountain peak, and began their journey back down off the mountains. This side of the mountain had consistent rains, and at sometimes storms. Tsigler told them these rains were when formed the waterbed for the river. Now that they have Tsigler and the rain with the day and night, Grechko believes they should travel day and night, with just short naps. They are zigzagging to stay on safe paths; therefore, night travel is not that dangerous. When they find a seldom cave, they will go in dray off and rest for a few days, then begin once more. Even the birds and wild animals kept low in all this rain. The one special tool they now possess is Tsigler's lights, which shine through the windiest storms. Tsigler guides them close to the river, as the terrain is not as chaotic, yet tends to have meaner storms. They concentrate totally on the route and push until they reach the foothills. Having solely dark skies, Grechko map to the north remains forever incomplete.

They soon move out of the heavy rain zone and start walking among the tall brush again with all its dangers that Tsigler neutralizes for them. She tells her party that they are hardly one week away now. Their night travels, offset by the extended cave days could trim one week from their updated projected arrival date. Grechko asks Tsigler to find a pleasant cave in this area because he wants to do a little scouting and mapping. This is too close to their home not to have any detailed information. The girls agree and use these days pull themselves back together. If their emergency kits had not included the thin waterproof garments, they believe the last few weeks would have been impossible. The pounding rain gets old extremely fast, and the torment of freezing clothing invites sickness. They overcame this challenge, and Grechko attests; he never plans to suffer through that another time. If ever they go to the northern coast once again, it will be through the forest or by sea. After spending a few days here, they move forward. Grechko feels they need a cave within one day of the little girls cave. He wants to start setting it up, as a backup, in case they have trouble. Tsigler asks him why he believes there will be trouble. He tells her that Emsky has two headstrong women who are about to clash. Someone will have to budge, and Datsishin solely budges for him. She would not budge again. Tsigler tells him she knows of a cavern less than one hour from Teplov, and rests above a small cliff along a stream. It has plenty of fruit trees and berry patches, plus a few close large meadows for vegetation. It also has one of my favorite flower patches. Datsishin comments that this will be great if they can afford the rent. Tsigler tells them, that if they get lucky, a few lions will pass through, and they can yank them for their fur. Grechko tells her that these sounds fine, and they can get selected firewood stored so he can stay there if he needs to do a little hunting or tracking in this first winter. They found the cave and decided to live there for two weeks setting up the basics. The new couple actually fought two more lions and skinned them. Grechko kept the furs in this cave and placed leaves to cover the firewood while it dried. Datsishin and Tsigler combed the cave for any unwelcome guests and removed as much dust and insect webs as possible. They left the high webs, believing this would help control any flying insects. Grechko made a charming door to the cave from one of the lion furs. He dug a shaft about five feet down that cut into their cave top. They would use this shaft as a chimney; therefore, he stacked stones around the top to help prevent it from closing. Their cave was snuggled up, notwithstanding they decided to visit the little girl.

Teplov's initial hostility calmed down as her spirit of curiosity and excitement took control. Each day, she waited for news from Tsigler. Subsequently, Tsigler informs Teplov that the couple is resting in a cave about one hour from here. The next day, she asked again and Tsigler reports to her the couple would be spending a few weeks in the cave resting and preparing to visit her. Teplov asks Tsigler why they must spend two weeks in a cave so close. Tolmachyov reminds her that her invitation was for scarcely one winter in her cave, which she expressed much hostility toward them, and thus they are protecting themselves. Thereafter, Teplov complains that she does not even realize if she likes them yet. Tsigler asks Teplov, "What if you do not like them, then what?" Teplov tells her that they can worry about that later. Tolmachyov enlightens Teplov that she is a young girl and that these are adults, and she should treat them with respect and then maybe things could work out, and she could have several new friends when she leaves. Teplov agrees if they are not too bossy. All the suspense continues to build on Teplov. Tsigler tells Teplov that the couple is fun, especially when talking. Teplov tells her that since they cannot see her, she has an advantage. It might be different since they can see her. Tsigler tells her that she has been fully visible, with permission, for over one month now. Teplov asks where her clothes are. Tsigler tells her, I appear to them as I appear to you. Teplov scolds her that she is a woman, and should never be nude in front of men. I will be the lone one, which he had not viewed nude, and that could give him ideas. Tsigler informs Teplov that her body has no special sex-related organs and is gendered neutral. Teplov argues that Tsigler's body is more female gender neutral than the male gender neutral. Tolmachyov tells Teplov to relax; Tsigler's appearance does not violate any form of morality.

Tsigler tells Teplov she hears the calling for her, and accordingly departs.

About two hours later, Tsigler comes crawling into the cavern's opening. Teplov asks her why she did not fly into her cavern. Tsigler tells her she has a surprise. Teplov calls for Tolmachyov who causally comes to her side and tells her everything will be okay. Teplov is trembling as a woman with a lion's scarf on her head comes walking in to meet her. Her powerful piercing eyes paralyze Teplov. Teplov keeps her eyes locked on this woman refusing to back down or retreat. Her break comes when the man comes in as she inspects him. Teplov walks forward to the man, having no desire to talk with the woman. She welcomes the man and introduces herself. Datsishin steps between them and introduces them to her. Teplov points to a corner they have decorated and tells her that they can put their things there. Datsishin and Grechko go to their corner as Teplov and Tolmachyov go to their area. Tolmachyov feels the early tension and takes selected fruit to their new guests making sure they have no trouble. Datsishin is taking a nap while Grechko comes over and asks both Tolmachyov and Teplov to show him a few places outside her cave. As they are wading in the river's waters, Grechko tells Teplov to relax, that Datsishin has trouble with new people. Once she likes you, you will never be able to find a better friend. Something happens inside Teplov as Grechko is talking with her. She feels the security of his voice as it matches her fathers, but also the warmth she has never before known. Grechko tells her to kiss him on his cheek and these things will work out overall. Teplov goes to kiss him on his cheek; however, as he rests his strong hands on her shoulders, she loses control and kisses him on his lips. Grechko finds himself caught off guard, yet does not want to offend Teplov, not knowing her customs, do he goes casually with it. With their lips sealed, a huge scream comes from behind them as Datsishin is running at them with a great branch. Tolmachyov tells Teplov to swim under water to where Demeris likes to rest. Datsishin begins hitting

Grechko who takes the club from her yelling at her to calm down immediately. The temperature of the river's water is rising.

Teplov makes it to the sunken tree, where she can come up and not exposed. She could hear a little screaming and see certain hitting. Each time the bad woman hits Grechko she feels worse. She does not understand what is making her depressed, Grechko's suffering, or the fast she just dumped herself on a man. Teplov is trying to figure why she acted accordingly strange. She never kissed a man on the lips previously, nor became so helpless at his touch. Tsigler flaps her wings causing the water to splash in Datsishin's hair. This slows Datsishin enough for Grechko to constrain her while she regained control of herself. Datsishin complains that she saw them kissing. Tolmachyov stands there silent. Grechko tells her they were sealing their agreement the child would have patience and try to understand you. He furthered, clarifies that this woman, pointing at Tolmachyov, was here with them and making sure it was normal. Datsishin tells Grechko that because he has no qualms seducing her in from of Tsigler, why kissing a new woman in front of another new woman be any different. Grechko tells Datsishin that she had better get control of herself, because this young teenage girl is too adolescent to be alone in a big world and that, she is fine enough to share what she has, and therefore, they are going to be polite to her. He spins her around, and kisses her on her lips. Teplov remains hidden. Grechko now tells Datsishin, that he and the new little girl must not be in love because she is not chasing them with a club. Datsishin and Tolmachyov begin laughing. Datsishin sees the foolishness of her overreacting. She asks Grechko how he knows exactly how to care for her. Datsishin then tells him that it was a fear of losing his love that scared her. Grechko tells her that might be understandable around other adults; however, this is with a kid and if the kid wants kisses, she deserves kisses. He tells her that his mother always kissed his friends when they did something good or were sad, and that is a tradition he wants to carry into the next generations.

He looks at Tolmachyov and asks her if she can bring the poor innocent little girl back to her home where they will be waiting to apologize. Datsishin asks what gave him the idea she was going to apologize. Grechko reveals that he will have to apologize then, and of course, help eases the pain with a long kiss this time. Datsishin instantaneously volunteers to do the apologizing. She afterwards kisses him explaining this is to ease her pain. Grechko adds that if this is the case, subsequently she deserves another one. Meanwhile, Tolmachyov finds Teplov hiding near the resting spot favored by Demeris. Teplov remains quiet when she arrives. Tolmachyov asks her if she is hurt. Teplov tells her she is not hurt, but she is so ashamed. Teplov wraps her arms around Tolmachyov and begins crying. Tolmachyov asks her why she is ashamed. Teplov explains that she does not realize why she behaved as her sisters did around men when in that man's arms. Tolmachyov realizes there are certain emotions in this event, so she guides Teplov to the shore where they will sit under a tree and talk. Tolmachyov asks Teplov to describe how she sees the new man. Teplov tells her that when he talks, her heart beats fast, and she feels dizzy. When he put his hands on her shoulders, she wanted him to touch her everywhere. Teplov asks Tolmachyov if this means she is odd. Tolmachyov tells her it means she is in love. Teplov asks what about his woman. Tolmachyov tells Teplov she must be patient and be strong for the next few years and may have to share him with Datsishin. She will need to obtain Datsishin's agreement so the best road to begin would be trying to gain Datsishin's friendship. Tolmachyov further explains that sometimes to get what we want we force ourselves to make many sacrifices. It is time for Teplov to use her brain to get what her heart wants. Teplov agrees and then asks how she can survive there without her. Tolmachyov reminds her that she can still visit her as an invisible voice. Now, before she leaves, as Siostra is on her way to put her in the special pouch just for her and Chemeris, she will get her settled back in the cave with her new family.

When they walk in Teplov stands behind Tolmachyov with her head down as they walk to her sleeping corner. Datsishin asks Tolmachyov if she brings Teplov over to talk with them. When they get in front of the couple, Grechko asks her them to sit down now. Once they seat themselves, Datsishin looks at Teplov and apologizes. She then leans over and gives Teplov a kiss, resting her hands on Teplov's shoulders. Teplov slowly reaches her hands up and calmly grips Datsishin's hands and tells her that she truly wants to be good friends with both. Datsishin gives her a strong hug and clarifies that they also want to save them. She looks at Teplov and tells her she could use a younger sister. Teplov tells her that is great, because she was looking for a new older sister because Tolmachyov is leaving to go back to her home. Datsishin tells her that this is terrible, to have her whole world, abandoning her little sister so quickly. Tolmachyov explains that the creation of her body exists simply for temporary use and beginning to fail. She will return to her body, such as Tsigler. They all appear the same; the lone difference is that she has her arm bracelets on her left hand. They will be watching them and helping them when they can do so. Tolmachyov changes into a body such as Tsigler and flies out the cave and continues out toward the sea. Teplov just sits where she is, and begins to cry. Datsishin guides her over to the wonderful furs that Teplov had prepared for them and lies Teplov down between her and Grechko. Teplov is too sad to notice and simply continues crying. Datsishin tells her to keep crying until the hurt is gone. She additionally advises her to cry all the hurt out and hold nothing back. Datsishin held her tight, as Teplov gave her full control and was exceptionally obedient. Datsishin enjoyed this, having a young heart to idolize her. She began completely to ignore Grechko, not intentionally, but from her extra tight bond with Datsishin. Teplov took her to the river place to show her where they bathed. She sat on the bank allowing Datsishin to go first. Once Datsishin was in, she ordered Teplov to join her. When Teplov removed her playing gown, Datsishin told her to hurry, and that she was relieved, they were identical. She asked Teplov a few personal biological questions and then agreed that they were the same. Teplov put herself in Datsishin's arms, and Datsishin began rubbing selected special oil she had that would help make her skin soft. When they left the water, Teplov could not believe how soft her skin was and just lie on the ground touching her legs then touching Datsishin's legs. Next, she grabbed her hairbrush and began to brush Datsishin's long beautiful black hair. She began to cry. Datsishin asked her why she cried and Teplov told her because her hair, face and everything was so beautiful; she would soon grow tired of her and cast her from her.

Datsishin then asked her if she should give her a chance to earn her favors. Teplov honestly told her anything. Datsishin told her the last few months of walking had made her muscles tense, and she needed certain little soft hands to massage her. Truthfully, she did not need a massage; nonetheless, she knew that Teplov was young and had the abundance of restless energy that needed burned. She felt good in that somehow, she could read Teplov so easily. Teplov had not realized how much she truly missed her mother and older sisters. They spent all their days together and at nights, Datsishin kept Teplov in her arms, as if she was the baby, who was somehow escaping her womb. Grechko complained one night that he wanted to take Datsishin outside for a private matter. Datsishin refused to, not wanting to leave her little Teplov unprotected. Teplov told them they could take care of their matter here in the cave. She promised that she would hide herself in her blankets and remain there until they came to get her. Grechko told her that Tsigler told them that she did not want them making love around her. Teplov informs them that were before she fell in love with her new bigger sister and that if her older sister needed this, she wanted her to have it. Datsishin refused, saying she could not do this and enjoy herself when her sister did not have a man. Teplov told her that time would settle everything and that now we had to reproduce their next generation. It was their responsibility. Teplov jumps in Datsishin's arms and tells her if she does not understand how, she will gladly teach her. Datsishin tells her that considering they allowed Tsigler to watch them, which she would be wise to take a few peeks and see how a master works. Teplov kisses her crazily all over her face telling her that she believes Datsishin can do this better than anyone could who ever lived. Grechko continually asks Datsishin what she did to this poor little girl. Datsishin tells him she is the baby who refuses to come out of her womb. Grechko realizes that Datsishin and Teplov share the same spirit and dreams. Teplov goes over to her corner and yells back to Datsishin, "Sister, show me how it is done," when she immediately jumps underneath her blanket and does not reappear until Datsishin pulls the blankets from her to take her back to sleep in her arms.

The next few years saw the new small family taking turns between the caves they lived. One thing was for certain, Datsishin and Teplov were one and never apart. Teplov heart and mind belonged to Datsishin that she grew apart from Tolmachyov and Chemeris. Datsishin handled all the communication with Tolmachyov and Tsigler. Teplov, surprising abandoned her original plans concerning Grechko, and totally ignored him. She solely talked with Datsishin and obeyed her unconditionally. Datsishin, likewise, lived to serve Teplov. She scrubbed and oiled her every day, even though the oil they used now was bear fat. Datsishin made sure she always had protection and care. Even Tolmachyov and Tsigler marveled at this relationship. Teplov barely slightly separated while Datsishin and Grechko procreated, because Datsishin made her lay beside her holding hands. After each attempt, they summoned either Tolmachyov or Tsigler, and occasionally Chemeris, to discover the bad news. This was tearing Datsishin apart. It was clear to all that merely Teplov was holding her together. Teplov could not believe that one as beautiful as Datsishin could be so miserable. One day, Datsishin fell on her knees crying for Tsigler to find out why her womb was barren. Tsigler had known the answer for a few days, but was afraid to tell her. This night, knowing that Datsishin would not endure much longer she called both Datsishin and Teplov to a tree beside the river. Tsigler braced herself as she prepared to tell Datsishin the truth.

Datsishin begged her to reveal this secret. Tsigler told her that she could never have any children, because of certain exposure to a chemical, she whiles in space school. Datsishin froze, not moving any muscle and spoke no words. Teplov stood in front of her and pressed her head again her womb petting her long black hair. They stood like that throughout the night, as Teplov remained locked to hers. Tsigler told Grechko the news. He knew that Datsishin would suffer greatly from this as she had humbled and surrendered her body so many times over these last few years. Next, Teplov laid her sister down and began massaging her exactly the way she enjoyed. Datsishin just laid on the ground as if in a coma. Teplov showered her with thousands of kisses, swearing how much she loved her, yet there was no response. Teplov begged Datsishin not to leave her. Finally, after one month, Datsishin told Teplov that her life was finished. Teplov told her that was so unfair, because destiny had given her to Datsishin as being from her womb, and because she will have no more children, she decides to leave her. Datsishin wraps her arms around Teplov, once more crying, telling her she could never leave her. Teplov sincerely tells her that she will always be with her and would do anything for her. Teplov tells her; spontaneously, that Datsishin can use her womb to make the babies she wants. When they are born, she will surrender them for life to Datsishin in exchange for the love she has given her. Datsishin braces both of her hands on Teplov's face and looks her straight in her eyes, studying her intensely. Datsishin then remarks that she believes Teplov would actually do this for her. She continues that since they will never be apart, the womb the baby came from would have no effect on their lives, as they will be caring for the baby, regardless of mother. Teplov assures her that she speaks the truth and swears she will do this for her, whenever she commands.

Datsishin reports that she would lay beside her and relax while Teplov would be letting that grunter moan like a pig over her. Teplov asks her why she always looked as if she liked it. Datsishin tells her that is the way of women and that, the women have to pretend to enjoy it so the man's ego, not hurt, and it would break their hearts if we told them how poor, that they really were. Datsishin tells Teplov not to worry; she will make sure that her gift from the heavens rightfully treated as an angel. Teplov then confesses that she is so scared and is worried if this is moral. Datsishin agrees to ask Tolmachyov. Tolmachyov tells them that this is moral, as among the three of them, they are responsible for repopulating Emsky. Teplov agrees and lays under Grechko, who himself is nervous because he knows how much Datsishin treasures and worships this young woman. Teplov survives the first time, next the second time, and after that gets a hit on the third time. Teplov kept her promise and gave her sons to Datsishin, who gave them to Grechko. As Datsishin had predicted the baby always had two mothers, side-by-side. Once her son got older, Grechko would take the boy with him on all his works. In the days of Teplov, she gave to Datsishin eleven sons. When the sons were older, Teplov complained to Tolmachyov that they needed wives. Tolmachyov took this rightful request to Borsod-Abaúj-Zemplén gave female bodies to eleven volunteer Spirits who were roaming around Emsky. He placed them in the forests beside their cave so that they could come out and introduce themselves to their fresh husbands. Tolmachyov and Tsigler having new temporary bodies conducted the marriages. Borsod-Abaúj-Zemplén promised to provide the wives for the first four generations of all tribes on Emsky. When Tsigler told Teplov this great news, Teplov asked her what she meant by all tribes. Tsigler told her that is a mystery not for her to know. There came a day when Grechko believed his body was too old for him to live among his children and not be a burden. He asked Tsigler if he could enter the land of the dead. Hearing this, Datsishin and Teplov joined in the request as they received approvals. Tolmachyov, Tsigler, and Chemeris helped them cross over the line as they laid down their bodies for their children to bury them. Because of their ancestors, their descendants continued to live solely on Álmosd and every nation on that northern continent allows men to have one or two wives.

Most of the marriages that have more than one wife are because of fertilization difficulties. Teplov is the one who gave up everything so Emsky could have its future generations. She did not realize the Power Spirits had additional plans for the other continents.

CHAPTER 05

Paskala and Pasqualino

A fter this window stopped its vision, I looked at Orosházi as she sat there with small tears flowing from her wonderful eyes. I asked her why she was crying. She looks at Pankrati who maintains her constant peaceful appearance and asks her if what we just saw was real for Emsky. I jump in and ask Orosházi why she asks this question. Orosházi tells me that was so much emotion and mystery, and included so many new species she never knew, such as the Benigna. She does not understand how such a species can be actual. Moreover, if they are existent, how they could remain hidden with today's modern technology. Pankrati tells us that the Benigna not solely continues on Emsky, but on many worlds throughout the universe. Orosházi looks at our map of Emsky and confesses that she has just witnessed several strange forms of truelove. She is so impressed with Teplov, who produced eleven sons; giving them to a woman, she first planned to dishonor. Teplov had all that power, yet for love gave it to a woman who had everything, except the one thing Teplov had. She gave her pure gift freely and because of love. Orosházi comments that either way Teplov chose, Álmosd still received its sons and history knows that Teplov is the mother. What this did was giving Datsishin honor and purpose for her life, and Teplov received her honor by knowing she had saved her friend or sister. She compares their love to the one she has with me. She had laid down all her beauty so one as ugly as me could have love. Orosházi prides herself is this great sacrifice so Emsky could have its chronicles. I glance at her shaking my head in agreement, then stare at Pankrati, and ask where Teplov's spirit is today and specifically if Borsod-Abaúj-Zemplén put them in their heavens. Pankrati tells that Teplov went with Datsishin and Grechko to the heavens of Zhutov, a right she had because of the eleven sons she gave to Grechko. I think how ironic the mother of Emsky resting in a neighboring galaxy. Pankrati informs us that Emsky's seventh stone had an even more dynamic beginning. Borsod-Abaúj-Zemplén had concerns with how the Ethelbert was, except for Teplov, wiped out by a single plague. They knew a wider genetic pool would reduce the chances of a single plague destroying all the people, as this was the reason; they waited for Grechko and his limp to Emsky. They decided for this stone to have more than one cradle of this civilization. This was a common occurrence on many of the other worlds, yet with Emsky being on the end of a spiral; they did not as many opportunities available. Many explorers avoided worlds with people already living on them because of immunization differences and the possibility of an unknown plague. Borsod-Abaúj-Zemplén knew they would have to help to the tide Emsky's way.

One method would be to stabilize Emsky's worldwide population dispersion. They accomplished this by retarding the advancements in developing ships and other forms of sea and air travel. This would provide them with a possible five cradles of civilization. The early rafts could barely reach another continent, and were primary to capture female slaves for breeding. This provided a method to inject the various genes from one cradle into another and through the ages slowly blended the cradles to where the later transportation developments permitted. Orosházi sets snug beside me now and I ask her if she will ever ignore me such as Datsishin did to Grechko. She tells me absolutely if the woman was as beautiful as Pankrati. Pankrati's skin tone turns red and she warns Orosházi that sort of talk will get us in big trouble. Orosházi asks her, "What can my relationship with Sénye matter?" Pankrati tells us that we are here for a reason. Orosházi looks at me and tells me she will keep me, because she wants citizenship in Emsky. I tell her that I am still getting the better end of this deal. She taps me on my face, followed by a wink. I ask her if everything is okay. She confesses the great ones we have just watched made her aware that others can give more than she can give. I divulge to her that she gives me more than I need, and I have been storing it, so if she goes through a slump, I can use what I have stored. I can understand how this is affecting her, because it touches me as well. I can see the importance of starting out with a solid foundation. I stare at Pankrati and ask her to describe what we have just witnessed. She smiles and looks at us and says, "I saw the same thing, I see in front of me, and that is the miracle of love." This is when it hit me that Pankrati is the real deal and represents something wonderful. I can see how this impressed Orosházi by her response, as this seems to be removing the tension she was holding. Orosházi lifts my left arm, slides under it, and rests her head on my shoulder. She knows this is her place. I almost wish that we could have our world and begin our legacy. At least what I see is making my boring world essentially exciting.

Our chamber once more becomes dark, and the window reveals a new vision. I saw before me two candles that burned bright and released warmth and wonderful dancing white smoke. The swerves and swirls in the smoke are astonishing. Afterwards, I notice a great wind come in and blow out the candles making the window I am looking at once more black and dark. The window now shared a warm orange and yellow peaceful cloud, and I saw before me two large wineglasses filled to the top with a bubbling red wine. The crystal glasses that held the wine were sparkling in a rhythm that made me be at ease. The two wineglasses slowly and calmly sank into the orange cloud, and a giant tower began to rise out of the cloud. The tower was strong and sturdy, and appeared to have a city at its peak, although I could not see it clearly, because it was so far from us. I did hear men say, "Great is the city and he who built it." Our window became dark as our chamber filled with light. Orosházi looks at Patrizius and asks her to tell us what we just witnessed. Patrizius explains that we will first see the two candles from which the wine came forth.

We now saw through the window as it took us deep into the universe, and we came on a giant planet that the Patrizius identifies as Itshak. This is a highly advanced world. All the buildings have the same square shape, being tall, wide, and square. They have a black shiny glass covering them. I have never seen so many buildings crowded together. As we float over this world, I notice no building had windows. I also noticed no roads, nor any movement of people on the outside. These buildings appear in clusters, separated by open space. We also see many huge sheets of the black glass lying above the ground. As we continue to float, I hear a big, loud crashing noise and see a huge laser beam from the sky blasting at one of the building clusters. Something above those buildings, such as a shield of various sorts is blocking it. I can experience the intense heat from where we are approximately two-hundred miles from where the strike was. Pankrati guides us down to the surface beside one of those large black sheets of glass that is out in the open wilderness. When we arrive on the ground, I am surprised at what is in front of us.

I can see in front of me a large group of people, with children playing, eating, a little singing while others are dancing. Pankrati begins telling us what we are witnessing. She begins by describing that this is an open picnic area for any in the Empire to bring their families and enjoy outdoor recreation. The black glass above them, just as the black glass around all their buildings are two-way mirrors. They can see out; however, no one can see what they are doing. This is especially true for intergalactic espionage. This glass is also able to reflect target scanners, protecting them from laser strikes. The large blast that we just witnessed was a locked-on target whose beam the glass reflected. The Itshak planet belongs to the Janvier Empire who rules the Joconde galaxy. The Janvier Empire has been at war with the Giocondo Empire for over two thousand years. The Giocondo Empire rules the Igorko galaxy. Each galaxy receives over ten-thousand target strikes each day; having an average death toll under one-hundred people. These deaths are most time odd coincidences, such as the misfortune of being in the redirected target strike area. If they stay under or inside the black glass, they will live a normal lifespan. Nevertheless, the mental toll and financial toll of this prolonged war are overwhelming and apparently never ending. The diplomatic channels broke down 500 years ago. The concern of each side is the other will attempt to expand in their galaxy. Although, both galaxies continue to expand, they expand in the opposite directions. They have no roads because there is no need for them. Large material transports are moving along deep underground tunnels. Human transport is through a version of what the Empire calls teeporting. People simply beam to where they wish to go. These beams have a three solar system limitation, and if they proceed through a laser attack, the individual will not rematerialize. The single visible form of transportation is their attack battle ships. They maintained these in the event; they occupy an area in the enemy's Empire and need to move war supplies to the target galaxy. Our story begins with one of these battleships.

The most elite battle force is their long-range fighter ships. These small ships, with a capacity of less than six people can outmaneuver a live attack laser beam. They have the latest and best battle technology that their Empire can offer. They are not large enough to host a long-range laser; nevertheless, they can hold multiple short-range lasers. These short-range lasers can destroy a city while orbits, their host planet. The difficulty lies in the power of their shields. A long-range laser can shatter through their shields and because of the space, they displace while flashing through the cosmos, these long-range lasers can detect their position, so any form of shifting is useless. Both Empires have agreed not to use these ships against nonmilitary ground targets, unless they provide prior notification to the Empire, they are going to strike. They agreed to this to reduce the loss of innocent civilian lives. Violation of the laws of war will result in massive attacks from neighboring Empires. Therefore, they use these small DD43's for information-gathering purposes and humanitarian missions. Occasionally, a high profile leader will wish to defect to his enemy's Empire. Most times, the Empire this leader wished to become a citizen will send a force into "free this innocent prisoner." Each side knows it will happen; thereby, they keep these prisoners away from civilian populations. Ironically, these traitors will receive a great highly publicized welcoming ceremony, after which are put in prison for the remainder of their lives, used simply for the occasional propaganda stream. Each Empire will search long and hard to find the bravest men to serve in this force. They are the ones who would save their Empire if under attack. DD43's are difficult to detect, as the scanner must have a confidence range to do the detailed space displacement calculations. A normal espionage mission is not worth the effort to detect, because, if one side clamps down on the espionage, the other side would follow suit. Both Empires depend on this espionage for their security concerns.

Itshak is famous for their DD43 warrior named Paskala. His fame came when the governor of Itshak decided to defect to the Giocondo Empire. This brought great shame on those who lived on Itshak. Giocondo sent in a fleet of eleven DD43s to retrieve this defector. A young space pilot in the small Itshak planetary guard force traced the eleven enemy DD43s and reported it to the Janvier Empire who refused to engage these ships. Paskala also reported it to his commanders, who became upset when the Empire refused to engage them. Itshak's defense consisted of just eight aged DD08s, who were no matches for the new DD43s. Paskala's commanders ordered him to retreat. Paskala was a young man always hungry for knowledge and knew his DD08 from the front to back. He asked his two of his comrades to join him, as he would engage these DD43s. They agreed if they could remain out of the shooting range of the DD43s. Paskala accepted this because his plan did not call for them to be in harm's way. Paskala locked in the invader's course. He knew exactly where they would go. To make sure they stayed on the same path, he released the communication where the Janvier Empire had ordered them to retreat and allow the rescue of the Itshak traitor. The invaders did as he projected and lowered their short-range shields, so they could collect this traitor and get back into their space faster. Their long-range shields would give them plenty of warnings. To offset this Itshak reprogrammed his three ships' reflectors not to reflect. A long-range signal would pass through, whereas scarcely a short-range signal would detect this abnormality. He could now be invisible in this battle. He needed one additional advantage, and that was a way for his missiles to attack these ships. He could not fire the missiles, as the defending DD43 weapon systems would detect this. He elected to use a strategy never before used. He would plant the missiles, with non-reflecting reflectors. The weapon system reflector's signals would slip through his missiles. Once a missile is within one-hundred miles, nothing can detect it. The detecting waves have too many arches in them to define any close items. This was where he needed his two friends. He needed them to help him make the final fine-tuning adjustments to get a perfect hit as the DD43 hit the missile. The enemy's formation was four-four-three. The first four would be slightly staggered in front of the second four. This was to allow the second row also to fire at the enemy and to provide back up in the first row, while at the same time protecting the important third row. Paskala knew his space plants would get the first four needing no adjustments. Their explosions could cause the space mines for the second row to shift slightly. This is where his two friends would help, as each one would monitor two of the mines and have their computers make the instantaneous adjustments. These adjustments were fine-tuned close range, or their signals would be jammed. Once their alarms beeped that the tweaked adjustments programmed, they could slide back out of range of the final three ships, which he had a special plan. Paskala would be sitting about fifteen miles from while the fleet would be passing with these reflectors reflecting. This was so sensitive, that even if he sneezed the invading DD43s would detect him. He had three missiles chained to the outside of his ship. Paskala knew the first thing that this three command DD43s would do is gaining access to the damage. This would give him enough time to plant two of the missiles in the antimatter's exhaust zone. When these ships accelerated the exhaust zone acted as an intake zone and would pull anything in that zone into the ship instantaneously. These two ships would explode at once. It was this last ship that would give him the problem. He would have to guess how it would react. He kept the third missile in case the last remaining ship came after him, he would plant it, and in the last, few seconds do a space drop while the DD43 hit that third missile. In order to get this ship to attack him, he would have to turn off his reflector and send a signal to that ship to surrender. He would reengage his reflector as he dropped. To drop fast he had an extra jet pack attached to the side of his ship. It would fire down and with the explosion above him pushing; he would be out of the danger area. The plan worked exactly like this forever to be the most famous and wisest warrior in Janvier's history. One little matter caused one or two temporary concerns.

Just before they were to set the mines, the commanding general of the small fleet of DD08s discovered three of his ships were missing. He ordered them returned or those who had them executed. Paskala jammed the signals and overloaded their circuits, another special skill that he had developed while he burned all the circuits in his home state through trial and error. That was the reason he was a DD08 pilot, part of his stay out of the jail package from the judge. Paskala always took advantage of any situation, finding ways to do things different. Even though he stopped this transmission and prevented its rebroadcast, the message still appeared in the ship's logs as received. Within minutes, the eleven mighty Janvier DD43s vanished. The last transmission sent back to Janvier showed one old small DD08 demanding surrender. Paskala had planted a space streamer to capture the entire event as he now rebroadcasted it throughout both galaxies. Paskala has one more job to complete his mission. If his calculations were correct, he could escape punishment for the most daring act of his life. He landed his DD08 in the Itshak governor's space doc. As he walked into the governor's house arrest chambers, the ten guards securing it stepped back and saluted him. Paskala asked them to turn on their security streamers and punch in a code he had. This code would broadcast it throughout all Itshak. He walked into the governor's private prison chamber, grabbed him by his head, and dragged him out into the open lobby outside his cell. He later told people he did this so as not to get any blood on the expensive furnishings. Once the streams activated, he declared, "I am Paskala, the one who just destroyed eleven Giocondo DD43s with my DD08. I am a proud citizen of the great planet Itshak and we will not hang our heads in shame because of a traitor. Traitors from Itshak who bring shame on the great Janvier Empire will be shot in their head until they are dead." He immediately pulled his pistol and began shooting the governor in his head, releasing four shots until he dropped. The guards were stunned, yet offered no resistance. They later told the Empire streamers that they were not going to risk their lives for a traitor. Within minutes, this great victory, coupled with the execution of a traitor eagerly streamed into every home in both galaxies. This was the greatest defeat that the Giocondo ever suffered. They could not blame the Javier Empire as they had copies of their orders to retreat. The name Paskala was now well-known name as children in both galaxies fought over who could be Paskala in their space games. Paskala unfortunately had one debt he had to pay or spend the remainder of his life in prison.

Javier needed a scapegoat to redeem the diplomatic honor. They found the loophole through the commanding general's orders to return the ships and Paskala's failed obey this order. The Empire wanted to keep their hands clean of this matter; therefore, they made several power deals with those who had their sights on the governor's position. Just before the trial began, the Itshak military court-martialed Paskala, taking away his rank, detaining him for unlawful appropriation of three armed space vehicles. They cut deals with the other two pilots for their testimony. Just before the trial began, the planet arrested him for the murder of the governor. They took him from the military, rushing him into public court. Many loyal Paskala followers were at the military court when the planet took him. They immediately released this information to the public who began serious riots. These riots soon took place throughout the Joconde galaxy. Subsequent groups began to deactivate the glass shields around government buildings. Within hours, the Janvier Empire was in serious trouble. The King had to act fast, so he sent three of his armies to free Paskala and to arrest all who were involved with this great injustice. He knew who was involved because he had established this plan and needed to silence these people quickly. He did this by ordering their executions on sight by the name of the King. Later, that day all the glass shields were back in place. The King was shocked the Giocondo had not invaded. The Giocondo public streams reported that their military had refused to invade under these conditions. Their military leaders reported that they would not fight a dishonorable enemy.

Paskala immediately found himself a freeman as the King pardoned all charges against him and assigned him to the DD43 fleet command as their senior ace. He walked among the fleet with eleven shinning diamond stars, each one representing a destroyed

DD43. No other warrior from either galaxy ever destroyed more than one DD43. His record stood for the eternity of both Empires, never even halfway matched. Paskala was wise enough to comprehend he had to keep a low profile so as not to anger his jealous King. He actually found this easy to do, as he would spend much time in the Empire's science labs. The King approved of this and gave him all the clearances he wanted, mainly to keep him out of the public's eyes. Paskala also felt the pressure of all his attention and flew most of his DD43 missions logged in as another pilot. He was fascinated with altering any form of signal. His favorite pastimes now included zipping through command transmissions from the Giocondo and sending them to their news agencies and public schools. He would float through the Igorko galaxy totally disrupting the transmissions. He decided to add a little excitement by placing a random target generator and mix up the receivers. He was thrilled beyond his wildest expectations at the reports he intercepted. A lot of which was done in the dark was shining bright in the light. He knew this game had its best results when concentrated in one area created the most embarrassments. One night when he released his transmissions, two separate stars randomly released dot twenty-three solar flares. This was a rare time that two dot twenty-three flares radiation frequencies merged jumping to a new galactic rate of recurrence jump for the region between these stars. Paskala had three transmissions floating in this area. There was a young woman named Pasqualino who was teeporting from her planet called Yasha to her university three planets from Yasha in the same solar system. Her materialization code mixed with the rate of recurrence jump flipped her code back into Paskala's DD43 port. The horrible result was she rematerialized with two heads, no legs, or arms. She was in full control her mental capabilities. Paskala was shocked at what had happened. His little game backfired, and he had no idea what to do with this Giocondo Empire citizen. If anyone saw her, it would escalate this war and defame him as a brutal beast of evil.

The problem he now faced was how to get this monster back to his labs where he could hide her. Every alarm would go off with her Giocondo chips that he could not surgically remove. He parked his ship, and began running his scientific reanalyzes to break the coding of her teeporter down into parts he could translate. Paskala linked his labs and ship through scrambled transmissions. He knew this was easy for the Janvier to catch, unless he was extremely careful. His first break came when he could scramble two links in her Giocondo Empire Chip. This would enable him to get her back into his Empire. Once to the rear, he would teeport her through his screeners, using the private labs provided by the King to run his preprogramed analytical test. He would afterwards return to his house, teeport her to him, and subsequently run his experiments in his exclusive labs. He requested his vacation time, which gave him five weeks to work on this situation. Finally, he isolated the code jump concerning her heads. Afterwards, he could run these through his screeners and filter the variations. Three weeks into his vacation, he could teeport her to his office and back to his home, reforming her as she was originally with one small problem. He could not readjust her Giocondo Empire Chip in his simulator. He had to assimilate it in his simulator and if fixed, shift back before the Janvier Empire alarms sounded. After over one billion attempts, he realized the new locked chip's code was permanent. He told Pasqualino the bad news. She was heartbroken, as she did not want to live among the killers and demons of the ages. This thinking resulted from her lifetime of propaganda programing. Paskala knew it was just a matter of time before the alarms reported her code as a close Giocondo code, and would alert the security forces to apprehend her. He had to do something quickly. Pasqualino requested that he take her to a neutral neighboring galaxy, and she would try to find a way to survive. He felt bad about this, her losing all her family and friends, starting or starving in a foreign land. He still had two weeks; therefore, he told her they would search together. What he would find changed his life taking him out of his glory and comfort zone.

He boarded her on his ship and throughout the Janvier Empire's western neutral border, they explored. He discovered the false name he was flying with was not loaded along this border's safe passage list. This list controlled the DD43s, the Empires highest priority guarded weapon. He could dock and then resign in as himself, as he had the clearance for over thirty-five pilot names. The Empire considered him their greatest hero and number one target of the Giocondo Empire. The trouble with this option would be that the King would recognize instantly where he was and try to capture him and his ship would undergo a detailed routine scan as part of each border transfer. This was primarily to inventory the weapons and scientific equipment. This detection would discover Pasqualino, who did not have an Empire clearance to be on a DD43 and thus detained. If he jumped the border, there would be no coming back. This was a question of his ethics and responsibility. He asked Pasqualino, who was a beautiful woman, what he should do, free himself, or free her. She would not answer him, but instead asked him a question, "Why cannot we both be liberated?" He smiled at her and asked her, in total confusion, "How can we both be free?" She answers by reminding him that he is an explorer and by spending so much time in the Giocondo Empire must love danger. Such behaviors to her would indicate an adventure into a new quadrant of the galaxy. She points her hand up and says, "Somewhere out there where they are not at war." He thinks for a second, turns on his emergency beacon, and sets his speed to the max as they do a double space wave jump, a feat that solely a DD43 can do. He knows the double space wave jump will set off the alarms in the DD43 headquarters, which is on the other border because the Joconde Empire does not keep the DD43s on the western border. This did not worry him, as the border jump would set off the alarms on the western border. To hedge himself, he sent back a kidnapping threat from an unknown terrorist agency for peace that if certain demands not met, they would kill the great Paskala. This would have authorities believe he was a victim. Once they passed the border, he had programmed his ship to drop eighty degrees. He was wise to do this, in that by the time the western armies discovered he had shifted course; he was long gone to well beyond any scanners. For the searchers, they could barely guess his course and whichever way they guessed; it would be years before they would recognize if they were on the correct course, based on the jump he currently had. Within a few minutes, it hit him that he was now without a world, without friends and no more great advanced labs. Then again, he was without having to hide because of his fame, now he would hide to save his life. He never trusted his friends anyway. Moreover, as in his labs, if advanced technology was having a naked woman with two heads, no legs or arms show up in your ship, he needs a new technology. He would learn to create with sticks and stones. He still had one problem; he did not understand how to handle.

This problem was sitting beside him, with her long curly blond hair. The Giocondo women all had golden hair, believing any other color represented wickedness. They were exclusively family oriented and industrious. The women controlled most of the marketing activities related to the homes and families. A woman could, at no time trade for a dress or food from a man. They would never purchase anything from a man. Their husband made those purchases. They never talked to any men, except relatives. For dating, their father or older brothers would accompany them and relay the messages between the dating couples. Paskala was aware of the Giocondo culture, and he knew that if Pasqualino were to return and any discovered she had been in his lab, or even worse his home lab, she faced execution in public. He was so surprised that she was talking with him. Paskala asked her, as they were both flashing into the unknown, why she was accordingly relaxed and talking with him. She smiled and said, "Are you an idiot, you are the great Paskala, the father of all great warriors." Paskala found himself surprised by the conviction that she answered this. She perceived him as being the man of all men. He asked her if the Giocondo still executed her for being with him. She smiled and told him, "Of course, yet

I would be smiling as each flame took me closer to the land of the dead." Paskala had trouble understanding this, so she clarified for him that a law was a law and had no exceptions. He explained to her that the Janvier let the people decide the immunities, as they had with his life for killing the governor. She laughs and tells him that all he did was moving his execution date forward, as the Giocondo would have executed him after creating his propaganda streams. Paskala was learning things about the Giocondo that he already knew.

He was puzzled at how he could learn something he already knew. Although he saw all these things while spying on the Giocondo, to have one beside him talking about these things as if they were everyday common things excited him. He recognized that he could explore Pasqualino and be exploring Giocondo at the same time. Instead of peeking through the windows, he was now standing in the living room. In his excitement, he blurted to her, "This is amazing; you sound almost like a real human." She slapped him immediately and cried, "I was beginning to think you were not a filthy dog. You understand the reason we do not have dogs is that they remind of us you Janvierians." Paskala looked at her and apologized, reminding her that the Janvierians had no blond-haired women and that this was strange for him. She accepted his apology and told him that he was the lone Janvierian that did not appear like a dog. Paskala felt the sincerity in what she was saying, thus he told her that he agreed most Janvierians not simply looked like dogs but also acted like dogs. Pasqualino disagrees with the acting like dogs part in that she admires the Janvierian women's ability to talk and deal with men. Paskala confides in her the Janvierian women can stand in front of a person and lie just as sincerely as a man and this has caused him undue pain to many times. Pasqualino asks him what the difference is between a man lying and a woman lying. Paskala tells her that needs to believe in the moral purity of a woman, especially if she were to be the mother of his children. He asks her if she has ever lied. She winks at him and sticks out her tongue. Paskala slaps himself for asking such a foolish question.

If Pasqualino had ever been caught lying, she would have no tongue. Paskala commented that he felt the Giocondo laws were too strict. Pasqualino rebuts that she feels the Janvierian laws were too vague and that the people found themselves in more trouble with the gray areas, whereas the Giocondo laws were precise, and if obeyed, no punishment would result. The Giocondo recognized what they can and cannot do. The Janvierian can fall prey to wicked leaders, as he did with his King, and face a punishment not deserved. She had him nailed to the wall on this one, as the Giocondo ensured all their people knew of the Janvierian King's desire to execute him out of jealousy. Paskala was beginning to understand Pasqualino's ability to relax while with him. The Giocondo considered Paskala a hero betrayed by the Janvierians and therefore, an enemy of your enemy must be your friend. Paskala asks Pasqualino if she knows why they are so comfortable with each other. Pasqualino tells him because for the first time in his life, he is with a real woman, as are all Giocondo women and not as the lying, deceiving, and wicked Janvierian women. Paskala could merely agree with what she was saying. Next, he asks her if she knows what we will find out there. She tells him that since the great Paskala is leading the way, she has no fear and closes her eyes for her nap. Paskala finds the absolute, black and white of her answers so enticing. She does not flirt with the gray areas that can have multiple answers and hide any possible misleading. She does not argue or grieve over what she has lost, she simply holds onto what she has. If somehow he could merely find a way to stomach her sunny blond hair, so much of his torment would vanish. He could barely hope that time would mend this weakness, because she was growing on him as each minute passed them. He wanted to learn how to examine something and say this is what I see and to see that, as Pasqualino did with such ease. When he looked at something, he saw one-thousand shades of gray and trapped with trying to see that thing with different shades of gray. He could now understand that if he saw it as black, the single question would be how it would appear as white. One variable, solve it, and then move on to the next equation. Naturally, he would have to leave several of the variables black, or else he would have all white, which would be the same as having nothing. No wonder Pasqualino could simply make a black or white statement and drift off into the peace of rest.

He looked into the deep dark black and white space before him. What Pasqualino saw in everyday life was what composed the surrounding universe. She was looking up, while he was looking into a fantasy realm. Accordingly, he decided it would be best to talk with her more before he continued his private evaluations. This time, he would allow her to make the black and white lines on a clean panel, instead of him trying to consolidate all his mangled, gray lines. He decided it was, time to release one of his special space wave tracker scramblers, which he used daily while in the Giocondo Empire spying. This time, he would use it on the Janvier Empire's DD43's, which would be tracking him. He felt comfortable knowing he had no less than the distance from the eastern DD43 stations to the western boarder lead before those who would track him. He also had the wave jump lead, which is the space and time it takes to make the jump, as he flashed by the western border in a complete wave jump. By now, the Janvier should have decoded Pasqualino's codes and would be ashamed to report a kidnapping of their great hero by a Giocondo woman. He was curious on how the King would handle this one. Paskala found it amusing that one again, he would be embarrassing the King, although this time the King would not be jealous but in danger of being shamed. Was he so weak that he could not protect his greatest warrior from a lone petite Giocondo woman, especially one from the planet Yasha, who had no great heroes? Paskala had programmed his course with a few directional changes so he could shift the horizontal and vertical plains of his path. He believed this would make it utterly impossible for anyone to track him. He never believed in the impossible, as he dedicated his life to changing the impossible into possible. Paskala knew that a possible special joint search force consisting of both Giocondo and Javier would search for them. The Giocondo protected their women and were willing to make any sacrifice to save one. He would have to travel to the absolute utter deep end of the universe for any chance of sanctuary. He knew that no less than ten years in this DD43 would find a place within the confidence range he needed. He still had a few things to neutralize.

His DD43 and body have a Janvier chip or program embedded, as Pasqualino also still had her chip embedded. He had his ship's code manipulators working on this problem as their maximum capacity. He froze all his other projects. Meanwhile, he had coded reflectors, which reflected their codes back into the deep universe in the opposite direction. He hoped this would lead those who were chasing him to believe he circled to the rear, a strategy; he was famous. He knew these codes were manipulative, as the Empire would alter his during his espionage trips. He also knew of another problem that could cause them great hardships. The Giocondo is family centered, and Pasqualino would suffer from the absence of her family soon. He had no family, and was the property of the Janvier Empire. All his searching to discover his parents and any siblings always failed. He knew of a great manufacturing facility that had craved in and killed many adults in his area. His guardians always told him and all the other children in his ward their parents died in that disaster, a disaster caused by the owners, not keeping their facilities' safe and bribed government officials to keep in business. Several habits appear to be universal. He currently believed that these things could not happen to the Giocondo Empire, from the vibes he was receiving from his sleeping partner. A lifetime of programing that all Giocondo was wicked and bloodthirsty beasts were not holding true for him now. Pasqualino was accordingly transparent; she was so easy to read, and did not waver on any position. Even so, he knew she would bend while moving into the new, unknown, where the laws had yet to rule. He wondered if they would be able to melt the walls of hate that had formed their ancestors.

Pasqualino wakes up and begins complaining that Janvier men are lazy like the Giocondo men. Paskala asks her to explain this statement, as it could be an insult or a compliment. She complains that he did not prepare their dinner while she was napping. Paskala looks at her and asks why she dyed her hair blond, because she is acting as a Javier woman now. She laughs and gets up going back to the food processor and asking him what he would like to eat. While she is sitting up his tray, because he cannot get out of the pilot's seat while they are at wave jump speed, their ship hits a space pocket vacuum and does a temporary double jump, which is much like a small jolt. The jolt shakes, open a storage door and what appears behind that door makes Pasqualino scream. Paskala tosses her back a weapon in which she catches perfectly. She points the weapon at the two unknown people hiding behind that door. Pasqualino orders them to come out where she can see them. They come out, and she cuffs their hands and feet and guides them up to Paskala. The man asks her if she is a Giocondo. She confesses to be a Giocondo. Paskala looks at the young couple and recognizes the female as being one of his comrade's daughters. He asks them what they were doing on his ship. The young man tells him this is the ship where they enjoy their relationship, and that his log reported he would not be using it tonight. Paskala scans and detects their Empire chips and begins deflecting them resetting his course for straight ahead. He tells the juvenile couple that thanks to them, those who are chasing them grasp where he is. The young man, called Osman and the woman called Rika are from Itshak as well. They ask Paskala why he is running. He explains that he did a great wrong with a Giocondo woman and is dedicating his life to repay her. He offers to drop them off at a planet and send a message back to Janvier where to find them. They ask whether instead he will allow them to serve on his ship. Paskala asks if they are willing to give everything up because of him. They ask if they can receive everything because of him. Paskala is the undisputed pride of the Itshak, the one who redeemed them. He knows that no Itshak person would betray him. He asks them if they can accept a Giocondo as a friend. Rika asks if there is anything, we can do about her terrible blond hair. Pasqualino volunteers to shave off all her sun colored hair if the three Janvierians shaves off all their dirt colored hair. They quickly reach a compromise and keep their hair. Pasqualino unlocks their cuffs and asks Rika to help her prepare the food for the men. Rika tells her that she does not serve food to the men. Pasqualino begins hitting her telling her that she will serve food to the men on this ship. Osman and Paskala quickly agree. Rika reluctantly also agrees. Rika asks Pasqualino why she enjoys serving men so much. Pasqualino asks Rika if she loves Osman or merely has sex with him to be cheap and worthless. Rika claims to love him. Pasqualino then asks her why she would not want to control what goes in him, so he would be stronger and have longer lives. She reminds Rika that if a man selects what he wants to eat, he will not select the healthy foods. Rika hugs Pasqualino and then runs around the inside their ship screaming for joy, "I just touched my first Giocondo and I did not burn alive." Paskala will scare her by recommending she sleep next to the shower tonight, in case the burning is a delayed action. Pasqualino confesses her surprise that she should already suffer from infestation with plagues from breathing the same air as the Janvierians. Paskala reminds her that the ship's air is filtrated. He could now detect evident concern from Pasqualino and Rika. To relax them, he tells the girls, they will be okay. Even though the air is filtrated it would tell him any new foreign particles were in the air, and as for the burning up from touching a Giocondo, he touched Pasqualino when they first met and has yet to burn. The girls begin shoveling the food on their spoons and into their men's mouths. Paskala did not believe he would enjoy being spooned-fed; however, finds himself enjoying this. This is the first time he has flown a non-training mission with four people aboard this ship. Usually such a crowd makes him uncomfortable, yet this time he is enjoying it. This packed cabin has so much excitement as this new crew is bonding, creating bonds that never before have existed. He wonders if it can get better than this. Then a beeper goes off that sends a chill down his back.

The beeper is to his program that is trying to reprogram their chips. The program has hacked the code and not fully reprogrammed them, but also has discovered the eject code, as all five chips, including the DD43's chip eject. Osman collects the chips, puts them in the ship's teeporter, and flashes them in reverse across the universe. Paskala knows that even with the chips hacked; they will struggle to revert to their original code, which he believes will take about four months. At that time, they will cause those who are seeking them to retreat to where the chips are, which would be about a four-year reversal. Without these chips in them, the posy will never find them. Any advanced programs, which try to project his location based on his previous random course selections will spin them in circles for the ages. This is why he reverted to a straight course after discovering his stole ways. During the next five months, the crew learned so much about each, another. They were emerging from the shame of their earlier hates to the curiosity of what they were missing from their age-old enemies. Rika, one day commented how that she hoped their children did not have as they had done most of their lives. This statement caught Pasqualino by surprise because she had never considered mating with Paskala, a Janvier. She began crying that she did not realize if she could ever do such a wicked thing to her ancestors. Osman reminded her that most of the things our ancestors had taught us were lying, and that it was our responsibility to change those lies into truths. She still did not realize if she could do this, what if the children did not have blond hair. Paskala asks what if they did have golden hair. Rika tells Pasqualino that when she sees her first child, she will change her mind. Pasqualino tells her that many of her girlfriends had decided to have babies after seeing their friend's babies. Paskala came out with the solid convincer when he asked Pasqualino what the Giocondo ancestors would think if they knew the son of Paskala had a Giocondo mother. She jumped and said, without hesitation, they would rejoice and claim this son as theirs. Rika smiles and then adds, "So they will rejoice at your son?" Pasqualino confessed that she might have a little pity on poor Paskala, because no other women wanted him. Everyone agreed with her on this point, wanting not to go through this long debate once more. Paskala informed his crew one morning that it was time for his big test.

This test would tell him if the posy was still chasing them. As with all equipment on board, he had at one time or another rigged it. He would set his long-range scanners to a six-month scan, and then his special invention, have the scans come back to him and not continue throughout the ages as the light from a star does. The danger of a scan was that if someone were in this range, he or she could trace it back to him. Either way, he had to know. He shot his first scan, and it returned negative. No one was chasing them. He would run another test following month and each month for the ensuing few months and then search for a planet to rest for a few days. Osman was his lifesaver now, as he would sit in the pilot's seat, giving him a chance to clean and walk around the ship, and even one night dance with Pasqualino. Pasqualino, as all Giocondo women had soft skin, the product of years of lotions and oils. This was their pride. Paskala knew of this tradition, yet never realized its impact until he held her for a dance. It erased from his heart any desire ever to touch another woman. Suddenly, her blond hair or brown freckles, no longer bothered him. Something was wrong with him, and he did not understand nor care what it was. He was regularly singing the Giocondo songs Pasqualino was teaching the crew. She appeared to appreciate all the enjoyable things to do, most likely from her deep family roots. She confesses to us the Giocondo depended on their family for support where the Janvier relied on their Empire. She was correct in that a family would provide better support than a King would give. One day, we asked her about her family. She confessed that she had no family. The government caught her mother with another man and executed her.

Her father shortly thereafter committed suicide. The Empire would never put siblings in the same child centers and thereby transferred her to Yasha. We ask her how she kept her strong family beliefs. She explains the Giocondo child centers have so many families that take the children for the weekends and holidays. During the week and at school, they would have the family oriented activities. Even many of their classrooms were set up as a family activity. They called all teachers either mother or father. Rika asked what they called police officers. She told them they called them hogs. Osman told her they had the same practice in the Janvier. It appears not everyone feels comfortable around the police. It was simply up to the crew to find out what all they had in common.

The things they had in common grew each day, as their excitement grew each time they passed the long-range scan. It was evident they were not being followed. Paskala decided he would run his next test in one year. It the meantime, he saw a galaxy quickly approaching, then bumped his DD43 out of space wave and into normal light-speed and began to scan the galaxy ahead. He found a quiet little planet with no moons and landed on it among several mountains along a giant lake. While approaching the landing area, he discovered a peaceful looking green-sanded beach. This looked interesting, and after his scanners told him, it was safe; he landed on it beside several giant black rocks. These rocks looked as if they were meteors. For the first time in his life, he did not care what they were, because the next few days were for fun and no exploration. Everyone applied a handful of special oil that would protect their skin from the sun, as they had been inside their ship for so long. A DD43 had an advanced environmental simulator that protected those aboard it, nevertheless, Pasqualino said to put it on and therefore, everyone did. What is so ironic us that the first steps taken on a new world visited by a blended crew would receive and obey orders from a Giocondo. Everyone knew that she was right and with her intense family bonding traits, would never allow one of us in a harmful situation if she could prevent it. The crew knew it and as such; she was the most sought after among the crew. Everyone was in competition for her attention. She finally claimed that whoever told her that the Janvierians hated the Giocondo lying. They should have warned her that they would try to talk her to death.

The crew just laughed at her and told her to deal with it. She told them that this problem, she hoped never to solve. This new space family soon found themselves splashing in the salt-free giant lake in front of them. Once more, Giocondo knew all the fun games to play, and soon they found themselves in the dark and decided to return to their ship. They passed their exterior scans and received clearance to enter the ship. Pasqualino asked Paskala an interesting question that if they had not passed those external scans, could they enter the ship. He told her he had a program that could bypass the lockout. His handprint would open the latch. This was a safety valve, which the Empire had placed in their DD43s, knowing that a stranded pilot lost them, both a pilot and the ship, as, both could sit in quarantine in a space dock. Paskala does find it strange that no life exists on this planet. Pasqualino tells him to relax, because all worlds had a stage where they had no life. He asks her where she learned that. She tells him in her first year of beginning school. He asks her that if she is so smart, then why is this sand green. Pasqualino looks at him as if surprised and asks him why he is teasing her with so many easy questions; the sand is green with the reaction with the space rocks that have changed the chemical balance of this beach. Rika looks at her and asks her, why they have not defeated the Janvier yet. Pasqualino winks at her and tells us because they do not want the Janvier to pollute their worlds. Osman looks at Paskala as; both wonder if there could be an element of truth in this. Rika asks Pasqualino to begin another song and soon the crew is sipping on selected special spirit liquors from the food generator, laying on the floor, and singing. The next day, they put on their gravity displacers. Afterwards, they went sightseeing above the cliffs, which surrounded them. Paskala decides to take a closer examination of the rocks in this cliff, and although breaking his vow not to research, cannot deny that something does not fit here. He motions for his family, as he knows them by now, to come to listen to what he sees. He shows them how the layers between each rock bed appear filled with the same material. The caves are also in perfect alignment for each padded coating between the rock levels. They ask him to tell him what this means.

He tells them it means they should go back to the ship. They rush back to the ship, and he launches it. The crew now demands a few answers. He explains the cliff as recently created and no one who could create something that massive was someone this crew did not need to meet. As they approach orbit, his sensors begin to sound an alert. He immediately makes his DD43 transparent as they pass through a fleet of ships undetected. Once pass them, he removes his transparency and jumps into a space wave. Rika asks Paskala if the jump onto the space wave gave away their secrecy. He tells her they are okay, as the ships are not chasing them, but now are landing on the beach. She wants to understand how he has this information. He points to a monitor and shows her the alarm calm. Next, he tells her that short-range scanners are not retraceable because of the planet's orbit. Paskala pushes another button that turns from red to green. He tells her he has jumped scrambled their jump wave; therefore, no one can ever find it. Pasqualino now comes up and sits beside him in the co-pilot seat. This is the first time; except for feeding and cleaning, she has ever sat beside him. She tells him that his detection of the cliff evidence just saved their lives. They would have been too far from their ship to make it back and would now be captives or maybe even deceased. Pasqualino tells him she is so amazed at his great abilities. Paskala reveals to her that is from spending too many lonely days and nights hiding in research projects. Pasqualino tells him to tell her when he becomes tired of the lonely nights. Paskala promises her that is one thing he will honestly tell her, and for her to be prepared, because he could be telling her when he finds a world for them to live securely. She asks him why they need a world; after all, it does not seem to be holding back Osman and Rika. Paskala tells her that he is not like those dirty Janvierians. Rika hits Osman and yells at him that she told him they knew. Osman then complains to Paskala that they have just ruined everything. Pasqualino looks at Rika and asks her how she has ruined everything now, because, if they stop, afterwards he has no chance breaking down Paskala. Rika looks at Osman and tells him they can continue, solely to break down Paskala. Paskala smiles at Rika and ironically thanks her. The gang was restless now that they had the taste of air in their lungs. Paskala could see the expression in their eyes and sense the tension in the cabin. He spots five galaxies in a row ahead and jumps out of his space wave just in time to catch the final one. The crew rush to their windows so they can once more see the stars of a galaxy. Soon, perhaps they will walk on another planet. Pasqualino asks him not to pick another barren planet that has a space fleet. Paskala finds one, even though populated; he will place their ship where no people live.

He spots a charming castle resting on a secluded mountain. Then he says sorry and pushes a special button that releases a spray over the entire region. Rika sees people dropping. Pasqualino becomes angry, calling Paskala a killer. He tells them to relax, because he has merely put everyone into a one-week sleep. They will be fine, although hungry, when they wake up next week. He then opened a drawer loaded with various laser pistols, pulled one out with its holster, and attached it to his belt. Afterwards, another device popped up out of the hole. He opened the box and extended the wand that appeared as it transformed into a long thin rifle laser device. Pasqualino asks Paskala what these weapons are. He explains the pistol is in case someone wakes up, it will put them back to sleep at x-7 with x being the number of sleep days past, and the rifle is to wake up people or animals. Rika asks why we would want to awaken an animal. Paskala recommend we do a little horseback riding. Pasqualino becomes excited telling Paskala that he must have read her mind and that this will be a great week, if no one dies. Paskala tells her that a week with death in it is never great. Paskala was about to learn a lesson in a class; he never wanted to take. What works in one galaxy does not hold true on the other galaxies.

Paskala lands his DD43 on this peaceful thick-fogged mountaintop beside a lake in front of a giant castle. As they step out of their space home, various horses go running, pass them. Rika comments how those horses must be running in their sleep. She gets a good laugh from Pasqualino and Osman before they begin to cough. Paskala tells everyone to get back inside the ship. They rush back inside as Paskala ejects selected new button panels from the walls and starts pushing buttons. The permeated orange fog cabin quickly subsided, as it flowed into an exhaust and dispensed outside the ship. Outside, it burned in midair. Everyone looks around in confusion. Numbers begin flashing on his panel. Paskala alerts his staff that they must leave this world because of biological hazards to can give them a deadly virus. He was withholding the truth, hoping for a fast getaway. The crew urged him to get back into orbit.

Paskala suspected that the sleeping spray may have actually killed these people and was heartbroken over this strange interaction. What pestered him the most now was that not all the rules of physics in which he based everything might apply anywhere else. He, therefore, began to run several scans of worlds, which had the same physical bases as his Itshak. To his surprise, many worlds appeared on his screen, with numbers ranking their compatibility. He now reran the scan solely on these worlds ranking them with the least population, with rankings for both the planet and the plant's solar system. He found a few with empty solar systems and lay in a course to explore these. There would be no more expeditious landings, mandatory now detailed scans before landing. He never conceived that a sleeping spray could kill people. Nevertheless, when an environment exists based on H_3O_2 basis, it interacts differently with sodium-based additives, and actually separates the H_2O from this equation, adding a $NaOH$ poison. This proved deadly as also was the normal water byproduct, which was too thin for their bodies to process, while similarly distributing the sodium-based poison expeditiously. He knew what had happened, yet it did not bring back all those innocent dead people. He would have to live with this mistake and would conceal it from the ones he now loved so they as well would not suffer. Paskala learned a valuable lesson and that was researching proceeds all actions in these new worlds. He went to select the solar system furthest from the one he was just in and at the last minute remembered on an old tale about how divine beings usually ruled one galaxy, therefore he jumped back onto his self-generated space wave, which flowed into the first real space wave and soon was flashing once again through space. He explained this to his crew as the space wave completely would clean the outside of the ship, and that his filters would run a few more tests on them, for precautionary purposes only.

He traveled for a couple of more days and then once more felt the urge for another world. He jumped from the space wave and reducing to be light-decade-speed, which is ten times faster than light-year-speed, while exploring a few neighboring galaxies. He ran his scans and found a few empty solar systems that were in the same section of the galaxy, thus felt safe with these. This time, Paskala asked his crew to help him select a planet. The planet scanned and was solely that compatible with Itshak and Tasha. They agreed on one and Paskala landed his ship on a grass beach that merged into a sandy beach. He had enough playing in the sand for a while and now looked for the grass to lie on while enjoying a little sun. The grass and sand beaches offered a large clear water lake in which they could swim. Not wanting to get caught off-guard again, Paskala activated a shield over this area, so that nothing could enter by air, sea, from underground or land. They swam and enjoyed certain walks on the beach. Paskala wanted specific time to speak with Pasqualino. He asked her what she had planned for the remainder of her life. Pasqualino explains to him that she will not think about tomorrow and will not begin thinking about such things until she has a home to live and family to serve. Paskala asks her who will be the father of that family. She slaps him lightly and asks him if he knows any volunteers. He smiles and shakes his head yes. She asks him why he had doubts about their relationship. Paskala tells her that he felt this way because of her frigid behavior on the ship. Pasqualino explains to her future mate that she is not going to behave romantically in front of adolescents. She reiterates there is behavior for the bedroom and behavior for social situations and that these behaviors should not blend past their boundaries. She gives him an enjoyable long kiss and then tells him if he wants more, we need to find a world and build our house. Paskala tells her he wants at least another three months in space and when they do find a place to run deep-space scans for at least one year thereafter. She smiles and winks, then closes this conversation with the word house. They return to the ship and begin to prepare for an outdoor picnic. Following the picnic, Pasqualino teaches the gang a few more games, which take them deep into this moonlit night. This world had one moon, as its orbit was close; thereby, allowing it to provide many night-lights.

Paskala tells this family that a reason no one settles here would relate to this moon's close orbit. They agreed to sleep outside tonight. Rika and Osman grab one sleeping bag and select a place somewhat close to the ship's door to sleep. Paskala goes to grab a sleeping bag when Pasqualino hits him, knocking the bag out of his hand. She selects the next one and tells him to follow her. She selects a spot between the ship and the beach on the opposite side of the ship from Rika. She opens the sleeping bag and tells Paskala to jump in as she follows him and reseals the bag. Paskala looks at her with a strange expression, which she simply asks him how he likes their new temporary home. She removes any doubts from his mind about her desire to have a life with him as a mate. Paskala is wise enough to realize the Giocondo women are one-man women. She is his for the remainder of her life, which, if the Giocondo found them, would not be long. The next day turns out to be a bit colder than the first day. The family builds a comfortable fire and enjoys the heat from it. They have studied this activity in their ancient history classes. The cold air turns out to be short lived. The summertime activities begin once more. The crew decides that today would be a fine day to play in the foothills of the mountain, which towers from the beach are ending.

Paskala moves the ships landing on a spot that is in the path they wish to explore. He resets his shields and scans. The area they are exploring is above the tree line, which makes it easier to see what is around them. A day hiking on the steep mountainside leaves this crew exhausted. They decide to sleep inside tonight with their muscle relaxers activated. They enjoy the next morning's breakfast outside and then agree it is, time to move forward. Paskala soon will have their ship riding a space wave and deep into the unknown; they once more proceeded. Three months later, he decides to reduce speeding and search for low populated planets. He notices an odd-looking galaxy that has an added extended spiral. The expanded spiral attracts him, as it offers the gravitational benefits of a galaxy, while offering certain extra privacy from the galaxy's core. Large Empires often neglect areas that do not have many worlds to offer and because of the additional defensive burdens. He enters the first solar system and discovers four planets with inactive space ships rotating around them. His scans warn of crews deceased from plague related deaths and that most bodies have been decaying for around five years. One of the four planets has just three people, and they live on a continent to the far north. He turns on his transparent shield so to remain invisible and begins rotating around the planet. They marvel how the planet still looks so untouched by man, with so many ships in their orbits. Paskala talks the crew into settling in the center, mountains by a river on the large continent, which occupies the northeastern corner of this planet. He takes his ship in for a closer landing when something goes wrong. His panels are out his control. He orders everyone to put on their antigravity jackets because they are going to jump immediately.

They dawn their jackets and he takes his laser pistol and fires at the cabin's door blasting it into the air. They all jump out of his ship, and a few seconds later they see a flash. His powerful DD43 had malfunctioned and self-destructed. When they meet on the surface, he explains that somehow, the DD43 command could activate the self-destruct through a spray scan. The scan locked onto their ship in the beginning; however, his massive speeds kept them just a few days ahead of it. The short visits to the other worlds gave it time to get closer to them, as they apparently departed the previous world just in time. Paskala is confident that another month in space it would have caught them. Destiny was on their side by circling this planet, so close to its surface. Even one more orbit around this planet would have been their dome. The few seconds in the delay caused by the panel malfunction was the result of the planet's gravitational pull. First, a close flight to the surface will give a panel flash on a self-destruct. Pasqualino believes this was more than a coincidence and that it is their destiny. She thereby calls this land Gyáli, which means destiny on Yasha. The crew agrees.

Paskala takes inventory of what each person grabbed on the way out of the ship. Osman grabbed his laser pistol belt and laser rifle. Pasqualino grabbed the medical bag that she always kept with her. Rika grabbed her camping bag, which had a tent, shovel, ax, sleeping bags, and so many more things, compact into small cubes packed tight in her bag. She had planned for Osman and her to spend a few extra days on the other side of the mountain on the planet they just departed. When everyone elected to return to space, she simply tossed the bag beside her chair. This proved to be the most valuable asset for these new pilgrims. They immediately began to clear a little space for their settlement. The crew had witnessed a few large beasts roaming the surface when in their orbits, thereby decided to build a wall made from trees that would surround their homes. Paskala would use his forever laser pistols to cut the trees, and could trim them into three-inch thick boards. His rifle had a tree bonder that bonded, would together. All warriors needed to make temporary wood fortifications as part of their stranded on a strange world training. Once they built their large fort, as they also constructed their homes and storage buildings. They were living off the fruit and vegetables that Giocondo was gathering for them. Although they were not the same as those on her Yasha, they were variations of the same plant families. She borrowed Osman's laser pistol one day and got the gang a bear, which she asked the men to help her process. She was wise enough to bury the extra organs, and when she got the beast to their camp, she removed its hide before clothing if the weather turned cold. Before hunting, she had created a stone fireplace. She also had long poles made from the branches of the trees Paskala was using to make boards. Pasqualino took the left over wood and stacked it beside her fireplace. She then began to smoke the bear meat, cutting it into chucks larger than normal. Once Pasqualino had, the outside smoked, she took Osman's laser pistol, and on a low, setting quickly dehydrated the meat. Soon she had a large quantity of bear jerky for the gang to eat with their vegetables and fruit. She was an expert fish spiker as on Yasha, they would wade in the creeks and with special spear-like, poles they called spikers would spike the fish as they passed by them.

She discovered a shallow bed in the nearby river and could walk out in the river and spike fish extremely easy. She used the fish as a fresh treat for the gang's meals. Her skills enhanced this new family's ability to survive in the wild, as the Giocondo's favorite family activity was camping, sometimes for weeks at a time. Once the houses were finished, the couples moved into their respective homes. Giocondo and Paskala exchanged their personal vows. Both women were soon pregnant and after the winter months passed, in early spring Giocondo gave birth to her initial daughter as Rika gave birth to her first son. They continued this routine for ten years when Giocondo had ten daughters and Rika had ten sons. Frustrated because he could not have a son, Paskala decided to spend a few weeks in the mountains and search for the answers. While walking along a path one day, a bright light came to him and temporarily blinded him. He fell to the ground holding his eyes. The voice told him that because he had killed the guiltless people on that green foggy planet, he could have no sons and that soon he would lose Pasqualino. He begged that they spare Pasqualino as she was innocent and for them to take her like, they would be taking the life of an innocent one. He offered his life in exchange. At this time, a giant bear came leaping on Paskala killing him quickly. The next month, one of his daughters with one of Osman's sons discovered his body. They brought it back to the camp where Pasqualino burned it, as was the custom of the Giocondo. Her hero no longer lived. Osman produced no more children with Rika with respect for the memory of Paskala and their love for Pasqualino. Pasqualino's daughters married to Rika's sons and they began many cities throughout Gyáli. Neither the Giocondo nor the Janvier ever discovered their runaways.

Orosházi argued with Pankrati that the punishment for Paskala was so harsh. Pankrati reminds her that the Empire has yet to rule Emsky and this is from their history. She agrees the punishment was harsh, yet at the same time feels sorry for all the blameless people who died of his chemical spray. Unfortunately, innocent people often pay for the deeds of others.

CHAPTER 06

The hidden mystery of Sénye and Orosházi

The window before us once more turns black and empty. Orosházi complains that she wants to see my life this time, as it is, time to lay the finishing foundation to her love so all the secrets now known. I argue that I have shared all secrets, and that it is not fair to see all my life and for me not to see my Orosházi's life. Pankrati tells me that she will go with Orosházi on this one, and that we will peek into her life afterwards. Orosházi face turns somewhat pale as I ask her what is wrong. She explains that much of her history is humiliating for her and brings great shame on her. Paskala explains that all history is as this. She looks at me and begins to play my book. I remember so little before the first traumatic event in my life. This is the record based on what I knew at the time of these events as recorded in my book. Even though we had no deity, all souls record their events. Orosházi revealed to me how to open my book. I recall so many talking about Emsky joining the Empire as a young boy. Nevertheless, we did not join during my lifetime. The Empire constantly swept our planet for demons and evil spirits, as they collected all who were in wicked, judged and erased them from existence. Emsky had an excess of lost spirits, and spirits, which were troubled. I never knew much about all their details, although we did cross paths more than I wanted. Closer to home, my parents were poor, and both worked in the fields most of their days. An elderly woman who lived next to us, named Boyarov or as I called her, monster Boyarov, because she always dressed me like my sisters. I was the single boy in our family and had three sisters, who believed their mission in life was to make sure I never had any boy fun. I begin my life's story in my seventh year. My three sisters were Blum, who was in her eleventh year, Antipin, who was in her tenth year, and Dultsev who was in her ninth year. They watched me as if I were their baby. They enjoyed beings clean with a strong well-mannered appearance, hoping that a few soldiers from the skies would stop, and visit. Our continent is in the center of Emsky, and even though we had no flying machines, the four continents that surrounded us did. Therefore, they travel by the sea and air. Emsky considers us the ancestral land where life began. Thus, the other continents treated us as a shrine and never pestered us. We lived identical as our ancestors did for the preceding one thousand years. The main exception was that we had hospitals and medical clinics with doctors trained elsewhere. These foreign medical people lived in the places they work, never socially mingling with the Emskies. This was an Empire pre-requirement, which demands all people treated equally, fed, and clothed.

We are one of the few lucky solar systems in that we just one sun. Our nights reveal the two moons we have. One is larger than the other is, accordingly we have little moon and big moon. The night sky is packed with so many small lights we call stars. Even though we live as our predecessors, the great nations on Emsky have built schools throughout our continent. This is also a mandatory prerequisite for entry into the EGaSOJAF. They have as well landed many hydro construction machines for building new roads and bridges. We do not let it bother us too much, because everyone wants to join the great Empire. We live in the Durov kingdom, which includes all lands above the Yolkin River. I am still adjusting to school, as it does conflict with my playtime, yet it also gives us time away from Boyarov and a chance to meet other children, a few good, and many bad. Several of the boys in my class pestered me because of the extra attention from my sisters; nevertheless, I must live with this, because they are not going to change. Compared to the other girls in our school, my sisters are among the prettiest. Boyarov helps them with the face paints and material to make their dresses. Our parents also provide her with material to make my pants. I will not wear any pants Boyarov makes with her material. The boys at school would crucify me if I wore them. She knows about girls, but not boys. Fortunately, my sisters backed me on this issue, so she ended using her material for my pants. School has been always tough, yet when I got out of our class, my three sisters are there, and any boy they see pestering me; they put them against the wall. The first few times the teachers who witnessed this attempted disciplinary action; nonetheless, their efforts went in vain. My sisters argue hard with the school administer who called the teachers in and ordered them to maintain control over their classroom bullies.

My sisters were my life, while I still lived in our family home. They appeared as sweet angels when in social situations, yet when we got home, they become extremely industrious, searching for food and finding new ways to feed us. Our parents went to the hospital a few days ago. I guess this is why I began my story here, because this was my first major life change. My parents overworked their bodies ruining their health. The doctors would not tell us anything; therefore, we plead for Boyarov to ask on our behalf. She relayed to us that the situation is merely days currently until they depart us. This feels so wrong to me, in that if we were in the Empire now, they would be in their new bodies and all this meaningless work no longer needed, as one of the field machines can do the work of so many. Boyarov finds one of our priests to ask the hospital to permit us to see our parents. We are uneasy about the priests because they select children for their blood sacrifices. Blum informs Boyarov of her concerns for our lives. Boyarov tells her a secret, "One of the priests is her special friend, and they will keep us safe." They allow us into the room where my mother and father are. I have so seldom seen them in my life. My father always promised us he would have a prosperous year, which would give us a little family time and maybe even a pilgrimage to the ocean. Our father favored me over my sisters; nevertheless, our mother favored my sisters. Therefore, everything balanced itself, as my sisters and our father never had any common interests. Accordingly, our mother tried four times to produce a son for her husband, finally gaining success with my birth. She always told me I was her savior, rescuing her from enduring another pregnancy, which was hard on her as she continually worked in our rocky slopping mountain fields. We had no other relatives, because our parent's families condemned them for marrying. They fled from the eastern green lands into the mountains, crossing the Yolkin River to our current home, which they built. Our cabin was a simple one with a loft, which my sisters and I slept. I always rushed up first, braced myself against the wall, so they did not crowd around me, and pester me all night with their stupid girl talks.

The issue at hand now is the imminent death of our parents. Our village, Velem had a big place that they keep all the children without parents. Those kids also attended our school, and they did not appear happy. This was a great fear facing us now. Antipin cried to Boyarov in sorrow at this prospect. Boyarov told my sisters, they might live with her, but without me. My three sisters refused to live with her, unless she included me in the package. They even volunteered to share their food with me. My sisters threatened to surrender their bodies to the priests for them to sacrifice. Boyarov, in fear, believed them and thereby agreed to take them and me. She lived alone in a big house. We had never been on her second floor because we are afraid of what might be up there. Boyarov told us the upstairs was no place for little people. Now that we have a home to live in, we turned our attention back to our parents. The doctors gave them certain of their medicines to take away their pain, as they were on the pain drip currently, whatever that means. Boyarov told us it meant they would sleep until they stop breathing. My mind was confused, as I could hold nothing against my parents for dying on us. They wore themselves out to keep a home for our family to live. A little better luck would have been delightful, yet that was for the ages to decide. The priest came out to Boyarov and explained the situation. She told us it was, time to go to her house. Along the way, we stopped by cremators, as we burn all our dead, returning them to our air for their eternal freedom. We realize that once the Empire takes, control, and we lived in their bodies and we could no longer burn them. I believed this to be good, as I did not understand for sure if the dead felt the burning or not. It would be terrible if they did. Another gift from the Empire is that all our priests must stop their practice and convert to regular citizens. That would be wonderful, not having to worry whether their long knife will have my head under it next. We became so immune to these sacrifices, as our fear of the great winds and sky tunnels that destroyed everything in front of them gave us no other choice. They tied the child and gagged her and her mouth, not removing the gags until they had sliced their throats. The priests always took one boy and one girl; subsequently, they could mate in the land of spirits and gave the spirits children; I had heard. I am not going to worry about the sky, as we had a lot more to worry about in our lives. Boyarov took us to her house, and invited us upstairs. It was nighttime when we arrived, hence we were too afraid to go upstairs. She understood and dropped a number of her quilts from upstairs down her stairway. We camped out in her, or I guess now, our living room, the first night. So many times, we played and studied in this room.

Tonight, I did not rush to any corners, and bravely lay down among them, enjoying my protective hens as for a peculiar reason this felt safer with me among them. Life could be strange at times. Boyarov was not our typical Durovian, as she had a few modern (Andocs) devices in her house. One thing she had was small lights that she has placed throughout the house. She told us they ran off batteries she recharged by the sun. Accordingly, we had long ago promised never to tell any one of these special home machines, such as her sewing machine, she used to make our clothes. Actually, I saw these machines in our books at school, nevertheless; I pretended as if I had never seen one. Even if I told people I had seen them, they would believe me to be insane. Her machines allowed her to cook simpler and to clean her clothes easier. My sisters sang me a song to help me go to sleep. Blum did not appear as if she had slept much our initial night. I usually woke up throughout the night, and our first night; I saw her lying down with tears in her eyes. When I sat up, she quickly turned her head. I crawled over to her other side and whispered, "Do not turn your face Blum, or I will scream." She looked at me, and I asked her what was wrong. She told me she was worried about our future. She knows that Boyarov is elderly, yet healthy. Nevertheless, she lived by herself for a long time, and may not adjust to all of us here. She grabbed and pulled me up beside her, and we slowly drifted back to sleep. We will wait for the challenges to face us tomorrow, although a few new creeks and other strange noises left us packed tighter than two coats of paint in the morning. A stranger would never recognize that we were from the same family, because our personalities were as different from a night and a day. Even though, the one thing we knew was that we belonged together, and being the younger one, I always wanted them to remember this. The morning came as I feared, and we worked our way downstairs to the smell of eggs and bacon. I looked on the counter where she had also made bread and had a couple of jars of her preserves open beside it. There were five plates on the stand beside her. She looked at Blum and asked her if she helped her load the plates, then asked Antipin to pour the juice and for Dultsev to place the silverware. Antipin asked Boyarov if she wanted Sénye to do anything. She looked at me, as my heart stopped beating and awaiting a verbal beating, and said to put the cats and dogs outside, and remember to chain the dogs. I jumped, joyful as a skunk on Sunday, grabbed her two cats from their hiding place, pleased that they liked me, pet them, gave them cookie chunks I had in my pocket and told them to hide, because I was going to bring the dogs. The dogs were easy because they followed me everywhere when they were unchained. They knew that I had something to eat in my pocket. So I took out the remainder of my cookie and out the door we went, chained them said goodbye to them and my emergency food reserve.

When I went back inside, I went to Boyarov's water basin beside the front door and washed my hands. I then went back into the kitchen, when Boyarov yelled for me to come in front of her. My sisters froze as they stared at me. What did I do wrong? Boyarov grabs my hands and smells them. Her face changed from an expression of hate to a cheerful happy expression. She tells me a good job for washing my hands and then looks at my pants pockets. She smiles at me and says, "You gave them your cookies?" I shook my head yes, as she reached over to the cookie jar and grabbed two more and handed them to me. She looked at my sisters and told everyone to eat breakfast. My sisters rushed to me and thanked me for washing my hands. I knew these things were going to be different now; however, if I was going to live in a house with four females, I knew whom the bosses were; nonetheless, the last thing that I wanted to do was hurt my sisters. I did not care if the boys at school teased me anymore, when I saw my sisters, I gave them big hugs, and we always kissed on our cheeks. The boys in my grade would follow us, calling us names. We ignored them. Then one day, five of Blum's girlfriends joined us. The boys began to call them names and one threw a small rock at one of the girls. This was clearly the wrong move. Her boyfriend saw it, grabbed his friends, and they thump these pestering idiots with a big thrashing. The boys never bothered us again as my sisters learned something that day.

They learned that the boys who were always flirting with them could gain protection. Boyarov knew this all so well, especially in her dealings with the priests. Protection totally went so far, because, if thieves raided us, everyone was on their own. We simply did not think about these things and tried to live our lives in little Velem. Blum asked Boyarov about using boys for protection. Boyarov told everyone to sit. I got up to go out the door, when she called me back. Boyarov tells me that anything to do with protecting my sisters is also my business, no matter how corny. Boyarov began by telling my sisters, they must always appear beautiful. Around the house and on her farm, it was acceptable to come across normal, because, if someone came to call on them, we would intercept them while she spruced up herself. Boyarov continued by adding never give extra than a soft hug or allow more than a pliable kiss on your cheek, unless with each other or your brother. This shows them that you will love harder for those who are in your life. Once your school days and boarding university days are finished, then the rules change because you will no longer be obligated to appear daily. Blum looked at her and said boarding university days? Boyarov told them absolutely, that all four of us would attend the best universities the Durov had, which were located in our largest city named Storby, which sat on a large plateau in the mountains along the northern coast. We believed that city undefeatable as it sat so high in the sky. Even aircraft that would later fly over our continent would fly around this city. We never worried about attacks from other lands beyond the waters; we clearly worried about invasions from other kingdoms on our continent, and they could not enter our mountains because our forts were ready to crush the armies if needed. As for us, Boyarov stresses that we will attend the best universities. Afterwards, we will build new lives away from Velem.

Dultsev asks her what she will do. Boyarov tells us she will grow old and die. This angered me as I jumped and shocked everyone by saying, "We will not allow that!" Boyarov smiled at us and told us we were the best adolescents' people she ever met. Antipin reminds her that we are her junior people. A tear flows from her eye as she reaches out to hug us.

Dultsev asks her why we must attend the university. Boyarov explains that we need this to fit in with the fresh age that is coming on us. When the Durov rebuilt our new nation, they will depend on their educated to guide them. We will need this for our future. Antipin asks her if she went to a university. Boyarov tells us she went to the same one that she is sending us. We thanked her, even though not sold on this idea; we knew that other kids bragged about the future colleges they would attend. We agreed not to brag. We had never even dreamed of such an opportunity. Blum tells us these universities are so expensive, and that you must study hard to get in them; therefore, from this day forward, everyone does their homework and studies for tests. We looked at her knowing she was right and gave our oaths. Life with the one I once believed to be a witch turned out to be life changing. She had people who came to help us study and clean the house. One night while we were studying a large group of priests came to our house. This could definitely mean one thing. We listened to them talk through our floor vents, which allowed the downstairs heat to go upstairs. They handed her the paper that had both my name and Antipin's name on it. She then went into our dining room, removed her clothes, and laid on the table, while the priests enjoyed her for over two hours. When they finished, she put her robe back on, and they stood around her fireplace where one of the priests threw the paper into the fireplace. We could not believe the great sacrifice she made for us. Blum told us never to mention this to any one, because, if anyone found out, he or she would declare us all demons and burn us. Boyarov truly loved us, and we loved her so much more after that day. We strived to be the greatest children anyone could have and at the same time that her loyal friend. We never knew where she got all her money; it was just always there when we needed it. About ten years later, our first traumatic life experience hit our family.

Before this event, we had perfect lives. Blum, Antipin, and Dultsev were studying in the university, and I was scarcely one month before taking my entrance exams. Boyarov and I lived well together, although she spent more time away than previously. This did not bother me, as I spent all my time studying. She returned one night with the special foods she had traded. We feasted like kings this night, sang a few songs, talked about our lives. She consistently thanked us for staying with her. I constantly told her that soon she would be staying with us, as this is the cycle of our lives. That night our luck vanished as the largest gang of Pirates, we had ever heard of attacking Velem. These Pirates were different, in that they barely took a few possessions. The one possession they took was our most valuable one, our lives. They killed everyone in Velem, including the priests, and they burned the temples. Next, they began to search the countryside. Boyarov and I hid in her basement's secret room. We heard them search our house quickly and then departed. The next morning, Boyarov wanted to go outside and see what the Pirates stole. I told her to stay in the basement for another day, as there are usually smaller bands of thieves who loot after the Pirates had looted. She was headstrong and pushed me to the side running up the steps and going outside to see if we were safe. I may have been able to stop her; however, it would have involved a fight. Instead, I kept the trapdoor open slightly high enough for me to see if she were to come running back into me. She did not return, and silence ruled our secluded ranch. I slowly and noiselessly walked around our home peeking through the sides of the windows scanning our yard. I saw both our dogs sitting beside the body of my love mother. They lightly tapped their tales. I thereby realized that she was dead and with the dogs being quiet, the area was clear. I walked outside, picked up her body, and walked over to a flowerbed that we loved dearly. Afterwards, I picked up a shovel and buried her in the ground. My heart would not allow me to cremate her; she loved this ranch and as such; I wanted her always to remain on it. I spent the next few days in tears, and then five days later a group of men, dressed in suits came to our house riding in large carriages. I had a sword that Boyarov had given me that she claimed belonged to her father. I vowed that the next who came here to steal would die.

The carriages stopped in front of our grand porch. I rushed out with my sword and put it to the neck of the first man who stepped on our ground. I told them that any who tried to steal or kill will die. The man tells me they have no weapons are here to visit with Boyarov. I point to our flowerbed where the dogs are lying and tell them I buried her there. Displaying their extreme wisdom, they ask me to show them where I buried her. They commend me on the excellent wood carving message of love that I placed on a stick above her grave and watch me pet the dogs. Accordingly, they pay their respects and ask if we can talk in the house. After they set at the table, I pour each of them, a cup of Boyarov's favorite tea, and soon join them. The men explain that Boyarov had established a plan that if she did not appear before them once each week, they were to visit her ranch and check how things were. I explain that if she were not so headstrong and committed to keep me a boy, she would still be alive. They chuckle, explaining they were surprised at my size from all the stories she told them, yet they suspected I had to be older, as she had set up the funds for my university. The men explain that she had a will and that once the police verified her body was in the grave I had shown them; they would open the will and read it to me. I asked them that since all the police and priests who knew her from Velem are dead, how can someone identify her except for them? They tell me the police in their village, which was one day away, recognized her, and would come to name her. I was reluctant about disturbing her rest; nevertheless, the men insisted these were her rules to protect her family. I reveal to them that I did not realize she had a family. They glance at me and qualify by saying my sisters and I. The police came a few days later and verified the body. After this, a few men came to take me to the men's village for the reading of her will. I never understood wills or legal things. I believed in squatters' rights, meaning who lived in a place owned it. Nevertheless, she will give everything to the four of us. Her father had left her a lucrative business that had a solid income flow. This was plenty for us to survive. They asked me if I wanted to sell her ranch, and we told them this was our home, the place we lived, loved, and occasionally cried. My sisters were also at the funeral. We agreed that this money would allow us to live together on the ranch, and as we married, we would divide the land and buy adjoining lands hoping someday to have four larger ranches. We knew the land was cheap now, so we told one of the administrators what we wanted to do, and he did it all for us. We divided the ranch into four squares, with the house belonging to none of the squares. We shared the house. We could purchase much cheaper land surrounding it and began building a large wooden wall to fortify it.

I told my sisters that no Pirates would raid us again. While building the wooden wall, several military men who were now civilians offered to build us large stone covered walls with wooden fighting positions on top of them, in exchange for a little land. We purchased land for them and kept this land inside our fort. Extra defenders were always welcomed. The walls were finished as I graduated from the university in Storby. They planted thistle bushes and berry patch along the outside of the wall, making it difficult for someone to climb the fifteen-foot walls from the ground. We had no gates, just one wide underground tunnel laced with knife-springs, razor floors, and that we could flood with water, which we could activate if needed. I knew that the Pirates would return someday, they were waiting for our town to rebuild. Ten of the original priests has escaped the primary raid and set up a new temple. They did not bother us, for the most part, because we wore robes to the priesthood in Storby, and openly declared the local priests to be false. Nevertheless, they missed having their clutches and privates in Boyarov and her wealth. One night the priests came to visit us and demanded that we pay the overdue donations. We refused. They threatened to tell the local people that we had placed a curse on them. This would cause them to attack us immediately. I calmly sat down and began reading a few parts of Boyarov's diaries. I then showed them her financial records where she recorded her donations and asked them if their records matched. I told them not to get any ideas, because we had copies of these journals in two other villages with the instructions in our wills that they be published, in a newspaper, we owned, if any of us were to die unexpectedly. I recommended that they keep guards with us to make sure any strange accidents did not happen. We never paid this one penny. Additionally, we seldom traded in Velem and if we did, we had the soldiers' trade on our behalf. We had our businesses ship us our supplies.

The one thing we discovered that was missing was potential spouses. Our creativity would not hold us back. Antipin and Dultsev lured a few university boyfriends to marry them. Blum was the restless one, and one day returned to Storby to live the remainder of her life. Surprisingly, she never married, nevertheless, was not lacking in the attention of men. I always pictured her as a copy of Boyarov. Now came the part that had Orosházi attention and interest. She knew this story, yet wanted to see how I presented it. I had to tell the story of my wife Estse and the two sons and our daughter. Estse was unlike any, I had ever met before this time. One day, I was riding along the road that led to the hills behind our ranch that I enjoyed hunting. While riding in the solemn still of a forest, the sound of a woman screaming filled the cool air. I leaped from my horse, pulled out my long sword and rushed down the small slopes in front of me, where there stood two men beating the unclothed woman. Diving in midair, I struck the head of the first man and then rolled quickly from the ground to my feat lunging forward stabbing the second man in his heart. As the men's bodies hit the ground, the terrified woman began begging for mercy. I motioned to her to relax, bent over and picked up her torn gown, and tossed it to her telling her to put it back on now. After she redressed, I asked her what she was doing in the forest and her name. She identified herself as Estse, telling me that her parents brought her here from a story where a woman named Blum wanted them to settle outside her family ranch. She gave them a deed and a letter to show her family for lodging while they settled. I asked her for those papers. Surprisingly, she handed them over to me. I looked at them, and they were in order. I then placed them in my pocket. She begged me to give the papers back to her. I revealed my identity to her and told her I would escort her parents and her back to the ranch. Estse began to cry, revealing the two thieves killed her parents.

I guided her back to my horse and took her back to our ranch, first stopping and showing her the new farm that Blum had purchased for them. It was a peaceful sloping slightly forested 200-acre farm with a few streams flowing through it. There was an old stone house and animal buildings that needed mending. I took her to our ranch house and introduced her to Antipin, Dultsev and their husbands. She relaxed with my sisters, and we began the healing process with the burial of her parents beside Boyarov. She was slightly taller than my sisters were, although a few inches shorter than I was. We had plenty of time on our hands around the ranch, and with both of my sisters now playing matchmakers, we found ourselves doing many couple activities, which seemed natural as there were three boys and three girls. I enjoyed not feeling like the odd man out, in that if I agreed with the boys, my sisters were mad, and if I agreed with my sisters, their husbands were angry with me. Now I could stick with the boys, as the three girls would argue back. I had to admit this was enjoyable. Even so, I also learned that I had to support Estse or she would give a cold shoulder. I learned about another relationship form with women, moving from sisters to mating. The mating relationship was not as easy that with sisters, because fighting with the sisters was fun, and I just could not be comfortable in fighting with Estse. I found myself apologizing and bribing to regain her friendship. It took little time to learn the things she enjoyed and the things that she opposed strongly. I pretty much knew her boundaries from the four years of university study in Storby. We were fortunate enough that Blum had done the prescreening before she sent her family to live beside us. Estse was hurt over the loss of her parents, yet we knew that was life in all Durov, except Storby. Although Storby did not have raiders, they still had the thieves, rapists, and murderers. They were more secretive in their strikes. Something was happening on our family ranch that was putting music in the air.

We began doing many activities together and avoiding the couples' activities. We needed a little time to blend our personalities and form our partnership. She enjoyed riding our horse once I shared the special techniques to fine-tune her new style. We spent two years together during the days. Her priests forbid her to sleep with a man unless first married. Every night, I tried to convert her to our local temple, as I did not even care about any back due donations. She stood strong to her beliefs to my misfortune. Either way, she always behaved as a woman, and we treated her as such. We talked concerning our entire lives; to my disadvantage, she knew so much regarding my life. Blum told her everything about my existence. I did not mind this because it told me I had a solid shot in a relationship with her. This was an age of questions, and Estse was a leader in this new style. She would not merely ask questions, but also answer questions. She was so great at seeing the real topic under investigation. Finally, after two years, she agreed to be my wife. I have already built our home; even though the sisters wanted me to stay in Boyarov's house, we needed something new. We never argued; I knew what she wanted, and she knew what I wanted. We worked as a team with one mind, and one goal. Our two sons and daughter gave us a new hope in life. Who needed air or water when a home packed with love and life encircled them? The mountains would vanish from us, and the streams dried up when the family was together as one. We enjoyed nature, especially Estse who had grown up in Storby. We would bundle up and go camping for weeks at a time. My sisters never worried when they did not see us around our ranch, they knew we were exploring the area. One day, our luck ran out as a gang of thieves and murders now from Velem robbed and killed my family. I was hunting at the time, and although it took me, three years to track down all eight of the killers, and for each chopped off their heads and buried them at the feet of my family. We believed that with their heads removed and placed at the feet of those they murdered the land of the dead would torment them for eternity. After I completed my revenge, the ranch haunted me day and night, therefore, one day; I got on my horse and rode. I rode from town to town throughout Durov, yet somehow the thought of another Durovian I would scream endlessly.

Therefore, I rode to the western green lands along the great sea, and went south out of the Durov Kingdom and into the Kharmats Kingdom. The Kharmats were darker than we were because of the hot sun. I, accordingly, lay in the grass and tanned within a few days. Then I explored the Kharmats Kingdom. They tended to themselves, and I kept my nose to myself. No one waved when passing. I knew about these customs from my university days, although sometimes strangely I would know. I always believed this was from having seen others do it and at the last second having it click in my mind. These were how they detected foreigners. Those who did not understand their culture would identify themselves through their awkward actions. I almost waved a few times, but at the last minute, something pulled my hand down. I ate solely fish, knowing the king had laws against hunting his beasts. I wonder if the fish was what this bird craved, and if this kept my lone trustful companion, a black raven who would sit afar and stared at me, on a tree nearby. Each day, he would appear. Soon I would toss the parts of the fish I could not eat. Subsequently, I hid in the day and walked at night. Finally, in the fall, I crossed the border from Kharmats into Chadov. The Chadov had many of the identical customs that we had. At one time, we were part of the same kingdom; however, the king had two sons who laid, claim to the throne on his death. To prevent war, the kingdom divided with the new kingdom called Chadov. I often worried how troubled my sisters must be suffering, not knowing where I was. My clothes were worn and dirty now, as was I. This kingdom was so similar that many times I felt as if I had walked here before somehow. I thought that this land was part of my past existence. Since I had never been below the Yolkin River, as forbidden by my parents who told me they had too many bad memories of their earlier life. One night, while I was sleeping in a tree, the owner of the land spotted me, with his spear stabbed, and killed me. What I had thought would be a long, comfortable, happy life turned out to end, tired, sad, and hungry. I decided that I could have nothing, because anything I had, someone who wanted it without earning it, would kill and take it. I noticed the same fears when I talked with those from Kharmats and Chadov. Things have stabilized just slightly now with the new schools and hospitals; however, the kings needed to protect the people, and they did not want to pay to provide this security. They could not see that this fear was holding back productivity, which I what produced the wealth they took in taxes. Durov beginnings had constantly been a mystery to all who lived on the island, as one year's tales of great dragon fighters from the skies settled here first, then the next week, it would be a couple from the sun with the flying woman. It was invariably something strange and unbelievable. I was curious myself to see the history of Durov, yet first it was my turn to see Orosházi dance on the needles. Shame filled me now, as I looked at her and remembered that I had loved once before, yet as destiny took my Estse, destiny gave me Orosházi.

The window new revealed a stream from a world I had not before witnessed. Orosházi removes the mystery by welcoming me to Jaroslaw. The world is much larger than Emsky, with a geographical layout unlike any, I had seen previously. They had just one continent that sloped slowly to one giant mountain, which covered the center lands. Most of the people lived around the seacoast, which ironically went nowhere except in a huge circle. I saw this planet as arranged logically and consistently. Her family was wealthy and among the aristocrats, routinely lending money to their crown. Orosházi was a speedster, both with her long legs and with her powerful wings. She was popular with her classmates and teammates. A competitive athlete, her teams enjoyed many extra wins because of her efforts. Orosházi was loyal to her close friends and immediate family members. She socialized with no one else, mainly as required by her social position and class rules. Jaroslaw was a regimented closed society and class lines were not crossed. Just the lowest two classes could marry as they wished. The upper two classes could not marry whom they wished, as all marriages were prearranged. Love for the upper classes was specifically with immediate family and pets. They did not believe nor want love between the husband and wife in these classes. These women did not reproduce, as most had their reproductive organs removed when they were born, and those who did not have them removed at marriage. The Jaroslaw upper class had a special breed of human females they used for reproduction. During one of her successful seasons, they were playing an important regional game she was resting before the game in her room. A group of wicked came in her room and kidnapped her. They hid her in the hygiene tunnels under the city and kept her for the remainder of that season, when they released her. She never again played sports, but in turn prepared for a future as a home administrator for the man the king assigned to her. The king favored Orosházi because of her sport's heroics and could capture her kidnappers. He burned them in the royal courtyard with their parents. Orosházi met her new husband officially, as the king's family administrators explained their official roles. The king had them assigned to his showcase city, region, which was to display the perfect harmony lifestyle. He created a place where others would strive and sacrifice to be a part.

Orosházi's husband was one who did not enjoy conforming. He had secret habits that he learned from a servant friend, such as the ways of the women of the night and the joys of spirit waters. Her husband would send her to her parent's home for the weekend and invite his carnal associates as they disgraced their home and her name. She did not realize that so many pitied or mocked her. Orosházi shows us a day when her friends told her what was happening in her home. Her friend had the home streams at which time Orosházi fed them to the king and went into hiding. She remembers seeing a black raven staring at her from a tree in the horizon. Sympathizers for her disgrace connected her with the cargo freights who gave her safe transport to another trading galaxy, where they offered her a position as a researcher on a deep-space exploration vehicle. When they arrived at her first planet research station, the institution requested for her assignment from their command. They granted Orosházi assignment. A few years later, she soon once again grew restless, complaining that something out there was calling her. One night she was sleeping in her room when a black raven appeared at her window. The ravens were not indigenous to the planet she was working; therefore, she went outside to trace this strange phenomenon. She followed the bird along a shallow creek bed, then up to a lightly snow covered barren hillside with a tiny grass hut on the top, under a tree. The raven went inside the hut through a minuscule window. Orosházi went inside the hut and fell into a deep sleep. When she awoke, she found herself chained in a small cage, where she remained for what she believes was four months. Then one day, she awoke floating in the space around Emsky. She had dreamed of a death, yet did not believe it was true. Unfortunately, Orosházi discovered quickly how hostile this new place was. Each day, she continued to battle and win, yet hauntings of a belief something special that belonged to her would soon arrive continued. When the new souls floated up from the world below, she would inspect them. Inspection was no more than a quick scan, even though she did not recognize what she was searching for, her subconscious knew. Boring days followed, as she had mastered survival in this child's game as she labeled it. I had scanned her life during our light exchanges and still wondered what was in her locked rooms. Nothing she revealed today gave me a reason to believe that she had suffered any additional traumatic events. Therefore, I asked her what was in her secret rooms. Orosházi turned to me and asked what was in my secret room. I told her there were no hidden rooms in me. Pankrati confirms that I have a clandestine room and put it in our window and asks for my permission to open this door. I am confused about this mysterious room, yet there it is before my eyes. Confused, I tell her to open this strange door. She clarifies with me if I am sure. This begins to worry me, what could be inside such a boring person as I am that would be a danger? In my hand appears a key that I give to Pankrati. She goes to the door and unlocks it. The room changed to a bright purple, and the stream in the window revealed a new world.

Moreover, on this world, an enormous war covered all the lands, as explosions sounded everywhere as deafening thunderstorms. We could hear people screaming and see them falling from tall buildings. Strangely, they also ejected from aircraft, as the plane would then become invisible. A dark black smoke covered all the land. Next, we saw a huge rocket ship launch into the air, shooting straight for the sky. As it reached the orbit, it began releasing giant bombs, which increased in size as they came closer to the surface. These enormous bombs crashed into the planet's surface, causing it to shatter into large loose rocks. The planet no longer existed as a whole, but as an ocean of meteors. Then from the meteors, we saw three small ships appear racing to stay ahead of them. The meteors crashed into one of the ships. Shortly thereafter, a meteor scraped the side of another ship. The craft struggled to maintain speed, nevertheless, continued to lose its speed until meteors crashed from behind it, destroying it. One ship remained, and on this ship, were two women and one man. They executed many astute moves outmaneuvering the blistering meteors that were chasing from behind them. Each minute, the meteors were beginning to slow while the small craft continued to gain speed. The first two hours were the dangerous ones, yet soon it was evident the crew would survive on this small ship. They were confused not knowing where to go or how to survive. While flashing toward the outside their galaxy, a bandit ship locked them in its beams and pulled them onto their ship. On arriving, the man began firing his laser weapon, killing the three guards of the loading dock, yet not before they executed one of the women. The remaining man and woman disabled the cameras and began for the upper deck, which was the next deck to this two-deck ship. When they arrived in the control room, an exchange of fire lead in a winner takes all battle. The man and woman killed four of those on the deck, while in the last few minutes of the fire exchange, the second female fell to her death. Now, solely the man remained on this intergalactic ship. He scanned their charts and programmed a course to one of the smaller out of the normal route's galaxy. As he sat in the captain's seat, alone on this large ship, the window focused the stream now on his face. The face we saw put a silence on our faces, as we sat there in a deep shock. Something was wrong here.

I set up in my seat. Orosházi looks at me and asks, "Who is that man who resembles you?" I tell her I have no idea. Orosházi asks me how I can have no idea of something in my room. I just gawk at her puzzled. Pankrati asks her to relax, that she will reveal the answers. I find myself astounded in watching someone who appears as me flying a giant ship throughout the universe. The stream once again begins. The ship is now flashing through space, zipping pass galaxies as if they are still. This Pirate ship is among the fastest in this quadrant of the universe. They fine-tuned it for speed; they needed for fast escapes after their raids. The pilot, whom they call by my name, Sénye records a diary of each day's activities. He calls himself Sénye, which sends a chill down my back. I am looking at myself, from so long ago in the ages accordingly in the far past cripples my stomach. I sense sweat profusely dripping down my face. My hand trembles, Pankrati pats me on my shoulder and whispers for me to relax. She knows the future; therefore, if she is telling me to calm down, I then release my tension and decide to discover my history with these two wonderful female spirits. I stress the two and females, so I can better define the completeness of Pankrati's support owning the higher humanity standards the women tend to endorse. Sénye packed all the dead Pirate bodies into boxes he had emptied. The Pirates stored their stolen booty in these boxes, supposedly for future sale, as if they already had buyers. He released these boxes into space without any words. Sénye next programmed the ship's heading and proceeded in a straight vertical course. He believed this would make all who were searching for the ship an equal distance of a safety zone would exist. At least, he would not be rushing into unknown enemy's ambush. He wrapped the female body of his comrade who lost her life in the battle for this ship in a fine linen and put her in a vacuumed sealed room. Sénye planned to bury her in his new home. The vacuum room was to delay her body decaying. Sénye continued flashing through space until one day a strange creature came flying through his ship. This creature was a black raven, a species of bird that was extinct on his world. Sénye guessed the bird was a stole way or a mascot for the Pirates. The bird would always land, its droppings on a certain spot on his guidance screen. The first time, he did not notice it; however, the second, third, fourth, and fifth time convinced him something was happening. Sénye reprogrammed his course to this spot, which he located the specific planet that the bird had repeatedly identified. Once he was in orbit around this planet, the bird vanished. He ran scans for any life forms, and could find no human, yet another type of human related form of being. His panel flashes while also locking in on this target. Sénye lands the ship on a plateau speckled with a few trees. The panel alarm continues until he drives the ship pass a small grass hut. Something inside is driving his panel crazy.

Sénye gets out and enters the hut, finding a woman laying on her belly with her four wings resting on her back. She is in a deep sleep. There is the water and a kind of soup beside her. He looks around as this identifies that something else could be around here. As he is searching, the black raven appears again, flying into his ship, then out once more. Sénye believed this meant for him to take the woman and leave. He carried her body into the ship, placing her in one of the private chambers. He then took his former shipmate's body, and placed her in the hut. Soon, he was once more in orbit and flashing out of this galaxy and on straight horizontal course. Sénye believed if any were searching for him, his lead was great enough he could pass horizontally pass them and then on a course that they could never track for eternity. His calculations were accurate, as his posy never found him, nor even the quadrant, he was. He soon discovered that his sole battle was not outside the ship, but also within it. The woman woke up in her chamber and began screaming for better clothing. He explained to her the lone female clothing they had was from one of the Pirate's mistresses. She designed her wardrobe for a specific service. The woman comes out to the ship's deck wrapped in towels, telling the ship's pilot that she does not perform those services. Orosházi now sits beside me with a strange stare on her face. She asks Pankrati if this is true. Pankrati asks her if she may open one of her remaining two doors. Orosházi hands her a key. She asks Pankrati if she will tell her what is in that one. Pankrati reveals to her that the room has the same story as Sénye's room. They cover the same period and events, except for a few minor exceptions. Orosházi takes hold of my hand and asks me what I think about the likelihood that we had met previously. I tell her that somehow it makes sense because the way we bonded was too complete. I explain that she scanned millions if not billions of spirits and miraculously and instantaneously selected me. One peek and spending eternity at my side standing in front of large groups of spirits declaring an everlasting love did not hit me right. I confess to her that this is the part, which is strange. Orosházi retreats behind a serious expression and tells me that she hopes she was not easy as the first time.

Pankrati reveals that our first meeting was extremely different. Orosházi looks at me and confesses the joy in her heart that our love may truly be predisposed. She asks Pankrati to begin the show once more. Orosházi throws an armful of the special clothing the ship's mystery woman had on, at Sénye. Sénye tells her to pick up the garments and to put them on, or he will remove her from this ship. She asks him where they are, and Sénye tells her that he has no idea. If he had known she was such a wicked troublemaker, he would have shot that black raven that guided him to her. Orosházi stairs with confusion all over her face at him; nevertheless, does not say a word. The part about the black raven had her confused. I ask Pankrati about this black raven that I have as well had seen. The Orosházi who is sitting beside me also expresses her curiosity concerning this mystery bird. Pankrati tells us to relax, and the window will explain everything. There is a proper time and place for certain information revealed. We nod our heads in agreement, and our windows begin once more. Orosházi puts on the revealing outfit as ordered by Sénye. Sénye glances quickly to verify her compliance and then tells her to wrap the towels around her once again, and go to her chamber, remove that outfit, and if she cannot find anything, use the towels, with fasteners. Orosházi at first was so humiliated while standing in front of a common or unquestionably lower class man revealing what she had always believed to be private. The humiliation turned to anger when he simply glanced at her and then told her to redress. Men were supposed to react different from what this mad beast had acted. She returned to her chambers, found underwear that had enough designs in it that truly, a woman would recognize what it was; nevertheless, it hid what she wanted it to hide. If this lower-class monster thought, he was her master, he was playing a game that she was going to change the rules and win.

She came back out to the deck, as Sénye smiled at her and told her he had hoped she would select that pair of underwear, as it is so stimulating. Orosházi walks in a sexy style pass Sénye and asks him what he would comprehend about stimulation. She walks pass him and sits in the chair beside him. Sénye asks her who gave her the right to sit in that chair. She looks around at chairs counting, saying, zero, zero, zero, and one-half or sissy, and afterwards pointing at herself says, one. She scratches her throat and after that says, one and one-half, or one woman and one sissy. That idiot is what says this seat is mine. I forbid you ever sitting in it. Sénye stands up, grabs her hand, flings her to the floor, and sits in that seat. Orosházi instantaneously leaps into the captain's chair laughing, while saying, "It works on idiots every time." Sénye tells her that he was getting ready to move to another seat as she was coming onto the deck. Orosházi tells him there is no reason in the universe that he would give up that seat. He tells her that various odd sorts of peculiar space mites were biting his behind. Sénye tells her he has the special salve that can heal these sores, as long as they did not go up his anus. He smiles and tells her how lucky that he is simply to have to drive these long skinny two-headed mites out of one hole. Orosházi jumps screaming that one of them just bit her. Sénye plays cool and explains that it must have been the thin underwear, which allowed them to penetrate so fast. Sénye he tells her it may be too late unless emergency penetration of the salve is applied. He pulls out a glove from a drawer beside his seat and a small jar of the specific sort of lotion. She begs him to tell her what she must do. He explains that I might be embarrassing to her, and that it probably would be better to allow them to destroy her insides. Orosházi tells him that nothing is embarrassing. He tells her that if he uses his finger to trap the mites on this glove and if they bite his finger she will owe him extra work as compensation. She agrees. He tells her to remove her panties, bend over, and brace both hands on the railing in front of our seats. Sénye asks her to promise him that if it hurts, she will forgive him. She agrees. He asks her if she wants him to do a little exploratory penetration first to see how high the infestation is. She begs him to do so.

He rubs a little of the salve around both of her private holes and tells her that he had good and bad news. Orosházi begs him for the news. Orosházi tells her that the anus is okay, but he can see the tracks of one into her other entry point. He thinks he can get in there and chase him out. Orosházi begs him to hurry. He inserts his finger moving it around, and other sporadic movements, occasionally saying she thinks he got it running. He asks her how it feels. She tells him that it does not hurt as if she thought it would. Sénye tells her that the lighting is not good from where he is, and they need to shift to their left. She scoots over and tells him to hurry and get this beast inside her. Sénye sits in the captain's seat, plays with her for a little while longer, and then tells her he got it, and she will live. Orosházi spins around, and leaps on him, kissing him, and thanking him for saving her. A few minutes later, she stands back up in front of him and puts back on her underwear. Then something hits Orosházi as she notices Sénye is sitting in the captain's seat and warns him believing he forgot. He smiles at her, wiggles his finger, and comments, "It works every time." Orosházi becomes extremely angry, telling him he has violated her and destroyed her dignity. Sénye reminds her that she called him an idiot and tricked him out of the captain's seat first. Orosházi argues that what she did should not have warranted rape. Sénye tells her that he purely did what she begged him to do. He further tells her not to be embarrassed, as he will not tell the crew. She reminds him that they have no crew. Sénye tells her then she has no need to worry about anyone finding out how easy she is. Orosházi begins crying, telling him that he is the first and single man that has ever been inside her. She runs off the deck.

Sénye has begun to rethink about the prank he just pulled. It was a common prank that they pulled when meeting new female warriors. He had assumed that with her athletic fine-tuned body, which she would have been the one all her species males would have wanted and competed to receive. He goes to the lower deck and stands by her doorway. Sénye tells her he is sorry and asks how he can redeem her honor. She reports that marriage would be the lone solution; however, she would never marry him. Her life is ruined. Sénye tells her that technically, her life is not ruined. He asked her if a doctor had ever examined her down there. She confirms that they have on many occasions. Orosházi reveals that they were examining her to remove her reproductive parts, which they usually removed when she married; however, she had many internal sports-related injuries that they wanted to heal first before removing these organs. Sénye tells her that he merely put his finger in her, and not the part that would have defiled her. He tells her she is nonetheless, clean, and he promises never to report this to anyone, because even though he does not like her, he still does not want to hurt her. Orosházi stops crying and appears to be thinking particularly serious thoughts. She looks at Sénye and asks him to tell her how she compared, as a question she could never ask her doctors. Sénye smiles at her and tells her that he was especially impressed with how well developed, strong, healthy, and clean that entire area was. He would honesty evaluate it as being clearly among the most elite. Orosházi smiles at him and says thanks, because she is from an elite class and if she was anything lower, her life would be shameful. Sénye invites her to the food generator room, where they can load up the food and have a party on the deck. Neither Orosházi nor Sénye are familiar with the Pirate's cuisine and punch in small bite sized samples before ordering their meal. They soon wiggle through it, select the water, and take their meals up to the deck, where Sénye offers Orosházi the captain's seat. She smiles and tells him that seat is his, and anyway she would like to sit in the seat where he bent her over and thrilled the strange man who hides in this ship. Sénye asks her if she at least just a little enjoyed it. Orosházi tells him she was worried about her life and therefore that took away any possibility of an erotic experience.

Sénye smiles at her and then asks whether she will explain the part about having a husband. Orosházi explained how the upper classes were married on Jaroslaw. Sénye said revealed that his world stood filled with war, and thus none was given in marriage. Each day to remain alive was a victory, most days spent with burying those who died the previous day. That was a great priority to keep down any widespread of diseases. The foods from the homes of the dead they distributed to the hungry along with their weapons. This was an ideological war; thereby no one knew who his or her enemies were. They were invisible and among them. An enemy who could walk beside you and in an instant drive a knife through your heart left all in constant fear and mistrust. Sénye was fortunate in that all warring sides feared invasion from the other worlds and established a combined space protection force. They staffed these ships with members of all ideological divisions and guarded their world. When the ending massive bombs were unleashed and the planet began to fall apart, a command came to flee the solar system. When the final explosions shattered his formatter world, they made their escape attempt. His ship was the lone ship of his small fleet to make it. Sénye knows there were three other fleets, yet has no status about how they fared. Sénye and Orosházi sat in their respective seats looking at the screen of space before them. Orosházi asked him if he knew anything about all these other empty seats. Sénye told he had not investigated them yet. She jumped and began exploring the other panels, occasionally making insignificant adjustments. Sénye eagerly asked her to explain each adjustment, which were for unimportant things such as temperature control and lighting intensities. Sénye offered no argument not caring about such minor details. Within one day, Orosházi understood enough about the controls properly to control the ship. Orosházi remarked how happy she was to comprehend the controls of her ship. Sénye argues that it is his ship, and because of his mercy, he is allowing her to stay. He fought for the ship and not giving up his rightful claim to it.

Orosházi explains to him that the black raven gave her a claim to this ship and that when he brought her aboard, and enjoyed her privates that gave her a rightful claim to this ship. Sénye tells her that she is making valid points, and that he would rather share this ship with her than to be on it alone. Orosházi tells Sénye that she will share the ship with him, so she will have someone to watch the deck when she sleeps, but that she would rather have the ship alone than share it with one who has such a low regard to the purity of a woman. Sénye tells her that true purity does not seek opportunities for impurity. He sees a tear begin to form in his eye and quickly adds this ship is consequently, lucky to have one who is so pure, without blemish such as hers. Orosházi sighs the relief and explains that she feared he would say she was impure. Sénye explains that he has no evidence of such an impurity, unless she wishes to provide him this. Orosházi slaps him and declares that she may not be able to ship break him. She tells him that it is time for her sleep. She will return in a few hours. He agrees and returns to reading the ship's logs, which are boring yet informative. This taught him much about the diversity, and complexity of the colonies and kingdoms spread throughout their vast territory, which was far away and would have no true benefit for him here. What it gave him was a feeling for other people and how interacted. He felt this could help him make decisions concerning and predicting future encounters. They continued to flash through the universe; both deciding that what was behind them ought to be as far back as possible. Something was happening in their ship, and that something was not what they truly wanted. They grew apart from each other, going days at a time without talking. Then one day, Sénye's monitor alerted him of a living creature drifting in space. He slowed the ship and discovered a small ship. Sénye received an emergency call from the ship and locked his scans pulling the ship's crew of one to his loading dock. He grabbed a weapon and greeted this newcomer. She was laying on the floor, her feet bound by tree roots. Her skin was green and hair that flowed beyond her feet. She had no clothing, with slightly flowers attached throughout her hair. Sénye asked her for her name. She reveals to him that her name is Be'SuD. She refuses to tell where she is from, telling Sénye that even if she told him, he would not be able to find it. She begins to tell him her shocking story, which Sénye pauses her.

Sénye sneaks into Orosházi's chamber and retrieves the female underwear; taking it back and having Be'SuD put them on herself.

First, she animatedly refuses. Sénye asks her why she would refuse this. Be'SuD explains that those who hide their skin on her world go to prison. Sénye reminds her that her world is way out there in a place we cannot find, and she is on this ship now and will follow this ship's laws. Be'SuD tells him that there are just two on this ship, and that I should be considerate of other people's customs. Sénye reports to her there are three people on this ship, and the other one is a female like her. Sénye continues by telling her that if catches her exposing those different parts, she will be deadly angry; therefore, it is two against one. Sénye tells her that to be honest, he wishes she would win, yet the moral thing is for her to put the underwear on until they can prepare something better. Be'SuD agrees to comply, for the sake of harmony. They go to sit down on the deck; she goes to the copilot's seat. Sénye enjoyed this respect. He took her to the food generator and feed her. Oddly, she was familiar with a few of the foods. She explained this by how mobile the Pirates were that they most likely collected foods that come from the collections of others. Sénye figured that somehow this made sense, in that she said it so calmly he could not form a logical argument against it. Accordingly, Sénye asked her about the roots that they had to cut from her feet. Be'SuD tells him the roots were to keep her in that ship and that if anyone cut them from inside the ship, the ship would have exploded. His scanners must have found the safe separation points. Sénye tells her that the scanners may have suppressed the explosion back on itself. The Pirates primarily designed their equipment for battle conditions. Sénye continues by questioning why he found her treed to a small space ship drifting in the middle of space. Be'SuD explains that she is a political prisoner. Her father was a high-level government official when their government fell to the rebels. They exiled her forever to drift in space and never again to be free. Sénye smiles at her and remarks that we must have ruined their plans. They sit there laughing and telling each other stories about their lives. The room suddenly grew still as the balance shifted.

Coming on the deck with a strange expression appeared Orosházi. She asked Sénye who our new crewmate was. Sénye told her to ask the newcomer. Orosházi stared at Be'SuD and asked her for her name. Be'SuD looks at her and refuses to talk. Orosházi asked her again, and moved toward her. Be'SuD firmly braces herself and blocks Orosházi advance. Sénye tells both to sit down now. Orosházi leaps into the copilot's seat, while Sénye gets up to go get a little rest on the lower deck. Orosházi notices that Be'SuD is following him. She asks Sénye where he is going. He tells her to sleep. Orosházi asks Sénye why the green thing is following him. Be'SuD explains to her that green things always sleep with the master of the ship. Orosházi yells out that Sénye is not the master and that this ship has no master. Be'SuD wraps her arm around Sénye and asks him, "Master, where shall we sleep?" Sénye points to the steps and they walk off the deck. As they leave the deck, Orosházi throws one of her bracelets at them, hitting the wall above the door and yells out, "At least I have values." Be'SuD tells her to keep her values because she has the valuable. Sénye does not tell Orosházi that Be'SuD had no genitals. They had yet to discuss the reproduction process, as Sénye thought that not to be an appropriate topic for a first meeting. Her breasts were the same, so somehow it was connected. Sénye was wondering about this sleep deal. He figured that he would offer her a sleeping space in one of the two spare rooms. This felt lucky to have four rooms. Sénye enthusiastically shows her the room next to his. He knows not to show the room next to Orosházi. Be'SuD smiles at Sénye and asks him if he is one of the low intelligent models of his species. Sénye tells her he is actually an extremely intelligent model of his species and quizzes her about why she asked this question. Be'SuD asks him what part of her sleeping beside the master of the ship he did not understand. Sénye tries to explain that in his culture sleeping together is a symbol of love and devotion.

Be'SuD tells Sénye that these are more of their foolish customs. She begins laughing and calling all Sénye's people fools when he explains that sometimes, they have no clothing on when they sleep. Be'SuD tells him that is when the person needs their clothing the most, to stay warm from the cold. She gives Sénye a choice; he must her grant either to have freedom from clothing or to sleep beside him; however, she has a right to one. Sénye tells her to take a few blankets from the spare room and for them to set things up for their sleep. They snuggle together and after Sénye removed Be'SuD's loose hair from his face, they fall to sleep. Approximately eight hours later, Orosházi comes in and dumps the cold water on them while declaring it was time for work. Sénye complains that the cold water was going overboard on the waking them up for nothing. His duty was not for another four hours. Orosházi tells him that the intensity they were sleeping told her that they were exhausted from something the previous night. Be'SuD tells her that they were just warming up for their big event that the next rest period. Sénye pretends to stretch his back and comments that he might not survive this succeeding round without many serious injuries. Orosházi calls them both animals and declares she will put them in cages if they do not behave. Sénye accuses her of being jealous. Orosházi tells him he is sick and that she would never sleep beside him, nor behave so low as Be'SuD. Be'SuD informs her that she is not behaving low, but is showing respect to someone who was kind enough to save her, and she should be thankful. Orosházi continues her anger by declaring that Sénye did not save her. Be'SuD tells her not to be angry with her because she is being considerate to someone who deserves respect. Be'SuD tells Orosházi that she needs to remember who fought and lost their friend for this ship. Orosházi looks at Sénye and reminds him of what she gave him believing that they were friends for her faith in his words. Sénye looks at the girls and tells them that we need each. Three people are much better than two people are; and who knows extra eyes and hands could save us during an intense battle.

The women stared at each other for a few seconds, and then both appeared to relax. Sénye thanked them for their contributions to the harmony of their mission. Be'SuD quickly readjusted to the panels and controls on this ship. She flew her kingdom's spacecraft. She passed all the simulator tests with perfect scores. Orosházi passed three quarters of the tests, while Sénye passed one-half. The women complained that they would have to carry the burden during a major attack. The joke turned into a reality within a few days when an alien attack force of four crafts swooped in from empty dark. They labeled them as alien because they were not from any local galaxies. They would search for easy lone targets to loot. They mistakenly struck at Sénye's craft during one of their practice defensive drills in which the girls demanded the equipment such as shields activated. They did everything in real time, except for the firing of the lasers and missiles. The invaders first missiles hit the shield, which confused Orosházi initially; however, Be'SuD quickly told them they were under a real attack and activated their emergency procedures and laser locks and she pushed the fire button knocking out two of them before they came within visual range. Orosházi locked in on one with a missile lock and fired knocking out the third. The Pirate shields would allow laser and missile outgoing fire, a feature they had not previously seen. The shields would not go down when they tried to take them down with the weapon's system operational. Fortunately, Be'SuD quickly put it together, telling the crew; she heard rumors of these advancements. Apparently, the Pirates had got a copy and remanufactured it. Meanwhile, Sénye had locked onto the last attack vehicle, elected to use laser on it, and had a direct hit. This time they had been lucky, in that the shields were up, yet they were going slow and practicing their military drills. If they had been going the higher speeds available on this craft, they would not have been an approachable target. Sénye recommended that the future battle drill done in pairs in the simulator. They agreed to intensify their radar scanners for extra security. The crew worked as a team as their confidence grew in their abilities.

Slowly, throughout this process Be'SuD reduced her role as the peacemaker or a conciliator function between Orosházi and Sénye.

Be'SuD socialized with each casually fitting into her third-person role, a function she enjoyed. She preferred to be alone, a feat that was difficult with Orosházi on one arm and Sénye on the other. Orosházi and Sénye learned so much about each other through Be'SuD who never held anything back when questions and feed her curiosity any information she could obtain. Her curiosity centered on personalities. She developed this through her indoctrination for a life in diplomacy and politics. Her crewmates felt her world had cheated her from a rightful destiny and came to appreciate their good luck. Their updated social climate left each knowing so much about the other. Orosházi found herself emotionally bonded with Sénye to the same degree, if not slowly passing her bond with Be'SuD. Orosházi began asking about finding a world to live. Sénye argued that settling on a world would be of no value if we cannot reproduce. Be'SuD could not reproduce based on her political status; reproduction would be illegal, and thus organs removed shortly after birth. Sénye was beginning to wonder if the rich who could not reproduce were really members originating from children of the lower classes. They explained their worlds had their special private sources for the reproducers. Be'SuD told the crew that Orosházi would have to handle the reproduction department. She accepted and invited Sénye into her private chambers. She eventually conceived and gave birth to a human boy. Sénye's species produced the dominant genes in the child. The human race would continue as the future generation. Sénye now had to keep his promise and discover a world for this crew. He discovered that something unexpected would make that choice for him. They had traveled in space now for two years at the second highest speed. One day, Be'SuD called the crew to the deck. She was concerned about the gradual decreasing levels of certain energy ingredients. She explained that their energy supply was depleting itself, usually caused by an energy stone rounding its tips and causing the beam to hit not solely its receptor, but also the surrounding tip. Be'SuD said we had to drop our speed to normal warp and begin exploring the galaxies that so rarely were appearing in this wide-open section of the universe. The first two galaxies did not offer anything they believed that would work. The third one looked promising. They explored it for days, running their matching criteria. While playing on the deck, they accidentally hit one of the course controls, which shifted their course from the center to the outside of this galaxy.

Sénye discovered this when he detected that the solar systems were spreading farther apart. As he reached the galaxy's border and began going into space, as determined by the gravitational readings reversing from a left-right spin to an in-out spin, he reversed his heading toward a sparsely populated spiral that was approaching. His alarms alerted him of a nearby solar system that had inhabitable planets. As he inspected the planets, he selected an orbit around a planet that was the fourth from the sun. On his second orbit, his female crewmates came to the deck and asked him what he would seek to find. Sénye found nothing wrong with the planet below them, yet behaved as if he did not care either way. The deal breaker came from an unexpected card, as their ship began to lose orbit. The alarms sounded as Be'SuD told them it was, time to head for the loading dock. Sénye asks her what they will find on the loading dock. She tells them an escape pod. Orosházi, while holding her son, asks Be'SuD why they must leave this ship. Be'SuD explains the ship is losing orbit and is lacking the energy to break the orbit. It was somewhat more than energy, because to escape the orbit, the ship had to reverse the gravitational directions, which this ship did not have the functional laser tips to make this reverse from the spray lasers from the high-speed burns. They were going down and would be crowded in a small space pod. Be'SuD asked them, which island below on the surface; they wanted to settle. Two had life and three did not. They agreed on the large island that was in the center, as Orosházi liked the center of it being mountain as was on Jaroslaw. It had a warm climate that appealed to Be'SuD. It did not have war, although still had empty space shells in its orbit, which appealed to Sénye. They proceeded to the space pod, taking emergency backpacks with them. Be'SuD recommended they eject from space and that way the ship would burn on reentry and not release any dangerous chemicals or elements into the planet's environment. What she actually had done was set the self-destruct with a delay set for three days. It would take months for the ship to fall to the surface, so she had plenty of breathing space.

Into the pod, they crowded and the ramp launched them out from their ship. Be'SuD commented on how large the ship was. It was now drifting away from them as this planet began to grow larger and closer. They were excited at the prospect of a new life in a fresh world. Their ship splashed down on the western bay coastline of a land that Be'SuD called Nógrád after her older brother and a river that Be'SuD called the Yolkin River after a river she played in as a child on the deserts of her home planet. She talked about the fun they had playing in the sand as children. Sénye and Orosházi looked at each other wondering what thrilled her from playing with sand. They just shook it off as being the joys from another culture and galaxy. They knew that what one world had plenty; other worlds may have little. They splashed into the sea, and Be'SuD jumped out with the raft and inflated it. She then secured herself and reaches up for little Wadich as Orosházi hands her son to him, and then she boards the raft and grabs hold of Wadich. Be'SuD stands up and begins receiving the bags and equipment that Sénye passed out to her. When he finished unloading everything to her, Be'SuD pointed at a lever for him to pull after pushing three buttons, which she pointed for him to push. He did as she said and the capsule sank into the sea. They rowed the boat toward the shore when Be'SuD told them to hold on for a minute as she jumped into the water, and a few minutes later came up with a bag she took with her packed with fish. Her crewmates were surprised when they pulled her back onboard. When they reached the shoreline, and saw the wonderful sandy beach Be'SuD begged them to camp here for the night, which was quickly approaching. Be'SuD unpacked the gear while Sénye went into the nearby forest to collect firewood. They prepared for their first name, a night on the sand, which Be'SuD giant smile shinned the entire beach. She was so at home in the sand. They had no idea why she enjoyed the sand with subsequently much enthusiasm, yet soon could face a challenge. What would put the pieces together?

The next morning, after Be'SuD and Wadich played in the water for about one hour, as she wanted to wear him down before the long day on the raft. They knew the river ran into the mountains. Sénye wanted to be about three ridges in the highlands. That would allow them to hunt the grasslands and still enjoy the mountain lands. Orosházi was the one who wanted the clan to live in the hills, just before the steep mountains. Because she was once again pregnant, Sénye and Be'SuD accommodated her wishes. They discovered a broad stream that feeds into the river and agreed this would be better. After going up the stream for a few hours, they see found a spacious meadow surrounded by a forest. Be'SuD remained on the raft, passing the equipment to Sénye, while Orosházi was watching Wadich. After finishing with the unloading, Be'SuD asked them was that green material was that they were walking on now. Sénye tells her it is grass and asks her if she has ever previously seen grass. She tells him now and jumps from the raft onto the green grass. When she touches the grass, her skin turns to a dark black with giant yellow spots speckled throughout her body. She stands up and walks back to the raft, as smoke now flows from her skin. She lays down on the raft as Sénye jumps into the stream and begins to splash water on her. He soon stops all the smoke and asks Be'SuD if there is something can be done to help her. She tells them, unfortunately, her insides burned as well. Orosházi asks her what happened. Be'SuD tells them that for a strange reason her species and grass do not mix, and instead the grass was burning her body by changing its molecular composition. This was something like a serious allergic reaction. Be'SuD told them that she was dying and would be dead soon. Sénye asks her why she never told them she was deathly allergic to grass, and that they could have lived on a beach, especially since they have the entire continent to themselves.

Be'SuD explains that she had never seen grass before, and did not realize it until it was too late. The chloroform in her green body was a negatively charged chloroform, whereas the chloroform in the grass was a positive charged chloroform. They did not react at all. The grass that she walked on completely burned as well. Be'SuD lay there crying as Sénye was grabbing the sandy mud from the stream's bed to cover her burns. This barely offered temporary relief from the terrible pain.

Sénye, Orosházi, and Wadich worked hard to comfort her, yet by nightfall, she died. Sénye dug a deep hole and placed her body in it. He spent the next two days cutting stones with his laser pistol. They covered an area twenty-five all around her grave with three layers of stone. They called the place, 'the bed of love.' It was not until two thousand years later the excavators found the letter Sénye and Orosházi had written and placed under Be'SuD. The letter explained how she had bridged the deep gap between the woman with the wings and the spaceman and gave them love. Be'SuD united them into one mind and heart. They bonded, particularly after the three days filled with tears in which they cried after Be'SuD's death. Orosházi was especially heartbroken, because at first she hated Be'SuD for enjoying what she had rejected. She revealed to her a love she had trapped inside her. She confessed not having the power to set this love in motion, and that once it was in motion, she would never stop loving the father of this land they called Nógrád; named in honor of the father of someone who had held their hearts, Be'SuD. They knew that sadness would follow them all the days of their lives if they remained there. Sénye loaded the raft, his family, and equipment, and they went back to the sea and sailed south, around the southern tip of the second river in this land and then sailed up this river until they found the mountains. They were happy to confirm that these ridges, just as the ones on the Yolkin River also ran north and south. This allowed the new river; they were on to slow with a slight slope as his rows kept the boat flowing inland. Once they reached the tip of the river, they traveled into the first ridge to the east. Sénye's spirit thought that the world to the west would give rise to children of impishness.

Sénye and Orosházi lived exceptionally cheerful together, as Sénye continued to create new games and jokes that kept his family happy. Sénye had dreams that caused him much grief and changed the way his family lived. He complained about having dreams of his wife and children dying, and therefore, with his laser pistol cut many stones and with the horses he had broken, pulled the stones back to their hilltop and built an eight-foot tall rock fort around a plateau that was in front of their cavern. Later generations discovered this fort after a large storm, fully excavated it, and became an important landmark for the Kharmats. This fort did not stop the dreams, and the nights continued to haunt Sénye. His days, filled with joy as Orosházi continued to produce sons and daughters. Their family grew too large for the caverns thereby Sénye took many of his sons and with laser pistols, built many small homes. The homes had rock walls and wooden roofs with chimneys for cooking. Sénye continued with the high walls, fearing the wild carnivorous beasts. He dug with his laser rifle underground tunnels, constructed brick, and wooden walls connecting these homes and storage buildings. He sat many traps for the carnivorous beasts, thinning their numbers immensely. Sénye worried about his grandchildren as with his children had a restless urge to explore. A few of his children told tales about seeing white angels flying at night. Orosházi believed their depressed Jaroslaw genes caused these visions. Sénye was proud of his children and the way they all loved the mother with wings from the sky. He told these children that one day she came down from the sky and tied him to a tree, starving him for many days until he promised to marry her. He became so hungry that it was sure death or marriage, and in his weakness, he chose marriage. Orosházi tells the children that Sénye caught her in one of his traps. He would not free her, until he made her pregnant. After she had her baby, she could not leave because she loved her baby too much. The children did not which story to believe and because their parents never argued with each other's story, so they could not at any time figure out who was right, forcing this one day to conclude they had united because of love. They cared for their family, instilling a solid moral foundation. Then one day, the harmony of the peaceful family suffered first major challenge.

Six of the nine brothers found themselves in a great disagreement in which their parents could not bring them to peace. Three brothers went to the east into the land called Chadov named by Be'SuD during the orbits after her brother and three went to the north into a land called Durov, named after Sénye's brother. Orosházi did not want any lands having the names of her family members, believing to do so would cause a curse. Three of the sons remained with their parents caring for them until their days were finished. Their parents soon moved to a new fort that Sénye built for them. They spent their remaining days writing songs and poems, taking hikes through the mountains and camping in the forests that before Sénye had feared. They would travel once each year and visit the sons who had left for the other lands on Nógrád. As their years, advanced Sénye found difficulty in walking and most places he went was on horseback. Orosházi began flying over the lands and eventually over the seas, though never more than thirty minutes out. She would return to Sénye claiming to have seen women swimming in the water yet when she would go down and get close to the surface they would vanish. The children feared her mind was beginning to leave her and made her promise solely to fly near their home. They believed these stories too strange even to record in their tales. As with all who walk in the lands of Emsky, their days' end. As the time was approaching, Sénye and Orosházi promised that they would find each in the land of the dead. They died within minutes of each other; nevertheless, as they were born in other galaxies, those deities took them into their realms. They both appealed to their gods, so they would reunite in Emsky. In order for them to be in the land of the dead around Emsky, the male had to be born on Emsky. Their deities placed them into a sleep and gave Sénye to Borsod-Abaúj-Zemplén who agreed to replant Sénye close to the end of time, as he was there in the beginning times. Orosházi's destiny was different, as her deities would not approve her spending eternity with other species, for fear they would mistreat and abuse her. The caste system believed Sénye to have been the father of a world, which was close, yet not far enough apart to argue. Therefore, the fellow caste saints pulled her aside and set her to drift in the universe knowing her subconscious soul would take her to Emsky. Sénye was reborn and lived another life on Emsky, this time as a native born. Orosházi came out of her space sleep as she entered Chuprin. She was familiar with this galaxy from their exploration so many ages previously.

Pankrati asked Orosházi and Sénye if any of these brought back memories. Orosházi confesses, with Sénye that the memories are coming back to them. They stared at each other not knowing, what to say or do. They had children and generations that they had created. A nation he had grown up in, actually the complete continent of Nógrád was their children. The thing that filled Sénye was the raiders, which killed his wife and children were as well his children, and the strangest was how his wife also was his daughter. At least there were enough ages, which had passed and the innocence of his ignorance justified this. Sénye worried now about his innocent children that the evil spirits destroyed who surrounded Emsky. Pankrati told them that when the Empire captures the wicked demons, they would free the righteous, they sent into sleep. The righteous shall never fall to evil. Orosházi now changed her position on Emsky's entry into the Empire. She wanted them to join quickly, as she was willing to give up her Jaroslaw features so she would resemble her children. Children have the power to pull a mother through any door. Sénye complained to Pankrati that he wanted to keep Orosházi the way she is, as he had twice fallen in love with her as she now appears. Pankrati explains the Empire has exceptions and dual appearance creations. This would have Orosházi appear as Jaroslaw to Sénye and as an Empire spirit to all others. Orosházi quickly asks if they can make Sénye appear decent for her to see, while the others continue to see his ugliness. I told her she had better be careful because I would tell the children the secrets about their mother. The gang enjoyed this joke as Orosházi realized that it might not be wise to tell jokes about their children's father. They were still in awe at being a part of such a dynamic planet's history. They needed a little time to let this soak inside their now complete souls. The connection and bond they had was cemented in a lifetime of love and devotion to each other, and the success they had in raising a large family, with eighteen children, nine sons, and nine daughters. Sénye felt better currently in knowing that this was just as much Orosházi' world as it was his.

CHAPTER 07

Lenti, the land down under

A new sense of belonging overshadowed the window chamber, especially with Orosházi recognizing that her children were among those who lived in the lands below Emsky's equator. The ancestry of the Lenti came forth in another manner, alike and not like from the other continents. The Borsod-Abaúj-Zemplén decided that they had planted enough from other parts of the universe to add the balance they wanted for this seventh stone and now wanted to add certain stabilization. They called on Tolmachyov and Siostra concerning their desire to form a fresh human race from life already part of Emsky. They wanted this new man and woman to have the Benigna-A and Benigna-B values. Tolmachyov explained that their genetic structure was unique and that any form of alteration would cause serious problems in the reproduction process for the future generations. Siostra recommended that they create new beings with clean slates and allow them to work with them, while also in human form, and thereby keep their species a secret on Emsky. She further recommends that he creates additional women to keep the gene pool somewhat blended. Borsod-Abaúj-Zemplén told them they would create them with the genetic recombination, such as the Jaroslaw whose reproductions receive a new genetic heritage to promote a stronger healthier species. They do this anytime the genetic coding between mother and father was higher than ten percent. They did agree that added mothers would help them build their generations quicker. The Power Spirits caused a great sleep to come on Tolmachyov and Siostra as they completely scanned, their genetic makeup, looking for any genes that could blend or enhance a human hereditary makeup. In disappointment, they discovered just three codes, with even these codes requiring numerous modifications. They would use these genes as dormant genes, merely activating if the species needed them. They sent Tolmachyov and Siostra back to Emsky, gathered the genetic coding from their creations, and decided to make a new human species from Emsky. They gathered dust from Emsky and poured within its blood; they made from the air. Once the blood formed the body from the dust, they placed inside, a spirit they had created. The spirit spread its light throughout the blood-filled body, trying to escape, yet instead the energy from the spirit hardened the dust forming bones and muscles. The coding the Power Spirits had put in this dust formed the organs, and once they formed; the Power Spirits knocked their creation to the ground, causing it to gasp for air and thus take his first breath. Emsky now had a man of the seventh stone created from the dust of the land and blood from the air. They told the man to take dominion over this land and declare it for the righteous. The man was at first excited about his new life and mission.

This excitement grew weaker each day, as the man witnessed the beasts walking as male and female through the fields. One day, the man whom the Power Spirits called Enuno, asked a rabbit why there were so many little copies of him everywhere. The rabbit called his female to stand beside him and explained that they made these young rabbits and protected them until they grew older. They told him that all the beasts that walked in the fields did as they had always done. Enuno walked among the deer, bears, lions, horses and cattle, seeing those were the rabbits had told him were true. He complained to the Power Spirits that this was not equitable. The Power Spirits asked him why it was not fair. Enuno told them because the beasts that they had created could create more of them, yet he would have to spend his life alone. Enuno's heart was heavy with burdens. He no longer desired to toil on the land, finding no purpose in his labors. Therefore, the Power Spirits caused a great sleep to come over him. They took large handfuls of dust and formed it into three piles. Next, they took three drops of blood from Enuno and gave each pile a drop of the blood. Afterwards, they poured water from the sea and ground several leaves from the nearby trees and blended the mud and drop of blood. The drop of blood flowed through the muddy lump reforming the genetic codes changing each part into flesh. The three bodies formed within minutes and created their spirits from the life in the blood. From the dust, they created them and vegetation of Emsky. The vegetation was to provide them with the gift to create new life. The Power Spirits named these women Kvinde, Mujer, and Naine. When Enuno saw these three women, he became so happy. He called for the bears and lions to celebrate. The bear called Enuno and told him that he would have to make skins for these women. Enuno asked them how he could make skins for women. The bear called the lions to join them. The lions, as with all the beasts, had a strong relationship with Enuno. They had shared in so many adventures and strange games they created. Enuno was their representative if other humans came to this land. The natural instinct of the animals was to distrust anything that walked on two legs. Enuno broke this barrier, for the most part, through his days of crying in loneliness.

The beasts learned to work with Enuno, knowing he also had to eat. They shared their prey, with was the feasts of the deer and buffalo, which roamed Lenti in large herds. Bear explained to Enuno that the skin of people was too thin to give warmth in the winter and protection against abrasive contacts. Enuno could not understand what they had in mind, as he had barely survived one winter and spent most of it around a fire inside his cave, never going out, as a lion would bring his meat for him to eat. The lions agreed not to eat any of the deer hides until they clothed the humans. The women were not comfortable around Enuno because their bodies looked different. When the collected the hides, they could make wrappings to hide the differences. Enuno refused to wear and form of clothing for his upper body until the cold weather began. The herds were becoming harder for the lions to trap, and therefore, as their catches decreased, they drifted further from the humans. Kvinde told Enuno that if they could not catch the deer while they were running they should try to catch them while they were resting. She dug a big hole and in the bottom, she erected pointed spears with the points facing up toward the sky above it, she lined several branches with fruit, and she placed the fruit along a path the lead to the main path of the deer. Her trap worked, as they caught their first deer. She resets the trap, and they caught another. They gave the second deer to the lions who tried to reform their alliance. Enuno took the advice of Kvinde and refused the partnership. She felt it was time for Enuno to spend time with his people and not with animals. Mujer and Naine agreed as well. They were creating their group as one against three, as Enuno would sleep in the open cavern on the inside front of their cave. The women slept in one of the tunnels about fifty feet inside the cave. One day while they were sleeping in the cave, a few eagles came into the cave and began laughing. They asked the eagles, why they were laughing, not knowing what they had done to create so much humor. The eagles told them that the males and females on Durov, Gyáli, and Nógrád sleep together, since they sleep apart. How will they ever learn to reproduce if they do not discover their hearts and love? Mujer asked the eagles, which one will sleep with the man. The eagles laugh at them once more and reveal that they must decide these things. People are supposed to take domain and control over the lands, not to be ignorant and dependant.

Enuno heard the eagles talk and in anger chased them from his cave. He was so angry the eagles would dare laugh at them. Enuno decided that day that he would build around the opening he had cleared in front of his cave a five-foot high wall. Their cave had another opening through its tunnels that came out on the other side of their hillside. The issue that truly puzzled Enuno was that he did not understand how to talk with the women who the Power Spirits created as his companions. They always did everything together, and when he came around them, they would become silent and turn their faces. This made him even lonelier than he was previously. They coexisted, solely in proximity, but not as those who belong together. He still walked alone, clearly now behind him walked three whom, he believed most times were more afraid of him than the beasts, he had declared his enemy. Enuno became more of a loner. He could never even figure out how to talk with them. When he would try to talk with them, they would laugh at him, or notwithstanding make strange faces. Whenever he would get serious, they would play. This made it impossible to get anything accomplished. He had to carry and stack all the stones for their walls. This was not what he had planned when he asked for a companion. This feeling was not of being alone, but also thought of as a reject or a fool. He wondered how they turned out this way. They gained their power by uniting. There had to be a method to get among them. He longed to have something they wanted.

The males among the beasts controlled their species, so Enuno set out one day to discover the answer to his problem. He told the women that he would be gone for a short time. They surprised him by appearing to be unhappy about his departure. He asked them why they seemed so depressing. They explained that this felt safe when he was among them, and they would be living in fear while he was not with them. Enuno walked about in the heavy forest with his wooden spear. He traveled over the hills, through the thick brush and crossed a few streams. His big scare was while walking beside a stream when he stepped on a snake. Enuno had never previously seen a snake. He was shocked when the log moved and even more surprised when it opened its mouth, and he saw the large fangs. From instinct, he ran his spear into the snake's mouth, ramming the tip out of the back of the snake's skull. This incident taught him that there was so much more to learn about this land, and fear filled his heart worrying if one of his women were to meet a snake. He knew his search would not last forever, and, considering they have never before seen a snake, they should be okay. Enuno had not faced an unknown danger before in his life. A new sense of appreciation flooded his heart presently. The trees looked taller, and the grass appeared greener. The air was fresh as he stood in place and took a deep breath. He saw a few small animals dash around in the trees. They played so well together, and displayed a spirit of amalgamation and were accordingly happy. They had the one thing that he wanted so much and that blended with his fellow humans. His difficulty came from seeing the final show in the acts these groups were performing. He missed the hard work and trust that took, time to develop. He would find out the stages in this process and dance in the trees with fellow humans, even though their bodies has differences, although this modification was consistent with the variation between the male and female animals. This convinced Enuno the creation of his women was the way they were supposed to create them; the trouble was that no one included an instruction manual. The female humans had personalities who created a wall between his women and him. His initial day of walking slowly turned into darkness, and was transforming into his first night. Enuno was searching for answers and always thought that the true answer would come from the high skies held the night white dots speckled the mysterious black painted the nighttime sky.

To receive his answer, he would have to sleep in the open where whatever was putting the sun to sleep at night could talk with him. Harboring his courage in the open, he fell to sleep. Late in the night, he heard the loud thunder. This brought him from his sleep causing him to jump to his feet. As he began to focus his eyes, before him came a bright light that descended before him. This light blinded Enuno, causing him the place his hands over his eyes and fall to the ground. Shortly thereafter, he could sense the heat from the light decreasing, and accordingly lowered his hands and before him appeared a gorgeous gray-skinned woman with long stringy black hair. Her female breasts had stunning silver painted upside-down flowers, as also did her shoulders. She wore no clothing, as his women did at first. The thing that confused him was the bottom women hidden part did not appear the same. Enuno asked her if she was a woman. She told him that she was not a woman, but a creation of another species. At this time, she flapped her two white wings. When Enuno saw this, he knew she was not like his three women. Nevertheless, with her wings had to be from somewhere in the sky. He achieved his goal. Enuno thought that even though her body was different, she had more knowledge than he did, and she was not laughing at him, which was a great step in the right direction. He asked this creature from the sky for her name. After lightly flapping her wings, she reveals, "I am called Tsigler." Enuno asked her since she was here. She revealed that she heard him crying for help. Tsigler then asked him what he needed so that his heavy burdened, would no longer plaque his heart. Enuno began to cry, telling Tsigler that the women he received would not give him the honor that the women of the beasts give their males. His females shun and then mock him. Daily walking in shame among the just other people in the world that he knew existed was spoiling any desire to continue with his life. He lived in a world that belittled and made him think he was worthless. He wanted to understand how to make them respect him, or even if such a thing was possible.

Tsigler told him that he had to do things that would make them want to honor him. He would have to learn to be himself and not seek to find himself in others. Learn to be happy inside and the happiness will roll outside to the world that surrounded him. When they joke about him, enjoy it with them. Do several of the things they enjoy, and soon they will do those things with you. Enuno had to think about the activities they enjoyed and work to be a part of this along with them. Tsigler said she had watched him at night avoid these women. He needed to be more receptive to them at night, because they had feared, and if he kept them safe, they would compromise to maintain that security. Enuno asked her if she knew when these women would do what creation, intended them to do and make children. Afterwards, Tsigler told him that he was the one who controlled those things. Enuno asked her how he could do such a thing, having no idea. Tsigler told Enuno to sit while she revealed to him a vision to teach him how to procreate. Enuno watched the stream confessed to Tsigler that this did not seem to be possible. He then asked how it would be imaginable to get his women to cooperate with this. Tsigler told him the protection at night would set the stage for this. Become their protector and provider and they will become his partners and work with him to create their family. She reminded them that he must be kind and behave as if he truly cares for them. The creators had given them to him, so he could build a family based on love. He had to learn about love. Enuno asked her what love was and how he could ever discover it. Tsigler explained that love would come once he surrendered himself to his women. Enuno, not understanding this, told her that if he surrendered, how they could be his women. Tsigler responded by informing him that love merely existed when those who were inside it surrendered all. If he believed her, and surrendered himself, they would submit to him as well. He had to remove the lines that divided them.

Those same lines that held him back also prevented the ones; he wanted to join him from reaching him. He would have to swallow his pride, and if they treated him as a joke, laugh with them. They also tease and play with each. When they played among themselves, rather than going off to be alone, he should stay and share in the joy of pestering their new victim. This would position him as a practical teaser, and they would not be so fast to oppose him, not knowing if her fellow sisters join him or her. Enuno thought about this and asked her how he could recognize her knowledge was accurate. Tsigler told him that she had lived in the realms of love all her long life, and it was because of the love, she had come to aid him. Enuno confessed to Tsigler that these women made him so nervous, and when he was around them, his mind did not work the way he wanted it to work. Tsigler smiled and told him this was natural and these women had to learn how to relate to the men just as the men had to learn to relate to the women. She told Enuno that if he first became friends with them and relaxed throwing away his pride and feelings of superiority, these women would give him the honor and the power he needed. His power would be with the joy in the love he created. Tsigler asked him why he would want power if it made the people created for him to suffer. Enuno told her this was never his purpose; he just did not want to be alone and shunned. Tsigler advises him to become fun and do things that they all can enjoy. She asked Enuno if he enjoyed singing and telling stories. He confirmed that he found these things enjoyable. Tsigler recommends that he tell the scary stories at night when it is dark. That is the time when these women would have their greatest fear. He would have to learn various acting skills and to learn how to make situations appear more intense than normal. Tsigler told him to keep his women under his wings, so when he flew they would fly beside him. Be approachable and understanding. He also had to realize when to turn the charm and fear generation off when his women were overloaded. Meanwhile, she would be hidden in the dark around him and help him, if possible. In any manner, she could not allow any of his women to detect her, as Enuno was the sole one permitted to see her.

Meanwhile, life for Kvinde, Mujer, and Naine's lives were not in the balance they had craved when Enuno was with them. The first day that he was gone, a large bear jumped over their wall and came after the women. They each had a knife and were quite good with it. When the bear leaped on Mujer, the bear found Kvinde and Naine jumped on her back and continued to stab while Mujer stabbed from below this bear. Kvinde could get both bear's eyes, while Mujer got a cut across its throat. They fought hard, and the struggle lasted just a few minutes as the bear died. The women rolled the bear of Mujer and cleaned the carcass, salting the meat and drying the hide. They decided to create a wonderful bear coat. This bear attack scared the women; they could not rest as every little noise brought fear into their minds. They agreed that their relationship with Enuno was not working the way that they thought it should. The first thing that they had to do was figuring out how their situation should be. That was almost as conceivable to them as how they would be able to change the night into day. They were hopelessly lost. A voice suddenly spoke to them, saying, "I understand what you must do." Kvinde looked around on the ground and saw nothing, then she looked up in the tree beside her and the lone thing that she saw was a little red bird. Kvinde asked the scarlet bird if it was she, who was talking. The crimson bird acknowledged that it was she, who knows what they must do. Mujer asks the small-feathered acquaintance how she could understand about such things, as all her children came from eggs. The bird agreed that her children came from eggs, nevertheless, reminded the women that the bear and most of the beasts in the field offspring did not come from eggs, but created within them. The cherry bird told these women that last year she lived on the large island north across the sea in a land called Gyáli and she saw the women there who had made little people. Naine subsequently pleaded with the small bird to reveal to them, what she saw. The rosy bird, afterwards agreed to tell them what she saw.

She began by telling them that the women in those lands treated their men with honor, and not shun them, as she saw them do for their man. Naine told the ruby bird that they did not understand how to do the things she had revealed they must do. They planned; however, to try working with their man when he returns. The rosy bird flapped her wings and asked the women how they knew their man would return. Mujer tells their feathered friend that their man told them he would return and with his word, he would honor his promise. The bird told them this was an important first step, that at least they were yet to become enemies. Kvinde asked the bird to explain how the women she saw produced more people. The crimson bird revealed to these future mothers was the Gyáli women would first become extremely fat, as if they had eaten the heads of a lion and a horse. Then a day would come when their belly was normal, and they would be carrying their new babies. They appeared so happy. They always kept, the babies close to them. Mujer asked how the woman got the baby out of her belly. The bird told her most likely; it was the same way that the beasts brought forth their newborns. Mujer asked the bird how the baby creation process started. The bird told these women that she did not understand for sure how. She did realize that the man was supposed to begin with the man somehow. Naine clarified it was the man who was supposed to begin the procedure. These women instantly became angry feeling as if Enuno had cheated them. They thanked the bird for helping them. This bird began to fly away, telling the women they need to get back inside the cave. Mujer looked around, and saw two lions looking at them. The human women were now petrified and remained motionless, not knowing when the lions were going to attack them. The lions then began to laugh at the human women. Kvinde inquired about why they were laughing at them. The lions tell the women they laugh at them because they do not grasp how to make babies, which is the number-one mission of females. Mujer explains to the lions that whatever created them did not teach this. Naine asks the lions how they cannot understand if birds taught their ancestors the first time. The lions discussed this privately for one minute and then turned and walked away.

Kvinde and Mujer congratulate Naine on her logic. They had never used their logic in an argument against someone other than Enuno. They had confidence when going against Enuno, because they knew he was gentle and when he was extremely bored with him, he would simply go to one of his corners. Now that they have a taste of the true danger in this world, they want Enuno back in their lives. Mujer recommends that they pick a few of his favorite vegetables and various spices with a selection of their bear meat and make a great stew for him to eat when he returns. This was if they were still living when he returned. Kvinde believed they should try to make this cave more of a home and to blend Enuno's belongings among theirs. This was going to take various readjustments, yet they knew that if they were to produce the newer generations, these adjustments would have to happen. They planned to teach Enuno how not simply to play their games, but also how to win them. They noticed how the male lion strutted around, and the females did all the hunting and work. Their male served as their protector. Kvinde told her sisters, they had been so lucky in that they had received both the protection and the work from their man. Mujer reminded her sisters that they now had nothing. Naine suggested that in the morning they went to search for him. Her sisters asked if she knew how to find them. Naine told them about a young wolf she had played with since he was born. He was smart when it came to find things. They would have him smell a few of Enuno's furs he slept on at night. The next morning, they began their journey, though merely traveling until midday, when the young wolf separated from them. He was too far ahead for the women to get to him, and therefore, they became stranded along this path. Kvinde told them they had to return to the cave, and make it there before nightfall. They would follow their tracts and explore for familiar landmarks. This worked fine when they were on hilltops, yet when they went into thick forests it became difficult. Nonetheless, they traveled along the path they came and later in the afternoon returned to their cave. With each step of their return trip filled with fear, they gained a new appreciation for their home. They searched for a sign to see if Enuno had returned during their departure. They found no evidence; therefore, they huddled for a chilly scary night ahead of them.

Little they knew that Enuno appears to them soon. One minute in the future will equal years in their minds. The fear was with them, and it would not depart from them. Enuno's second night on his journey had not fared as he had planned. This night he did not see his teacher, Tsigler. Instead, he had a series of disturbing bad visions that left him both confused and missing his cave. As he lay down under the open sky, a noise awoke him. He stood up and walked around his small open area, noticing that his sky no longer had the little white dots. At first, he believed this to be from a storm that could be coming his way, yet there was no wind, and this puzzled him. The sky was a darker shade of black, a shade he had never before seen. This caused him to slide back to where his spear was, quickly reach down, and grab it. Nonetheless, his weapon was no match for the darkness that controlled the sky. Next, a small fire appeared, as it became larger in front of him. When the fire was about five feet from him, it consolidated into a face, with the left side burning. It was the face of Kvinde and she was begging him to save her. He quickly reached down to the ground, grabbed two handfuls of dirt, and threw them on her face. This had the opposite effect, in that if caused her face to burn faster. He ran to her, and with his hands tried to wave air on the fire and kill it. The air made the fire faster. Enuno noticed that even though the fire burned faster, it did not burn deeper into Kvinde's face. This was strange, in that all the fires he had made; they always consumed, what they burned. What kind of fire would no more than burn, yet not consume what it burned. This was strange indeed. This was the first time he saw a fire that burned but did not consume. Kvinde continued to cry to him for help. Enuno asked her what happened to her body, because he just saw her head. She tells him the fire already took her body. Enuno told her that a head could not live without a body, as they knew from hunting the beasts. Kvinde reminded him that she was not a beast. Enuno asked her how her sisters were doing, and if they were safe. Kvinde told him they were doing fine. When she answered, she spoke in a harsh tone, which surprised Enuno because in any action that put the three sisters against him, they would speak warmly to reinforce their perception of sisterhood and unity. Enuno asked her how Noamity was doing. Kvinde tells him that she is doing well, although they are struggling to be free from the fire monster, which is trying to burn their cave.

Enuno looked at her and told her to hurry and burn the other side of her face, so the fire would quench itself, and that he could sleep. Enuno walked away going back to the tree and calling for Tsigler. Kvinde's burning face yells for him to save her, and that she will soon perish. Enuno ignores her keeping his back to her. He could see the shadows the fire creates and thereby monitors its movements for security purposes. The burning faces makes one last scream for help, and after Enuno does not respond, vanishes. When he no longer saw the shadow of the fire, he turned around, and discovered the burning face was gone. This caused a heavy burden took over his heart. He could not believe that his eyes would deceive him. Enuno now worried that Tsigler may have also been a false vision. The difference between her message of love and happiness and the burning face vision of pain and suffering was astronomical. It was the same as the difference between hot and cold, night and day. Enuno needed answers and continued to call for Tsigler, who would not appear. He believed this to be strange because he believed her to be from a place of love and kindness, yet why would she leave him now. He had so many questions that needed answering. The one thing he knew was the time had arrived for him to depart this area, even though the single place he had spoken with Tsigler; it was apparently now a place for lies and deceit. He believed the risk of seeing another false vision was so greater than a reward from a Tsigler visit. She was not here, so there was no need for him to be nearby either. He grabbed his things and began his walk home in the late hours of the night.

This forest had extra noises he heard for the first time. He somehow had wandered from his original path, yet knew he was going the correct direction because of the stars in the sky. Many times, while hiding from his women, he would sit outside their cave and study the stars. The stars were his roadmap, and in the morning, he would walk south to line up on his original path. He had kept the mountain ridge to his north when walking on his journey, as a safety valve, if he became lost, as he had now done. The path took a surprising turn dropping in a downward slope. He slipped as he was walking and fell into a deep hole. While, dropping he feared the bottom may have spikes as the holes he dug. To his great delight, the bottom had merely small pebbles, which sunk into the loose dirt that they covered, softening his crash. He dropped his spear when he fell, which now left him defenseless and confused. He wondered who else on this island would dig deep traps. His women and he were the sole humans living on this large island. Enuno survived one mystery earlier tonight, one last night, and now a second one this night. He would try to figure a plan to escape in the morning, as for currently he was safer down in the hole, so he believed. While trying to go back to sleep, he felt a tremble in this hole as the dirt from the wall in front of him dissolved. A strange wall that he could see through appeared in front of him. Water filled from behind this wall and slowly a woman he never before had known came forward. Her hair was, pitch black and waiving in the water. He saw air bubbles rising from below beginning at a point close to the invisible wall. There were no bubbles forming from her mouth. She had many long then pines covering her shoulders, above her eyes and on her cheeks. Slowly, she moved her right hand to the wall, with her palm and fingers extended facing him. Her black wide opened eyes stared at him as if a lion ready for his kill. Enuno could not determine how this woman could be alive, living in the water. Enuno wondered was thus a type of life he did not know. He was finding himself in many unknown situations since he escaped from his cave. He may have enjoyed the security of knowing longer than his life programmed its path to receive. His expedition for answers instead created more questions.

Enuno stared into the face of the women in the water before him. She moved her mouth as if to be begging him to save her. He felt around the three remaining walls when he discovered a part of a rock. Using his fingers, he dug around the rock and finally could work it loose. While pulling the stone from its solid encasement his arms hit the wall behind him, forcing him to release the stone. The stone thumped onto his foot, though not hard enough to break any bones, but strong enough to deliver a few cracks. This was enough to make Enuno extremely angry. He lowered his knees and reached down, grabbing the stone. Then, holding the rock with two hands smashed it against the invisible wall. The wall shattered into many sharp small pieces of clear rocks. Afterwards, the water came into the hole flooding it. Enuno looked at the woman who began to shrink into a dry piece of shriveled fruit, screaming as she shrank that he had killed her. Sure, she asked him to save her. He wondered if she expected him to walk through the invisible wall. Whatever she wanted; he did all that he could do, and that was to break through, and try to free her. There were greater questions now that needed answered, such as how they met first and why was she in a tube of water, other than for her survival. If she needed, water to survive, and he was not in the water, why would she want him to save her? To appreciate the truth, Enuno did not care if he ever found the answers for any of these questions. He had a mission that was more important, and that was to return to his home. Meanwhile, he waded in the water as it rose and soon could anchor himself on the hole's sides and crawl out of the hole. He knew that for what is left of the night he would walk slowly and cautiously, as he did not want to meet any more water women living underground. The night moved little by little, as he elected to move higher up the hill closer to the ridge and fewer trees, which meant more moonlight.

More moonlight meant a greater chance of being in his cave the next night, and maybe be among women who were human as was he and not anymore light women with wings, water women or burning women. Enuno found himself filled with joy in knowing that the sky once again had those white dots, which were his map home. He had separated himself from what he once believed to be his tormentors, yet now had a new sense of hope that they could build a relationship. He was willing to surrender, and if they had to make fun of him, he would give these family members more reasons to laugh at him. He truly missed their laughter. We wriggled through the rest of the night, as the forests began to be thin to his south; he worked his way southwest, hoping to save a little time in the morning in finding his path. When the sun began to bring in another day, he shifted his course straight south, knowing he would run into his path. He had carefully followed a path in which many herds used so that it would be easy to find in case he would be in a situation as he now was. His heart filled with joy when he discovered his path within one short hour. Excitement rushed through his body as new wells of energy filled his body. He would be home in his cave before nighttime came. While walking along his path, he discovered a woman's footprints. He saw the footprints of wolves, in fact, an entire pack running over these prints. Enuno feared the worse now, that perhaps they came looking for him and found themselves attacked by beasts. He thought for one minute and then relieved that the tracks were over two sets of female footprints, one going in each direction. Enuno believed that for a certain reason, they turned back to the cave. His guess was that they might have deemed such a journey as too dangerous for them, which he agreed was equally important threatening. He scanned the available vegetation and saw no bloodstains, which indicated to him there was not a fight. The one thing fact, he knew was that these girls were fighters when their backs were against the wall or their lives were in danger. He hoped that such a short absence did not cost him all his people. Enuno began running toward his cave, yet soon detected that several dangerous beasts were tracking him.

He would have to continue cautiously so as not to give an unfair advantage to the hungry beasts after him. Even so, he kept his spear visible and walked in the middle of this path, strong and head turning to keep awareness of any movements around him. A movement not detected, could mean his death.

One lion decided to test his alertness. He came prancing face-to-face down the middle of the path. Enuno braced his spear and pretended to be afraid. This gave his attacker a false sense of superiority and easy prey. The lion opened his mouth to release a loud roar so that all could see his great victory. As his mighty roar rushed from his mouth, Enuno charged him, driving his spear into his mouth and up through his brain. The roar ceased as he pulled back his spear and push it in another part of the lion's upper mouth. When the lion closed his eyes, Enuno pulls his spear from the lion's mouth as his jaw clamped shut. The lion's body hit the ground dust splashed riding on the thump of the ground stopping the collision. The area around Enuno grew deadly silent. He continued his walk holding his bloodstained spear, as the scavengers behind him rushed to consume the carcass who just moments before claimed his victory over a human. The buzzards and other large birds no longer flocked over him, but now raced against those who would feast on the lion's cadaver. He recognized the surroundings as soon he was within his normal hunting range. This meant that he would be back to the cave in a few hours, and no longer had to worry about making it to his cave before nightfall. He returned much quicker than his trip to the night spirit. Enuno's earlier confidence in his ability to build a new relationship with his females was now beginning to erode. He had to find a way to restore this confidence because he did not want to appear feeble before his fellow humans. If he appeared weak, he could be shamed for the rest of his life. Nevertheless, the words for Tsigler that told him to surrender to his women and begin a new life based on caring, and sharing kept ringing through his mind. Enuno tried to determine how surrendering could not appear weak, but seem strong.

Enuno remembered the loneliness his corner had to offer him. He committed himself never to sit in that corner alone again. Enuno hoped he would be sufficiently strong to surrender, and not foolish enough to hang on to nothing. Each step he walked closer to the cave made his heart beat harder. Why was he so afraid of the people the sky gave him? He looked around him and noticed that all things had lost their colors. The grass was grayish, as the sky was a lighter shade of gray. The trees were a darker shade of gray. The warm air was getting hotter than normal. Enuno was sweating so much that his steps were turning into mud baths. He stopped and rested under a tree. When his body hit the ground, he fell into a deep sleep. Before him now appeared a vision. Afterwards, he saw three worlds and three burning fires in the space above them. The giant balls appeared as if ice covered them. Enuno wondered how they could have ice with the fire in the sky above them. Thenceforth, appearing above him was a white line that continued to circle the sky. Then from the burning space appeared a dark black tiger with bright yellow eyes and long white whiskers from each side of his chin. His eyes stared at Enuno as if they were staring to attack him. Filling with confusion, Enuno knew just to stand tall and firm. The stare down lasted precisely for a few minutes when the tiger asked him what he saw. Enuno, not wanting to offend the tiger spoke about the worlds and the balls of fire. The tiger told him that his life was now this picture. He was the black tiger, and the worlds were his women. The tiger further tells him the four balls of fire represented their loves. I looked around for the fourth ball of fire and finally discovered it behind the tiger. The tiger asked Enuno what was wrong with the image he saw. Enuno told the tiger that he should not his have back to the women and the worlds not frozen. The tiger asked him if he knew of anything in the picture that could make the worlds warm. Enuno noticed the tiger's fire eyes turned a bluish-black. The tiger raised himself and slowly turned his back to Enuno and sat his back end down and turned his head backward to face Enuno with another important question.

The tiger asked Enuno why the fires were in the sky and not inside the worlds. Enuno asked the tiger what he thought had to be done. The tiger tells him that love can make all things possible. All Enuno would have to do is moving the fire into the worlds with his love. The tiger told Enuno to talk with his heart. The tiger slowly vanished.

Enuno looked at the fires and asked them to move into the worlds. The fires did not move. Enuno wondered why the tiger would have told him that he could do this. His words did not move them. He believed that this vision had to have a truth in it; therefore, he tried again by saying, "By the name of my love, while the fires take their heat to the worlds so those on the worlds may not be cold but warmed with love." The fires began to move into the worlds. The tiger appeared from behind him, congratulated him for using his love to bring warmth to others, and asked him if he saw how love could take away the pain of others. Enuno asked him if that was the mission of love. The tiger told him that after we give our love to others, their new love would return to us. Our love grows, in others and that love saves us. Enuno thanked the tiger for teaching him about the power of love. Enuno looked with great pride as he saw the worlds before him turn bright blue. He felt fine, as he had never before seen the power of love. He still wondered how this would work with his women, but he did realize that he wanted them to have the warmth that he gave these worlds. Enuno was excited once again about the prospect of building a new life for his family. He would take possession of them as his family because he would plant his love in these three gifts from the heavens. The bluish worlds began to vanish as he could see the daylight returning to his eyes once more. He jumped, grabbed his spear, and with great excitement proceeded to his cave. He would be there in just a few minutes. Soon he was at the bottom of the hill in which the entrance to his cave was. He sat down to rest and took a little water from his water bag washing his face and hands. He wanted to appear presentable to his women, and they consistently made fun of him when he was dirty, as they constantly cleaned, themselves first. He looked up at the hole and noticed it appeared to be quiet. When the women were in the cave, they would make much noise. Enuno feared that something might be wrong. His fear repressed itself when he heard several voices coming up the path from behind him.

He looked out and saw Kvinde, Mujer, and Naine walking toward him. They were laughing and had collected a bundle of vegetables and various fruits. They assembled the vegetables and fruits that he enjoyed. As they walked closer to him, his heart began to beat harder. He was becoming dizzy and confused. There was so much that he wanted to say to them, yet currently he could not remember any words or actions. If they saw him meanwhile, they would believe him to be a fool. Kvinde looked up and saw him. They came running to him, welcoming him home. Mujer told him that they missed him so much. Naine told him they thought he would arrive here later tonight or maybe even tomorrow, and that they were going to make him a huge bear stew. Enuno looked at them, confessed also to miss them, and promised not to leave again unless they all agreed it was necessary. He apologized for being away so long, and did not realize how important they were in his life until he was without him. Kvinde confessed for the women that they also missed him and were afraid while he was gone. Enuno promised to protect them the best that he could. Mujer asked him why they did not have any little people yet. Enuno explained that before he did not understand how, but that a woman angel taught him how to make it, so they could make little people. Naine became angry, wanting to understand why he left them to be with another woman. Enuno explains to her that he had never seen nor even known of this woman before she appeared in the night sky. He also tells them that they must keep her a secret because she was from the world of the spirits and not a human as they were. He owes her so much, because their creators did not teach him about procreation and love. Naine asks him what love is. Enuno tells them that it is so wonderful, and that he used his love to move fire into three worlds just like the black tiger from the sky had told him to do. Mujer asks him if he had been eating any peculiar mushrooms or drinking any odd water. He told them that his mind was clear, and that the reason he went on this pilgrimage was so that he could build a stronger relationship with them.

Mujer asks him if this means that he likes them now. Enuno tells them that he actually loves them and wants to surrender himself to them so that they can make a new union based on caring and sharing. Kvinde revealed to him that they also wanted this type of relationship and had even agreed not to make fun of him any longer. Enuno told them that from this day forward when they made fun of him, he would laugh with them. Enuno told them that he had been so afraid of them, because they treated him as if he were not a part of their group. Mujer confessed that what they had done was cruel and wrong, and that they just did not recognize how they were supposed to act. Naine asks Enuno if they surrender to him, will he teach them how to make him become comfortable and a member of this family. Enuno tells them that he believes this is the beginning of a happier life for all of them, and once the little people come out of them, they will be building the future generations for this large land on Emsky. Kvinde asks him how little people can come out of them. Enuno tells them not to worry, because they will have to mate for him to begin creating life in them. When they go through this activity, he will explain it to them one at a time. Naine asks him why it must be one at a time. Enuno tells them that this is a sacred activity, and that he wants it to be as special as possible for each mother of his little people. Mujer rubs her belly and tells her sisters that she believes that Enuno's babies will grow in their bellies. Enuno confirms what she is telling them. Naine asks why it is Enuno's baby and not theirs. Mujer tells her that the father is the provider and protector, and that he will work harder to provide and protect what is his. Kvinde agrees, saying that the father is the one who begins this life, and thus it should be his. Enuno tells them the little people belong to both the mother and father because the mother and father must love each other and in love, there is caring and sharing. Both surrender to each other, therefore both share and care in their loving. Naine tells her sisters and Enuno that she is getting excited about this love concept, and that they have their man back to protect and love them. Life will be so much grander now. She looks at Enuno and asks him if he enjoyed helping them make his stew for dinner.

Enuno looks at them and yells in excitement that he would so much enjoy this, and that they need to start fast before he starves to death. He furthers, asks them if they have enough wood. The sisters tell him they could use a little more wood. He looks at Kvinde and asks her if she would like to help him. Kvinde asks him since when did he need any help with gathering wood. Enuno tells them that he just would like to keep at least one with him, so he would not be lonely. Kvinde rushes to his arms, kisses his cheek, and tells him she would love to help him. Naine asks if she can help the next time, and Mujer ask if she can help the time after that. He agrees with a great smile. The women ask him why he is smiling, and he tells them because he is feeling love move in and take control of their lives. Naine tells him she does not understand how love feels; however, does appreciate that this is wonderful. Naine and Mujer rush up to the cavern to prepare the vegetables and to clean the fireplace while Enuno and Kvinde stroll around the forest floor looking for small branches and dry wood for their cooking fire. They gathered it and returned into the cave. Kvinde told Enuno that if he were to become confused about what to say or do to consider her, and she would help him. If she winked at him, he would be quiet, and she would answer for him. Enuno gave her a big hug and kiss telling her that he wanted to earn their respect, especially as they would be making children he fathered. She told him that she understood, and that they wanted to make their peace with him as well. She confessed that they never wanted to live again without him. The short separation had rebuilt this division of unknowns into a family of known, yet the final unification would take form when Enuno taught them the skills that he had learned while on his pilgrimage. Enuno and Kvinde delivered the firewood as Enuno began the fire. He told the women that they would keep a fire burning outside their cave at night to prevent any wild beasts from entering their home.

The family enjoyed their stew. Enuno complimented them on how fresh the bear meat was, and that he did not realize they still had meat remaining. Mujer told him they had to kill a bear while he was on his pilgrimage. The bear attacked soon after he was gone, hoping for selected easy prey. Naine then rose and walked to her corner bringing back a wonderful new fur coat and gave it to him telling him it was from his women. Enuno was so surprised and happy. This was the first gift that he had ever received. He began crying and thanking them for such a wonderful gift. The women also overcome with emotion as the group had its first sincere hug filled with passion. Enuno confessed now to the entire group that he needed to learn so much about them, so they would all live lives filled with love and as much happiness as possible. Enuno noticed it was beginning to rain outside and looks at Naine and asks her if she wants to help him. He tells her that because it is raining, she can join him the next time if she desires. She jumps and tells Enuno that someone needs to watch him even in the rain and rushes to his side. He looks at her and confesses that he forgot they were bear hunters. Mujer tells him not to worry, if they have to defend him, they would with their lives. Enuno tells them that they are never to die to save him; they are to live for their family. Kvinde informs him that they will never stand by, and watch him die. She claims they have the right to decide when to risk saving a member of this family, and that they would die for each, another, thus they would also die for him. This was their right. The women stared at him, and he wiggled out of this jam by hoping that never a situation such as this would confront them. He took Naine, and they went into the dark to find the wood. Enuno told her the driest wood was under the trees and that because it was dark, they had to stay together. He also warned her about a new discovery that he made, called snakes. They were logs that were alive. Their skin felt different and if she touched anything unusual to let it go to call him. Fortunately, they collected the wood and returned to the cave, as Naine came walking in wearing Enuno's fur coat. Her sisters looked at her strangely, and she told them that he insisted she wear the coat. Enuno confessed to this new form of sharing.

Enuno told the women that he would much rather they have comfort rather than him. He scooped up much of the coal from their dinner fire and used them to start their small nighttime fire. With the fire burning for security, Enuno asked Kvinde to join him in one of the private tunnels where Naine and Mujer could not see them. Once alone, he explained to Kvinde the procreation process. She was puzzled, yet wanted to make a new person, so she agreed to follow him. She found that this was surprisingly an enjoyable experience. Her loud moans of excitement puzzled her two sisters, and once they had finished; she was so thrilled to tell her sisters that she at once rushed to them, before replacing her body wrappings. Naine and Mujer were accordingly surprised at how happy Kvinde was as she explained the wonderful experience to them. This actually left Enuno somewhat embarrassed to return to the women. Kvinde noticed he was slow to return, so she went to bring him back to the group. When he returned both Naine and Mujer asked him if they could join with him tonight. Enuno sadly explained to them that he had to make new seeds and he wanted each of his women to receive the same number of seeds. He told them that they would have to try many times and then if they had a month in which they were not their special way that they were each month. His angel friend had explained this to him as a sign they would know. They would continue trying until they were successful. Each night one would join him, as they continued until one by one they, each became pregnant. When their pregnancies progressed, and they began to enjoy this new life moving inside them, they bonded with the father of their babies. They all now agreed the babies were Enuno's children because his seed created them. They also wanted the security of not being alone while raising their new little people who would lay the foundation for their future generations. Naine and Mujer question their decision when they were helping pull the baby out of Kvinde. She laid there screaming in great pain, even so when her first son came from her, and she saw her new child that she cheered in great excitement thanking Enuno for this great gift of life. Naine asked her if she remembered the pain. She swore to them that she remembered no suffering and the sole thing she knew was the greatest thing ever in her life was now in her arms. Enuno had previously explained about the feeding process. The sisters watched as Kvinde's son drank her milk. They were so amazed that an angel spirit had taught their man these great things and wondered what great new knowledge lay in their future.

Enuno wondered about their futures as well. He knew that the wild beasts would be quick to attack the new little people as they attacked and killed the newborns of their fellow beasts. They would have to develop more precautious security habits. He did not worry about this, because he knew the mothers would do whatever they needed to do to keep their children safe. Naine and Mujer both delivered sons and soon the three mothers were begging Enuno for more children. Enuno would never again worry about them making fun of him or considering him to be of no value. They wanted and needed him, as did the future generations that would create their homes in the Lenti lands. Now that they knew what to do, they have done it. They would soon need to think about another place to raise this growing tribe, yet Enuno wanted to keep this cave; therefore, he searched deeper into the tunnels of the cave discovering other entrances. These additional entrances worried him, yet he knew that he could roll several rocks in front of them, and that would hold back any intruders in the dark, as most beasts did not enjoy scrapping their noses are rubbing their furs while trying to push the rocks aside. He felt better in knowing about these entrances. The thing, which he feared currently, was if he had discovered all the entrances. Each day now he would explore by himself, as none of his women would part with their children. One day, he discovered an outlet high above him. There was no path to this hole, yet just to kill the time he tried a few of the side tunnels and working toward the light above, he marked the path upward that lead to an opening beside the hole. It concluded in a comfortable cavern on a high mountain with a peaceful secure meadow. He walked around the meadow enjoying the wide-open space, plus the sharp cliffs that led up to it. He could stack many rocks to protect the children. They could easily switch back and forth from this new place to their current home. He felt this would be the perfect expansion of his family. They needed more time outside and the freedom to enjoy this land. Enuno knew that he would have a confrontation with the beasts who waited patiently for their prey, and to establish a few new boundaries in their relationship, boundaries that ensured they understood his revenge.

Enuno returned to his women and told them of his plan. He would move one family at a time and build ground markers for each turn so the children would not get lost if they traveled alone. Once they were all secure in their new home with its pleasant open cavern and plenty of small side tunnels for individual rooms, he called for his three oldest sons to join him. They were eleven years old now and the leaders of their younger brothers and sisters. The names of these three sons were Pancratius, Waldek, and Onufrys. The clan had agreed that the children could mate when they become of age for new populations, and that would be at age thirteen. These boys would be much older, in that they had to wait until the daughters they would join with reached this agreed adult age. These three sons were the closest to Enuno, for the most part, because they were the first-born and the oldest whenever he needed help. The boys naturally had their differences, in which Enuno strived hard working to avoid. Pancratius was the strongest of the three, causing Waldek and Onufrys fighting for second place. Moreover, they did fight constantly, and neither appeared without a bruise. In the early days, Enuno would attempt to stop them; however, the next day that they would be fighting once more. Thereafter, he learned to ignore it, neither condemning the loser nor congratulating the winner. He consistently had Pancratius walk ahead of them with Waldek on one side and Onufrys on the other side. He accepted their faults because they also had special qualities. Waldek was the wise one who provided the family with so much new information from his visions of education. He developed a method of representing speech sounds with what he called letters and used a black stone writing on flat stones that he stored in their caves. Onufrys was the strategic and industrial son. He enjoyed working with mud with fire, and his long knife that he created from melting certain stones, that he used to carve new things from wood. He was creative and while he worked with Waldek could astonish his parents. The difficulty lies in their constant fighting.

Their mothers were not as calm as their father was, and were constantly punishing them. The boys accepted this as a way of women, because their sisters also behaved in this manner. They cooperated when with their father and for Enuno this would work. He wanted considerable creativity in the border around their new play area on top of the hilltop; in addition, he needed a few fresh weapons against the beasts. Waldek believed that if they put a little food, the beasts liked they would go into the trap for the food. Onufrys created the new straps with the ropes; he created from the tree vines. Their first few days gave them many kills. Pancratius suggested they tied the beasts they did not want to eat to the vine ropes and allow their carcasses to hang in the air as a warning sign to the other beasts. Enuno agreed to do this after they had a few more kills that are successful. He wanted these large herds to travel other paths. Waldek suggested that they created fresh paths that would lead away from their hilltop. Pancratius and Onufrys began creating this new path. Onufrys created a new concept of planting thick branches into the ground and tying thin logs horizontally to create a fence. He also transplanted several berry vines that would grow on these logs adding thorns. The sons explained to Enuno that soon this would make a barrier to keep many of the beasts out of the area he wanted protected. The project to create the new path required the help of all children old enough to work. They could complete these two projects before the cold seasons came. He would rest much better this winter as the beasts wore in their fresh path walking along his long fence. Enuno wanted this winter to be special, one once he finished his annual mating duties; he asked Waldek to create several new songs and dances that they could enjoy with the wines that Onufrys had made for the winter. This would be a time of celebrating, as he was now able to work through his sons and daughters. The new little people were eager to do things with him, and their mothers, not just supported, but also vastly encouraged this bond.

Kvinde, Mujer, and Naine were strong and sharing mothers. Enuno spent most of his time with the children as they were busy defining the next generation. Outside of the battles between Waldek and Onufrys, all the others in this family lived in harmony. His first night of drinking wine went well as he played with his children, sang the songs, and played their games. The next day, Enuno's head gave him pains as he had lost count of the quantity of wine, which he drank the previous night. This night, he drank merely water while he played. He enjoyed the excitement of these contests, even though he constantly allowed one of his children to win. As he lay down, this season with his wives, for when they gave, birth to this year's babies, they would sleep with their newborns for three seasons. As Enuno drifted into a deep sleep, he beheld a new vision. This vision was not as his others were, for nothing in it moved. He saw a rock bridge that led to a stone floor. The rocks were yellow, while the stones covered with blood. On the rocks was a white-haired man wearing a lengthy white robe that floated in the wind while also fluffing in the air behind him. He had a long silver rod in his right hand and a shining silver sword in his left hand. These instruments intersected above his head, causing many rays of bright lights to outshine all around him. He appeared as if he was attempting to prevent something from crossing over the bridge. Enuno looked over and saw before him a raging red and yellow fire. Consequently, he saw three yellow rays of fire, proceed toward the man, yet as they approached the lights from his sword, the fire moved around him. This man had protection against the fire. Enuno looked again into raging fire and saw beasts that he could not identify. He could see how they were struggling to escape from the fire, yet most could not. Then one comes rushing from the fire. Enuno went to jump back in fear; however, the burning beast stops before the silver sword and rod. Enuno could see a deep hole in this burning inferno. Deformed creatures would jump to raise their head above the fires and cry out in great pain. Enuno tried to count the creatures in this conflagration; nevertheless, he finally lost track of the number. This was something beyond his understanding.

Enuno woke up in the morning greatly disturbed. This vision had to mean something, as it was so out of place. He sat down his women, and explained this vision to them. Naine asked him why nothing moved in this vision, for if it were a true vision with a message and meaning, they would have moved and explained it to him. Enuno told his pregnant women, as he was once again successful in his annual duty, that this stillness, except for the bobbing heads in the burning hole, was what puzzled him the most. Kvinde recommended that he ask his three oldest sons. Enuno called on Pancratius, Waldek, and Onufrys explaining this vision to them. In his wisdom, Waldek told him, that the eye sees what it brings the power to see. The vision was not as important to Waldek as was the power that gave it to him. Pancratius explains that the vision hides in its gladness and sorrow. Onufrys quickly expands that if our future is to bring sorrow, then they should seek the answer so they could prevent this sorrow and have a better future. The sons asked their father if he knew where they could find answers from the unseen world. Enuno looked at his sons and answered that the past was unchangeable, but the future is still in their power. They would go today and seek out the one he knew of as Tsigler. Enuno told his women that they had to go find the one called Tsigler and find this answer. He called the remaining children who could speak and told them that they must stay in the protected areas and obey their mothers while he and the three oldest sons were on this journey. He then departed with his sons walking past their normal hunting territory. Enuno told them that they must be careful, for the wildest beasts would be watching for an opportunity to attack them. They walked the initial day traveling deep into the lands of the west. That night they slept in tree branches, as Enuno was not as daring this time as he was the first time he made this journey. He remembered the strange visions that this land could bring to them. This time, he wanted to make sure his sons were safe. The next morning, they found a stream and with their long knives spiked a few fish, for their first meal, catching extra for the other meals during this day. Enuno told his sons that this would allow them to travel quicker toward their destination, wherever this could be.

The second night, he found a small meadow where he could sleep under the stars. He remembered that by sleeping in the open, Tsigler could find him quickly. She also had revealed to him, that she merely appeared in the nighttime hours. The second night, she once again, she did not appear. They began their march once more on the third day. Enuno was not familiar with the land they now were traveling. The stars and sun were telling him they were traveling north and south. Any time he attempted to go west, the paths would end and the forests would end. He had to go south to stay in the trees. Enuno would not walk in the open with his three sons. He would not take that risk. If the path simply opened to the south, then he would go south. He believed this to be part of his answer. The exam, nevertheless, did not have the questions he was searching for, and if it did, the probe headed in a direction, which confused him. That next day they fought and killed three lions, one of which scrapped a large cut into his left arm. They had to use one of Onufrys tree vine ropes to stop his blood from pouring. Waldek used one of his knife's needles he had made for his mother so she could sew their garments, and sewed his father's gashing cut in his arm. They traveled for a few more hours until reaching the top of a hill, where Enuno said they would camp that night. He hoped that by being higher, maybe he would be closer to Tsigler and she could hear him. That night, he called out for Tsigler throughout all the hours of darkness. His answer came one hour before sunrise when a voice said to him that on the fifth night of his journey before the great waters, she appears before him and his sons. Enuno took his sons and walked for two more days until they reached a wonder that they had never seen previously. Before them, the land turned into water for as far as they could see. They walked to the water, and waded just to their waist not trusting this new phenomenon. They walked back to the sizable sandy beach and began to gather the wood for their nighttime fire. Enuno wanted a large fire, as he feared this sand would make it easier for the beasts to attack them.

When the sun set that evening, a dark long cloud covered the horizon about one mile from the ocean waters. The sunlight that flooded below the cloud was a penetrating yellow. The light the escaped from above the cloud was a passionate white. The water came to the beach in layers as the water turned into bubbles splashing against the beach. They could hear the splashing all night long. It had a peaceful rhythm that added a tranquilly that oozed them into a serene sleep. As the moons cast their lights on the great sea during the late-night hours, a light appeared waking up Enuno and his sons. The light continued toward them forming into the gray beautiful angel whom Enuno knew. Pancratius, Waldek, and Onufrys all bowed to the ground not knowing what this spirit was going to do to them. Enuno told them not to worry. Tsigler welcomed them each by name. Pancratius asked her how she knew their names. Tsigler told them that she had watched them many times. Enuno asked her why they had to travel five days to meet her. Tsigler told them that they needed to see the great waters and the beauty of the life of the water and the air and the vastness of their powers. Enuno told Tsigler about his vision. Tsigler looked at him in surprise. She told him that he saw a place in which those on Emsky were not to see, for it was from other worlds. Tsigler explained that other deities punished their sinners with eternity in lakes of fire. Each had their specific manners in which they kept the damned imprisoned for their eternities. Tsigler was confused because the Borsod-Abaúj-Zemplén did not monitor the dead spirits from Emsky, as most drifted off into other galaxies. Tsigler told Enuno that since he had received the vision, he could include this story in his tales. No one knows when the heavens will change, and if they were to change, the wicked severely punished. This was a warning for his generations, and he should take advantage of this great wonder.

Tsigler spent the next few hours speaking with Pancratius, Waldek, and Onufrys telling them several tales about the old days on Emsky and about the people on the other lands. The sons were fascinated with her and promised not to tell others about Tsigler. She wanted to keep her contact with the humans a secret. They promised to honor her wishes. Enuno asked her to help them on their journey back. She agreed to watch over them at night and to screen the lands before them. When morning arrived, they began their five-day trip back to their home. The sons were so excited, believing they had seen the greatest beauty of a female and an angel beyond their wildest dreams. Enuno knew they were fascinated with this spiritual meeting. This was an encounter far grander than with a human. Their faces glowed. Enuno knew they would have trouble with this secret. Nonetheless, Tsigler did make it into their legends as the one who translated the vision of Enuno and forewarned that those of evil would someday face spiritual punishment. Enuno understood how this felt. He understood and was proud that he could share such an experience with his sons. This was the greatest moment in their family history. They had an experience with another life form. The giant sea would divide their family, as Pancratius swore to his father that he would someday begin his family on the sea.

A few years later, he kept his promise as the entire family moved their first to establish their security and homes. They set this new settlement up calling the city Tsigler. Three of the younger brothers and three younger sisters stayed with Pancratius. It was hard for the mothers to let their babies go; however, Enuno told them that the entire land was for them to have a domain. Kvinde was the first to agree telling the other mothers that they had to let go. Enuno took his remaining family and returned to his hilltop in the mountains. Eight years later, Waldek discovered a great sea to the north past the end of the mountains on the forestlands. When he returned, he took his wife and six brothers and six sisters to his new settlement in which the family from the hilltop helped him build. Enuno once more took the remainder of his family back to the hilltop. The years finally established a new truism, and those were the mothers' bodies became too old to bear any children. They helped their daughters as they began to have children. The reigns slowly converted occupied by the next generation.

Enuno spent his remaining days with his women and as a group; they visited the new families that were building their homes. The beasts ignored the humans now, so Enuno was thankful for this. Enuno had new worries, for he had seen how the beasts would grow old and die, or no longer be strong and alert enough to escape the predators. He did not worry about this too much about the predators, as he always had a few of his sons with him when he ventured beyond his expanded walls. The first miseries came with the death of Mujer. This was when reality began to set into their lives, or the reducing number of years ahead of them. The death of Mujer effected Naine more than Kvinde. Kvinde was a realistic woman and accepted that death was a part of life and therefore, eagerly worked helping Mujer's children. Nonetheless, the following winter took Kvinde and in the spring, Naine passed away. Enuno stood tall as their father for the subsequent two years, until his death. He knew that he prepared the children well for their mission of adding human life to the continent of Lenti.

CHAPTER 08

The Andocs

The window became silent as Pankrati smiles at the two she was hosting. Sénye and Orosházi also sat silently with puzzled stares in their eyes. Pankrati asks them if they have any questions or comments. Orosházi reveals that the story of the Lenti was wonderful, as Orosházi enjoyed the manner in which Enuno worked hard to build his family. They lived long lives, and set their children up with cities and safe places to exist. Sénye adds that the Lenti were the most secluded as they stayed on their lands and if any attempted to invade them, repelled them with constantly a superior force. For most of the history of Emsky, everyone stayed clear, except for minimal trading. The Andocs could set up schools and hospitals; however, unlike the remainder of Emsky they filled these hospitals with their individual medical people and the schools with their own teachers and subjects. They had always had schools, but never created the public buildings to present these subjects. The Lenti instead constantly maintained a low number of students each teacher and therefore, smaller classes. Lenti had many more teachers than any other continental world on Emsky. They were family centered and the unquestionable lowest number of wicked people. Tsigler's warning about the wicked, filled their sacred tales, and each generation accepted this without any question. Pankrati told her attendees the window would now show the beginning of the most advanced people to live on Emsky, the people who were the most involved with the Chuprin in preparing Emsky for integration into the Empire. They wanted it the most, and were willing to bring the rest of the secluded Emsky world up to speed with the universe that surrounded them. The Andocs were from a huge ancient civilization that colonized empty worlds or lands. They were the Ruumi from a vast collection of galaxies on the far side of the universe. Their civilization had reached its peak and had expanded their borders as much as possible. They then decided to spread out throughout the universe and plant their future children on other worlds. This would as well make sure they would survive long past their Empire, which was constantly involved in large-scale wars. Because they had shifted away from acquiring galaxies, they now had to defend their vast Empire of over 500 galaxies. During the age when time switched from the negative time to positive time, the universe had many large Empires. The shift from the negative time to the new time direction caused many Empires to decline. Mass diseases, technological disruptions, and political collapse left many of the large Empires powerless to provide for their starving masses as forced themselves to move from the comfort of advanced life to survive as their ancestors had millions of years earlier. Planets spun from their solar systems drifting in the freezing empty space. Many stars exploded, causing other planets to crash or splatter. The center of the universe was now a large black hole that was sucking all it could into it. What it could not pull in, it shifted destroying the life on it. The collapse ended within a few millennia as the force of the new time direction caused the black hole to cough up what it had inside it for a fresh big bang that exploded this mass into deep space. The gasses were a hot liquid that began to reform into new worlds, and galaxies.

This great reorganization naturally did not affect all the galaxies in the same manner. Many of the galaxies could survive this time shift with merely global disasters such as earthquakes, floods, and loss of life through the extinction of food sources such as vegetation. The ripple of the time waves continued for many millennia, and in a sense, continues in the deep parts of the universe, although not as destructive in intensity or duration. It could never end. It, nevertheless, will reach a point where it will collapse returning to its original point many billions of years in the future making another time line shift. This evolutionary story happened before the first stone of Emsky, thereby did not have any relationship directly with the seventh stone except for the Andocs. The Ruumi traveled the universe planting their giant eggs in the oceans or great bodies of water on worlds that had the gasses that they needed to live. These eggs could remain dormant for almost one billion years. They planted these eggs on Emsky before the first stone in the history of Emsky's ages. The Ruumi were the number-one race to repopulate most of the worlds consumed and reformed by the current big bang. A special material that could condense to the size of an atom and expand accordingly to its genetic code size energized their eggs. Their extensive colonization efforts added a degree of standardization to the newest part of the universe that was regenerating itself. These creations were not interested in being a member of a large Empire, and just as the continents on Emsky wanted to enjoy their solitude. Their lone exception was incorporation into the Empire of the good, which soon would annex Chuprin.

They planted their eggs on Emsky with so many other worlds in Chuprin. The Ruumi planted them in the deepest part of the ocean so they would endure the planet's long evolution cycles. The first six stones did not trigger any alarms, as the eggs lay dormant. They remained, hidden to the worlds who hosted them. Their covert domain fell, prey to a special species. The Benigna-A roamed all the seas always searching for any artifacts from the earlier worlds to add to their hidden collections. Siostra was playing with Demeris one night swimming in the deep middle of the ocean. They had agreed to enjoy a few weeks exploring the ocean and thus picked up Tolmachyov and Chemeris in the middle of the ocean for their daily hibernation. There came one night when Demeris discovered a small shining white, ivory-coated stone. She used her hands to pull away several rocks that were locking it to the ocean's floor. She finally called for her mother to help her. Siostra knew it was not native to Emsky, yet that was all she knew. It did not appear to have any value, except maybe, as a unique ornament in her decorated under the ocean cavern. Siostra loved her cavern as it led to an underground river that had plenty of air pockets for her beloved Tolmachyov and Chemeris. They finally removed the rocks and pressed dirt and before them was a large ivory egg. It was five feet long. This was the largest egg that they had ever seen. Strangely, it took both Siostra and Demeris to pry the egg out of its hole. Depression overtook them sourced by the egg's enormous weight. Notwithstanding when they went to lift it on their underwater vines, expecting a great struggle, they met with a surprised instead. They did not want to ask for any help, for fear that, others would want to break the egg and share its parts for their personal home decorations. When they lifted the egg in the open water with their vines, they gave a hard yank hoping their strength would give this enough elevation from the ocean floor to transport this egg to their cavern. Nevertheless, when they yanked the egg, it offered no resistance and thus flung high into the water as they snapped their long vine. Their momentary confusion quickly turned into joy as they realized they could now bring this egg home without any sharing or having to destroy what they currently felt to be something special. They shortened their vines and hurriedly carried it back to their cavern. Once back, Siostra tucked it into a safe hidden place in an underwater river close to her entrance. Siostra told Demeris that they needed to search that area for more of these special stones. She believed that this stone was not a fluke of nature.

She was true in her belief that the creation of this stone was not from anything on Emsky. Her problem lay in trying to determine what created them. Siostra believed that there had to be more of these special stones. She did not understand why she believed this, just that she had too strong of a thinking that there was more to discover. She took Demeris with her and off they went to continue their extended vacation hunt, leaving Chemeris on the underground riverbank to guard their new treasure. Siostra had special invisible dust on her hands from touching the egg. This dust mysteriously led them to the next three eggs that they secured in their underground riverbank. Tolmachyov believed that they should move these rocks to a mountaintop on the still vacant Andocs continent. She alleged that these stones had something special inside them that she believed was a life form. Tolmachyov was strong with these forms of suspicions, as if she had that special sense. Siostra agreed, and they began moving the eggs up the river this time with the help of Tolmachyov and Chemeris, because the river was shallow most of the way there, as they were going upstream working their way from the deep-ocean bed to the shorelines of Andocs. Here they would scoot it up to the longest river in the Andocs, which led to the highest mountains. They would set the eggs out in the forest under the tall trees. Tolmachyov and Chemeris would keep a watch on them at various times in the night and Siostra with her Demeris sticking their heads out of the river during the days. There was no need to worry, as merely animals lived in Andocs, and they were not in search of any large white ivory stones. They had no knowledge that these eggs came from the one-time powerful Ruumi.

The Ruumi planted these eggs long before their tragic fall. The Ruumi held on longer than many other Empires, as their 500 galaxies were in more of a string formation, many areas barely two galaxies wide. This gave a forewarning to the galaxies on the opposite end of the black hole. The black hole could not consume all its galaxies, yet did affect each one much worse than the others were. Their great Empire lost most of their space power with the collapse of so many galaxies and with the shifts in the other planets' orbits; they rushed their rescue attempts, overloading many planets with as much as ten times their original populations. They lost too much of their military power when their earlier galaxies collapsed, their military believed this to be a raid into these territories and sunk their power into this newly perceived battlefield. Their ships zapped forward into this empty black just to vanish. Their powerful space missiles that they shot into this black mass simply slipped into oblivion. This created more panic in the nearby galaxies as these spaceports saw a mass exodus flooding their open space with refugees. Many believed their Empire faced punishment for the bloodshed it created in obtaining these galaxies. Even though they had shed blood, the Empire worked hard to rebuild these worlds. After a few centuries, their occupation ended as the motherland forces returned to the new battlefields, knowing the newer generations now gave their allegiances to the Ruumi to whom, they currently were part. The Ruumi central government fell to corruption as, so many gave way to their greed. They purchased Armies and fought among each other. The blood spilled in the Ruumi central galaxy more than any other galaxy, which was common in places where power existed. Little they knew that the real power was in the genetic coding that they placed in their eggs they were planting on the outer parts of the universe. Their greatest scientists and most glamorous women contributed to this gene pool. They were exceedingly careful not to include public administrators or military in this pool by order of their King, who wanted the new ages to be composed of an unknown breed of people. More importantly, the King did not want royal genetic coding blended with regular genes.

Although there was nothing wrong with the Ruumi majestic genes, the King provided a blessing to the prospective universe's generations by removing these genes from the genetic pools that would reseed many future galaxies. The royal genes actually did not contribute to the intellectual or beauty of their gene pools. The public administrators and military leaders professed to be corrupt stealing all that they could through the myriad of gray laws the plagued the public. This was one of the reasons, why the Ruumi who was invincible; their infrastructure collapsed as the black hole was also sucking away their frontiers. As the military weakened, revolution broke out throughout all the capitals. The public pulled the planet governors from their offices with their staffs and executed in public. It did not take long for other public scammers, and especially the Empire's revenue generators, to hide in exile on the moons, which had breathable gasses. Certain radical groups launched random raids on these moons, when they had a breather between the natural disasters, which intensified as the black hole grew. Ruumi learned that when an Empire takes too much from the people that when the chains find themselves loosened, they would break free and take back what they lost. The royalties, who were merely figureheads at this time, escaped the impact of these rebellions, totally losing their large annual allowances. Their subjects enjoyed seeing them struggle as the former royalty struggled. Food was now available solely to those who would fight the hardest. Meanwhile, the hardest did fight hard, scarcely rewarded with harder struggles for dwindling resources. Ruumi, although hard fighting warriors, avoided greed in these times of uncertainty. There was no need to accumulate property, as the blood that they would shed to protect it took away any gain or peace that came with it. The widespread decentralization made it possible for small civilizations to continue through all the climate changes, floods, fires, powerful earthquakes, and tornados. Most of their history perished at the hands of nature and battles. The remainders of their history, except for a few pages, in summary, most of the survivors remained forgotten over the ages.

Siostra and Tolmachyov checked on the eggs daily. The white eggs gave them their first surprise when they turned green within a few days. The shade of green matched the terrain that secured it. Tolmachyov believed this was a sign that life existed with it. She became even more protective of this special form of life that was burning her mind with curiosity. Their first summer was extremely hot. One day in the middle of this scorching season, Chemeris discovers small cracks in the four eggs, appearing in the same places. Siostra orders that their surveillance now become covert in that no chance of detection will be possible for whatever is inside them. Benigna law forbids any contact with other humanoid life forms. This was especially applicable with here until they could confirm what species existed inside these eggs. They at the present officially classified them as eggs and doing so requires additional protocols. This discovery was too great now to keep a secret, as all the Benigna received their briefings. This was an added safeguard to prevent any Benigna from accidentally exposing themselves to this mystery. The Benigna secured the area watching the eggs continue to crack and while they cracked completely open releasing two men and two women. They emerged as young adults and with a special garment covering their gender-specific differences. They implanted these as being one of the methods to pass down a beginning of Ruumi culture, yet the rest the new people would have to learn on their own. The names of the four adults were Patrikas male, Rika female, Kalka male, and Olimpisia female. When they first emerged, fearing each, they rushed into the forests. Hunger forced them to seek food. Vegetation and fruits were the first things they tested. Their natural instinct moved them away from the flesh of animals, as they had no way of capturing these beasts even if, they so desired to consume them. Rika's fear of being alone forced her to begin tracking Patrikas. Patrikas senses that something is different in the world surrounding him, by the response of birds and their delay in reforming behind him. One night he set a trap by digging a hole and covering it with grass. He hopes this ambush will discover the mystery that if following him.

The next day, he walks to the center of his trap and quickly leaps over it, yet whatever follows him mimics the same action. Rika did not see his footprints in the brush and noticed the depth of the footprints on the other side, thus jumped herself. That night, Patrikas returned to this site and placed a false footprint in the middle of the brush ambush using mud on leaves. He attaches a vine on a tree limb that hangs over the snare. Patrikas secured the rope, so he could swing from it, nevertheless, when he released it, the rope would hang over the brush footprint. This proved to advance for Rika to escape, as she stepped on the brush reaching for the vine, which was too high for her to grab, as her jump for it snapped the brush, she stood. She fell into the trap screaming. Patrikas rapidly realized the scream was from his species and rushed back to the hole discovering an extremely hostile Rika. He manages to overpower and bind her. He takes her back to a cave he made his home, making Rika his prisoner. Patrikas soon determines that Rika is not a threat to him, yet still has concerns about her flight risks. He believes that by feeding and caring for her, they will become friends. Both are surprised about their natural tendency to bond as companions and soon Patrikas takes his chance and releases her. Rika stays with him, becoming his helper. They work as a team and soon their hormones teach them the new uses for their bodies. Their first mating experience left Patrikas confused and demanding answers. He believed this experience took away his independence and control of his own body. One minute, his mind was on survival, and the next minute he was behaving as an animal begging on his knees and dependant on the mercy of another. Patrikas had to find the answer for this question and mystery. One night, he departed on his mission of discovery, not knowing the answer was developing in his cave at his side in the womb of Rika.

Kalka and Olimpisia did not have the save capture process to find themselves living as one. Kalka discovered the terrain that he selected also had carnivorous beasts claiming this land. Kalka survived his first beast attack slightly with the use of a large stone was he able instinctively to kill the aged tiger. His injuries were minimal, as Olimpisia witnessed this battle. She rushed to the tiger grabbing another stone and beating it until it stopped moving. Olimpisia applied mud to his wounds wrapping them in leaves. Next, they studied the tiger to determine why it no longer moved. Accordingly, they both agreed the tiger wanted to damage Kalka. It was not until later they could accurately to define this killing process. For the time being, they knew that a form of a weapon had to be developed. They elected to use strong clubs with sharp stones attached to them. One day, they were watching two large lions fighting viciously. They continued to fight until one dropped to the ground dead. They also watched how the tigers hunted the deer and afterwards ate that animal flesh. Kalka invented a bow that would shoot the arrows he gave sharp ends with that could outrun the fleeing beasts. The arrows, aimed for the neck and a leg, as Kalka and Olimpisia would shoot at the same animal, knowing that they had to injure a limb with the neck injury. The neck injury, they hoped to disrupt the animals control over its body, and the limb shot designed to slow the beast. Once they had it slowed, either they would shoot additional arrows into the creature, or if they could catch it, then beat it with their clubs. They learned, through trial and error to cook the meat and to salt it for storage. They discovered the salt when a rodent died in their cave on a bed of salt, and another scavenger tore it open consuming selected parts. The remaining parts did not rot as the other carcasses in the open. This discovery opened a new realm of survival tools for this couple. When their first summer ended, and the days grew colder and the vegetation vanished, the consumption of meat kept them alive, with the burning wood, introduced to them by a surprise source.

Patrikas departed from Rika in his quest for answers. Rika could not remain in hiding and therefore, began hunting for those who were in the other eggshells. She had not seen them, yet believed they existed. She searched throughout the summer, finally one day discovering Olimpisia. At first, Olimpisia had reservations about Rika; however, the need to have another as she removed her fear and gave her the courage to welcome her into their family. Olimpisia gained Kalka's approval as the new family of three formed. Rika surprised them in the middle months of the winter months when she gave, birth to her first son, whom she called Yubkin. Olimpisia fell in love with little Yubkin and wanted to realize how she could have one of those boys come out of her. Rika explained this to Kalka and Olimpisia. They at once began their mating process. Their hormones were not as active as Rika and Patrikas who were more involved in hunting and hormonal fluctuations relieved through the brutality of their hunt. Rika had another mystery she had discovered during her days alone. One night while she was sleeping in a tree, because of the rain, lighting hit a few branches on the ground, beginning a fire. She went to the ground, studied the fire, and experienced the heat from it. The next day, she rubbed new sticks together, and began her first fire. Rika brought this knowledge to Kalka and Olimpisia, making the first fire that they had seen. They were thrilled with the heat, which took away much of the discomfort of the cold. That winter also found Rika mating with Kalka, because she did not have enough faith that Patrikas would return. Rika offered her cavern to her new roommates; however, Kalka wanted to keep the rock house he had constructed. He had stacked rock walls and formed them into the house. Kalka stacked logs that he used as their ceiling and sealed it with mud and straw that he made by the tall grass, he found. The door was from the hide of a deer they had eaten. Kalka also created a small wall around the border of their secure meadow. Olimpisia and Rika had prepared the meat that they could eat the rest of the winter. Kalka had discovered how sharp stones could cut the meat and sharpen their spears and arrows. Rika would wonder at night where Patrikas was, and if he was in good health.

Patrikas worked his way over many ridges and the deep valleys between them. His zigzag path within one month prevented him through total confusion of finding a path back to his home. He traveled the green lands reaching the great sea. He followed the sea throughout the cold months, finding this area became warmer the further he walked south. Patrikas could not follow the stars and after a few years made it to the deepest part of the southern lands of the Andocs continent. Patrikas learned to sleep in trees, as the available caves were scarce and not located in strategic places. Patrikas was vegetarian and lived from the year-round supply of vegetation and fruit trees. Fortunately, this southerly land did not have large herds of animals and the predators that followed them. Heavily populated with gorillas, apes, and monkeys, the southern lands, presented Patrikas with a world that confused him. Patrikas believed these to be different forms of human life. He allowed his head and facial hair to grow. One day, he discovered the carcass of a large bear, took a sharp rock, and tore off its hide. He cleaned it in the ocean and using another rock formed bodysuit from this hide. He used bands cut from the discarded parts of the hide to tie the hides; he used to cover his arms and legs. Over the years, Patrikas began to refocus his social norms and soon found himself working with a group of gorillas. He attached himself with a few female gorillas, and they began to reproduce his children. The Gorilla women began to prefer bearing this new species to bearing gorillas through Gorilla fathers. This caused a few fierce fights with the other males in this small clan. Patrikas could use his spears and arrows to remove the other male threats. He became the sole breeder to this group and within a few years had many children of this new species. His children were born with a small part of his intelligence and complete ability to use their hands. They also could fly through trees, and perform the normal functions of the Gorilla. They were powerful in their territorial battles against the other groups of apes and gorillas.

They never could develop language skills, which hindered their capacity of create a civilization. Their one advantage lay in an instinct they had as the comradeship among themselves, they united among each other, yet their union was more than a non-aggression among themselves and holding onto their lands. The other animals were no match for Gorilla Ruumi as their teamwork made penetration impossible. The Gorillas spread themselves strategically throughout their lands and held fast to their family unit as the solid foundation of their civilization. They were fine stewards of their land, tending to their trees and vegetation. The choice of their mates was also ritual and controlled by their mothers. The fathers had nothing to do with this mating process. The mothers

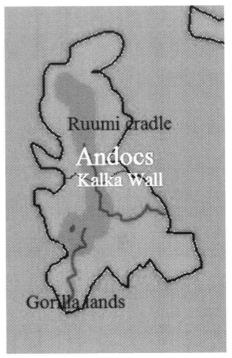

controlled the surrender of their daughters and the mates for their sons. Kalka's generations fared much better, creating cities and forts for their security against an invisible enemy. Their intuitions inclined them to set up a code of behavior so they could have cities, which depended on the vegetation farmers and the hunters. The cities processed what the farmers gave them and then distributed it those who needed it. The city dwellers helped the farmers work their lands. Farmers stood exempted from the military service. The primary source of labor was building stone roads and walls. They named this wall after the father of the Ruumi.

The Kalka Wall ran from the western ocean through the mountains to the eastern sea. The wall began with Kalka, as he could extend it for ten miles before his death. He died while working on this wall. Olimpisia recorded in her writings that he wanted to make sure that his descendants stayed in the north and did not travel in the south. Her sons worked hard and finally, the fourth generation completed the wall. They stacked the stones ten feet tall and dug a deep trench in front of it. They planted in front of this trench rose plants and berry vines. The descendants never truly knew why they had to stay in the northerly part of the Ruumi cradle. The northern section offered so much land providing the newer generations with many opportunities to expand. There came a day when a man known as Pásztói created the first rafts. Fifty people could stand in this wide raft. They gave the people on the sides long poles to push against the shallow ocean floor. They built these rafts to move people from the east shore to the northern shore, western shores, and the opposite for their return trip. This allowed them to bypass the mountains in the middle lands. There came a day when Pásztói wanted to explore below the wall into the forbidden lands. He built a smaller raft and took ten men with him as he mapped the lower half of the continent. The Ruumi gorillas remained, hidden when the raft passed by their lands. Pásztói used the stars and measured their distance by the number of pushes with their rods into the shallow ocean floor. He precisely mapped the border and the mouths of the two rivers plus the shallow end of the two rivers. He could not accurately define the limitations of the mountains from the sea, yet he did recognize these lands were overflowing with game and beautiful open lands. Pásztói recommended that their crown sends and expedition through the mountains to make sure no hidden enemy kingdoms shared this large continent. The King formed the first expedition, a force of twenty men, with their supplies to survey the mountains. He ordered that no men leave the mountains and walk on the green lands. Without reason the writings of Rika forbid any foot to touch the green lands to the south. She also warned that any who walked in the mountains would be in great danger. The men of this expedition at first were nervous; however the land on the other side of the wall looked the same, the trees were similar, even the beasts that inhabited the area were the same, as they simply jumped over the wall apparently without any worries. The first day over the wall, the twenty soldiers hunted and killing a small deer. The meat cooked the same on their fire and tasted the comparable. At the end of their week, they found a beautiful valley and a place they marked on the map as the Garden of Emsky. This site had a wide dark-green stream that swelled into a heart at its top basin. The heart is broken, half on the top and the other half about fifty feet below the cliff. The waterfall sparkled the landscape with a pure white glow. The water in the lower basin was a lighter green and rushed around the large black rocks that stayed within its stream. The northwestern bank of the stream slowly formed from a brush and green trees with a walkable slope. The northern bank passes the waterfalls where a steep cliff that existed coated with the lines of a raging time. The southern bank stood stocked with a myriad of trees of many colors. The bad smell flooded the land that surrounded it with an exotic sense. The explorers marked this on their map, as the place where people could relax and find happiness. The sound of the water splashing added to the serenity of this place. They allowed their horses to graze on the rich grass in this area, while the men relaxed on the soft meadows. They enjoyed this to such a high degree that their commander sent four of his men back to their King's city and share this great study. This commander stood high on a nearby peak, saw the mountain ridges for miles, and saw no danger. He felt no fear and wanted all his fellow compatriots to enjoy this beauty. The King rushed back with his harem and they found this place to be all that the explorers claimed it would be. The King decided now to send two groups of explorers, with twenty men each, into this deep unknown. He wanted a group on each of the four ridges before him, telling them to go down one ridge and return on another. This way the two groups could map all four ridges and document the wonders between them.

The two groups departed, with the second delayed, as they had to return to the city to collect their provisions. The leader of the first group was the King's son, Prince Ecser and the leader of the second group was the princess's cousin Aristov. These young men coexisted highly competitive against each other and were committed to discover the greatest treasures for their King. To make sure fairness, the Prince advanced three hours ahead and waited for cousin to catch up with them. They agreed to exchange reports daily, considering that whoever made a discovery did not truly matter, as it was ridge specific and therefore dependent totally on fortune. A few days later, they both discovered something special in a valley that sunk between their ridges. They stumbled on two red trees with branches that existed intertwined. There remained no leaves on these trees, as their roots were also this eerie red. The mysterious aspect of these two intertwined trees was how they formed a human hand with the branches representing blood-filled veins. They stopped to allow their artists to paint this fluke of nature. That night in their dreams, both Ecser and Aristov had dreams. In this dream, a white spirit appeared in front of them. This spirit warned them that if they left the mountains, they would die. The spirit also warned them not to travel down the outside of the two outer ridges. They were solely to scout the four inner ridges therefore; they had no plans about these extra outer ridges. The puzzle for Ecser revolved around this same age-old warning. He asked the spirit, why they could not step foot on the green grasslands. The spirit told Ecser that the grasslands existed inhabited by a sin of nature. The beasts had survived, protected, as they were neither human nor animal. Their actions and customs have gained them the right to survive. Ecser asked this spirit how these animals could be human and animal. The spirit revealed the ancestor of these beasts was Patrikas, a Ruumi. Ecser spoke to the spirit disclosing that they had a tribe that came from the descendants of Patrikas and Rika, from her first son. The spirit acknowledged that tribe as honorable and repeated its warning not to walk in the green lands. Ecser and Aristov discussed their dream and agreed not to enter the green lands, not so much from the spirit's warning, but from the warning of the King.

The next six days, they traveled the ridges, documenting the difference from a land never before occupied by a human, noting the one drawback was the crowding overabundance animals. This day, thousands of predators attacked both groups. They fought hard as no member escaped without an injury. Ecser lost seven men, while Aristov lost nine men. They agreed to return to their homelands, taking their dead men with them. They did not want to leave them among all the animals the explorers had to kill in the attacks. The number was shocking for them, as they looked over all the malodourous carcasses. They were sick, which such a waste of Emsky's bounty lay in waste. The two leaders agreed not to change their ridges on their retreat. The King was furious at their early return. He could not accept defeat by animals nor would he allow a tale about the honorable Patrikas to be the father of an animal race. He declared to them that any who divulged this story he would execute. This story stayed unrevealed until after the official discovery during the later reign of Ecser. His father never again when beyond the Garden of Emsky during the remainder of his life, nor let anyone else to go pass this garden that he kept heavenly guarded. Prince Ecser had a personal urge for revenge against the animals that had shamed him before his father. When Prince Ecser happened to receive his crown as King, he began to create the first Andocs Army. His nights were haunted by dreams of that day when he suffered so many lives to the animal raid. This was not acceptable, especially by being Ruumi humans, who were supposed to be a superior breed. No one knew what the special features of being Ruumi were. All they knew was a short comment from Rika in her tales that she had the words Ruumi written with a golden thread on the inside of her clothing that she was born wearing. Olimpisia as well wrote about this, which added to the credibility of this word. King Ecser had a score to settle, as equally important did Aristov who the King made his high general.

The King knew his Army had to have a huge arsenal of weapons. He developed an exceptional archery division that would be able to fire five thousand arrows. He covered his spear and long knife division with special animal furs knowing that the beasts would attack fiercely trying to rip their body apart. Ecser and Aristov began their raid to clean Andocs of any threats to human security. This march contained most of every man from the King's kingdom. Ecser took the extremely young and exceedingly old as supply reserves, knowing the immense quantity of animal flesh that they would harvest. They brought forth wagons filled with salt and returned with wagons filled with field-harvested meat. They removed the hides back in the home territories for use as clothes and other household uses. Ecser would not leave so much life-sustaining bounty to waste a second time. Ecser and Aristov lead their giant fleets into the mountains in the southern lands. Once more, six days pass the Garden of Emsky; the land became flooded with animals as they began raiding nonstop for days. Ecser and Aristov's troops had plenty of arrows and weapons. The sky would rain arrows, and then when a new wave of beasts swarmed in above those dead from the previous wave. The animals could not launch another raid on the open meadow before them as the stacked carcasses prevented them from attacking. They next launched their attacks on Ecser and Aristov's side flanks and rear. These avenues were hindered brush and trees. Their spear and long knife divisions fought perfectly in these conditions. Meanwhile, the front line saw his harvesting reserves cleaning the animals from their line working outward to keep a barrier wall. They did not harvest all the animals, as they did not harvest lions, except to remove their hides. They dug holes to store the nonedible organs. They tossed the heads and hoofs on the open ground, to add obstacles if of another wave would come. Another wave did not come. Ecser and Aristov moved forward one hill, to avoid the smell and sniper any scavengers attempting to feast on the earlier day's battle. The reserves rushed the harvest back to the north to offer food for all the people. As they continued south, the intensity of the raids began to thin. Ecser did not realize that the worse is still waiting for them.

When they reached the south of the mountains and saw the green lands before him, he decided that if Patrikas had a sin living in this land, it was the time to face it. His men spread through the forests and after two days, finally killed a few of these special creatures, and brought them back to Ecser. He was horrified and declared that they had to ensue erased from the surface of Emsky. Their bows and arrows allowed them to kill the Patrikas hiding in the trees. The first few weeks saw few kills, yet Aristov insisted that by guarding the water sources, they would be able to thin them. The fighting continued for one year, when King Ecser had to return to his kingdom. He took one small company back with him. On his way back, a group of Patrikas caught and slaughtered the King and his company. They delivered the King's head back to Aristov. He was angered and sent a division to take the King's head back and request two more divisions with more ammunition. The new King, Ecser's oldest son, Prince Pankrati, brought back two divisions and winter clothing for his soldiers serving under Aristov. They joined these forces stretching into a long line that stood designed to do a solid flush to the sea, with advance elements to ambush water sources. They return from the sea, pushing the Patrikas north, as many went pass their northern border where wild beasts attacked them. King Pankrati discovered that the Patrikas had borders, they stayed in, and the animals avoided. He sent scouts out to map this border. King Pankrati told his large Army not to go into the animal lands, as he did not want to fight them at this time. He knew it was important to keep an eye on them, in case they would try to raid as the animals in the mountains had done. The best they could determine now was that these beasts wanted to see the Patrikas killed off first. The King and Aristov swept back to the sea, and then back inland and made their concluding sweep along the animal border. They spread their men out twice as wide and made one concluding sweep down and back up to the mountains. He left two large battalions to do an ongoing sweep for the remainder of his life. The important issue was that no chance could exist that even one remained. King Pankrati knew that the animal kingdom would rush to occupy this new land. This would serve his interests.

The animal kingdom did enter this now vacant land. They would serve for any Patrikas and kill them, as they did not want to chance their numbers to multiply and would battle to regain their lands. Ten years later, Aristov took a division, and this time worked his way down the eastern shoreline. He hunted down all the predators that he could, citing that they were eating the game reserved for human consumption. He felt confident to divide his force into many small hunting groups and within one year, cleaned out a large portion of the predators, leaving the edible game protected. He mapped the terrain and discovered the huge lake south of the northern great river. His force swept through the southern lands, making the last sweep to the Patrikas, who were now extinct and reduced the predators stunting their expansion by also eight hundred years. He assembled all his King's soldiers, and led them back to their northern homes. King Pankrati remained resolved to keep his people above their historical coast-to-coast Kalka Wall. When the hunters returned to their homes telling how they had killed the tree people, as they called them, many people became angry. They demanded to learn more about this other race of people and the reason this needed extermination. They argued that killed other people without cause was morally evil. King Pankrati used as justification the head of his father and warned that any who challenged his morality would have their head placed beside his father. This did not stop the continuous complaints. King Pankrati finally declared that any who would not swear alliance to him and receive their white star tattooed on their head or faced being cast over the wall and then banished from the northern lands the rest of their lives along with their children and all their future generations. It took two years to reorganize his loyal base, at a cost of one-third of his people who now forever survived cast over the wall. This caused so much depression and sadness over all the land, as many families lost their sons or father, while others their daughter or mother.

Aristov finally revealed the reason to King Pankrati as to why his father wanted the tree people destroyed. When the King discovered the true reason, he agreed with his father's decision to clean the Andocs of this sin against the creators. He stood fast to his decision, the remainder of his days, keeping his secret locked in his private diaries, to stay locked until all who currently lived had died. He believed their lack of patriotism and sense of the true morality of protecting the honor of the ancestors took away many of their basic rights to understand the truth. The truth would strangely paralyze them. His younger brother, led the people of the southern lands becoming their first King, crowned as King Bercik. His older brother refused to reveal to him their father's reason, simply telling him that it was their father's wish. Moreover, as his sons, the divine spirits bound them to obey their father. King Bercik refused to accept this, as he had a taste for power and had a throne he did not want to surrender. He established a standing Army, which he used to create the new roads needed to establish an infrastructure for his new kingdom. King Bercik moved his people southward until they reached the eastern river, using the river as their primary form of transportation for their trading. He created most of his roads to connect this river with the southern ocean and river. He discovered huge herds of horses as they began to break them in and established a sizeable reserve for all his soldiers and transportation wagons. He could move his Army quickly anywhere along the Kalka Wall and move large amounts of raw resources to build the new cities they needed. It took them merely ten years to construct their cities and set up their security, when one day a large group of soldiers came over the wall to speak with King Bercik bringing him an unusual gift. King Bercik opened the box and pulled out his brother's crown. The group notified him that King Pankrati was dead, and that he had to return and accept his father's kingdom. King Bercik notified his courts and returned to the north to accept his new kingdom, solely to find a shocking surprise to greet him.

As King Bercik entered his father's house, he saw his mother's body and not his brother's body. Instead, soldiers came to bound him, taking him outside to hang with his last view because of his brother who came over and took back his crown. Several among the kingdom believed this to be dangerous, as it left the throne without a spare Prince, as the lone sibling who remained was a younger sister, who had married and moved away from her family. A few cities saw riots; nevertheless, the soldiers rushed in and bound them, releasing those who pledged their allegiance to their King. When the southerly lands discovered their King was dead, they demanded their Armies attack in revenge. The southern Armies climbed over the wall, and because of time, constraints, did not pull their horses over the walls, and elected to attack on foot. They happened to meet many surprises when they crossed the wall, as they fell into King Pankrati's ambushes. His policy was to kill on sight. The southern Armies did not go down without a fight, as they fought with all their might and survived much longer than the King had originally expected. The King used several of his reserves to speed up the massacre. The King received what he wanted, and that was the complete defeat of the first Army from the south to invade. He would face two added southern Armies, though not as large, they were initially successful. One of the two Armies crossed the wall where it met the eastern ocean shore, with a company coming over the wall to secure an unloading area. Accordingly, other soldiers brought the horses around the wall in the shallow ocean waters. Once they had all crossed this unguarded area, they began their cavalry raids. King Pankrati was preparing to ambush the second Army slowly to cross over the wall in the mountains. He never thought about this Army being split, believing that the first Army's defeat cost the southern kingdom, most of their fighting force. Because his people had objected to the way he massacred the first Army, he decided this time to march his captives deeper into the mountains to a place that rested above a giant cliff. He would have his soldiers fling them over this cliff. Meanwhile, the third Army was raiding the small villages putting extreme pressure on the King to face them.

This choice forced the King to split his Army. The King could not accept this option, and instead killed all his prisoners and dumped their bodies into the nearby hillsides. The prisoners did not drop as animals before a butcher, but fought as raging animals, making this elimination extremely difficult, actually obtaining a kill rate of one to three. This disturbed the King, with this second Army being one-half his Army and for three of these to average one death among his warriors was beyond his comprehension. One-sixth of his Army now lay dead. He would currently have to fight an armed Army. The mystery now was how many more will he lose. His scouts reported to him that this Army was on horses, and they could strike at will. He knew that open meadows were no longer an choice. The King would have to stay in the forests, yet the cavalry would not fight in the forests. He could not ignore them, as this third Army would continue to hit cities and large farms. The destruction of farms, which supported cities, could cause that city to starve for the next year having no harvest. The King had to meet them between cities, yet they were not willing to engage him. The King had just had a few options available. One was to form and send a cavalry to the south to raid. The other part of his plan was to train farmers and city dwellers based on the three to one the prisoners unleashed on him. The last part of his plan was to intercept them at the sea with, they tried to bring their horses south with them. This would be his finest ambush with so many traps and his greatest secrecy. He would have another standing Army around his palace city as a decoy. When news reached the southern cavalry that the north was raiding the south, and the cities were putting up a harder fight now, they elected to return and save their families. They rushed to the seacoast wanting to return south before the King moved his palace Army to the ocean. Their rush to the sea put their precautionary measures to the side. The third Army rushed the King's trap, as he could slaughter the soldiers and capture the horses, which gave him an ability to form another cavalry that he at once unleashed on the south.

The King took the remainder of the Army back to his capital. He first built a third cavalry and then was the original to break an opening in the Kalka Wall. He filled the hole in with a strong gate made from wood. He also enclosed a small meadow around the gate with another rock wall and second gate that lead into a military fort. These gates would permit him to launch his cavalry in the mountains and not have to walk them in the ocean around the wall borders. The north now had three cavalry groups raiding and torturing the south. The northern cities began to riot once again over the brutality of their southern raids. The Queen forced the King to bring back the cavalries and to keep his kingdom above the Kalka Wall. The King gave in and brought back his military. King Pankrati and the Queen went on to have seven more children, all of which were females. This angered the King, as he decided to clean up those who were born with deformities, believing these babies were cursing his country. When he started these selective murders, two of his daughters became sick and died. The King now became suspicious concerning invisible spirits. He slowly slid into insanity, and his courts finally voted to have the Army execute him. The crown went to the son of the King's sister. This new King immediately established peace with separation, with the south. The south did not trust the north and therefore, created the second son law. All families gave their second son of to the southern King who raised them in his children's camps and used them for public works and his military. This policy remained for over two centuries, when the southerly King had many great Armies. He decided the launch a war against the north. The war became out of control early in its stages. The southern King refused to walk on northern soil, claiming it would defile him. The invading soldiers believed that they had to extract a large booty to compensate the cost of them existing defiled. The populace did not surrender their family members or property without a fight. The King of the north rushed his cavalries to the raided areas, and the battles continued. The invading Armies found themselves surrounded inside their enemies. The north had dedicated itself that no property or raider would return to the south. This turned into a war without borders. The citizens would not rest until their homelands were once more safe. Even the soldiers who tried to flee, they hunted and killed.

There was no such thing as surrender, which also resulted in death, although they experienced their death in a more humane method. The northern raiders in the southern lands fared no better as they also met, the citizen's revenge.

The one trait that all the Ruumi descendants on Emsky shared was that they would not allow their homes to coexist with invasions. The raiders that made it to the Kalka Wall were trapped in the walls fort on the northern side and there executed. The Ruumi left the northerly lands uninhabited for the following two centuries. Extremely few ventured to the north to settle, as most believed this land stood cursed. The Andocs were the first to build the boats and sail the seas. They had adopted stringent laws against invasion, declaring that no person from their kingdom could set foot on another land. They accepted this as the beginning of troubles, because, once they knew of other lands, greed would lead them to lust for it. Therefore, no ship of theirs could come close enough to another land to create stories of the possessions they saw. They were also empowered to kill any aboard any boat that saw them. The Andocs had the largest and fastest ships. They also developed cannons and gunpowder. They authorized these solely for open sea use and not shot onto land. One they considered to be saving the peace, while the other considered an act of war. They struggled to stop the spread of greed and lust, two things that their instincts hated as much as death. Andocs never allow belongings to accumulate above what for what one family requires to live one life. At death, all property goes back to the King who would sell it back to the public, using the profits to finance the kingdom. This prevented any from accumulating too much wealth, which they considered the cause of all wickedness. The public, who voted on all large expenditures, controlled even the kingdom's treasure. The people craved education and public works. This form propelled the Andocs to become the lead civilization on Emsky, as Emsky's protection by the Andocs strong love for the independence of all people, which kept all free from one overpowering wicked power, although a few tried.

CHAPTER 09

The Dispositions of the Seventh Stone

The special chamber once again became silent as Sénye and Orosházi sat braced in their positions. Orosházi looked at her true husband and next looked at Pankrati as if to ask why the window was no longer sharing visions. Pankrati inquires if they have any questions. Sénye who no longer told this story, stares at Pankrati, and pleads that she summarize what they saw, and clarify what Emsky's Chronicles includes. Pankrati reveals the foundation of the seventh stone was a separate five-based civilization. This was an intentional strategy to prevent one source to set up the basis for another worldwide collapse. Emsky now had a wide base and universal gene pool for its humans, and fortunately, the Benigna to help the Borsod-Abaúj-Zemplén keep various exciting life on his favorite Emsky, Emsky4. The advantage to the multi-source civilization proved to be the disadvantage as well. The vast numbers of civilizations remained separated and fell prey to laments of space. The balance of the cosmos permits many challenges to face a world as the odds or dice do not fall as preferred. The first catastrophe to hit Emsky4 or the favored Emsky came from an unexpected return of the Ethelbert. The galaxy had smashed all their ships, except for one, through Chuprin's belts of meteors, which rotated around the solar systems in the center of the galaxy. Galactic gravitational pulls occur by designed to clean their empty space and by it protect their worlds. A large meteor smashed one Ethelbert ships into a nearby moon. Here, it remained for one thousand years, when another small meteor bounced off the seated meteor exposing the previously trapped Ethelbert ship. This planet had seven moons, and each cycle had a special point when the other six moons aliened on the opposite side of their orbit. This had a surface pulling effect on this moon, and each cycle would loosen the ship. There came a day when the ship was swept back into space. The ship flung into the planet's orbit, which after one-half orbit flipped it into space. This ship slipped through to the bottom of the Chuprin and floated in the space just outside this galaxy. Each time the ship tried to escape Chuprin's gravity it failed. Accordingly, the extended spiral that contained Emsky swept through this area. The ship returned to the Emsky solar system, and as if it sensed life, fell into Emsky4's orbit and crashed in the mountains of Álmosd. It crashed hard against one of the cliffs and shattered for miles in the area below it. Emsky was to meet its first external catastrophe.

The plague that took the innocent lives on this Ethelbert ship sunk into the skeleton remains of the carcasses that at first masked them. This virus then turned itself off lying dormant. When these skeletons stood sandwiched between the cliff and disintegrating ship, they exploded into unidentifiable fragments that coated the land below the cliff. A wind spread the fragments throughout the eastern part of the continent. The one planet saving aspect of this virus was that when submerged in water it died. It was a surface and air contact virus, and spread quickly. The virus had mutated into a form in which more than one-half of the humans could develop an immunity. The plague killed one third of the children of Álmosd. Many families befell completely destroyed, as other families lost no one. The medicine men believed this came about based on the gene pool of the families and warned that these bodies needed to burn unconditionally. These forced neighbors burning the neighbors' bodies and friends disposing of their earlier special people. The cold seasons came after the body burnings, this season cycle. This disaster alerted the Álmosd the dangers existed in all parts of their world, several beyond, their control. They had, through a fortunate gene in their composition, survived a deadly plague, that no fewer had their ancestors overcame, placing the hidden gene in their available chromosomal pools. Although all who survived stood affected by this pandemic, at least it stayed in families, wiping out their grandparents, parents, and children. This left other families intact and the remaining population completely protected in case this cursed plague returned. No one knew that an entire multi-planet civilization had lost the battle against this epidemic. The visions scanned over the empty homes and unoccupied seats in the schools. It was easy to see the populace had a large piece missing, as unfilled spots existed between parked carriages, and the way people sat in their dispersed groups during town meetings. Their records called this the Sky Plague. The Álmosd King ordered all ships destroyed and that no one leave this continent, and if any ever set foot on it that, they be executed and at once burned. He had signs warning others not to trespass on their land. They could use animal hide to create waterproof bags with strange, terrifying tales of giant monsters who lived in the northern waters and lands. These small watertight bags made it to all Emsky's continents and shaped to exploratory policies of the other lands, as they feared plagues and unknown killers.

Emsky believed unknown killers now roamed throughout the great seas. The Andocs knew different; however, did all they could to spread these stories, enhancing them whenever they had an opportunity. This helped carry out their wish to keep the continents separated. The second disaster to raid Emsky was a species known as the Polpo befell Gyáli. The Polpo was a species that was from a neighboring galaxy whose world underwent a series of earthquakes that released toxic gasses from the planet's core. The Polpo fed on humans as their primary source of food. They would land on a planet in groups of ten-thousand and search the globe humans to harvest. The Polpo would thin the planet's human population and then travel to another planet or solar system that they detected humans and feast there, for while they could do so. They probed the humans on Emsky, identifying the difference in the genetic makeup and decided those on Gyáli were the closest match for their culinary preferences. The appearance of the Polpo had several basic features that resembled human, such as face, arms, and legs. Their torso was scaly, and had a tail, which resembled an octopus with three arms and two rows of suckers. Its head had twelve horns of arms each arm with three rows of suckers. They could run faster than a deer and leap thirty feet in one bound. The suckers would also siphon dirt trying to extract any human decaying remains or bones. Merely one thing could kill them, and that was pure salt. Because the Gyáli suffered through cold winters and the cold-water currents intensified the winter weather throughout all their coastlines and mountains, they stored extra game if of another occasional long winter. The Polpo invaded Gyáli from the seacoast, as standard attack formation, and then work their way inland. They attacked their first seaport capturing all the humans they could find. They decided this time to collect humans in centralized points and feed them with their stored meat until the able to transport them back to their hunting reserves. The Polpo could not stay on Emsky for any longtime without a lung cleaning as the Emsky gasses contain small traces of a gas, which caused respiratory reactions. To their surprise, these gases were not the threat that would make this collection effort different from their predictions.

One camp attempted an escape by first throwing their uncooked meat on the Polpo. When the salt from this meat burned through them as an acid, the rebels quickly discovered their saving weapon. In this camp, they each grabbed a piece of meat, and the thin animal skin hides that it was stored in and attacked their guards burning them with this salt. They were now free and began to plan for a complete coastline sweep. These rebels soaked their furs in salt and soaked the ends of their spears with saltwater. Subsequently, they would bring a wagon of salt with them as they began to spread this ledge throughout their entire continent. Next, they rushed on their horses throughout all the land and at each station, sent additional bands in the other directions. The Polpo was astonished when these white sands ate through them as if they were no more than air. The Gyáli destroyed all the Polpo who remained in the open or as guards over their captives. Most Polpo herded their current stock into their ships and escaped Emsky as quickly as their crafts could take them. Once the Polpo consolidated in Emsky's orbit, they at once returned to their home galaxy. They believed themselves to be safe while on board, yet the Gyáli had such high concentrations of salt in the systems that when the Polpo eat their flesh, they suffered from internal salt burns, The crippled crew on return to their home planets, they ejected their remaining human stock into open space. Meanwhile, back on Gyáli all Polpo remains remained burned as the nations tried to begin their lives once more. This invasion struck hard across family lines. This was the first time the Gyáli faced a foe that was so powerful. The site of moons descending to the surface in the open day and creatures appearing that had raging snakes dancing from their scalps. The sucking stingers paralyzed all who came in person with them. The stories spread throughout their villages, sending many into the nearby hills. The Polpo had special harnesses that could transport them above the surface. This allowed them to chase the helpless humans that tried to escape. Those humans, who stood their ground and shot their arrows, still lost their lives, yet took at least one Polpo with them. Sadly, not all had the fortitude to fight for what was theirs.

Those who did formed merely a small dent against the Polpo, but embellished a huge boost in the enthusiasm. When the salt from the deer meat burned the first Polpo, excited with this news spread as fast as their winds blew. The initial obstacle was over their human face and the way their eyes flashed as the salt burned their bodies. This was a preferred appearance over the expression they had when they were preparing to capture a Gyáli human. The entire ordeal lasted for one week. Unfortunately, this week saw one of each three die or leave captured, because the Polpo suffered almost one-half to death. When they discovered the salt weapon, the Gyáli attacked with all they had. Even children ran up to the Polpo and threw salt at them. They did not need much salt to immobilize a Polpo. The chemical reaction of the salt with the Polpo arms, created an acid the spread throughout their bodies in their blood veins, destroying the veins and arteries in the process. It ended in a complete liquidation of their internal organs, bones, and muscles. Their outside appearances did not change any. This is why the Gyáli burned their bodies. This process took three weeks, as delays occurred when they held special services for their dead humans. The Gyáli had united and with their national spirit stood tall and steady as they survived a mysterious invader and saved their people. A new spirit of unity spread throughout their continent as their nations shared resources and bonded strength as they chased down this common enemy. Many held onto homes and lands. In spite of this, many failed to win this last battle, as they became food for the invaders. Usually the invaders took both the property and killed, leaving the dead to rot. This was not the normal battle or fought with the typical weapons. The battle; however, laid the foundation for a secluded Gyáli that quickly created a technology that protected them from anything that flew in their airspace. They survived also calling this their Sky Plague. When comparing their Sky Plague with the Álmosd, they attributed it to the opposites. The Gyáli plague used something small to kill a large enemy, whereas the Álmosd suffered from a small enemy killing something large.

Nógrád faced their special challenge, which turned to be more bloodthirsty than the other continents suffered. Borffor was an escaped prisoner from a civilization in the depth of the universe. She orchestrated her escape by injecting a virus among the guards. They lay dead before her as she walked pass the gate, allowing the other escapes to board the speedy spacecraft. These packed vessels flashed through the cosmos while those aboard believed that their thirst for freedom quenched. Unfortunately, their Kingdom felt different and within days led them into an ambush. They designed this trap so none would escape; therefore, all these prisoners faced their executions. Borffor used another avenue for her escape. She had a few prison servants nail her inside a box as a finished prison manufactured product, which had a destination. Borffor kept her peace in the box as it passed to her associates. After they freed her, she slashed their throats one by one until all no longer lived. Afterwards, she escaped in one of their ships leaving the solar system and then her galaxy. Their spaceships stood not designed for intergalactic travel. Borffor was daring and never retreated when a fresh opportunity lay in front of her. She pointed her ship to the brightest group of lights and drifted into the deep dark emptiness. One day, many months into her voyage, while asleep in her captain's seat her ship flashed into a strange hole in the middle of space. This wormhole zoomed her into a different quadrant of space. Once her ship exited the wormhole, the hole vanished, merely to reappear at random elsewhere among the heavens.

Borffor was from a race called the Viollu, a hairless purple humanoid related species. They had the power of speech with the intellect that comes with this. The initial tasks she faced were to remove the attached tracking device bound at her feet, and a special one drilled behind her eyes. The secret band that placed her in the escape box removed the two devices from her feet and disabled the one behind her ear. They worried about removing it while attached to her brain. The disabler the prison installed remained linked to her brain and central nervous system. They carefully replaced two of the biological links with new links, which reversed themselves canceling the transmitter by sending it into an endless loop. Borffor no longer had to worry about this, as she now existed in another quadrant of space. She discovered this to be both a source of good and bad information. Borffor no longer worried about any Viollu from her galaxy discovering her, unless the mysterious wormhole opened once again. The opposite side was that her scanner did not detect any Viollu life forms. The Viollu existed as the unique hairless purple-skinned people. It was difficult to blend in, especially as their skin would glow when it contacted any sun or star. To offset this, the Viollu would oil themselves to distort the color absorption spectrum and reflect a compatible color pattern based on the light energy surrounding it. Borffor wore her prison garments, which were rags, which barely, when properly held in place, qualified as clothing. The Viollu collected necklaces for accomplishments, either good or bad. Borffor had a collection of fifteen large dark necklaces that the government dictated she displayed. As with most government body mandates, these necklaces were biologically welded into her nervous system and a special connection to her lungs, causing them to fill with her body fluids. Therefore, she could never remove them. This seldom was an issue among the other humanoid life forms. Borffor's main embarrassment rested on the white rags she wore. She did not worry about her wardrobe during the escape. Borffor's taste of freedom controlled her total conscience. She forced herself to wipe everything else from her mind. If it was not on the road to independence, she ignored it. As all who appear before a criminal court claimed their innocence, Borffor flooded the courtroom with her tears as she pleaded her innocence. Her defense could not prove her innocence, and to prison, she went. There she learned the skills of crime as the greatest criminals shared their expert knowledge with her.

Borffor created a virus, which she first developed an antidote so her chosen inmates would not suffer from this poison. When she released this virus, it killed the guards and prison staff clearing the way so Borffor and her chosen ones could simply walk straight to the loading docks and enter the ships. Borffor was officially now a murderer; however, she would not let this change her perception of herself. She was the innocent; the Kingdom took her freedom, and her freedom was worth killing to obtain. Her family, friends, and history would label her, as her support team would reveal, as the mastermind murderer. Borffor's justification was that today's freedom was worth tomorrow's history. To her credit, she prepared a huge antidote, with instructions, to save the population at large. She actually warned her partners about overcrowding on selected vehicles, and escape in a convoy. Nevertheless, there were those who knew more than she did and pulled the masses to her. Her fortune laid with a few friends who nailed her and needed supplies in a marked export box and placed her with the inventory. A few days later, the box was loaded on an outgoing freighter and shipped to another planet for distribution. A mistake at the receiving end allowed the receiving company's personnel to open the box. Fortunately, one crew removed the boxes' nails after unstacking them. The next day, another crew unloaded the boxes. Borffor used the stillness of the night to slip through the factory and to her contacts, who also lived in this middle solar orbit world. They had her shipped to this world so her exit from this solar system would not be accordingly obvious. They had set her up, left her out for the Kingdom to recapture. Their faces seemed to be looking at death when she walked into their station. She was calm and greeted them with courtesy and thankfulness. Once she gained their trust, accidents began to occur. She killed them within a few days, securing her escape craft that slowly took her from this staging world.

Borffor's ship glided through space as she stumbled into the wormhole that pulled her from any grasp of her captures into her new home, forever removed from the lands held by the Viollu. She ventured into the unknown, a place to make a free life. Borffor welcomed this opportunity for a fresh beginning. She would try to make peace in this new land and manifest her lifelong dream of freedom to search for love. Borffor selected Emsky4 because of the division of the lands. She selected Nógrád as it appeared in the center of this world. Borffor did not intend to live the remainder of her life in hiding. Here she would start from the middle and work her way to the remaining places. When her ship was orbiting this Emsky, her ship smashed into a cluster of meteors with the impact working loose one of the lower side panels. As the ship entered the atmosphere, the panel burned separating from the exterior. This exposed many of the ship's circuit boards frying them. This disconnected Borffor's controls from the ship's systems. She could initiate emergency backup to control the ship enough to crash into the ocean off the Nógrád. Once she hit the water, her seat ejected the seat she was sitting. She flew about twenty feet into the air and returned to the sea. Here, Borffor swam to the shoreline and walked on the land after that. She walked on the sand until the daylight hours arrived. She spotted a pleasant tree and began eating the leaves. Borffor enjoyed the taste of this matter as it began to fill her food-processing organs. It had been too long that she enjoyed the fresh vegetation. This vegetation had a special crisp pollution-free taste. The vegetation in her solar system lost its fresh green appearance centuries ago during their industrial ages. Although they evolved technologically beyond the primitive fossil-fuel era, the residual pollution left a lingering misfortune. Unfortunately, it takes at least a millennium to reduce the newly gas to levels than plants can form a green color. The pollution was still dangerous to breathe; therefore, when going outside they wore masks. All homes had air purifiers. The vegetation that grew was a pale shade of brown, and when ran through food purifiers could be eaten by the Viollu.

Borffor was stumbling in disbelief that so much vegetation was available. She crawled on the ground while eating the grass. There was a wide variety of leaves, plants, and even flowers. Borffor began to explore the forests nearby this sandy beach. While she was walking, she heard a noise and hurriedly hid. She saw a man walking on the path in front of her. Borffor followed the man to his home. She watched his home for two days, as he came and then went on tending to his daily tasks. She found enough courage to approach the man while he was in his yard. This was ironic, that she would fear an introduction to a lone man, yet she could cripple one of the toughest prisons in her Kingdom. The man introduced himself as Tryndin when Borffor introduced herself. The first thing that he did was prepared an animal hide outfit. Borffor appreciated this act of kindness. They sang songs and exchanged a few heroic tales. Borffor felt her defenses erode and a few drops of happiness flow from her face. Her prosperity was short lived, as the next morning when she awoke, Tryndin body was motionless. Her efforts to revive him proved fruitless. Borffor dug a hole and placed Tryndin's blister covered body in it. This was such an unexpected turn of events. Happy and singing one day, next morning, dropping to rest in the ground. Borffor was careful when she buried the body not to touch the blisters. She feared it could be contagious; whatever he was causing his death. Borffor decided to continue her search on this what appeared a friendly world. Her next encounter did not go as well as her first. She discovered a family and when she approached a child in the family, the mother became alarmed, and then shouted for her mate, who began shooting arrows at her. Borffor scrambled to pass the arrows and dashed back into the forest. The man continued to chase her, tracking her as if he knew her every move in advance. She tried for two days to escape from his tacking; therefore, she took the lone evasive action she knew. With her special knife, she sharpened a branch to form a three-pronged point. She doubled back on her tracks and lay flat in the dirt along the path. When the man moved passed her, she tripped him and then stabbed him multiple times until he moved no longer.

Borffor felt bad about taking a child's father, yet he would not stop. He backed her into a corner, and she came out swinging. It always puzzled her how fools consistently chase someone wiser than they are. She came in peace and departed with a victory. She would not cheer in triumph as this also represented the loss of a mate and father. She would continue her search as loneliness was filling her world. The search, instead, found her. She stumbled into an ambush, or became the fool meeting the wiser one. They bound her and dragged her back to their village. Here, the villagers tied her to a tree in the middle of the village and formed large circles surrounding her feeding their curiosity. Borffor detected early that they meant no harm, so she smiled at the children and winked at their mothers. The village finished their mystery celebration, and under the clear moons retired to their huts. Borffor eagerly awaited the next morning when she anticipated the children would play around her, followed by their parents. Unfortunately, the children reappeared looking as monsters with their skin covered with large boils and blisters. Their parents followed shortly after them, with their bodies also plastered with lesions. Borffor was puzzled as, so many people lie around her gaggling for their last breaths. She had survived the pain of watching the others gag for their terminal breaths when she plagued the guards. The thing that disturbed her this time was the cries of the children and their mothers. The screech and pain the in their voices as they agonizingly dimmed into the close distance and ripped her heart from her soul, causing her to wonder if ever again would she hold her head high. She won the village with her charm and inner self, no more than to see them die this mysterious death. All who had contacted her died, yet just one by her hand. Either way, if she killed them or not, they lost their lives, as this was not the tranquility that she searched to find. She had a choice that she was not going to accept. Someone was to blame, and she was not going to take the blame for this. No one would believe her; therefore, this time she was not going to remain sitting with her hands in the cookie jar. Last time, she trusted in the good faith of civilization's justice. She would not this instance. She noticed several mountains towering in the horizon. She would try to hide in those distant highlands.

Borffor traveled at night and hid during the day. This timed she was extremely concerned about her tracks, because she knew these people were outstanding trackers. Even though she knew no guilt lie with her, the question remained, who killed these people. Regretfully, knowing who took their lives would not bring back the innocent curiosity of living children. Even though she believed she was not at fault, she could not shake the liability she gave herself. The winds that blew through the forest at night would whisper the names of these children tormenting even her mildest of dreams. Borffor wondered now, which was the greater punishment, was it necklaces tied to her heart or all those dead images engraved in her mind. Why would one wish to walk a path if on that, the path was nothing but sorrow? Someone was going to suffer, be it the victim or survivor. The survivors merely watched another suffer, and then wait their own suffering, which at times felt like the unending procrastination of the misery. She wondered if something supreme could be this cruel to those it created, or did they take turns inflicting grief on each another's creation. The joy the families shared among themselves created a longing for such a delight in her empty life. As she began her trek to the mountains, her first night, she stumbled through these peculiar trees and lopsided hills with rocky streams and small creatures nipping at her feet. She danced on the slippery rocks, as her feet did not follow her mind's instructions. Borffor wondered if she was still alive, because on this night, the sole thing, she saw that moved was her mind playing a trick on her. She looked up and saw an angel hovering over her. She knew this was false, because the primary thing that followed her was death and white Angels represented life. She believed that life must have been playing tricks on her, perhaps from all the distress that hounded each step. The battle now changed its battlefield and moved from reality to her mind. She at present had the right to question if the people of this world had actually died from a strange plague, which eerily matched her created plague released on the Viollu guards. Borffor ruled this correlation out, noting that her ship would have filtered this virus, and the people she killed during her escape with her by force, and they failed to suffer from a virus.

Borffor's nights panned out repeatedly in a similar manner, except for the angel, which did appear twice again. The days began to puzzle her because she would awaken and see dead animals around her. She was fortunate to meet a kind young man and spend a few hours talking with him. He invited her to spend the next night in his cabin with him. She needed a break, so Borffor accepted his invitation. When they awoke in the morning, she discovered that he was extremely sick with the same plague that killed the village she just escaped. He died shortly after she woke up on this day. She woke up late in this morning, the reason being her extreme exhaustion. She was surprised to see this man dying in front of her. At least now, she had a rested mind and body to evaluate her situation. Borffor had no reason to rule out that she was hosting an odd mutation of her plague, one in which she had no vaccination, the single exception being herself being an inoculation source. This hypothesis would prove itself in time; she would place herself in another prison. This was a prison with no walls. She would hide from people to avoid killing them. The torment of forfeiting socialization for the sake of saving socialization for others laid a heavy burden on Borffor. One night, after she climbed a steep cliff and crawled onto a wide-open meadow on the hilltop, she realized that this hilltop lacked any trees. The sole thing that offered cover was the meadow's high grass. The grass would not stop any weapon unleashed against her. To avoid this sure death, Borffor elected to move making no noise. This night was different from the earlier ones. On this hilltop, she would find the answers to her questions, although not the answers she was looking forward to finding.

The lights from the moons gave the night blindness the eyes it needed to see. Subsequently, a bright light was descending on her. Borffor looked up and saw a beautiful angelic woman descending on her. Borffor fell to her knees begging for mercy. The spiritual told her there

was no need for any mercy. Borffor asked her for her name. This spirit told her, "I am Tsigler and have been sent to warn you that your body is a death weapon with those who live on Emsky." Borffor asked

Tsigler why she was a death and how she became one. Tsigler told her it was a part of all Viollu, and was simply a process of her natural immunity or ability to battle a virus by having that virus in her planetary humanoid's immune system. This relieved Borffor to a degree; however, a degree, she could not change. Death stood, hidden inside her refusing to give its power. Borffor begged for a ride to another world. Tsigler told her that the virus would kill all humanoid life forms anywhere in Chuprin. Borffor asked Tsigler if there was a way to hide somewhere on Emsky. Tsigler revealed to Borffor about a large land that was isolated in the southwestern part of Emsky. Tsigler asked her if she could take her to this land.

Borffor agreed as Tsigler took hold of her hand and took her over the great sea to explore this new land. Tsigler flew low to the ground weaving around trees. Tsigler knew this area from a higher view and in this, paltry altitude lost, track of where she was and accidentally found herself over a village. This was not a good night to fly so low over a village because of so many bright moons. This village had another surprise in that they had domesticated a breed of wild dogs for their protection. These dogs began barking hysterically as their masters came running out with their weapons. Instantly, villagers began shooting arrows. Tsigler had no choice except to release Borffor, as she could not risk existing as seen by a living Emsky. Borffor fell to the ground as for body spun in circles. Fortunately, if there is a fortune in disasters, her body pushed the arrows out of her body when she hit the ground. The villagers placed her in their village cage as their medicine man dressed her wounds. Borffor woke the next morning to see the villagers preparing for her execution. She had survived the night among villagers, and none showed signs of the plague. Of course, the ones who planned to execute her would have the immunity. She sat in her cage while the villagers prepared for her execution. The children played around her cage, casting rocks at her calling her names. Their parents offered no disciplinary action. Borffor found disappointment in this. She believed the people on this planet to be special. Borffor realized that the Emsky was the same as the Viollu at heart, extremely few that cared, many cruel. That night, while the dogs barked all-night, and prided themselves in showing her their teeth, foolishly believed they were scaring her. She marveled at their idiocy. She dreamed of a chance to be face-to-face with these scared animals, as she would free them from their ragged teeth. She smiled at, and teased them throughout the night, consequently much, so their masters came, beat them, and put them in a separate cage. Borffor marveled at how these dogs would bark subsequently fiercely before a stranger as if to appear vicious and yet one small call of their name or yell from their master left them whimpering as if begging for mercy. She delighted in their whimpers as the whips lashed against them.

Borffor peacefully fell into a deep sleep, expecting, awaking in the morning by their work on her execution or the children's rocks flying into her cage aimed for her head. This morning was different, as it was the sun above her head burning her hair, which awoke her. She looked around her to find the children who should have been playing by this time simply to see their bodies plagued with blisters and large black boils gasping for their breaths. She laughed aloud at them, asking these little monsters to cry louder in their misery for her pleasure. Soon, their parents came out before her, as they too suffered from this curse. They began to tear down her execution station hoping it would remove what they believed to be a punishment for shooting at a sky person. One man opened her cage begging her to leave. Borffor yelled at them in anger because this shot at her angel. The people believed her to be mad and ignored Borffor as she rushed from their camp. Borffor looked for a high peak to stand and wait for Tsigler's return. Tsigler returned the night after the last villager died and once more took Borffor's hand to guide her over the great sea to her new home. When they arrived over this large land, Borffor saw the snow-covered forests under her. Tsigler took her to a cave she had previously discovered. She helped Borffor find selected wood and gave her an ax to split the wood. Soon, she had a comfortable fire burning. Borffor asked her how long that the cold season was in this land. Tsigler told her it would last three months, yet it would be one-half the seasons; therefore, she must store her food during the three warm months for the succeeding three cold months. This cycled deterred the Emsky from settling here. Tsigler advised her to cook pinecones and to catch fish for her protein. The vegetation grew twice each year in this forsaken land. She could travel the underground caves on this sizeable island and learn how to transport herself throughout this area with the advantage of concealment and to reduce any chance of accidental contact her the humans on Emsky. Borffor survived on the island that forever bore her name, because she carved her name on many substantial rocks on the island. Her social life revolved around the Benigna who received permission for contact with her because she was in exile from another part of the universe. She continued for another thirty-five years, finally dying of the flu she could not overcome.

Nógrád was not free from its surprises from the sky. Nógrád became the home of the succubus named Pankraz. She had a long history of tormenting men throughout Chuprin. Pankraz had two images, her true form, and her visible to the Emsky form. These forms had barely a few differences. Both of them gave her a strong female body with long blond hair. She wore a strapless red dress, which exposed her shoulders and legs. Pankraz never exposed her right hand. She had a long red cape that she wore tied around her waist. She also wore a flexible two-inch wide gold band around her right leg. Her eyes had a fierce appearance of strength. Her real appearance had pointed ears and a large two-headed tail. Each head resembled a dragon's head with giant razor-sharp jaws. This tale gave her the power to destroy any who threatened her. The two dragonheads would lash out and consume any enemy stretching up to twenty feet surrounding her. She appears as the dragon's tail in the middle of villages and unleashes a bloodbath in just a few minutes. This sent a great fear throughout the village. She warned that unless a child's sacrifice made each week with her in her village alter that they erected for her. After the sacrifice, all had to leave the area, for any who she found inside her boundary line would die. She established the priesthood and gave them her laws, especially the rules for her sacrifice. She roamed throughout all Nógrád setting up her priesthood. Pankraz established differences in each of these clans. She did not want unity, and believed by making these differences they would not form a union. This division made it so much easier to control her. Pankraz terrorized Nógrád for two centuries before she got an urge to torture another continent. When she tried to fly over the oceans, the Benigna-B attacked her without mercy. Her dragonheads had no effect on eating spirits. Each time, she angrily rushed back to Nógrád and demand added sacrifices. If the spirits were going to hold her on Nógrád then she would torment the weak subjects until they would beg that she leave. Pankraz began to burn their crops and kill their livestock. The people went to their priests and demanded that the sacrifices stop. They would instead put their burned crops and dead non-harvested livestock on the altars. The priests agreed, and the human sacrifices stopped. Pankraz lost her servants.

Pankraz's anger reached a level that began to distort her ability to reason. She decided to wage a great war on these rebels. Instead, she stood confronted with a surprise that proved to be more than she could handle. The Benigna-B swarmed over her during the night time hours, and during the day others from her species. They fought her and could finally to capture her and remove her from Emsky. The people of Nógrád did not comprehend much about Pankraz's departure. The priests of Nógrád wanted to keep their status and position. When they noticed that the fires and livestock killings had stopped, they joined and discussed their plans. Many believed that she had left Emsky deciding they were no longer important or worth her time. They agreed to wait one month and then once more meet. One month passed and still no more punishments, so they devised a plan to declare she was satisfied and would cease her punishments when the child sacrifices again given to her. The priests returned to their temples and declared that Pankraz was now so pleased that she invited other gods from her heavens to join the Nógrád, as she would share them with the other gods and protect the people from a great invasion that was in the seas currently. The people at once sacrificed quite a few children to gain their favor. The priests changed many minor details to establish differences between the fifty-two temples. These priests could declare three months later that these new gods had destroyed sea invaders. The next two years they enjoyed great crops, and the livestock reproduced healthy beasts. The people now felt the gods were blessing them. The priests enjoyed extra gifts for them and their temples.

The people could replace their emergency stocks in their grains. The next decade Nógrád enjoyed extra crops and their livestock regained their pre-punishment levels. The priests grew strong, and their temples became the sanctuary for the believers. After pronounced storms, the priests would declare the people had lost their great love for their god and that he or she was disappointed. The Benigna-B began to place documents that taught the people how to use roots and herbs for healing processes. At first, the priests lived shocked by these documents, yet began to take these serious as they began to release these manuscripts to the elders who developed these roots and applied them as the papers instructed. The Nógrád used these potions and shared them with the other temples, who also shared their documents. Several reports instructed them how to improve their crops and build stronger homes. Nógrád within a few decades, they became the leaders in primitive technology. They had roads made from stones, which the mysterious papers taught them how the cut, discover, and mine the special stones they used. These roads exist in mint condition even during the current age. They built medium-size fishing boats with nets made from ropes they could create from the wool of their sheep. They also learned a method that would effectively salt and smoke their meat. Then they learned how to create the jerky from it. They could take with them when exploring and mapping their lands. They also built strong nets across the mouths of their rivers, in which after the sea fish left in the springtime, and they returned in the late fall; they would lift the bottom of the net because these fish traveled the bottom of rivers solely during the springtime. This provided a great harvest in the fall of the trapped ocean bound fish. The river fish and their predators traveled between the surface and about fifteen feet below the surface. The net prevented their predators from entering the river and the river fish to stay in the river, which increase their numbers and offer a rich stock that, could feed their people. The Nógrád also hunted the predators on their continent enjoyed a reduction in over eighty percent of their population. They allowed the bears to remain and any predator they could eat. They concentrated on the lions, tigers, wolves, and certain snakes. The manuscripts instructed them to leave a few to keep the rodent numbers under control. They also collected rabbits to keep in cages and reproduce another source of meat. The Nógrád continued to stock their abundant crops and livestock. They were enough sufficient and began universities for advance training of future elders. They still did not have elementary and high schools for the general population, nor hospitals, as all medical needs they corrected through their local medicine men.

The Andocs established the hospitals and schools for the population, so they could make Emsky compliance with the Empire's least requirements. The Andocs became able to create sea ships, which could travel throughout all of Emsky. They worked on Nógrád first, copying many of their documents on the construction of buildings, roads and raising both crops and livestock. The Nógrád had an overflowing grain and livestock inventory that they could trade with the Andocs who would distribute it among other parts of Emsky who were suffering. Therefore, the Nógrád had a great impact on Emsky. Although their technology was primitive, it stood advanced for that era. They had roads and strong buildings, plus the most advanced crops, and strongest livestock. Their ability to harvest the river fish actually proved to provide immediate food to the other continents. Not all continents used these nets, as several had priests who forbid this. Notwithstanding before, they joined the Empire; they found themselves employing these nets, so they would not starve. The roads and large temples finally reduced the priest's resistance to this change. The Andocs always insisted that if they had used any changes without this primitive tone, the other lands would have rebelled and refused any upgrades. The Nógrád had the perfect upgrades that allowed the humans to build with their hands and from their lands. When they saw their livestock and crops improve, and they built stronger homes and established universities plus their secondary schools and hospitals, which they stocked with their continent's roots and herbs. The Andocs upgraded Emsky with the Nógrád primitive technology that made Emsky qualified to join the great Empire. Chuprin still had worlds to upgrade and added the Nógrád technology throughout their galaxy.

The Nógrád priests discovered that the documents, slowed down to a drizzle. The Empire approached the Benigna and requested that they no longer interfere with the Emsky priests. The Empire feared that the people would discount the benefits of joining them. The Benigna agreed and began to provide documents that supported joining the Empire. This began after the death of Sénye. He sat proud beside his mate Orosházi who also rested proud. They were witnessing how their descendants had such a great impact on Emsky. Emsky now felt so such a part of those who were now living on Emsky. Pankrati noticed the joy they were enjoying. She asked them if they would enjoy an official Empire wedding. They both perched up, as they now saw their original ceremony performed by their children. Pankrati told them to jump into the window that provided the streams. They were now in front of the Master's throne as millions of Angels formed the giant walls and ceiling around this amazing place. Subsequently, there appeared before them, an old man, whose white beard grew down to his feet, wearing a pure white robe. He yelled out that all bow now, as Saint Acsa, daughter of the master would soon appear. Sénye and Orosházi fell to their knees and bowed their heads. This Saint now declared the arrival of Pusztaszentlászló, the Goddess of Great Love from the Eternal Throne. Pusztaszentlászló walked over, bowed beside Orosházi, and told this couple to have no fear, because she appears beside them when the master's daughter appeared. The Saint now declared the arrival of Queen Grandmother Goddess Tompaládony and Vice Commanding god of the Rødkærsbro War. Tompaládony walked over and knelt beside him telling the couple not to have fear, but instead enjoy the visions they would soon witness. Next, the Saint declared the arrival of Queen Mother Goddess Julia, who knelt beside Pusztaszentlászló. She began to sing a great love song from the Empire, as the Angels played their heavenly instruments. When she finished her song, the Saint declared the arrival of Queen Sister Goddess Julia who knelt beside Tompaládony. They watched a presentation from the Power Spirits who spoke of his great pride in the couple whom the throne would join in this day. Afterwards a group of beautiful Angels appeared and began to sing selected special love songs. Tears of joy began to flow from both Sénye and

Orosházi's eyes. The couple could not believe how beautiful this place was. Orosházi asked how such a wonderful place could exist.

Pusztaszentlászló released a flood of love on this group. Orosházi fell on the floor praising this great throne. Shortly thereafter, Tompaládony declared that one who can sit on this greatest throne would soon appear. Pusztaszentlászló pulled back the flood of love. Orosházi regained her composure and gripped Sénye's hand. The Saint now motioned for the Angels to begin playing their songs signifying the throne was to sit. The Saint at present declared the arrival of Saint Acsa, daughter of the master. She currently began to walk in front of the master's throne and sat on it. Tompaládony provided a video stream that revealed the Empire's throne in which meanwhile, sat Penance sister Goddess Amity. Tompaládony explained that this was the greatest and private throne of the master. The Empire's goddesses managed the Empire's business, and this throne managed by Queen Lilith, the number one servant to the master, Bogovi the master, and sometimes by the queen grandmother, queen mother, and queen sister. Specifically, the master or his family could sit on the throne. The throne treated Acsa as the master's daughter and therefore, the same as the master. Saint Acsa walked now escorted to the throne by a special species that lived entirely in the holy of holies. Once the Saint seated her, Saint Acsa apologized for the non-availability of her father and his wife. She explained that they were with their armies, destroying wicked spirits. Saint Acsa as well officially announced no evil entities in Chuprin now existed. Chuprin was now safe for all righteous spirits who were currently joining the abundance of available heavens. Saint Acsa told the couple before her that their cave is vacant, as all the spirits had joined the heavens. She also revealed that the master and Lilith had success in freeing most prisoned virtuous spirits that unfairly suffered punishment. The rescue of innocent, blameless souls was the master's greatest mission. All deployable armies were on this mission. Good would win once more over evil.

Saint Acsa now showed to the couple before her how impressed that she was with the power of their love. She was impressed that after being separated in the universe and rediscovering themselves once again, currently being from different species. The Power Spirits hid them from the evil spirits of Chuprin who considered them a high priority to add to their prisons. They sought hard to capture them. Orosházi displayed divine skill in evading their massive attempts. She also was instrumental in saving her mate from the evil forces. She battled the demons in her ability to predict their plans and chose alternative actions. For this reason, the throne is enormously interested in protecting and awarding Orosházi and Sénye. Saint Acsa looks at them and reveals that both Lilith and Bogovi will try to recruit them. She asks Orosházi to show how she was so successful. Orosházi reports that she knew her destiny lay somewhere on Emsky and that she had no choice but to survive until she could solve this mystery. She solved the mystery when she saw Sénye. She still did not recognize why her love exploded demanding she become his slave and collaborate for the rest of eternity. She had searched millions of spirits who gave her no interest. Once Orosházi saw Sénye, she knew he was what she searched to find. After Pankrati divulged she was the mother of Nógrád and Sénye was the father, and the descendants were their children she was amazed. The planet she traveled through so much of the universe to find was the home of her children. With the latest report of the great contributions, their children made, they were accordingly happy. If just they remembered their children, this would add so much to their lost identities. Saint Acsa tells Orosházi that all their children were righteous and are living in the Empire's heavens. Orosházi rejoiced when she heard this news. Saint Acsa also told the couple that one of the sister goddesses would introduce them so these Saints will understand how great and important that their parents are to this Empire. They will comprehend their parent's wedding was held in the master's throne. The Angels began to sing once more while playing their instruments. After a few songs, Saint Acsa raised her arms. The throne became quiet once more. Saint Acsa looked at the couple and asked them to declare their eternal love for each other and loyalty to the throne. Both eagerly declared their love for each other. Orosházi further declared her love and loyalty to the Empire citing the greatest reason for her change of heart was because of her children and their future with the Empire. Sénye eagerly pledged his allegiance to the Empire and his family. Saint Acsa then declared by the power of the master's throne that they now existed united for eternity. The Angels began to celebrate in joy. Orosházi declared she had found herself at last. Saint Acsa, while smiling for joy herself, declared that she must now find one as great as Sénye to be her mate and departed from the throne. She also thanked them for preparing the Chronicles of Emsky.

Tompaládony volunteered to show them the heavens and find their children. Pankrati agreed the Chronicles of Emsky were now complete. Sénye asked her about the long history of great leaders and wars that were not included in these Chronicles. Pankrati explains to them that any may read the volumes of history books written on Emsky, but the Chronicles searched to reveal the heart of Emsky, and they had done with great success. She predicts that many will enjoy this chronicle, especially as it ends in an extremely rare wedding before the master's throne. Tompaládony took the reborn couple in search of their children and exploration of the heavens for their new home. Therefore, this is the Chronicles of the Emsky before they joined the Empire.

INDEX

THE ADVENTURES IN THIS SERIES

Prikhodko, Dream of Nagykanizsai

Search for Wise Wolf

Seven Wives of Siklósi

Passion of the Progenitor

Mempire, Born in Blood

Penance on Earth

Patmos Paradigm

Lord of New Venus

Tianshire, Life in the Light

Rachmanism in Ereshkigal

Sisterhood, Blood of our Blood

Salvation, Showers of Blood

Hell of the Harvey

AUTHOR BIO

James Hendershot, D.D. was born in Marietta Ohio, finally settling in Caldwell, Ohio where he eventually graduated from high school. After graduating, he served four years in the Air Force and graduated, Magna Cum Laude, with three majors from the prestigious Marietta College. He then served until retirement in the US Army during which time he earned his Masters of Science degree from Central Michigan University in Public Administration, and his third degree in Computer Programing from Central Texas College. His final degree was the honorary degree of Doctor of Divinity from Kingsway Bible College, which provided him with keen insight into the divine nature of man.

After retiring from the US Army, he accepted a visiting professor position with Korea University in Seoul, South Korea. He later moved to a suburb outside Seattle to finish his lifelong search for Mempire and the goddess Lilith, only to find them in his fingers and not with his eyes. It is now time for Earth to learn about the great mysteries not only deep in our universe but also in the dimensions beyond sharing these magnanimities with you.

.